W9-BQX-652

Praise for the novels of

Karen Marie Moning

the dark highlander

"Darker, sexier, and more serious than Moning's previous
time-travel romances . . . this wild, imaginative romp takes
readers on an exhilarating ride through time and space."
—*Publishers Weekly* (starred review)

"Pulsing with sexual tension, Moning delivers a tale
romance fans will be talking about for a long time."
—*The Oakland Press*

"*The Dark Highlander* is dynamite, dramatic, and utterly
riveting. Ms. Moning takes the classic plot of good vs.
evil . . . and gives it a new twist."
—*Romantic Times*

kiss of the highlander

"Moning's snappy prose, quick wit and charismatic
characters will enchant."
—*Publishers Weekly*

"Moning is quickly building a reputation for writing
poignant time travels with memorable characters. This may
be the first book I've read by her, but it certainly won't be
my last. She delivers compelling stories with passionate
characters readers will find enchanting."
—*The Oakland Press*

TO TAME A
HIGHLAND
WARRIOR

KAREN MARIE
MONING

A DELL BOOK

TO TAME A HIGHLAND WARRIOR
A Dell Book

PUBLISHING HISTORY
Dell mass market edition / December 1999
Dell mass market reissue / June 2004

Published by
Bantam Dell
A Division of Random House, Inc.
New York, New York

This is a work of fiction. Names, characters, places, and incidents
either are the product of the author's imagination or are used fictitiously.
Any resemblance to actual persons, living or dead, events, or
locales is entirely coincidental.

ISBN 0-440-24236-3

Manufactured in the United States of America
Published simultaneously in Canada

OPM   10   9   8   7   6   5   4   3   2   1

This one is for Rick Shomo—Berserker extraordinaire;
and for Lisa Stone—Editor extraordinaire.

ACKNOWLEDGMENTS

Chasing a dream is a risky venture, one made considerably richer by the company and counsel of family and friends. My heartfelt thanks to my mother, who endowed me with her formidable will and taught me never to give up on my dreams, and to my father, who demonstrates daily the nobleness, chivalry, and infinite strength of a true hero.

My deep appreciation to Mark Lee, a repository for the universe's trivia, whose bizarre tidbits feed the writer's soul, and to the special ladies of RBL Romantica for their friendship, insight, and of course the "Bonny and Braw Beefcake Farm."

Special thanks to Don and Ken Wilber of the Wilber Law Firm, who created the perfect fit for my dual careers, allowing them to work in synthesis with each other.

Eternal gratitude to my sister, Elizabeth, who keeps my feet on the ground in so many crucial ways, and to my agent, Deidre Knight, whose professional guidance and personal friendship has enriched both my writing and my life.

And finally, to the booksellers and readers who made my first novel a success.

A CELTIC LEGEND

Legend tells that the power of the Berserker—preternatural strength, prowess, virility, and cunning—can be bought for the going rate of a man's soul.

In the heather hills of the Highlands, the Viking god Odin lurks in shadowy places listening for the bitter howl of a man, brutalized beyond mortal endurance, to invoke his aid.

Legend holds that if the mortal is worthy, the primal breath of the gods blows into the man's heart, making him an undefeatable warrior.

Women whisper that the Berserker is an incomparable lover; legend holds there is a single true mate for him. Like the wolf, he loves but once and for all time.

High in the mountains of Scotland, the Circle Elders say that the Berserker, once summoned, can never be dismissed—and if the man does not learn to accept the primitive instincts of the beast within, he will die.

Legend tells of such a man . . .

PROLOGUE

Death itself is better than a life of shame.
Beowulf

THE SCREAMING *HAD* TO STOP.

He couldn't endure it another minute, yet he knew he was helpless to save them. His family, his clan, his best friend Arron, with whom he'd ridden the heather fields only yesterday, and his mother—oh, but his mother was another story; her murder had presaged this . . . this . . . barbaric . . .

He turned away, cursing himself for a coward. If he couldn't save them and he couldn't die with them, at least he owed them the honor of scribing the events into his memory. To avenge their deaths.

One at a time, if necessary.

Vengeance doesn't bring back the dead. How many times had his father said that? Once Gavrael had believed him, believed *in* him, but that had been before he'd discovered his mighty, wise, and wonderful da crouched over his mother's body this morning, his shirt bloodstained, a dripping dagger in his fist.

Gavrael McIllioch, only son of the Laird of Maldebann, stood motionless upon Wotan's Cleft, gazing down the sheer cliff at the village of Tuluth, which filled the valley hundreds of feet below. He wondered how this day had turned so bitter. Yesterday had been a fine day, filled with the simple pleasures of a lad who would one day govern these lush Highlands. Then this cruel morning had broken, and with it his heart. After discovering his da crouched above the savaged body of Jolyn McIllioch, Gavrael had fled for the sanctuary of the dense Highland forest, where he'd passed most of the day swinging wildly between rage and grief.

Eventually both had receded, leaving him oddly detached. At dusk, he'd retraced his path to Castle Maldebann to confront his sire with accusations of murder in a final attempt to make sense of what he'd witnessed, if there was sense to be made. But now, standing on the cliff high above Tuluth, the fourteen-year-old son of Ronin McIllioch realized his nightmare had only begun. Castle Maldebann was under siege, the village was engulfed in flames, and people were darting frantically between pillars of flames and piles of the dead. Gavrael watched helplessly as a small boy sped past a hut, directly into the blade of a waiting McKane. He recoiled; they were only children, but children could grow up to seek vengeance, and the fanatic McKane never left seeds of hatred to take root and bear poisonous fruit.

By the light of the fire engulfing the huts, he could see that the McKane severely outnumbered his people. The distinctive green and gray plaids of the hated enemy were a dozen to each McIllioch. *It's almost as though they knew we'd be vulnerable,* Gavrael thought. More than half the McIllioch were away in the north attending a wedding.

Gavrael despised being fourteen. Although he was tall and broad for his age, with shoulders that hinted at exceptional strength to come, he knew he was no match for the burly McKane. They were warriors with powerfully developed, mature bodies, driven by obsessive hatred. They trained ceaselessly, existing solely to pillage and kill. Gavrael would be no more significant than a tenacious pup yapping at a bear. He could plunge into the battle below, but he would die as inconsequentially as the boy had moments before. If he had to die tonight, he swore he would make it mean something.

Berserker, the wind seemed to whisper. Gavrael cocked his head, listening. Not only was his world being destroyed, now he was hearing voices. Were his wits to fail him before this terrible day ended? He knew the legend of the Berserkers was simply that—a legend.

Beseech the gods, the rustling branches of the pines hissed.

"Right," Gavrael muttered. As he'd been doing ever since he'd first heard the fearsome tale at the age of nine? There was no such thing as a Berserker. It was a foolish tale told to frighten mischievous children into good behavior.

Ber . . . serk . . . er. This time the sound was clearer, too loud to be his imagination.

Gavrael spun about and searched the massive rocks behind him. Wotan's Cleft was a tumble of boulders and odd standing stones that cast unnatural shadows beneath the full moon. It was rumored to be a sacred place, where chieftains of yore had met to plan wars and determine fates. It was a place that could almost make a stripling lad believe in the demonic. He listened intently, but the wind carried only the screams of his people.

It was too bad the pagan tales weren't true. Legend claimed Berserkers could move with such speed that they seemed invisible to the human eye until the moment they attacked. They possessed unnatural senses: the olfactory acuity of a wolf, the auditory sensitivity of a bat, the strength of twenty men, the penetrating eyesight of an eagle. The Berserkers had once been the most fearless and feared warriors ever to walk Scotland nearly seven hundred years ago. They had been Odin's elite Viking army. Legend claimed they could assume the shape of a wolf or a bear as easily as the shape of a man. And they were marked by a common feature—unholy blue eyes that glowed like banked coals.

Berserker, the wind sighed.

"There is no such thing as a Berserker," Gavrael grimly informed the night. He was no longer the foolish boy who'd been infatuated with the prospect of unbeatable strength; no longer the youth who'd once been willing to offer his immortal soul for absolute power and control. Besides, his own eyes were deep brown, and always had been. Never had history recorded a brown-eyed Berserker.

Call me.

Gavrael flinched. This last figment of his traumatized mind had been a command, undeniable, irresistible. The hair on the back of his neck stood up on end and his skin prickled. Not once in all his years of playing at summoning a Berserker had he ever felt so peculiar. His blood pounded through his veins and he felt as if he teetered on the brink of an abyss that both lured and repulsed him.

Screams filled the valley. Child after child fell while he stood high above the battle, helpless to alter the course of events. He would do anything to save them: barter, trade, steal, murder—*anything*.

Tears streamed down his face as a tiny lass with blond ringlets wailed her last breath. There would be no mother's arms for her, no bonny suitor, no wedding, no babes—not a breath more precious life. Blood stained the front of her frock, and he stared at it, mesmerized. His universe narrowed to a tunnel of vision in which the blood blossoming on her chest became a vast, crimson whirlpool, sucking him down and down . . .

Something inside him snapped.

He threw his head back and howled, the words ricocheting off the rocks of Wotan's Cleft. *"Hear me, Odin, I summon the Berserker! I, Gavrael Roderick Icarus McIllioch, offer my life—nay, my soul—for vengeance. I command the Berserker!"*

The moderate breeze turned suddenly violent, lashing leaves and dirt into the air. Gavrael flung his arms up to shield his face from the needle-sharp sting of flying debris. Branches, no match for the fierce gale, snapped free and battered his body like clumsy spears hurled from the trees. Black clouds scuttled across the night sky, momentarily obscuring the moon. The unnatural wind keened through the channels of rock on Wotan's Cleft, briefly muffling the screams from the valley below. Suddenly the night exploded in a flash of dazzling blue and Gavrael felt his body . . . change.

He snarled, baring his teeth, as he felt something irrevocable mutate deep within him.

He could smell dozens of scents from the battle below— the rusty, metallic odor of blood and steel and hate.

He could hear whispers from the McKane camp on the far horizon.

He saw for the first time that the warriors appeared to be moving in slow motion. How had he failed to notice it

before? It would be absurdly easy to slip in and destroy
them all while they were moving as if slogging through wet
sand. So easy to destroy. So easy . . .

Gavrael sucked in rapid breaths of air, pumping his
chest full before charging into the valley below. As he
plunged into the slaughter, the sound of laughter echoed
off the stone basin that cupped the valley. He realized it
was coming from his own lips only when the McKane
began to fall beneath his sword.

* * *

Hours later, Gavrael stumbled through the burning remains
of Tuluth. The McKane were gone, either dead or driven
off. The surviving villagers were tending the wounded and
walking in wide, cautious circles around the young son of
the McIllioch.

"Near to threescore ye killed, lad," an old man with
bright eyes whispered when Gavrael passed. "Not even yer
da in his prime could do such a thing. Ye be far more
berserk."

Gavrael glanced at him, startled. Before he could ask
what he meant by that comment, the old man melted into
the billowing smoke.

"Ye took down three in one swing of yer sword, lad," another man called.

A child flung his arms around Gavrael's knees. "Ye
saved me life, ye did!" the lad cried. "Tha' ole McKane
woulda had me for his supper. Thank ye! Me ma's thanking
ye too."

Gavrael smiled at the boy, then turned to the mother,
who crossed herself and didn't look remotely appreciative.
His smile faded. "I'm not a monster—"

"I know what ye are, lad." Her gaze never left his. To

Gavrael's ears her words were harsh and condemning. "I know exactly what ye are and doona be thinking otherwise. Get on with ye now! Yer da's in trouble." She pointed a quivering finger past the last row of smoldering huts.

Gavrael narrowed his eyes against the smoke and stumbled forward. He'd never felt so drained in all his life. Moving awkwardly, he rounded one of the few huts still standing and jerked to a halt.

His da was crumpled on the ground, covered with blood, his sword abandoned at his side in the dirt.

Grief and anger vied for supremacy in Gavrael's heart, leaving him strangely hollow. As he stared down at his father, the image of his mother's body surged to the forefront of his mind and the last of his youthful illusions shattered; tonight had birthed both an extraordinary warrior and a flesh-and-blood man with inadequate defenses. "Why, Da? Why?" His voice broke harshly on the words. He would never see his mother smile again, never hear her sing, never attend her burial—for he would be leaving Maldebann once his da replied, lest he turn his residual rage upon his own father. And then what would he be? No better than his da.

Ronin McIllioch groaned. Slowly he opened his eyes in a blood-crusted squint and gazed up at his son. A ribbon of scarlet trickled from his lips as he struggled to speak. "We're . . . born—" He broke off, consumed by a deep, racking cough.

Gavrael grabbed his father by handfuls of his shirt and, heedless of Ronin's pained grimace, shook him roughly. He would have his answer before he left; he would discover what madness had driven his da to kill his mother or he would be tortured all his life by unanswered questions. "What, Da? Say it! Tell me why!"

Ronin's bleary gaze sought Gavrael's. His chest rose and fell as he drew swift, shallow gasps of smoky air. With a strange undertone of sympathy, he said, "Son, we canna help it . . . the McIllioch men . . . always we're born . . . this way."

Gavrael stared at his father in horror. "You would say that to me? You think you can convince me that I'm mad like you? I'm not like you! I'll not believe you. You lie. You *lie*!" He lunged to his feet, backing hastily away.

Ronin McIllioch forced himself up on his elbows and jerked his head at the evidence of Gavrael's savagery, the remains of McKane warriors who had been literally ripped to pieces. "You did that, son."

"I am *not* a ruthless killer!" Gavrael scanned the mutilated bodies, not quite convinced of his own words.

"It's part of . . . being McIllioch. You canna help it, son."

"Doona call me son! I will never be your son again. And I'm not part of your sickness. I'm not like you. I will *never* be like you!"

Ronin sank back to the ground, muttering incoherently. Gavrael deliberately closed his ears to the sound. He would not listen to his da's lies a moment longer. He turned his back on him and surveyed what was left of Tuluth. The surviving villagers huddled in small groups, standing in absolute silence, watching him. Averting his face from what he would always remember as their reproving regard, his glance slid up the dark stone of Maldebann castle. Carved into the side of the mountain, it towered above the village. Once he had wished for nothing more than to grow up and help govern Maldebann at his da's side, eventually taking over as chieftain. He'd wished to always hear the lovely lilt of his mother's laughter filling the spacious halls, to hear his da's answering rumble as they joked and talked. He'd dreamed of wisely settling his people's concerns; of marrying one day and having sons of his own. Aye, once he had believed all those things would come to pass. But in less time than it had taken the moon to bridge the sky above Tuluth, all his dreams, and the very last part of him that had been human, were destroyed.

* * *

It took Gavrael the better part of a day to drag his battered body back up into the sanctuary of the dense Highland forests. He could never go home. His mother was dead, the castle ransacked, and the villagers had regarded him with fear. His da's words haunted him—*we're born this way*—killers, capable of murdering even those they claimed to love. It was a sickness of the mind, Gavrael thought, which his father said he, too, carried in his blood.

Thirstier than he'd ever been, he half crawled to the loch nestled in a small valley beyond Wotan's Cleft. He collapsed for a time on the springy tundra, and when he wasn't quite so dizzy and weak he struggled forward to drink, dragging himself on his elbows. As he cupped his hands and bent over the sparkling, clear pool he froze, mesmerized by his reflection rippling in the water.

Ice-blue eyes stared back at him.

CHAPTER 1

DALKEITH-UPON-THE-SEA
THE HIGHLANDS OF SCOTLAND
1515

GRIMM PAUSED AT THE OPEN DOORS OF THE STUDY AND gazed into the night. The reflection of stars dappled the restless ocean, like tiny pinpoints of light cresting the waves. Usually he found the sound of the sea crashing against the rocks soothing, but lately it seemed to incite in him a questing restlessness.

As he resumed pacing, he sifted through possible reasons for his unrest and came up empty-handed. It had been by choice that he remained at Dalkeith as captain of the Douglas guard when, two years ago, he and his best friend, Hawk Douglas, left Edinburgh and King James's service. Grimm adored Hawk's wife, Adrienne—when she wasn't trying to marry him off—and he doted upon their young son, Carthian. He had been, if not exactly happy, content. At least until recently. So what ailed him?

"You're wearing holes in my favorite rug with your pacing, Grimm. And the painter will never be able to finish this portrait if you won't sit down," Adrienne teased, jarring him from his melancholy reverie.

Grimm expelled a breath and ran a hand through his thick hair. Absentmindedly he fiddled with a section at his temple, twisting the strands into a plait as he continued to contemplate the sea.

"You aren't looking for a wishing star out there, are you, Grimm?" Hawk Douglas's black eyes danced with mirth.

"Hardly. And anytime your mischievous wife would care to tell me what curse she laid upon me with her careless wishing, I'd be happy to hear it." Some time ago, Adrienne Douglas had wished upon a falling star, and she steadfastly refused to tell either of them what she'd wished until she was absolutely certain it had been heard and granted. The only thing she would admit was that her wish had been made on Grimm's behalf, which unnerved him considerably. Although he didn't consider himself a superstitious man, he'd seen enough odd occurrences in the world to know that merely because something seemed improbable certainly didn't render it impossible.

"As would I, Grimm," Hawk said dryly. "But she won't tell me either."

Adrienne laughed. "Go on with the two of you. Don't tell me two such fearless warriors suffer a moment's concern over a woman's idle wish upon a star."

"I consider nothing you do idle, Adrienne," Hawk replied with a wry grin. "The universe does *not* behave in a normal fashion where you're concerned."

Grimm smiled faintly. It certainly didn't. Adrienne had been tossed back in time from the twentieth century, the victim of a wicked plot to destroy the Hawk, concocted by a vindictive Fairy. Impossible things happened around

Adrienne, which was why he wanted to know what bloody wish she'd made. He'd like to be prepared when all hell broke loose.

"Do sit down, Grimm," Adrienne urged. "I want this portrait finished by Christmas at the latest, and it takes Albert months to paint from his sketches."

"Only because my work is sheer perfection," the painter said, miffed.

Grimm turned his back on the night and reclaimed his seat by Hawk in front of the fire. "I still doona get the point of this," Grimm muttered. "Portraits are for lasses and children."

Adrienne snorted. "I commission a painter to immortalize two of the most magnificent men I've ever laid eyes upon"—she flashed them a dazzling smile, and Grimm rolled his eyes, knowing he would do whatever the lovely Adrienne wished when she smiled like that—"and all they can do is grumble. I'll have you know, one day you'll thank me for doing this."

Grimm and Hawk exchanged amused glances, then resumed the pose she insisted displayed their muscular physiques and dark good looks to their finest advantage.

"Be certain you color Grimm's eyes as brilliantly blue as they are," she instructed Albert.

"As if I don't know how to paint," he muttered. "I *am* the artist here. Unless, of course, you'd like to try your hand at it."

"I thought you liked *my* eyes." Hawk narrowed his black eyes at Adrienne.

"I do. I married you, didn't I?" Adrienne teased, smiling. "Can I help it if the staff at Dalkeith, to the youngest maid of a tender twelve years, swoons over your best friend's eyes? When I hold my sapphires up to the sunlight, they look exactly the same. They shimmer with iridescent blue fire."

"What are mine? Puny black walnuts?"

Adrienne laughed. "Silly man, that's how I described your heart when I first met you. And stop fidgeting, Grimm," she chided. "Or is there some reason you want those braids at your temples in this portrait?"

Grimm froze, then slowly touched his hair in disbelief.

Hawk stared at him. "What's on your mind, Grimm?" he asked, fascinated.

Grimm swallowed. He hadn't even realized he'd plaited the war braids into his hair. A man wore war braids only during the blackest hours of his life—when he was mourning his lost mate or preparing for battle. So far, he'd worn them twice. What had he been thinking? Grimm stared blankly at the floor, confused, unable to vocalize his thoughts. Lately he'd been obsessed with ghosts of the past, memories he'd tossed savagely into a shallow grave years ago and buried beneath a thin sod of denials. But in his dreams the shadow corpses walked again, trailing behind them a residue of unease that clung to him throughout the day.

Grimm was still struggling to answer when a guard burst through the doors to the study.

"Milord. Milady." The guard nodded deferentially to Hawk and Adrienne as he hastily entered the room. He approached Grimm, a somber expression on his face. "This just came for ye, Cap'n." He thrust an official-looking piece of parchment into Grimm's hands. "The messenger insisted 'twas urgent, and to be delivered into your hands only."

Grimm turned the message slowly in his hand. The elegant crest of Gibraltar St. Clair was pressed into the red wax. Suppressed memories broke over him: *Jillian*. She was a promise of beauty and joy he could never possess, a memory he'd consigned to that same uncooperative, shallow grave that now seemed determined to regurgitate its dead.

"Well, open it, Grimm," Adrienne urged.

Slowly, as if he held a wounded animal that might turn on him with sharp teeth, Grimm broke the seal and opened the missive. Stiffly, he read the terse, three-word command. His hand fisted reflexively, crumpling the thick vellum.

Rising, he turned to the guard. "Prepare my horse. I leave in one hour." The guard nodded and left the study.

"Well?" Hawk demanded. "What does it say?"

"Nothing you need to address, Hawk. Doona worry. It doesn't concern you."

"Anything that concerns my best friend concerns me," Hawk said. "So give over, what's wrong?"

"I said nothing. Leave it, man." Grimm's voice held a note of warning that would have restrained a lesser man's hand. But the Hawk had never been, and would never be, a lesser man, and he moved so unexpectedly that Grimm didn't react quickly enough when he whisked the parchment from his hand. Grinning mischievously, Hawk backed away and uncrumpled the parchment. His grin broadened, and he winked at Adrienne.

" 'Come for Jillian,' it says. A woman, is it? The plot thickens. I thought you'd sworn off women, my fickle friend. So who's Jillian?"

"A woman?" Adrienne exclaimed delightedly. "A young, marriageable woman?"

"Stop it, you two. It's not like that."

"Then why were you trying to keep it a secret, Grimm?" Hawk pressed.

"Because there are things you doona know about me, and it would take far too long to explain. Lacking the leisure to tell you the full story, I'll send you a message in a few months," he evaded coolly.

"You're not getting out of this so easily, Grimm Roderick." Hawk rubbed the shadow beard on his stubborn jaw thoughtfully. "Who is Jillian, and how do you know Gibraltar St. Clair? I thought you came to court directly from England. I thought you knew no one in all of Scotland but for those you met at court."

"I didn't exactly tell you the whole story, Hawk, and I doona have time for it now, but I'll tell you as soon as I get settled."

"You'll tell me now, or I'm coming with you," Hawk threatened. "Which means Adrienne and Carthian are coming as well, so you can either tell me or prepare for company, and you never know what might happen if Adrienne comes along."

Grimm scowled. "You really can be a pain, Hawk."

"Relentless. Formidable," Adrienne agreed sweetly. "You may as well give in, Grimm. My husband never takes no for an answer. Believe me, I know this."

"Come on, Grimm, if you can't trust me, who can you trust?" he coaxed. "Where are you going?"

"It's not a question of trust, Hawk." Hawk merely waited with an expectant look on his face, and Grimm knew he had no intention of relenting. Hawk would push and poke and ultimately do exactly as he'd threatened— come along—unless Grimm gave him a sufficient answer. Perhaps it was time he admitted the truth, although the odds were that once he did, he wouldn't be welcomed back at Dalkeith. "I'm going home, sort of," Grimm finally conceded.

"*Caithness* is your home?"

"Tuluth," Grimm muttered.

"What?"

"Tuluth," Grimm said flatly. "I was born in Tuluth."

"You said you were born in Edinburgh!"

"I lied."

"Why? You told me your entire family was dead! Was that a lie too?"

"No! They are. I didn't lie about that. Well . . . mostly I didn't lie," he corrected hastily. "My da is still alive, but I haven't spoken to him in more than fifteen years."

A muscle twitched in Hawk's jaw. "Sit down, Grimm. You're not going anywhere until you tell me all of it, and I suspect it's a tale that's long overdue."

"I doona have time, Hawk. If St. Clair said it was urgent, I was needed at Caithness weeks ago."

"What relevance has Caithness to any of this, or to you? Sit. Talk. *Now.*"

Sensing no possibility of reprieve, Grimm paced as he began his story. He told them how, at the age of fourteen, he'd left Tuluth the night of the massacre and wandered the forests of the Highlands for two years, wearing his war braids and hating mankind, hating his father, hating himself. He skipped the brutal parts—his mother's murder, the starvation he'd endured, the repeated attempts on his life. He told them that when he was sixteen he'd found shelter with Gibraltar St. Clair; that he'd changed his name to Grimm to protect himself and those for whom he cared. He told them how the McKane had found him again at Caithness and attacked his foster family. And finally, in the tone of a dreaded confession, he told them what his real name had been.

"What did you just say?" Hawk asked blankly.

Grimm drew a deep breath into his lungs and expelled it angrily. "I said Gavrael. My real name is Gavrael." There was only one Gavrael in all of Scotland; no other man would willingly own up to that name and that curse. He braced himself for the Hawk's explosion. He didn't have to wait for long.

"McIllioch?" Hawk's eyes narrowed disbelievingly.

"McIllioch," Grimm confirmed.

"And Grimm?"

"Grimm stands for Gavrael Roderick Icarus McIllioch." Grimm's Highland brogue rolled so thickly around the name, it was a nearly unintelligible burr of *r*'s and *l*'s and staccato-sharp *k*'s. "Take the first letter of each name, and there you have it. G-R-I-M."

"Gavrael McIllioch was a Berserker!" Hawk roared.

"I told you you didn't know so much about me," Grimm said darkly.

Crossing the study in three swift strides, Hawk bristled to a stop inches from Grimm's face and studied him, as if he might uncover some telltale trace of a beast that should have betrayed Grimm's secret years ago. "How could I not have known?" Hawk muttered. "For years I'd been wondering about some of your peculiar . . . talents. By the bloody saints, I should have guessed if only from your eyes—"

"Lots of people have blue eyes, Hawk," Grimm said dryly.

"Not like *yours*, Grimm," Adrienne remarked.

"This explains it all," Hawk said slowly. "You're not human."

Grimm flinched.

Adrienne leveled a dark look at her husband and linked her arm through Grimm's. "Of course he's human, Hawk. He's just human . . . plus some."

"A Berserker." Hawk shook his head. "A fardling Berserker. You know, they say William Wallace was a Berserker."

"And what a lovely life he had, eh?" Grimm said bitterly.

* * *

Grimm rode out shortly thereafter, answering no more questions and leaving the Hawk immensely dissatisfied. He left quickly, because the memories were returning of their own accord and with fury. Grimm knew he had to be alone when full recollection finally reclaimed him. He didn't willingly think about Tuluth anymore. Hell, he didn't willingly think anymore, not if he could help it.

Tuluth: in his memory a smoky valley, clouds of black so thick his eyes had stung from the acrid stench of burning homes and burning flesh. Children screaming. *Och, Christ!*

Grimm swallowed hard as he spurred Occam into a gallop across the ridge. He was impervious to the beauty of the Highland night, lost in another time, surrounded only by the color of blood and the blackness of soul-disfiguring desolation—with one shimmering spot of gold.

Jillian.

Is he an animal, Da? May I keep him? Please? He's an ever-so-glorious beastie!

And in his mind he was sixteen years old again, looking down at the wee golden lass. Memory swept over him, dripping shame thicker than clotted honey off a comb. She'd found him in the woods, scavenging like a beast.

He'd be fiercer than my Savanna TeaGarden, Da!

Savanna TeaGarden being her puppy, all one hundred forty pounds of Irish wolfhound puppy.

He'd protect me well, Da, I know he would!

The instant she'd said the words, he'd taken a silent vow to do just that, never dreaming it might one day entail protecting her from himself.

Grimm rubbed his clean-shaven jaw and tossed his head in the wind. For a brief moment he felt the matted hair again, the dirt and sweat and the war braids, the fierce eyes brimming with hatred. And the pure, sweet child had trusted him on sight.

Och, but he'd dissuaded her quickly.

CHAPTER 2

GIBRALTAR AND ELIZABETH ST. CLAIR HAD BEEN RIDING toward their son's home in the Highlands for over a week before Gibraltar finally confessed his plan. He wouldn't have told her at all, but he couldn't stand to see his wife upset.

"Did you hear that?" Elizabeth said accusingly to her husband as she rounded her mare and cantered back to his side. "Did you?"

"Hear what? I couldn't hear a thing. You were too far away," he teased.

"That's it, Gibraltar. I've had it!"

Gibraltar raised an inquiring brow. "What's it, love?" Flushed with outrage, his wife was even more alluring than she was when calm. He wasn't above gently provoking her to enjoy the show.

Elizabeth tossed her head briskly. "I am sick of hearing men talk about our flawless, saintly, unwed—as in nearly a spinster—daughter, Gibraltar."

"You've been eavesdropping again, haven't you, Elizabeth?" he asked mildly.

"Eavesdropping, schmeavesdropping. If my daughter is being discussed, even if only by the guards"—she gestured in their direction irritably—"I have every right to listen. Our fearsome protectors, who I might point out are perfectly healthy full-grown men, have been trading tributes to her virtues. By virtues they don't mean her breasts or any of her lovely curves, but her sweet temper, her patience, her calling to the cloister, for goodness' sake. Did she breathe a word to you about this sudden inclination to devote herself to the nunnery?" Without waiting for an answer, Elizabeth reined in her mount and glared at him. "They go on and on about how flawless she is and not one of them says a word about tupping her."

Gibraltar laughed as he drew his stallion to a halt beside her mare.

"How dare you think this is funny?"

Gibraltar shook his head, his eyes sparkling. Only Elizabeth would take offense that men didn't talk about seducing their only daughter.

"Gibraltar, I must ask you to be serious for a moment. Jillian is twenty-one years old and not one man has seriously tried to court her. I vow she's the most exquisite lass in all of Scotland, and men walk quietly worshipful circles around her. *Do* something, Gibraltar. I'm getting worried."

His smile faded. Elizabeth was right. It was no longer a laughing matter. Gibraltar had reached that conclusion himself. It wasn't fair to let Elizabeth continue worrying when he'd taken action that would soon put both their fears to rest. "I've already taken care of it, Elizabeth."

"What do you mean? What have you done this time?"

Gibraltar studied her intently. At the moment he wasn't

completely certain which would upset Elizabeth more: continued worry over their daughter's unwed state, or the details of what he'd done without consulting her. A uniquely masculine moment of reflection convinced him she would be dazzled by his ingenuity. "I've arranged for three men to attend Caithness in our absence, Elizabeth. By the time we return, either Jillian will have chosen one of them, or one of them will have chosen her. They are not the kind of men to give up in the face of a wee bit of resistance. Nor are they the kind of men to fall for her 'nunnery stories.' "

Elizabeth's horrified expression deflated his smug pose. "One of them will choose her? Are you saying that one of these men you've selected might compromise her if she doesn't choose?"

"Seduce, Elizabeth, not compromise," Gibraltar protested. "They wouldn't ruin her. They're all honorable, respectable lairds." His voice deepened persuasively. "I selected these three based in part on the fact that they're also all very . . . er"—he searched for a word innocuous enough that it wouldn't alarm his wife, because the men he'd chosen could be patently alarming—". . . masculine men." His perfunctory nod was intended to soothe her concerns. It failed. "Exactly what Jillian needs," he assured her.

"Masculine! You mean randy inveterate blackguards! Probably domineering and ruthless, to boot. Don't prevaricate with me, Gibraltar!"

Gibraltar sighed gustily, any hope of subtle persuasion debunked. "Do you have a better idea, Elizabeth? Frankly, I think the problem is that Jillian has never met a man who wasn't intimidated by her. I guarantee you not one of the men I've invited will be even remotely intimidated. Captivated? Yes. Intrigued? Yes. Ruthlessly persistent? Yes. Precisely what a Sacheron woman needs. A man who is man enough to *do* something about it."

Elizabeth St. Clair, née Sacheron, nibbled her lower lip in silence.

"You know how you've been longing to see our new grandson," he reminded her. "Let's just go on with our visit and see what happens. I promise you that none of the men I've chosen will harm a hair on our precious daughter's head. They might muss it up a bit, but that will be well and good for her. Our impeccable Jillian is long overdue for some mussing."

"You expect me to just go off and leave her with three men? *Those* kind of men?"

"Elizabeth, those kind of men are the only kind of men who will not worship her. Besides, I was once one of those kind of men, if you'll recall. It will take an uncommon man for our uncommon daughter, Elizabeth," he added more gently. "I aim to find her that uncommon man."

Elizabeth sighed and blew a tendril of hair from her face. "I suppose you've the right of it," she murmured. "She truly hasn't met a man who didn't worship her. I wonder, how do you think she'll react when she does?"

"I suspect she might not know what to do at first. It may throw her badly off balance. But I'm wagering one of the men I've selected will help her figure it out," Gibraltar said smoothly.

Alarm vanquished Elizabeth's despondence instantly. "That's it. We'll just have to go back. I can't be somewhere else when my daughter is experiencing these woman things for the first time. God only knows what some man will try to teach my daughter or how he'll try to teach it to her, not to mention how shocked she's certain to be. I can't be off visiting while my daughter is being bullied and bamboozled out of her maidenhead—it simply won't do! We'll have to go home." She gazed expectantly at her husband, awaiting his nod of agreement.

"Elizabeth." Gibraltar said her name very quietly.

"Gibraltar?" Her tone was wary.

"We are not turning back. We are going to visit our son to attend our grandson's christening and spend a few months, as planned."

"Does Jillian know what you've done?" Elizabeth asked icily.

Gibraltar shook his head. "She hasn't a suspicion in her pretty head."

"What about the men? Don't you think they will tell her?"

Gibraltar grinned wickedly. "I didn't tell them. I simply commanded their attendance. But Hatchard knows and is prepared to inform them at a suitable time."

Elizabeth was shocked. "You told no one but our chief man-at-arms?"

"Hatchard is a wise man. And she needs this, Elizabeth. She needs to find her own way. Besides," he provoked, "what man would dare bamboozle a lass's maidenhead with her mother hovering at her elbow?"

"Och! My mother, my da, my seven brothers, and my grandparents being in attendance didn't stop you from bamboozling mine. Or abducting me."

Gibraltar chuckled. "Are you sorry I did?"

Elizabeth gave him a steamy look from beneath her lashes that assured him to the contrary.

"So you see, sometimes a man knows best, don't you think, my dear?"

She didn't reply for a moment, but Gibraltar didn't mind. He knew Elizabeth trusted him with her life. She just needed some time to get used to his plan and to accept the fact that their daughter needed a loving push over the edge of the nest.

When Elizabeth finally spoke, resignation buffered her words. "Just which three men did you choose without my discerning insight and consent?"

"Well, there's Quinn de Moncreiffe." Gibraltar's gaze never strayed from her face.

Quinn was blond, handsome and daring. He'd sailed black-flag for the King before he'd inherited his titles and now commanded a fleet of merchant ships, from which he'd trebled his clan's already considerable fortune. Gibraltar had fostered Quinn when he'd been a young lad, and Elizabeth had always favored him.

"Good man." A lift of a perfect golden brow betrayed grudging admiration for her husband's wisdom. "And?"

"Ramsay Logan."

"Oh!" Elizabeth's eyes grew round. "When I saw him at court he was clad in black from head to toe. He looked as dangerously attractive as a man could be. How is it that some woman hasn't snatched him up? Do go on, Gibraltar. This is becoming quite promising. Who's the third?"

"We're lagging too far behind the guards, Elizabeth," Gibraltar evaded glibly. "The Highlands have been peaceful lately, but we can't be too careful. We must catch up." He shifted in his saddle, grasped her reins, and urged her to follow.

Elizabeth scowled as she plucked the reins from his hand. "We'll catch them later. Who's the third?"

Gibraltar frowned and gazed at the guards, who were fading out of sight around a bend. "Elizabeth, we mustn't tarry. You have no idea—"

"The third, Gibraltar," his wife repeated.

"You look especially lovely today, Elizabeth," Gibraltar said huskily. "Have I told you that?" When his words evoked no response but a cool, level stare, he wrinkled his brow.

"Did I say three?"

Elizabeth's expression grew cooler.

Gibraltar expelled a breath of frustration. He mumbled a name and spurred his mount forward.

"What did you just say?" she called after him, urging her mare to keep up.

"Oh hell, Elizabeth! Give over! Let's just ride."

"Repeat yourself, please, Gibraltar."

There was another unintelligible answer.

"I can't understand a word when you mumble," Elizabeth said sweetly.

Sweet as siren song, he thought, *and every bit as lethal.* "I said Gavrael McIllioch. All right? Leave it, will you?" He rounded his stallion sharply and glared, savoring the fact that at least for the time being he'd rendered her as close to speechless as Elizabeth St. Clair ever came.

Elizabeth stared at her husband in disbelief. "Dear God in heaven, he's summoned the Berserker!"

* * *

On the sloping lawn of Caithness, Jillian St. Clair shivered despite the warmth of the brightly shining sun. Not one cloud dotted the sky, and the shady forest that rimmed the south end of the lawn was a dozen yards away—not close enough to have been responsible for her sudden chill.

An inexplicable sense of foreboding crept up the back of her neck. She shook it off briskly, berating her overactive imagination. Her life was as unmarred by clouds as the expansive blue sky; she was being fanciful, nothing more.

"Jillian! Make Jemmie stop pulling my hair!" Mallory

cried, dashing to Jillian's side for protection. The lush green grass of the lawn was sprinkled with the dozen or so children who gathered every afternoon to cajole stories and sweets from Jillian.

Sheltering Mallory in her arms, Jillian regarded the lad reprovingly. "There are better ways to show a lass that you like her than pulling her hair, Jemmie MacBean. And it's been my experience that the girls whose hair you pull now are the ones you'll be courting later."

"I didn't pull her hair because I *like* her!" Jemmie's face turned red and his hands curled into defiant fists. "She's a *girl*."

"Aye, she is. And a lovely one at that." Jillian smoothed Mallory's luxuriant, long auburn hair. The young lass already showed promise of the beautiful woman she would become. "Pray tell, why *do* you pull her hair, Jemmie?" Jillian asked lightly.

Jemmie kicked at the grass with his toes. "Because if I punched her the same way I punch the lads, she'd probably cry," he mumbled.

"Why must you do anything to her at all? Why not simply talk to her?"

"What could a *girl* have to say?" He rolled his eyes and scowled at the other lads, wordlessly demanding support with his fierce glare.

Only Zeke was unaffected by his bullying. "Jillian has interesting things to say, Jemmie," Zeke argued. "You come here every afternoon to listen to her, and *she's* a girl."

"That's different. She's not a girl. She's . . . well, she's almost like a mother to us, 'cept she's a lot prettier."

Jillian brushed a strand of blond hair back from her face with an inward wince. What had "prettier" ever done for her? She longed to have children of her own, but children required a husband, and one of those didn't appear to be on the horizon for her, pretty or not. *Well, you could stop being so picky,* her conscience advised dryly.

"Shall I tell you a story?" She swiftly changed the subject.

"Yes, tell us a story, Jillian!"

"A romantic one!" an older girl called.

"A bloody one," Jemmie demanded.

Mallory scrunched her nose at him. "Give us a fable. I love fables. They teach us good things, and some of us"— she glared at Jemmie—"need to learn good things."

"Fables are dumb—"

"Are not!"

"A fable! A fable!" the children clamored.

"A fable you shall have. I shall tell you of the argument between the Wind and the Sun," Jillian said. "It's my favorite of all the fables." The children jostled for the seat closest to her as they settled down to hear the tale. Zeke, the smallest of them, was shoved to the back of the cluster.

"Don't squint, Zeke," Jillian chided kindly. "Here, come closer." She drew the boy onto her lap and pushed the hair out of his eyes. Zeke was her favorite maid, Kaley Twillow's, son. He'd been born with such weak eyesight that he could scarcely see past his own hand. He was forever squinting, as if it might one day work a miracle and bring the world into focus. Jillian couldn't imagine the sorrow of not being able to clearly see the lovely landscape of Scotia, and her heart wept for Zeke's handicap. It prevented him from playing the games the other children adored. He was far more likely to be hit by the bladder-skin ball than to hit it, so to compensate Jillian had taught him to read. He had to bury his nose in the book, but therein he'd found worlds to explore he could never have seen with his own eyes.

As Zeke nestled into her lap, she began. "One day the Wind and the Sun were having an argument over who was stronger, when suddenly they saw a tinker coming down the road. The Sun said, 'Let us decide our dispute now. Whichever of us can cause the tinker to take off his cloak shall be regarded as the stronger.'

"The Wind agreed to the contest. 'You begin,' the Sun said, and retired behind a cloud so he wouldn't interfere. The Wind began to blow as hard as it could upon the tinker, but the more he blew, the tighter the tinker clutched his cloak about his body. That didn't deter the Wind from giving it all he had; still the tinker refused to yield his cloak. Finally the Wind gave up in despair.

"Then the Sun came out and blazed in all his glory upon the tinker, who soon found it too warm to walk with his cloak on. Removing it, he tossed the garment over his shoulder and continued on his journey, whistling cheerily."

"Yay!" the girls cheered. "The Sun won! We like the Sun better too!"

"It's a stupid girl story." Jemmie scowled.

"I liked it," Zeke protested.

"You would, Zeke. You're too blind to be seeing warriors and dragons and swords. I like stories with adventure."

"This tale had a point, Jemmie. The same point I was making about you pulling Mallory's hair," Jillian said gently.

Jemmie looked bewildered. "It did? What does the Sun have to do with Mal's hair?"

Zeke shook his head, disgusted by Jemmie's denseness. "She was telling us that the Wind tried to make the tinker feel bad, so the tinker needed to defend himself. The Sun made the tinker feel good and warm and safe enough to walk freely."

Mallory beamed adoringly at Zeke, as if he were the cleverest lad in the world. Zeke continued seriously, "So be nice to Mallory and she'll be nice to you."

"Where do you get your halfwit ideas?" Jemmie asked, irritated.

"He listens, Jemmie," Jillian said. "The moral of the fable is that kindness affects more than cruelty. Zeke understands that there's nothing wrong with being nice to the lasses. One day you'll be sorry you weren't nicer." *When Zeke ends up with half the village lasses hopelessly in love with him despite his weak vision,* Jillian thought, amused. Zeke was a handsome young lad and would one day be an attractive man possessing the unique sensitivity those born with a handicap tended to develop.

"She's right, lad." A deep voice joined their conversation as a man spurred his horse from the shelter of the nearby trees. "I'm *still* sorry I wasn't nicer to the lasses."

The blood in Jillian's veins chilled and her cloudless life was suddenly awash with thick, black thunderheads. Surely *that* man would never be fool enough to come back to Caithness! She pressed her cheek into Zeke's hair, hiding her face, wishing she could melt into the ground and disappear, wishing she had put on a more elegant gown this morning—as ever, wishing impossible things where this man was concerned. Although she hadn't heard his voice in years, she knew it was he.

"I recall a lass I was mean to when I was a lad, and now, knowing what I know, I'd give a great deal to take it all back."

Grimm Roderick. Jillian felt as if her muscles had

melted beneath her skin, fused by the heat of his voice. Two full timbres lower than any other voice she'd ever heard, modulated so precisely it conveyed intimidating self-discipline, his was the voice of a man in control.

She raised her head and stared at him, her eyes wide with shock and horror. Her breath caught in her throat. No matter how the years changed him, she would always recognize him. He'd dismounted and was approaching her, moving with the detached arrogance and grace of a conqueror, exuding confidence as liberally as he exhaled. Grimm Roderick had always been a walking weapon, his body developed and honed to instinctual perfection. Were she to scramble to her feet and feint left, Jillian knew he'd be there before her. Were she to back up, he'd be behind her. Were she to scream, he could cover her mouth before she'd even finished drawing her breath in preparation. She'd only once before seen a creature move with such speed and repressed power: one of the mountain cats whose muscles bunched in springy recoil as they padded about on dangerous paws.

She drew a shaky breath. He was even more magnificent than he'd been years ago. His black hair was neatly restrained in a leather thong. The angle of his jaw was even more arrogant than she remembered—if that was possible; jutting slightly forward, it caused his lower lip to curl in a sensual smirk regardless of the occasion.

The air itself felt different when Grimm Roderick was in it; her surroundings receded until nothing existed but him. And she could never mistake those eyes! Mocking blue-ice, his gaze locked with hers over the heads of the forgotten curious children. He was watching her with an unfathomable expression.

She lunged to her feet, tumbling a startled Zeke to the

ground. As Jillian stared wordlessly at Grimm, memories
surfaced and she nearly drowned in the bitter bile of humiliation. She recalled too clearly the day she'd vowed never
to speak to Grimm Roderick again. She'd sworn never to
permit him near Caithness—or near her vulnerable heart
again—as long as she lived. And he dared saunter up now?
As if nothing had changed? The possibility of reconcilia-
tion was instantly squashed beneath the weighty heels of
her pride. She would not dignify his presence with words.
She would not be nice. She would not grant him one ounce
of courtesy.

Grimm worried a hand through his hair and took a deep
breath. "You've . . . grown, lass."

Jillian struggled to speak. When she finally found her
tongue, her words dripped ice. "How dare you come back
here? You are not welcome. Leave my home!"

"I can't do that, Jillian." His soft voice unnerved her.

Her heart racing, she drew a slow, deep breath. "If you
don't leave of your own accord, I'll summon the guards to
remove you."

"They won't do that, Jillian."

She clapped her hands. "Guards!" she cried.

Grimm didn't move an inch. "It won't help, Jillian."

"And quit saying my name like that!"

"Like what, Jillian?" He sounded genuinely curious.

"Like . . . like . . . a prayer or something."

"As you wish." He paused the length of two heartbeats—
during which she was astonished he'd capitulated to her
will, because he certainly never had before—then he added
with such husky resonance that it slipped inside her heart
without her consent, "Jillian."

Perish the man! "Guards. Guards!"

Her guards arrived on a run, then halted abruptly, studying the man standing before their mistress.

"Milady, you summoned?" Hatchard inquired.

"Remove this iniquitous scoundrel from Caithness before he breeds . . . *brings*"—she corrected herself hastily—"his depravity and wicked insolence into my home," she sputtered to a finish.

The guards looked from her to Grimm and didn't move.

"Now. Remove him from the estate at once!"

When the guards still didn't move, her temper rose a notch. "Hatchard, I said make him leave. By the sweet saints, toss him out of my life. Banish him from the country. Och! Just remove him from this *world*, will you, now?"

The flank of guards stared at Jillian with openmouthed astonishment. "Are you feeling well, milady?" Hatchard asked. "Should we fetch Kaley to see if you've a touch of the fever?"

"I don't have a touch of anything. There's a degenerate knave on my estate and I want him off it," Jillian said through gritted teeth.

"Did you just grit?" Hatchard gaped.

"Pardon?"

"Grit. It means to speak from between clenched teeth—"

"I'm going to scream from between clenched teeth if you disobedient wretches don't remove this degenerate, virile"—Jillian cleared her throat—"*vile* rogue from Caithness."

"Scream?" Hatchard repeated faintly. "Jillian St. Clair doesn't scream, she doesn't grit, and she certainly doesn't have fits of temper. What the devil is going on here?"

"He's the devil," Jillian seethed, motioning to Grimm.

"Call him what you will, milady. I still can't remove him," Hatchard said heavily.

Jillian's head jerked as if he'd struck her. "You disobey me?"

"He doesn't disobey you, Jillian," Grimm said quietly. "He obeys your da."

"What?" She turned her ashen face to his. He proffered a crumpled, soiled piece of parchment.

"What is that?" she asked icily, refusing to move even an inch closer.

"Come and see, Jillian," he offered. His eyes glittered strangely.

"Hatchard, get that from him."

Hatchard didn't budge. "I know what it says."

"Well then, what does it say?" she snapped at Hatchard. "And how do you know?"

It was Grimm who answered. "It says 'come for Jillian' . . . Jillian."

He'd done it again, added her name after a pause, a husky veneration that left her oddly breathless and frightened. There was a warning in the way he was saying her name, something she should understand but couldn't quite grasp. Something had changed since they'd last fought so bitterly, something in him, but she couldn't define it. "Come for Jillian?" she repeated blankly. "My da sent you that?"

When he nodded, Jillian choked and nearly burst into tears. Such a public display of emotion would have been a first for her. Instead, she did something as unexpected and heretofore undone as gritting and cursing; Jillian spun on her heel and bolted toward the castle as if all the banshees of Scotland were nipping at her heels, when in truth it was the one and only Grimm Roderick—which was far worse.

Sneaking a glance over her shoulder, she belatedly remembered the children. They were standing in a half-circle, gaping at her with disbelief. She stormed, absolutely mortified, into the castle. Slamming the door was a bit difficult, since it was four times as tall as she was, but in her current temper she managed.

CHAPTER 3

"INCONCEIVABLE!" JILLIAN SEETHED AS SHE PACED HER chambers. She tried to calm down, but reluctantly concluded that until she got rid of *him*, calm was not possible.

So she stormed and paced and considered breaking things, except that she liked everything in her room and didn't really want to break any of her own belongings. But if she could only have gotten her hands on him, oh—then she'd have broken a thing or two!

Vexed, she muttered beneath her breath while she quickly slipped out of her gown. She refused to ponder her urge to replace the plain gown and chemise that had been perfectly suitable only an hour before. Nude, she stalked to her armoire by the window, where she was momentarily distracted by the sight of riders in the courtyard. She peered out the tall opening. Two horsemen were riding through the gate. She studied them curiously, leaning into the window. As one, the men raised their heads, and she gasped. A smile crossed the blond man's face, giving her the impression he'd glimpsed her poised in the window, clad in nothing but temper-flushed skin. Instinctively she ducked behind the armoire and snatched up a gown of brilliant green, assuring herself that just because she could see them clearly didn't mean they could see her. Surely the window reflected the sun and permitted little passage of vision.

Who else was arriving at Caithness? she fumed. *He* was bad enough. How dare he come here, and furthermore, how dare her da summon him? *Come for Jillian.* Just what had her da intended with such a note? A shiver slipped down her spine as she contemplated the possessive sound of the words. Why would Grimm Roderick respond to such a strange missive? He'd tortured her ceaselessly as a child and he'd rejected her as a young woman. He was an overbearing lout—who'd once been the hero of her every fantasy.

Now he was back at Caithness, and that was simply unacceptable. Regardless of her da's reasons for summoning him, he simply had to go. If her guards wouldn't remove him, she would—even if it meant at sword point, and she knew just where to find a sword. A massive claymore hung above the hearth in the Greathall; it would do nicely.

Her resolve firm, her gown fastened, Jillian marched out of her chambers. She was ready to confront him; her body was bristling with indignation. He had no right to be here, and she was just the person to explain that to him. He'd left once before when she'd begged him to stay—he couldn't arbitrarily decide to come back now. Snatching her hair back, she secured it with a velvet ribbon and made for the Greathall, moving briskly down the long corridor.

She drew to a sudden halt at the balustrade outside the solar, alarmed by the rumble of masculine voices below.

"What did your message say, Ramsay?" Jillian heard Grimm ask.

Their voices floated up, carrying clearly in the open Greathall. The tapestries were currently down for a cleaning, so the words reverberated off the stone walls.

"Said the lord and his lady would be leaving Caithness and called upon an old debt I owe him. He said he wished me to oversee his demesne while he was not here to do it himself."

Jillian peeked surreptitiously over the balustrade and saw Grimm sitting with two men near the main hearth. For an eternal moment she simply couldn't take her eyes off him. Angrily she jerked her gaze away and studied the newcomers. One of the men was tossed back in his chair as if he owned the keep and half the surrounding countryside. Upon closer scrutiny, Jillian decided he would likely act as if he owned any place he deigned to be. He was a study in black from head to toe: black hair, tanned skin, clad in a length of black wool that was unbroken by even one thread of color. Definitely hulking Highland blood, she concluded. A thin scar extended from his jaw to just below his eye.

Her eyes drifted over the second man. "Quinn," she whispered. She hadn't seen Quinn de Moncreiffe since he'd fostered with Grimm under her father years ago. Tall, golden and breathtakingly handsome, Quinn de Moncreiffe had comforted her on the many occasions Grimm had chased her away. In the years since she'd last seen him he had matured into a towering man with wide shoulders, a trim waist, and long blond hair pulled back in a queue.

"It would seem just about every man in Scotia and half of England is indebted to Gibraltar St. Clair for one thing or another," Quinn observed.

Ramsay Logan folded his hands behind his head and

leaned back in his chair, nodding. "Aye. He bailed me out of more than a few tight spaces when I was a younger lad and more prone to thinking with the wee head."

"Och, so you think you've changed, Logan?" Quinn provoked.

"Not so much that I couldn't knock you senseless still, de Moncreiffe," Ramsay shot back.

Ramsay Logan, Jillian mused; she'd been right about his bloodline. The Logans were indeed Highlanders. Ramsay certainly looked like one of those savage mountain men whose notoriety was exceeded only by their massive holdings. They were a land-rich clan, owning a large portion of the southern Highlands. Her eyes crept back to Grimm, despite her best intentions. He relaxed in his chair regally, composed as a king and acting as if he had every bit as much right to be there. Her eyes narrowed.

The corners of Grimm's mouth twitched faintly. "It's like old times with the two of you poking at each other, but spare me your dissension. There's a puzzle here. Why did Gibraltar St. Clair summon the three of us to Caithness? I've heard of no trouble here in years. Quinn, what did your message say? That he needed you to serve Caithness in his absence?"

Above them, Jillian frowned. That was a good question—why *would* her parents bring these three men to Caithness while they attended their grandson's christening? Hatchard, Caithness's chief man-at-arms, commanded a powerful force of guards, and there hadn't been trouble in these parts of the Lowlands for years.

"It said that he wished me to watch over Caithness in his absence, and if I couldn't take the time away from my ships to come for him, I should come for Jillian. I found his message rather odd but got the impression he was worried about Jillian, and truth be told, I've missed the lass," Quinn replied.

Jillian jerked. What was her deceitful da up to?

"Jillian—the Goddess-Empress herself." Ramsay flashed a wolfish grin.

Jillian's nostrils flared and her spine stiffened.

"What?" Grimm looked puzzled.

"He's referring to her much-lauded reputation. Didn't you stop at the stables when you rode in?" When Grimm shook his head, Quinn snorted. "You missed an earful. The lads there prattled on and on about her before we even had a chance to dismount, warning us not to defile her 'saintly' mien. The 'Goddess-Empress Jillian,' one of the young lads called her, saying mere 'Queen' was too commonplace."

"Jillian?" Grimm looked dubious.

Jillian glared at the top of his head.

"Bespelled," Ramsay affirmed. "The lot of them. One lad told me she's the second Madonna, and he believes if she bears children, it will surely be the product of divine intervention."

"I must say, any intervention with Jillian would be divine," Quinn said, grinning.

"Aye, right between those divine thighs of hers. Did you ever see a lass more well fashioned for a man's pleasure?" Ramsay kicked his feet up on the hearth and shifted in his chair, dropping his hands in his lap.

Jillian's eyebrows climbed her forehead, and she placed a hand over her mouth.

Grimm glanced sharply at Ramsay and Quinn. "Wait a minute—what do you mean by 'her divine thighs'? You've never met Jillian, have you? You doona even know what she looks like. And Quinn, *you* haven't seen her since she was a wee lass."

Quinn looked away uncomfortably.

"Does she have golden hair?" Ramsay countered. "Masses of it, falling in waves past her hips? Flawless face and about yay-tall?" He held his hand slightly above his seated head to demonstrate. "Is her bedroom on the second floor, facing due east?"

Grimm nodded warily.

"I *do* know what she looks like. Quinn and I saw her in a window as we rode in," Ramsay informed him.

Jillian groaned softly, hoping he wouldn't continue.

Ramsay continued, "If she's the woman who was changing her gown, the one with the breasts a man could—"

Jillian's hands flew protectively to her bodice. *It's a little late for that,* she rued.

"You did *not* see her getting dressed," Grimm growled, glancing at Quinn for reassurance.

"No," Ramsay supplied helpfully, "we saw her undressed. Framed in the window, sun spilling over the most splendid morning gown of rosy skin I've ever seen. Face of an angel, creamy thighs, and everything golden in between."

Mortification steeped Jillian in a furious blush from the crown of her head to her recently viewed breasts. They *had* seen her; all of her.

"Is that true, Quinn?" Grimm demanded.

Quinn nodded, looking sheepish. "Hell, Grimm, what did you expect me to do? Look away? She's stunning. I'd long suspected the wee lass would ripen into a lovely woman, but I'd never imagined such exquisite charms. Although Jillian always seemed like a younger sister to me, after I saw her today . . ." He shook his head and whistled admiringly. "Well, feelings can change."

"I didn't know Gibraltar had such a daughter," Ramsay hastened to add, "or I'd have been sniffing around years ago—"

"She's not the sniffing around kind. She's the marrying kind," Grimm snapped.

"Aye, she is the marrying kind, and the keeping kind, and the bedding kind," Ramsay said coolly. "The dolts at Caithness may be intimidated by her beauty, but I'm not. A woman like that needs a flesh-and-blood man."

Quinn shot Ramsay an irritated look and rose to his feet. "Exactly what are you saying, Logan? If any man is going to be speaking for her, it should be me. I've known Jillian since she was a child. My message specifically mentioned coming for Jillian, and after seeing her, I intend to do *precisely* that."

Ramsay came to his feet slowly, unfolding his massive frame until he stood a good two inches above Quinn's six-foot-plus frame. "Perhaps the only reason *my* message wasn't worded the same way is because St. Clair knew I'd never met her. Regardless, it's past time I take a wife, and I intend to give the lovely lass an option besides hanging her nightrail—if she ever wears one, although I'm certainly not complaining—beside some common Lowland farmer."

"Who's calling who a farmer here? I am a bleeding merchant and worth more than all your paltry skinny-ass, shaggy-haired cows put together."

"Pah! My skinny-ass cows aren't where I get my wealth, you Lowland skivvy—"

"Aye, raiding innocent Lowlanders, more likely!" Quinn cut him off. "And what the hell is a skivvy?"

"Not a word a *flatlander* would know," Ramsay snapped.

"Gentlemen, please." Hatchard entered the Greathall, an expression of concern on his face. Having served as chief man-at-arms for twenty years, he could foresee a battle brewing half a county away, and this one was simmering beneath his nose. "There's no need to get into a brawl over this. Hold your tongues and bide a wee, for I have a message for you from Gibraltar St. Clair. And do sit down." He gestured to the chairs clustered near the hearth. "It's been my experience that men who are facing off rarely listen well."

Ramsay and Quinn continued to glare at each other.

Jillian tensed and nearly poked her head through the spindles of the balustrade. What was her father up to this time? Shrewd, red-haired Hatchard was her father's most trusted advisor and longtime friend. His vulpine features were an accurate reflection of his cleverness; he was canny and quick as a fox. His long, lean fingers tapped the hilt of his sword as he waited impatiently for the men to obey his command. *"Sit,"* Hatchard repeated forcefully.

Ramsay and Quinn reluctantly eased back into their chairs.

"I'm pleased to see you've all arrived promptly," Hatchard said in an easier tone. "But, Grimm, why is your horse wandering the bailey?"

Grimm spoke softly. "He doesn't like to be penned. Is there a problem with that?"

Like man, like horse. Jillian rolled her eyes.

"No, no problem with me. But if he starts eating Jillian's flowers, you may have a bit of a skirmish on your hands." Hatchard lowered himself into a vacant chair, amused.

"Actually, I suspect you're going to have a bit of a skirmish on your hands no matter what you do with your horse, Grimm Roderick." He chuckled. "It's good to see you again. It's been too long. Perhaps you could train with my men while you're here."

Grimm nodded curtly. "So why has Gibraltar summoned us here, Hatchard?"

"I'd planned to allow you all to settle in a bit before I passed on his message, but the lot of you are already onto the right of it. St. Clair did bring you here for his daughter," Hatchard admitted, rubbing his short red beard thoughtfully.

"I knew it," Ramsay said smugly.

Jillian hissed softly. *How dare he?* More suitors, and among them the very man she had vowed to hate until death. Grimm Roderick. How many men would her da throw at her before he finally accepted that she would not wed unless she found the kind of love her parents shared?

Hatchard leaned back in his chair and regarded the men levelly. "He expects she will choose one of you before they return from their visit, which gives the lot of you till late autumn to woo her."

"And if she doesn't?" Grimm asked.

"She will." Ramsay folded his arms across his chest, a portrait of arrogance.

"Does Jillian know about this?" Grimm asked quietly.

"Aye, is she duplicitous or is she an innocent?" Quinn quipped.

"And if she is innocent, to what degree?" Ramsay asked wickedly. "I, for one, intend to find out at the earliest opportunity."

"Over my dead body, Logan," Quinn growled.

"So be it." Ramsay shrugged.

"Well, whatever he intended, I don't think it was for the three of you to be killing each other over her." Hatchard smiled faintly. "He merely intends to see her wed before she passes another birthday, and one of you shall be the man. And no, Grimm, Jillian doesn't know a thing about it. She'd likely flee Caithness immediately if she had the vaguest inkling what her father was up to. Gibraltar has brought dozens of suitors to Jillian over the past year, and she drove them all away with one shenanigan or another. She and her da relished outwitting each another; the more unusual his ploy, the more inventive her reaction. Although, I must say, she always handled things with a certain delicacy and subtlety only a Sacheron woman can effect. Most of the men had no idea they'd been . . . er . . . for lack of a better word . . . duped. Like her father, Jillian can be the very image of propriety while planning a mutinous rebellion behind her composed face. One of you must court and win her, because the three of you are Gibraltar's last hopes."

Impossible, Jillian silently argued her case with shaky conviction. Her da would not do this to her. Would he? Even as she denied it, the long, considering glances her da had been giving her before he'd left surfaced in her mind. Suddenly his somewhat guilty expression, his last-minute hugs before he'd left made sense to Jillian. By the saints, as dispassionately as he matched his broodmares, her da had locked her in the stables with three hot-blooded studs and gone visiting.

Make that two hot-blooded studs and one cold, arro-gant, impossible heathen, she amended silently. For surely as the sun rose and set, Grimm Roderick wouldn't deign to touch her even with someone else's hands. Jillian's shoulders slumped.

As if he'd somehow read her mind, Grimm Roderick's words drifted up, inciting more of that witless fury she suffered in his presence.

"Well, you doona have to worry about me, lads, for I wouldn't wed the woman if she was the last woman in all of Scotia. So it's up to the two of you to make Jillian a husband."

Jillian clenched her jaw and fled down the corridor before she could succumb to a mad urge to fling herself over the balustrade, a hissing female catapult of teeth and nails.

CHAPTER 4

MALDEBANN CASTLE
THE HIGHLANDS, ABOVE TULUTH

"MILORD, YOUR SON IS NEAR."

Ronin McIllioch surged to his feet, his blue eyes blazing. "He's coming here? Now?"

"No, milord. Forgive me, I did not mean to alarm you," Gilles corrected hastily. "He is at Caithness."

"Caithness," Ronin repeated. He exchanged glances with his men. Their gazes reflected concern, caution, and unmistakable hope. "Have you any idea why he's there?" Ronin asked.

"No. Shall we find out?"

"Dispatch Elliott, he blends in well. Discreetly, mind you," Ronin said. Softly he added, "My son is closer than he's come in years."

"Yes, milord. Think you he may come home?"

Ronin McIllioch smiled, but it did not reach his eyes. "The time is not yet right for his return. We still have work to do. Send with Elliott the young boy who draws. I want pictures, with great detail."

"Yes, milord."

"And Gilles?"

Gilles paused in the doorway.

"Has anything . . . changed?"

Gilles sighed and shook his head. "He still calls himself Grimm. And as nearly as our men have been able to ascertain, he has never bothered to ask if you're still alive. Nor has he ever once looked west to Maldebann."

Ronin inclined his head. "Thank you. That will be all, Gilles."

* * *

Jillian found Kaley dicing potatoes in the kitchen. Kaley Twillow was a motherly woman in her late thirties; her curvaceous body couched an equally spacious heart. Originally from England, she'd come to Caithness upon the reference of one of Gibraltar's friends when her husband had died. Maid, cook's assistant, confidante in place of a scheming mother—Kaley did it all. Jillian plunked down on the edge of a chair and said without preface, "Kaley, there's a thing I've been wondering."

"And what might that be, dear?" Kaley asked with a tender smile. She laid her knife aside. "As a rule, your questions are quite peculiar, but they are always interesting."

Jillian edged her chair nearer to the cutting block where Kaley stood, so the other servants in the busy kitchen wouldn't overhear. "What does it mean when a man 'comes for a woman'?" she whispered conspiratorially.

Kaley blinked rapidly. "Comes?" she echoed.

"Comes," Jillian affirmed.

Kaley retrieved her knife, clutching it like a small sword. "In just what context did you hear this phrase used?" she asked stiffly. "Was it in reference to you? Was it one of the guards? Who was the man?"

Jillian shrugged. "I overheard a man saying he was told to 'come for Jillian' and he planned to do just that, precisely to the letter. I don't understand. He already did it—he came here."

Kaley thought a moment, then chortled, relaxing visibly. "It wouldn't have been the mighty, golden Quinn, would it, Jillian?"

Jillian's blush was reply enough for Kaley.

She calmly replaced her knife on the cutting board. "It means, dear lass"—Kaley bent her head close to Jillian's—"that he plans to bed you."

"Oh!" Jillian flinched, eyes wide. "Thank you, Kaley." She excused herself crisply.

Kaley's eyes sparkled as Jillian beat a hasty retreat from the kitchen. "A fine man. Lucky lass."

* * *

As she raced for her chambers, Jillian seethed. While she could appreciate her parents' desire to see her wed, it was their fault as much as hers that she wasn't. They hadn't started encouraging her until last year, and shortly thereafter they'd dumped a barrage of candidates upon her with no warning. One by one, Jillian had brilliantly discouraged them by convincing them she was an unattainable paragon, not to be considered in a carnal, worldly sense—a woman better suited for the cloister than the marriage bed. A declaration of such intent had cooled the ardor of several of her suitors.

If cool civility and frigid reserve failed, she hinted at a family disposition toward madness that sent men scurrying. She'd had to resort to that on only two occasions;

apparently her pious act was pretty convincing. And why shouldn't it be? she brooded. She'd never done anything particularly daring or improper in her entire life, hence she'd acquired a reputation as "a truly good person." "Yuck," she informed the wall. "Chisel that on my headstone. 'She was a truly good person, but she's dead now.' "

Although her efforts to dissuade her suitors had been successful, she'd apparently failed to stop her parents from scheming to marry her off; they'd summoned three more suitors to Caithness and abandoned her to her own straits. Dire straits indeed, for Jillian knew these men were not the kind to be put off with a few cool words and an aloof demeanor. Nor would they likely accept her claims of inherited madness. These men were too confident, too bold . . . *oh, hell's bells,* she dusted off another childhood curse, they were far too masculine for any woman's peace of mind. And if she wasn't careful, these three men could cause her to reclaim all the childhood epithets she'd learned while skipping at the heels of Quinn and Grimm. Jillian was accustomed to gentle, modest men, men gelded by their own insecurities, not swaggering, uncut bulls who thought "insecure" meant an unstable fortress or a weak timber in a foundation.

Of the three men currently invading her home, the only one she might hope to persuade to consider her plight sympathetically was Quinn, and that was far from a certainty. The lad she'd known years ago was quite different from the formidable man he'd become. Even at the far reaches of Caithness she'd heard of his reputation throughout Scotland as a relentless conqueror, both of trade and women. To top it off, if Kaley's interpretation could be trusted and Quinn had truly been making an innuendo about bedding her, his youthful protectiveness had matured into manly possessiveness.

Then there was the intrepid Ramsay Logan. Nobody had to convince Jillian the black-clad Ramsay was dangerous. He dripped peril from every pore.

Grimm Roderick was another matter. He would certainly not push for her hand, but his simple presence was bad enough. He was a constant reminder of the most painful and humiliating days of her life.

Three barbarians who had been hand-selected by her own da to seduce and marry her lurked in her home. What was she going to do? Although it appealed to her immensely, fleeing didn't make much sense. They'd only come after her, and she doubted she'd ever make it to one of her brother's homes before Hatchard's men caught up. Besides, she brooded, she would *not* leave her home just to get away from *him*.

How could her parents do this to her? Worse yet, how could she ever go downstairs again? Not only had two of the men seen her without a stitch of clothing on, they were obviously planning to pluck the overripe, or so her parents had concluded without so much as soliciting her opinion, berry of her virginity. Jillian squeezed her knees together protectively, dropped her head in her lap, and decided things couldn't get much worse.

* * *

It wasn't easy for Jillian to hide in her chambers all day. She wasn't the cowering sort. Nor, however, was she the foolish sort, and she knew she must have a plan before she subjected herself to the perils of her parents' nefarious scheme. As afternoon faded into evening and she'd yet to be struck by inspiration, she discovered she was feeling quite irritable. She hated being cooped up in her chambers. She wanted to play the virginal, she wanted to kick the first person she saw, she wanted to visit Zeke, she wanted to eat. She'd thought someone would appear by lunchtime, she'd been certain loyal Kaley would come check on her if she didn't arrive at dinner, but the maids didn't even appear to clean her chambers or light the fire. As the solitary hours passed, Jillian's ire increased. The angrier she became, the less objectively she considered her plight, ultimately concluding she would simply ignore the three men and go about her life as if nothing was amiss.

Food was her priority now. Shivering in the chilly evening air, she donned a light but voluminous cloak and pulled the hood snug around her face. Perhaps if she met up with one of the oversized brutes the combination of darkness and concealing attire would grant her anonymity. It probably wouldn't fool Grimm, but the other two hadn't seen her with clothes *on* yet.

Jillian closed the door quietly and slipped into the hallway. She opted for the servants' staircase and carefully picked her way down the dimly lit, winding steps. Caithness was huge, but Jillian had played in every nook and cranny and knew the castle well; nine doors down and to the left was the kitchen, just past the buttery. She peered down the long corridor. Lit by flickering oil lamps, it was deserted, the castle silent. Where was everyone?

As she moved forward, a voice floated out of the darkness behind her. "Pardon, lass, but could you tell me where I might find the buttery? We've run short of whisky and there's not a maid about."

Jillian froze in mid-step, momentarily robbed of speech. How could all the maids disappear and that man appear the very instant she decided to sneak from her chambers?

"I asked you to leave, Grimm Roderick. What are you still doing here?" she said coolly.

"Is that you, Jillian?" He stepped closer, peering through the shadows.

"Have so many other women at Caithness demanded you depart that you're suffering confusion about my identity?" she asked sweetly, plunging her shaking hands into the folds of her cloak.

"I didn't recognize you beneath your hood until I heard you speak, and as to the women, you know how the women around here felt about me. I assume nothing has changed."

Jillian almost choked. He was as arrogant as he'd always been. She pushed her hood back irritably. The women had fallen all over him when he'd fostered here, lured by his dark, dangerous looks, muscled body, and absolute indifference. Maids had thrown themselves at his feet, visiting ladies had offered him jewels and lodgings. It had been revolting to watch. "Well, you are older," she parried weakly. "And you know as a man gets older his good looks can suffer."

Grimm's mouth turned faintly upward as he stepped forward into the flickering light thrown off by a wall torch. Tiny lines at the corners of his eyes were whiter than his Highland-tanned face. If anything, it made him more beautiful.

"You are older too." He studied her through narrowed eyes.

"It's not nice to chide a woman about her age. I am *not* an old maid."

"I didn't say you were," he said mildly. "The years have made you a lovely woman."

"And?" Jillian demanded.

"And what?"

"Well, go ahead. Don't leave me hanging, waiting for the nasty thing you're going to say. Just say it and get it over with."

"What nasty thing?"

"Grimm Roderick, you have never said a single nice thing to me in all my life. So don't start faking it now."

Grimm's mouth twisted up at one corner, and Jillian realized that he still hated to smile. He fought it, begrudged it, and rarely did one ever break the confines of his eternal self-control. Such a waste, for he was even more handsome when he smiled, if that was possible.

He moved closer.

"Stop right there!"

Grimm ignored her command, continuing his approach. "I said *stop*."

"Or you'll do what, Jillian?" His voice was smooth and amused. He cocked his head at a lazy angle and folded his arms across his chest.

"Why, I'll . . ." She belatedly acknowledged there wasn't much of anything she could do to prevent him from going anywhere he wished to go, in any manner he wished to go there. He was twice her size, and she'd never be his physical match. The only weapon she'd ever had against him was her sharp tongue, honed to a razor edge by years of defensive practice on this man.

He shrugged his shoulders impatiently. "Tell me, lass, what will you do?"

Jillian made no reply, mesmerized by the intersection of his arms, the golden slopes of muscle flexing at his slightest movement. She had a sudden vision of his hard body stretched full length above hers, his lips curving, not with his customary infuriating condescension but with passion.

He sauntered nearer, until he stood mere inches from

her. She swallowed hard and clasped her hands inside her cloak.

He lowered his head toward hers.

Jillian could not have moved if the stone walls of the corridor had started crumbling around her. If the floor had suddenly ruptured beneath her feet, she would have hung suspended on dreamy clouds of fantasy. Mesmerized, she stared up into his brilliant eyes, fascinated by the silky dark lashes, the smooth tan of his skin, the aquiline, arrogant nose, the sensual curved lips, the cleft in his chin. He leaned closer, his breath fanning her cheek. *Was he going to kiss her? Could it be Grimm Roderick might actually kiss her? Had he truly responded to her da's summons—for her?* Her knees felt weak. He cleared his throat, and she trembled with anticipation. What would he do? Would he ask her permission?

"So where, milady, pray tell, is the buttery?" His lips brushed her ear. "I believe this ridiculous conversation began by my saying we're out of whisky and there's not a maid about. Whisky, lass," he repeated in a voice oddly roughened. "We men need a drink. Ten minutes have passed and I'm no closer to finding it."

Kiss her, indeed. When pine martens curled up on the hearth like sleepy cats. Jillian glared at him. "One thing has not changed, Grimm Roderick, and don't you ever forget it. I still hate you."

Jillian pushed past him, retreating once again to the safety of her chambers.

CHAPTER 5

THE MOMENT JILLIAN OPENED HER EYES THE NEXT morning, she panicked. Had he left because she'd been so hateful?

He's supposed to leave, she reminded herself grimly. She *wanted* him to leave. Didn't she? Her brow furrowed as she pondered the illogical duality of her feelings. As far back as she could recall, she'd always suffered this vacillation where Grimm was concerned: hating him one moment, adoring him the next, but always wanting him near. If he hadn't been so unkind to her she would have consistently adored him, but he'd made it painfully clear that her adoration was the last thing he wanted. And that obviously hadn't changed. From the first moment she'd met Grimm Roderick, she'd been hopelessly drawn to him. But after years of being brushed away, ignored, and finally abandoned, she'd given up her childhood fantasies.

Or had she? Perhaps that was precisely her fear: Now that he was back she would make the same mistakes again and behave like an adolescent fool over the magnificent warrior he had become.

Dressing quickly, she snatched up her slippers and hastened for the Greathall. As she entered the room, she halted abruptly. "Oh, my," she murmured. Somehow she'd managed to forget there were three men in her home, so consumed had she been with thoughts of Grimm. They gathered near the fire, while several maids cleared dozens of platters and dishes from the massive table centered in the Greathall. Yesterday, safe behind the balustrade, Jillian had been struck by how tall and broad the three of them were. Today, standing only a few feet from them, she felt like a dwarf willow in a forest of mighty oaks. Each man stood at least a foot taller than she did. It was downright intimidating to a woman who was not easily intimidated. Her gaze wandered from one man to the next.

Ramsay Logan was an inch short of terrifying. Quinn was no longer the stripling son of a Lowland chieftain, but a powerful laird in his own right. And Grimm was the only man not looking at her; he stood gazing intently into the fire. She took advantage of his distraction and studied his profile with greedy eyes.

"Jillian." Quinn moved forward to greet her.

She forced herself to drag her gaze away from Grimm and concentrate on what Quinn was saying. "Welcome, Quinn." She pasted a cheerful smile on her lips.

"It's so good to see you again, lass." Quinn took her hands in his and smiled down at her. "It's been years and . . . och, but the years have been generous to you— you're breathtaking!"

Jillian blushed and glanced at Grimm, who was paying no heed to the conversation. She stifled the urge to kick him and make him notice that someone thought she was lovely. "You've changed yourself, Quinn," she said brightly. "It's no wonder I've heard your name linked with one beautiful woman after another."

"And just where would you be hearing that, lass?" Quinn asked softly.

"Caithness isn't exactly the end of the earth, Quinn. We do get visitors here on occasion."

"And you've asked them about me?" Quinn probed, interested.

Behind him, Ramsay cleared his throat impatiently.

Jillian sneaked another glance at Grimm. "Of course I have. And Da always likes to hear about the lads he fostered," she added.

"Well, although I wasn't fostered here, your father *did* ask me to come. That must count for something," Ramsay grumbled, trying to jostle Quinn aside. "And if this dolt would recall his manners, perhaps he'd see fit to introduce me to the loveliest woman in all of Scotland."

Jillian thought she heard Grimm make a choking sound. Her gaze flew to him, but he hadn't moved a muscle and still appeared oblivious to the conversation.

Quinn snorted. "Not that I don't agree with his assessment of you, Jillian, but beware this Highlander's tongue. He's got quite a reputation with the lasses himself." Reluctantly he turned to Ramsay. "Jillian, I'd like you to meet—"

"Ramsay Logan," Ramsay interrupted, thrusting himself forward. "Chieftain of the largest keep in the Highlands and—"

"My ass, you are." Quinn snorted. "The Logan scarcely has a pot to"—he broke off and cleared his throat—"cook in."

Ramsay jostled him aside and moved into his place.

"Give it up, de Moncreiffe, she's not interested in a Lowlander."

"*I'm* a Lowlander," Jillian reminded.

"Merely by birth, not by choice, and marriage could correct that." Ramsay stepped as close to Jillian as he could without actually standing on her toes.

"Lowlanders are the civilized lot of the Scots, Logan. And quit crowding her, you're going to back her right out of the hall."

Jillian smiled gratefully at Quinn, then flinched as Grimm finally looked sidewise at her.

"Jillian," he said quietly, nodding in her general direction before turning back to the fire.

How could he affect her so intensely? All the man had to do was say her name, one word, and Jillian was unable to form a coherent sentence. And there were so many questions she wanted to ask him—years and years of "whys." *Why did you leave me? Why did you hate me? Why couldn't you adore me like I adore you?*

"Why?" Jillian demanded before she knew she'd opened her mouth.

Ramsay and Quinn gazed at her, puzzled, but she only had eyes for Grimm.

She stomped over to the fire and poked Grimm in the shoulder. "Why? Would you just tell me that? For once and for all, why?"

"Why what, Jillian?" Grimm didn't turn.

She poked him harder. "You know 'why what.' "

Grimm glanced reluctantly over his shoulder. "Really, Jillian, I haven't the faintest idea what you're blathering about." Ice-blue eyes met hers, and for a moment she thought she glimpsed a blatant dare in them. It shocked her to her senses.

"Don't be ridiculous, Grimm. It's a simple question. Why have the three of you come to Caithness?" Jillian quickly salvaged the remnants of her pride. They didn't know she'd overheard her father's despicable scheme, and she'd soon discover if any of them would be honest with her.

Grimm's eyes flickered strangely; in another man Jillian might have called it disappointment, but not in his. He scanned her from head to toe, noting the slippers clutched in her hands. When he looked at her bare toes she curled them under her gown, feeling oddly vulnerable, as if she were six again.

"Put your slippers on, lass. You'll catch a chill."

Jillian glared at him.

Quinn moved to her side and offered his arm for her to lean on while she donned her slippers. "He's right. The stones are cold, lass. As to the why of it, your da summoned us to look after Caithness in his absence, Jillian."

"Really?" Jillian said sweetly, adding "liar" to the list of nasty names she was calling men in the privacy of her thoughts. She stuffed one foot in a slipper, then the next. She doubted Grimm would care if she died of a chill. *Put your slippers on,* he ordered, as if she were an unruly toddler who couldn't complete the simple task of dressing herself. "Is there trouble expected in these parts of the Lowlands?"

"It's better to be safe than sorry, lass." Ramsay offered the platitude with his most charming smile.

Safe, my arse, she thought mulishly. Safe certainly wasn't this, surrounded by circling warriors who were inflamed by the mere scent of a woman.

"Your da didn't wish to take the chance trouble might befall Caithness in his absence, and now seeing you, lass, I

understand his concern," Ramsay added smoothly. "I'd select only the finest to protect you too."

"I'm all the protection she needs, Logan," Quinn said
dryly. He took her by the hand and led her to the table.
"Bring breakfast for the lady," he instructed a maid.

"Protection from what?" Jillian asked.

"From yourself, most likely." Grimm's voice was low
but still carried clearly in the stone hall.

"*What* did you just say?" Jillian whirled around in her
seat. Any excuse for an argument with him was a welcome
excuse.

"I said protection from yourself, brat." Grimm met her
gaze with a heated one of his own. "You're forever walking
into danger. Like when you wandered off with the tinkers.
We couldn't find you for *two days*."

Quinn laughed. "By Odin's spear, I'd forgotten about
that. We were nearly mad with worry. I finally found you
north of Dunrieffe—'

"I would have found her if you hadn't insisted I go
south, Quinn. I told you they'd gone north," Grimm reminded him.

Quinn glanced sideways at Grimm. "Hell's bells, man,
don't brood about it. She was found, and that's all that
matters."

"I wasn't lost to begin with," Jillian informed them. "I
knew exactly where I was."

The men laughed.

"And I am not always getting into danger. I just wanted
to feel the freedom of the tinkers. I was old enough—"

"You were thirteen!" Grimm snapped.

"I was fully in control of myself!"

"You were misbehaving as usual," Quinn teased.

"Jillian never misbehaves," Kaley murmured as she

entered the room and caught the last of the conversation. She placed a steaming platter of sausage and potatoes in front of Jillian.

"A shame, if it's true," Ramsay purred.

"Then there was the time she got stuck in the pigpen. Remember that one, Grimm?" Quinn laughed, and even Grimm couldn't begrudge him a smile. "Remember how she looked, backed into the corner, jabbering away to the enraged mama pig?" Quinn snorted. "I swear Jillian was squealing louder than the sow was."

Jillian leapt to her feet. "That's quite enough. And quit smiling, Kaley."

"I'd forgotten that one myself, Jillian." Kaley chuckled. "You were a handful."

Jillian grimaced. "I'm not a child anymore. I'm twenty-one years old—"

"And why is it that you haven't wed, lass?" Ramsay wondered aloud.

Silence descended as all eyes, including several curious maids', focused on Jillian. She stiffened, mortification staining her cheeks with a flush of pink. By the saints, these men held nothing back. Not one of her past suitors would have dared such a direct frontal attack, but these men, she reminded herself grimly, weren't like any men she'd ever known before. Even Grimm and Quinn were unknown variables; they'd become dangerously unpredictable.

"Well, why haven't you?" Quinn said softly. "You're beautiful, witty, and well landed. Where are all your suitors, lass?"

Where, indeed? Jillian mused.

Grimm turned from the fire slowly. "Yes, Jillian, tell us. Why *haven't* you wed?"

Jillian's eyes flew to his. For a long moment she was unable to free herself from the snare of his gaze and the strange emotions it incited in her. With an immense effort of will, she averted her gaze. "Because I'm joining the cloister. Didn't Da tell you?" she said cheerfully. "That's probably why he brought you all here, to escort me safely to the Sisters of Gethsemane come fall." She studiously ignored Kaley's reproachful look and plunked down in her seat, attacking her breakfast with newly discovered relish. Let them chew on that. If they wouldn't admit the truth, why should she?

"Cloister?" Quinn said after a stunned silence.

"The nunnery," she clarified.

"As in wed to the Christ and none other?" Ramsay groaned.

"As in," Jillian confirmed around a mouthful of sausage.

Grimm didn't say a word as he left the Greathall.

* * *

A few hours later Jillian was wandering the outer bailey, quite aimlessly, certainly not of a mind to wonder where one specific man might have gotten off to, when Kaley ducked out the back entrance of the castle just as she passed.

"The cloister, is it? Really, Jillian," Kaley reprimanded.

"By the saints, Kaley, they were telling stories about me!"

"Charming stories."

"Humiliating stories." Jillian's cheeks colored.

"Endearing stories. True stories, not outrageous fibs like you told."

"Kaley, they're men," Jillian said, as if that should explain everything.

"Mighty fine men, at that, lass. Your da brings the cream

of the crop here for you to choose a husband, and you go and tell them you're destined for a nunnery."

"You knew my da brought them here for that?" Kaley flushed.

"How did you know?"

Kaley looked embarrassed. "I was eavesdropping from the solar when you were spying over the balustrade. You really must stop doffing your clothes in front of the window, Jillian," she chided.

"I didn't do it on purpose, Kaley." Jillian pursed her lips and scowled. "For a moment I thought Mother and Da had told you, even though they hadn't told me."

"No, lass. They didn't tell anyone. And maybe they were a bit heavy-handed, but you can approach this in one of two ways: You can be angry and spiteful and ruin your chances, or you can thank Providence and your da for fetching you the best of the best, Jillian."

Jillian rolled her eyes. "If those men are the best, then it's the cloister for certain."

"Jillian, come on, lass. Don't fight what's best for you. Choose a man and quit being mulish."

"I don't want a man." Jillian seethed.

Kaley measured her a long moment. "What are you doing wandering around out here, anyway?"

"Enjoying the flowers." Jillian shrugged nonchalantly.

"Don't you usually ride in the morning, then go to the village?"

"I didn't feel like it this morning. Is that a crime?" Jillian said peevishly.

Kaley's lip twitched in a smile. "Speaking of riding, I believe I saw that handsome Highlander Ramsay down by the stables."

"Good. I hope he gets trampled. Although I'm not certain there's a horse tall enough. Perhaps he could lie upon the ground and make it easier."

Kaley searched Jillian's face intently. "Quinn told me he was going to the village to fetch some whisky from MacBean."

"I hope he drowns in it," Jillian said, then looked at Kaley hopefully.

"Well," Kaley drawled, "I guess I'll be heading back to the kitchens. There's a lot of food to cook for these men." The voluptuous maid turned her back on Jillian and started walking away.

"Kaley!"

"What?" Kaley blinked innocently over her shoulder.

Jillian's eyes narrowed. "Innocent doesn't suit you, Kaley."

"Peevish doesn't suit you, Jillian."

Jillian flushed. "I'm sorry. So?" she encouraged.

Kaley shook her head, chuckling softly. "I'm sure you don't care, but Grimm's gone to the loch. Looked to me like he planned to do some washing."

The moment Kaley was gone, Jillian glanced around to make certain no one was watching, then doffed her slippers and raced for the loch.

* * *

Jillian ducked behind the rock and watched him.

Grimm was crouched at the edge of the loch, scrubbing his shirt with two smooth rocks. With a castle full of servants and maids to do the washing, the mending, his every bidding—even rush to his bed if he so much as crooked a seductive finger—Grimm Roderick walked to the loch, selected stones, and washed his own shirt. What pride. What independence. What . . . isolation.

She wanted to wash the worn linen for him. No, she wanted to wash the muscled chest the soft linen caressed. She wanted to trace her hands over the ridges of muscle that laced his abdomen and follow that silky dark trail of hair where it dipped beneath his kilt. She wanted to be welcomed into his solitary confinement and release the man she was convinced had deliberately walled himself behind a façade of chill indifference.

One knee in the grass, his leg bent beneath him, he scrubbed the shirt gently. Jillian watched the muscles in his shoulders flexing. He was more beautiful than any man had the right to be, with his great height and perfectly conditioned body, his black hair restrained by a leather thong, his piercing eyes.

I adore you, Grimm Roderick. How many times had she said those words safely in the private chambers of her head? *Loved you since the day I first saw you. Been waiting for you to notice me ever since.* Jillian dropped to the moss behind the rock, folded her arms on the stone, and rested her chin upon them, watching him hungrily. His back was bathed golden by the sun, and his wide shoulders tapered to a trim waist, where his kilt hugged his hips. His plunged a hand into his thick, dark hair, pushing it out of his face, and Jillian expelled a breath as his muscles rippled.

He turned and looked directly at her. Jillian froze. Damn his acute hearing! He'd always had unnatural senses. How could she have forgotten?

"Go away, peahen." He returned his attention to the shirt he was washing.

Jillian closed her eyes and dropped her head on her hands in defeat. She couldn't even get to the point where she worked up the courage to try to talk to him, to reach him. The moment she started thinking mushy thoughts, the bastard said something remote and biting and it deflated the sails of her resolve before she'd even lifted anchor. She sighed louder, indulging in a generous dose of self-pity.

He turned and looked at her again. "What?" he demanded.

Jillian lifted her head irritably. "What do you mean, 'what'? I didn't say anything to you."

"You're sitting back there sighing as if the world's about to end. You're making so much noise I can't even scrub my shirt in peace, and then you have the gall to get snippy with me when I politely inquire as to what you're mooning about."

"Politely inquire?" she echoed. "You call a barely grunted and entirely put-upon-sounding 'what' a polite inquiry? A 'what' that says 'how dare you invade my space with your pitiful sounds?' A 'what' that says 'could you please go die somewhere else, peahen?' Grimm Roderick, you don't know the first damned thing about polite."

"There's no need to be cursing, peahen," he said mildly.

"I am *not* a peahen."

He tossed a scathing look over his shoulder. "Yes, you are. You're always pecking away at something. Peck-peck, peck-peck."

"Pecking?" Jillian shot to her feet, leapt the stone, and faced Grimm. "I'll show you pecking." Quick as a cat, she plucked the shirt from his hands, twisted her hands in the fabric, and ripped it down the center. She found the sound of the cloth tearing perversely satisfying. "That's what I really feel like doing. How's *that* for invading your space? And why are you washing your own stupid shirt in the first place?" She glared at him, flapping the tails of his shirt to punctuate her words.

Grimm sat back on his heels, eyeing her warily. "Are you feeling all right?"

"No, I am not feeling all right. I haven't been feeling all right all morning. And stop trying to change the subject and turn it around on me, like you always do. Answer my question. Why are you washing your own shirt?"

"Because it was dirty," he replied with calculated condescension.

She ignored it with admirable restraint. "There are maids to wash—"

"I didn't wish to inconvenience—"

"The shirts of the men who—"

"A maid by asking her to wash—"

"And I would have washed the stupid thing for you anyway!"

Grimm's mouth snapped shut.

"I mean, that is . . . well, I would have if . . . if all the maids were dead or taken grievously ill and there was no one else who could"—she shrugged—"and it was the only shirt you owned . . . and bitterly cold . . . and you were sick yourself or something." She snapped her mouth shut, realizing there was no way out of the verbal quagmire into which she'd leapt. Grimm was staring at her with fascination.

He rose to his feet in one swift graceful motion. Mere inches separated them.

Jillian resented having to tilt her head back to look up at him, but her resentment was quickly replaced by a breathless awareness of the man. She was mesmerized by his proximity, riveted by the intense way he was eyeing her. Had he moved even closer? Or had she leaned into him?

"*You* would have washed my shirt?" His eyes searched hers intently.

Jillian gazed at him in silence, not trusting herself to speak. If she opened her mouth, God only knew what might come out. *Kiss me, you big beautiful warrior.*

When he brushed her tense jaw with the back of his knuckles, she nearly swooned. Her skin tingled where his fingers had passed. His lips were a breath away from hers, his eyes were heavy-lidded and unfathomable.

He wanted to kiss her. Jillian felt certain of it.

She tilted her head to receive his kiss. Her lids fluttered shut, and she gave herself fully over to fantasy. His breath fanned her cheek, and she waited, afraid to move a muscle.

"Well, it's too late now."

Her eyes flew open. *No, it's not,* she nearly snapped. *Kiss me.*

"To wash it, I mean." His gaze dropped to the tattered shirt she still held. "Besides," he added, "I doona need some silly peahen fussing over me. At least the maids doona rip my shirts, unless of course they're in a hurry to remove them from my body, but that's an entirely different discussion which is neither here nor there, and one I'm sure you wouldn't be interested in having with me anyway. . . ."

"Grimm?" Jillian said tightly.

He looked out over the loch. "Um?"

"I hate you."

"I know, lass," he said softly. "You told me that last night. It seems all our little 'discussions' end on those words. Try to be a bit more creative, will you?"

He didn't move a muscle when the remains of his wet shirt slapped him in the face and Jillian stomped away.

* * *

Grimm came to dinner wearing a clean tartan. His hair was wet, slicked back from a recent bath, and his shirt was ripped cleanly in two down the center of his back. The loose ends flapped above his tartan, and entirely too much muscled back could be seen for Jillian's comfort.

"What happened to your shirt, Grimm?" Quinn asked curiously.

Grimm gazed across the table at Jillian.

Jillian raised her head, intending to scowl self-righteously, but failed. He was looking at her with that strange expression she couldn't interpret, the one she'd seen when he'd first arrived and had kept saying her name—and she swallowed her angry words along with a bite of bread that had become impossibly dry. The man's face was flawlessly symmetrical. A shadow beard accentuated the hollows beneath his cheekbones, sharply defining his arrogant jaw. His wet hair, secured by a thong, gleamed ebony in the flickering light. His blue eyes were brilliant against the backdrop of his tanned skin, and his white teeth flashed when he spoke. His lips were firm, pink, sensuous, and presently curved in a mocking expression.

"I had a run-in with an ill-tempered feline," Grimm said, holding her gaze.

"Well, why don't you change your shirt?" Ramsay asked.

"I brought only the one," Grimm told Jillian.

"You brought one shirt?" Ramsay snorted disbelievingly. "Odin's spear, Grimm, you can afford a thousand shirts. Becoming a miser, are you?"

" 'Tis not the shirt that makes the man, Logan."

"Damn good thing for you." Ramsay carefully straightened the folds of his snowy linen. "Have you considered that it may be a reflection of him?"

"I'm sure a maid can mend it for you," Quinn said. "Or I can lend you one."

"I doona mind wearing it this way. As for reflections, who's to see?"

"You look like a villein, Roderick." Ramsay sneered.

Jillian made a resigned sound. "I'll mend it," she muttered, dropping her gaze to her plate so she didn't have to see their stunned expressions.

"You can sew, lass?" Ramsay asked doubtfully.

"Of course I can sew. I'm not a complete failure as a woman just because I'm old and unwed," Jillian snapped.

"But don't the maids do that?"

"Sometimes they do and sometimes they don't," Jillian replied cryptically.

"Are you feeling all right, Jillian?" Quinn asked.

"Oh, will you just hush up?"

CHAPTER 6

IT INFURIATED HER. EVERY TIME SHE GLIMPSED THE LINE of uneven stitches puckering the center of Grimm's shirt, she felt herself turning into an irascible, beady-eyed porcupine. It was as humiliating as if he'd stitched the words "Jillian lost control of herself and I'm never going to let her forget it" across his back. She couldn't believe she'd torn it, but years of suffering his torment as a child had proved her undoing, and she'd simply snapped.

He was back at Caithness, he was hopelessly attractive, and he still treated her exactly the same as he had when she'd been a child. What would it take to make him see that she wasn't a child anymore? *Well, stop acting like one, to start with,* she remonstrated herself. Since the moment she'd tenderly mended his shirt, she'd been longing to waylay him, divest him of the pernicious reminder, and gleefully burn it. Doing so, however, would have reinforced his perception that she had a penchant for witless action, so instead she'd procured three shirts of finer linen, with flawless stitching, and instructed the maids to place them in his room. Did he wear them?

Nary a one.

Each day that dawned, he donned the same shirt with the ridiculous pleat down the back. She'd considered asking him why he wouldn't wear the new ones, but that would be as bad as admitting that his ploy to make her feel stupid and guilty was working. She'd die before she betrayed another ounce of emotion to the emotionless man who was sabotaging her impeccable manners.

Jillian dragged her eyes from the dark, seductive man walking in the bailey, wearing a badly mended shirt, and forced herself to take a deep, calming breath. *Jillian Alanna Roderick*; she rolled the name behind her teeth, a whisper of exhaled breath. The syllables tumbled euphonically. *I only wish . . .*

"So it's the cloister for you, eh, lass?"

Jillian stiffened. The throaty rumble of Ramsay Logan was not what she needed to hear at this moment. "Umhmm," she mumbled in the direction of the window.

"You won't last a fortnight," he said matter-of-factly.

"How dare you?" Jillian whirled about to face him. "You don't know a thing about me!"

Ramsay smiled smugly.

Jillian blanched as she remembered that he'd seen her naked at the window the day he'd arrived. "I'll have you know that I have a calling."

"I'm sure you do, lass," Ramsay purred. "I simply think your ears are plugged and you're hearing the wrong one. A woman like you has a calling to a flesh-and-blood man, not a God who will never make you feel the joy of being a woman."

"There are finer things in life than being a man's brood-mare, Logan."

"No woman of mine would ever be a broodmare. Don't misunderstand me: I don't belittle the Kirk and Christ's chosen, I simply don't see you being drawn to such a lure. You're too passionate."

"I am cool and collected," she insisted.

"Not around Grimm," Ramsay said pointedly.

"That's because he irritates me," Jillian snapped.

Ramsay cocked a brow and grinned.

"Just what do you think is so funny, Logan?"

" 'Irritates' is an interesting word for it. Not the one I might have chosen. Rather, let's see . . . 'Excites'? 'Delights'? Your eyes burn like amber in the sunlight when he enters the room."

"Fine." Jillian turned back to the window. "Now that we've debated our choice of appropriate verbs, and you've selected all the wrong ones and obviously don't know a thing about women, you may continue on with your day. Shoo, shoo." She waved her hand at him.

Ramsay's grin widened. "I don't intimidate you a bit, do I, lass?"

"Aside from your overbearing attitude, and the fact that you use your great height and girth to make a woman feel cornered, I suspect you're more bull than bully," she muttered.

"Most women like the bull in me." He moved closer.

Jillian shot a disgusted look over her shoulder. "I'm not most women. And don't be standing on my toes, Logan, there's only room enough for me on them. You can trundle back home to the land of the mighty Logan, where the men are men and the women belong to them. I am not the kind of woman you're used to dealing with."

Ramsay laughed.

Jillian turned slowly, her jaw clenched.

"Would you like some help with Roderick?" He gazed over her shoulder, out the window.

"I thought we'd just established you're not a cold-blooded murderer, which means you'd be of no use to me."

"I think you need help. That man can be dense as sod."

When the door to the Greathall opened a scant instant later, Ramsay moved so quickly that Jillian had no time to protest. His kiss was swiftly delivered and lingeringly prolonged. It raised her to her tiptoes and left her strangely breathless when he released her.

Jillian gazed at him blankly. Truth be told, she'd had so few kisses that she was grossly unprepared for the skillful kiss of a mature man and accomplished lover. She blinked.

The slam of the door caused the timbers to shudder, and Jillian understood. "Was that Grimm?" she breathed.

Ramsay nodded and grinned. When he started to lower his head again, Jillian hastily clamped her hand over her mouth.

"Come on, lass," he urged, catching her hand in his. "Grant me a kiss to thank me for showing Grimm that if he's too stupid to claim you, someone else will."

"Where do you get the idea I care what that man thinks?" She seethed. "And *he* certainly doesn't care if you kiss me."

"You're recovering from my kiss too fast for my liking, lass. As for Grimm, I saw you watching him through this window. If you don't speak your heart—"

"He has no heart to speak to."

"From what I saw at court I'd wager that's true, but you'll never know for certain until you try," Ramsay continued. "I'd just as soon you try, fail, and get it over with so you can start looking at me with such longing."

"Thank you for such brilliant advice, Logan. I can see by your own blissfully wedded state that you must know what you're talking about when it comes to relationships."

"The only reason I'm not blissfully wed is because I'm holding out for a good-hearted woman. They've become a rare commodity."

"It requires a good-hearted man to attract a good-hearted woman, and you've likely been looking in the wrong places. You won't find a woman's heart between her—" Jillian broke off abruptly, mortified by what she'd almost said.

Ramsay roared with laughter. "Tell me I could make you forget Grimm Roderick and I'll show a good-hearted man. I would treat you like a queen. Roderick doesn't deserve you."

Jillian sighed morosely. "He doesn't want me. And if you breathe one word to him about what you think I feel, which I assure you I don't, I shall find a way to make you miserable."

"Just don't be tearing my shirts." Ramsay raised his hands in a gesture of defeat. "I'm off to the village, lass." He ducked quickly out the door.

Jillian scowled at the closed door for a long moment after he'd gone. By the saints, these men were making her feel like she was thirteen again, and thirteen had not been a good year. A horrid year, come to think of it. The year she'd watched Grimm in the stables with a maid, then gone to stand in her room and gaze sadly at her body. Thirteen had been a miserable year of impossible duality, of womanly feelings in a child's body. Now she was exhibiting childish feelings in a woman's body. Would she ever gain her balance around that man?

* * *

Caithness. Once Grimm had considered the name interchangeable with "heaven." When he'd first arrived at Caithness at the age of sixteen, the golden child who "adopted" him had been lacking only filmy wings to complete the illusion that she could offer him angelic absolution. Caithness had been a place of peace and joy, but the joy had been tainted by a bottomless well of desire for things he knew could never be his. Although Gibraltar and Elizabeth had opened their door and their hearts to him, there had been an invisible barrier he'd been unable to surmount. Dining in the Greathall, he'd listened as the St. Clairs, their five sons, and single daughter had joked and laughed. They had taken such obvious delight in each step along the path of life, savoring each phase of their children's development. Grimm had been acutely aware of the fact that Caithness was not his home but another family's, and he was sheltered merely out of their generosity, not by right of birth.

Grimm expelled a breath of frustration. *Why?* he wanted to shout, shaking his fists at the sky. Why did it have to be Ramsay? Ramsay Logan was an incorrigible womanizer, lacking the tenderness and sincerity a woman like Jillian needed. He'd met Ramsay at court, years ago, and had witnessed more than a few broken hearts abandoned in the savage Highlander's charming wake. Why Ramsay? On the heels of that thought came a silent howl: *Why not me?* But he knew it could never be. *We canna help it, son . . . we're born this way.* Senseless killers—and worse, he was a Berserker to boot. Even without summoning the Berserker, his father had killed his own wife. What would the inherited sickness of the mind, coupled with being a Berserker, make him capable of? The only thing he knew with any degree of certainty was that he never wanted to find out.

Grimm buried both hands in his hair and stopped walking. He pulled his fingers through, loosening the thong and reassuring himself his hair was clean, not matted with dirt from living in the forests. He had no war braids plaited into the locks, he was not brown as a Moor from months of sun and infrequent bathing, he no longer looked as barbaric as he had the day Jillian found him in the woods. But somehow he felt as if he could never wash away the stains of those years he'd lived in the Highland forests, pitting his wits against the fiercest predators to scavenge enough food to stay alive. Perhaps it was the memory of shivering in the icy winters, when he had been grateful for the layer of dirt on his skin because it was one more layer between his body and the freezing temperatures. Perhaps it was the blood on his hands and the sure knowledge that if he was ever fool enough to let himself feel for anyone it might be his turn to come to awareness with a knife in his hand and his own son watching.

Never. He would never hurt Jillian.

She was even more beautiful than he remembered. Jillian was a woman full grown now, and he had no defenses against her but his will. It had been his formidable will alone that had brought him this far. He'd trained himself, disciplined himself, learned to control the Berserker . . . for the most part.

When he'd ridden into the courtyard a few days ago and seen the golden, laughing woman surrounded by delighted children, regret for his lost childhood had almost suffocated him. He'd longed to insert himself into the picture on the gently sloping lawn, both as a child and as a man. Willingly he would have curled at her feet and listened, willingly he would have taken her in his arms and given her children of her own.

Frustrated by his inability to do either, he'd provoked her. Then she'd raised her head and Grimm had felt his heart plummet to the soles of his boots. It had been easier for him to recall her with a younger, innocent face. Now the saucily tilted nose and sparkling eyes were part of a sultry, sensual woman's features. And her eyes, although still innocent, held maturity and a touch of quiet sorrow. He wished he knew who had introduced that into her gaze, so he could hunt and kill the bastard.

Suitors? She'd likely had scores. Had she loved one?

He shook his head. He didn't like that idea.

So why had Gibraltar summoned him here? He didn't believe for a minute that it had anything to do with him being a contender for Jillian's hand. More likely Gibraltar had recalled the vow Grimm had made to protect Jillian if she ever needed it. And Gibraltar probably needed a warrior strong enough to prevent any possible trouble between Jillian and her two "real" suitors: Ramsay and Quinn. Aye, that made perfect sense to him. He'd be there to protect Jillian from being compromised in any way and to break up any potential disputes between her suitors.

Jillian: scent of honeysuckle and a mane of silky golden hair, eyes of rich brown with golden flecks, the very color of the amber the Vikings had prized so highly. They appeared golden in the sunlight but darkened to a simmering brown flecked with yellow when she was angry—which around him was all the time. She was his every waking dream, his every nocturnal fantasy. And he was dangerous by his mere nature. A beast.

"Milord, is something wrong?"

Grimm dropped his hands from his face. The lad who'd

been on Jillian's lap when he'd first arrived was tugging on his sleeve and squinting up at him.

"Are you all right?" the boy asked worriedly.

Grimm nodded. "I'm fine, lad. But I'm not a laird. You can call me Grimm."

"You look like a laird to me."

"Well, I'm not."

"Why doesn't Jillian like you?" Zeke asked.

Grimm shook his head, begrudging a rueful twist of his lips. "I suspect, Zeke—it is Zeke, isn't it?"

"You know my name," the lad exclaimed.

"I overheard it when you were with Jillian."

"But you remembered it!"

"Why wouldn't I?"

Zeke stepped back, gazing at Grimm with blatant adoration. "Because you're a powerful warrior, and I'm, well . . . me. I'm just Zeke. Nobody notices me. 'Cept Jillian."

Grimm eyed the lad, taking in Zeke's half-defiant, half-ashamed stance. He placed his hand on the boy's shoulder. "While I'm here at Caithness, how would you like to serve as my squire, lad?"

"Squire?" Zeke gaped. "I canna be a squire! I canna see well."

"Why doona you let me be the judge of that? My needs are fairly simple. I need someone to see to my horse. He doesn't like to be penned, so his food and water must be brought to him wherever he happens to be. He needs to be brushed and groomed, and he needs to be ridden."

With his last words, Zeke's hopeful expression vanished.

"Well, he doesn't need to be ridden for some time yet, he had a good hard ride on the way here," Grimm amended hastily. "And I could probably give you a few lessons."

"But I canna see clearly. I canna possibly ride."

"A horse has a great deal of common sense, lad, and can be trained to do many things for his rider. We'll take it slowly. First, will you care for my stallion?"

"Aye," Zeke breathed. "I will! I vow I will!"

"Then let's go meet him. He can be standoffish to strangers unless I bring them around first." Grimm took the lad's hand in his own; he was amazed by how the tiny hand was swallowed in his grip. So fragile, so precious. A brutal flash of memories burst over him—a child, no older than Zeke, pinioned on a McKane sword. He shook it off savagely and closed his fingers securely around Zeke's.

"Wait a minute." Zeke tugged him to a stop. "You still didn't tell me. Why doesna Jillian like you?"

Grimm rummaged for an answer that might make sense to Zeke. "I guess it's because I teased and tormented her when she was a young lass."

"You picked on her?"

"Mercilessly," Grimm agreed.

"Jillian says the lads only tease the lasses they secretly like. Did you pull her hair too?"

Grimm frowned at him, wondering what that had to do with anything. "I suppose I might have, a time or two," he admitted after some thought.

"Och, good!" Zeke exclaimed, his relief evident. "So you're courting her now. She needs a husband," he said matter-of-factly.

Grimm shook his head, the merest hint of an ironic grin curving his lips. He should have seen that one coming.

CHAPTER 7

GRIMM CLAMPED HIS HANDS OVER HIS EARS, BUT IT didn't help. He tugged a pillow over his head, to no avail. He considered getting up and slamming the shutters, but a quick glance revealed that he was to be deprived of even that small pleasure. They were already closed. One of the many "gifts" that was part and parcel of being a Berserker was absurdly heightened hearing; it had enabled him to survive on occasions when a normal man couldn't have heard the enemy stealthily approaching. Now it was proving a grave disadvantage.

He could hear *her*. Jillian.

All he wanted to do was sleep—for Christ's sake, it wasn't even dawn! Did the lass never rest? The trill of a lone flute drifted up, scaling the stone walls of the castle and creeping through the slats of the shutters on a chill morning breeze. He could feel the melancholy notes prying at the stubborn shutters on his heart. Jillian was everywhere at Caithness: blooming in the flower arrangements on the tables, glowing in the children's smiles, stitched into the brilliantly woven tapestries. She was inescapable. Now she dared invade his sleep with the haunting melody of an ancient Gaelic love song, soaring to a high wail, then plummeting to a low moan with such convincing anguish that he snorted. As if she knew the pain of unrequited love! She was beautiful, perfect, blessed with parents, home, family, a place to belong. She had never wanted for love, and he certainly couldn't imagine any man denying her anything. Where had she learned to play a heartbreaking love song with such plaintive empathy?

He leapt from the bed, stomped to the window, and flung the shutters open so hard they crashed into the walls. "Still play that silly thing, do you?" he called. *God, she was beautiful.* And God forgive him—he still wanted her every bit as badly as he had years ago. Then he'd told himself she was too young. Now that she was a woman fully grown he could no longer avail himself of that excuse.

She was standing below him on a rocky cleft overlooking the loch. The sun was a buttery gold crescent, breaking the horizon of the silvery loch. Her back was to him. She stiffened; the bittersweet song stuttered and died.

"I thought you were in the east wing," Jillian said without turning. Her voice carried as clearly to his ears as had the melody, despite her being twenty feet below him.

"I choose my own domain, peahen. As I always have." He leaned out the window slightly, absorbing every detail of her: blond hair rippling in the breeze, the proud set of her shoulders, the haughty angle at which she cocked her head, while she looked out over the loch as if she could scarcely bear to acknowledge his existence.

"Go home, Grimm," she said coldly.

" 'Tis not for you that I stay, but for your da," he lied.

"You owe him such allegiance, then? You, who gives allegiance to none?" she mocked.

He winced. "Allegiance is not beyond me. 'Tis merely that there are so few deserving it."

"I don't want you here," she flung over her shoulder.

It irritated him that she wouldn't turn about and look at him; it was the least she could do while they said nasty things to each other. "I doona care what you want," he forced himself to say. "Your da summoned me here, and here I will remain until he releases me."

"I have released you!"

Grimm snorted. Would that she could release him, but whatever kept him bound to Jillian was indestructible. He should know; he'd tried for years to destroy the bond, not to care where she was, how she fared, if she was happy. "The wishes of a woman are insignificant when weighed against a man's," he said, certain insulting the feminine gender at large would bring her around to face him so he could savor the passion of her anger, in lieu of the sensual passion he desperately longed to provoke in her. *Berserker*, his mind rebuked. *Leave her alone—you have no right.*

"You are such a bastard!" Jillian unwittingly accommodated his basest wishes, spinning so quickly she took a spill. Her brief stumble presented him with a breathtaking view of the swell of her breasts. Pale, they sloped to a gentle valley that disappeared beneath the bodice of her gown. Her skin was so translucent that he could see a faint tracing of blue veins. He pressed against the window ledge to hide the sudden rise of his kilt.

"Sometimes I vow you aim to provoke me." She scowled up at him, pushing off the ground with her hand as she stood up straight, stealing his glimpse of cleavage.

"Now, why would I bother to do that, brat?" he asked

coolly—so coolly it was counterpoint and insult to her raised voice.

"Could it be that you're afraid if you ever stopped torturing me, you might actually like me?" she snapped.

"Never suffer that delusion, Jillian." He splayed his hand through his hair and winced self-consciously. He could never manage to tell a lie without making that gesture. Fortunately, she didn't know that.

"Seems to me you've developed an overwhelming fondness for your hair, Grimm Roderick. I hadn't noticed your little vanities before. Probably because I couldn't see that much of you beneath all the dirt and filth."

It happened in a flash. With her words he was dirty again—mud-stained, blood-soaked, and filthy beyond redemption. No bath, no scouring could ever cleanse him. Only Jillian's words could make him clean again, and he knew he didn't inspire absolution.

"Some people grow up and mature, brat. I woke up one day, shaved, and discovered I was a bloody handsome man." When her eyes widened, he couldn't resist pushing her a little harder. "Some women have said I'm too handsome to have. Perhaps they feared they couldn't hold me in the face of so much competition."

"Spare me your conceit."

Grimm smiled inwardly. She was so lovely, temper-flushed and disdainful, and so easily provoked. Countless times he'd wondered what kind of passion she'd unleash with a man. With a man like him. His thoughts took a dangerous segue into the forbidden. "I've heard men say you're too beautiful to touch. Is that true? *Are* you untouched?" He bit his tongue the instant the words escaped.

Jillian's mouth dropped in disbelief. "*You* would ask me that?"

Grimm swallowed. There'd been a time when he'd known from firsthand experience precisely how untouched she was, and that was a memory he'd do well to bury. "When a lass permits virtual strangers to kiss her, it makes one wonder what else she permits." Bitterness tightened his lips, clipping his words.

Jillian stepped back as if he'd flung something more substantial than an insult in her direction. She narrowed her eyes and studied him suspiciously. "Curiously, it sounds like you care."

"Not a chance. I simply doona wish to have to force you into marrying Ramsay before your da returns. I suspect Gibraltar might like to be present to give the *maiden* away."

Jillian was watching him intently, too intently for his liking. He wondered desperately what was going on inside her head. She'd always been far too clever, and he was perilously close to acting like a jealous suitor. When she'd been young, he'd needed every ounce of his will to carry on a convincing charade of dislike. Now that she was a woman grown, drastic measures were necessary. He shrugged his shoulders arrogantly. "Look, peahen, all I want is for you to take your bloody flute off somewhere else so I can get a bit of sleep. I didn't like you when you were a wee lass, and I doona like you now, but I owe your da and I will honor his missive. The only thing I remember about Caithness is that the food was good and your da was kind." The lie practically burned his tongue.

"You don't remember anything about me?" she asked carefully.

"A few things, nothing of any significance." Restless fingers twined through his hair, tugging it free from his thong.

She glared at him. "Not even the day you left?"

"You mean the McKane attacking?" he asked blandly.

"No." She frowned up at him. "I meant later that day, when I found you in the stables."

"What are you talking about, lass? I doona recall you finding me in the stables before I left." He caught his traitorous hand in mid-rise to his hair and crammed it into the waistband of his kilt.

"You remember nothing of me?" she repeated tightly.

"I remember one thing: I remember you following me around until you nearly drove me mad with your incessant chattering," he said, looking as bored and long-suffering as possible.

Jillian turned her back on him and didn't utter another word.

He watched her for a few moments, his eyes dark with memories, before pulling the shutters closed. When a few moments later the haunting silvery notes of her flute wept, he held his hands over his ears so tightly that it hurt. How could he possibly hope to remain here yet continue to resist her when every ounce of his being demanded he make her his woman?

I doona recall you finding me in the stables before I left.

He'd never uttered a greater lie. He recalled the night in the stables. It was seared into his memory with the excruciating permanence of a brand. It had been the night twenty-two-year-old Grimm Roderick had stolen an unforgettable taste of heaven.

After the McKane were driven off and the battle was over, he'd desperately scrubbed the blood from his body, then packed, flinging clothing and keepsakes without care for what they were or where they landed. He'd nearly brought destruction upon the house that had sheltered him freely, and he would never again subject them to such danger. Jillian's brother Edmund had been wounded in the battle, and although it seemed certain he would recover, young Edmund would bear scars for life. Leaving was the only honorable thing Grimm could do.

He found Jillian's note when his fingers had closed upon the book of Aesop's fables she had given him his first Christmas at Caithness. She'd slipped the note with her big, looping scrawl between the pages so it protruded above the binding. *I will be on the roof at gloaming. I must speak to you tonight, Grimm!*

Crumpling the note furiously, he stomped off for the stables.

He dared not risk seeing her before he left. Filled with self-loathing for bringing the McKane to this sacred place, he would not commit another transgression. Ever since Jillian had started to mature, he'd been unable to get her out of his mind. He knew it was wrong. He was twenty-two years old and she was scarcely sixteen. While she was certainly old enough to be wed—hell, many lasses were wed by thirteen—he could never offer her marriage. He had no home, no clan, and he was a dangerously unpredictable beast to boot. The facts were simple: No matter how much he might want Jillian St. Clair, he could never have her.

At sixteen he'd lost his heart to the wee golden lass; at twenty-two he was beginning to lose his head over the woman. Grimm had concluded a month ago that he had to leave soon, before he did something stupid like kiss her, like find reasons to justify carrying her off and making her his woman. Jillian deserved the best: a worthy husband, a family of her own, and a place to belong. He could offer her none of that.

Strapping his packs on the horse's back, he sighed and

shoved a hand through his hair. As he began leading his horse from the stable, Jillian burst through the doors.

Her eyes darted warily between him and his horse, not missing a detail. "What are you doing, Grimm?"

"What the hell does it look like I'm doing?" he snarled, beyond exasperated that he'd failed to escape without encountering her. How much temptation was he expected to resist?

Tears misted her eyes, and he cursed himself. Jillian had seen so much horror today; he was the lowest of bastards to add to her pain. She'd sought him out in need of comfort, but unfortunately he was in no condition to console her. The aftereffects of Berserkergang left him unable to make clear choices and sensible decisions. Experience had taught him that he was more vulnerable after a Berserker rage; both his mind and body were more sensitive. He needed desperately to get away and find a safe, dark place to sleep for days. He had to force her to leave this instant, before he did something unforgivably stupid. "Go find your da, Jillian. Leave me alone."

"Why are you doing this? Why are you leaving, Grimm?" she asked plaintively.

"Because I must. I never should have come here to begin with!"

"That's silly, Grimm," she cried. "You fought gloriously today! Da locked me in my room, but I could still see what was going on! If you hadn't been here, we wouldn't have had a chance against the McKane—" Her voice broke, and he could see the horror of the bloody battle fresh in her eyes.

And Christ, she'd just admitted that she'd watched him when he'd been berserk! "If I hadn't been here—" he began bitterly, then caught himself on the verge of admitting *he* was the only reason the McKane had come at all.

"If you hadn't been here, what?" Her eyes were huge.

"Nothing," he muttered, staring at the floor.

Jillian tried again. "I watched you from the win—"

"And you should have been hiding, lass!" Grimm cut her off before she could prattle glowingly about his "bravery" in battle—bravery that sprang from the devil himself. "Have you no idea what you look like? Doona you know what the McKane would have done to you if they'd found you?" His voice cracked on the words. It had been fear of what the McKane might do to his beloved lass that had driven him even deeper into Berserkergang during battle, turning him into a ruthless killing animal.

Jillian nervously tugged her lower lip between her teeth. The simple gesture shot a bolt of pure lust through him, and he despised himself for it. He was strung tighter than a compound bow; residual adrenaline from the battle still flooded his body. The heightened arousal attained in Berserkergang had the unfortunate effect of lingering, riding him like a demon, goading him to mate, to conquer. Grimm shook his head and turned his back on her. He couldn't continue looking at her. He didn't trust himself. "Get away from me. You doona know what you risk, being here with me."

Straw rustled against the hem of her gown as she moved. "I trust you completely, Grimm Roderick."

The sweet innocence in her young voice nearly undid him. He grimaced. "That's your first mistake. Your second mistake is being here with me. *Go away.*"

She stepped closer and placed a hand on his shoulder. "But I do trust you, Grimm," she said.

"You can't trust me. You doona even know me," he growled, his body rigid with tension.

"Yes, I do," she argued. "I've known you for years. You've lived here since I was a wee lass. You're my hero, Grimm—"

"Stop it, lass!" he roared as he spun and knocked her hand away from him so roughly that she stepped back a few paces. His glacial blue eyes narrowed. "So you think you know me, do you?" He advanced on her.

"Yes," she insisted stubbornly.

He sneered. "You doona know a bloody thing. You doona know who I've killed and who I've hated and who I've buried and how. You doona know what happens to me because you doona know what I really am!"

"Grimm, I'm frightened," she whispered. Her eyes were wide pools of gold in the lantern light.

"So run to your bloody da! He'll comfort you!"

"He's with Edmund—"

"As you should be!"

"I need you, Grimm! Just put your arms around me! Hold me! Don't leave me!"

Grimm's limbs locked, freezing him clear to his marrow. *Hold me.* Her words hung in the air. Oh, how he longed to. Christ, how often he'd dreamed of it. Her deep amber eyes shifted with fear and vulnerability, and he reached for her despite his resolve. He caught his hands in mid-reach. His shoulders bowed, he was suddenly exhausted by the weight of the internal debate he waged. He could not offer her comfort. He was the very reason she needed comforting. Had he never come to Caithness, he would never have brought destruction on his heels. He could never forgive himself for what he'd brought upon the people who'd

opened their hearts to him when no one else had cared if
he'd lived or died.

"You doona know what you're saying, Jillian," he said,
suddenly immensely weary.

"Don't leave me!" she cried, flinging herself into his arms.

As she burrowed against his chest, his arms closed instinctively around her. He held her tightly, offering her
shuddering body the shelter of his damned near invincible one.

He cradled her in his arms while she sobbed, suffering a
terrible sense of kinship with her. Too clearly he recalled
the loss of his own innocence. Eight years before he'd
stood and watched his own clan fight the McKane. The
sight of such brutality had rendered him nearly senseless
with grief and rage, and now his young Jillian knew the
same terrors. How could he have done this to her?

Would she have nightmares? Relive it as he had—at
least a thousand times?

"Hush, sweet lass," he murmured, stroking her cheek. "I
promise you the McKane will never come back here.
I promise you that somehow I will always look after you,
no matter where I am. I will never let anyone hurt you."

She sniffled, her face buried in the hollow between
his shoulder and his neck. "You can't protect me if you're
not here!"

"I spoke with your da and told him I'm leaving. But I
also told him that if you ever need me, he has only to summon me." Although Gibraltar had been angry with him for
leaving, he'd seemed mollified that he would know where
to find Grimm should the need arise.

Jillian turned her tearstained face up to his, her eyes
wide.

He lost his breath, gazing at her. Her cheeks were flushed and her eyes were brilliant with tears. Her lips were swollen from crying and her hair tumbled in a mane of gold fire about her face.

He had absolutely no intention of kissing her. But one moment they were looking into each other's eyes and the next moment he'd bent his head forward to press a pledge against her lips: a light, sweet promise of protection.

The moment their lips met, his body jerked violently.

He drew back and stared at her blankly.

"D-did you f-feel that?" she stammered, confusion darkening her eyes.

Not possible, he assured himself. *The world does not shake on its axis when you kiss a lass.* To convince himself— he kissed her again. The earthquake began just beneath his toes.

His innocent pledge took on a life of its own, became a passionate, soul-searing kiss between a man and his mate. Her maiden lips parted sweetly beneath his and she melted into the heat of his body.

Grimm squeezed his eyes tightly shut, recalling that long-ago kiss as he listened to the trill of Jillian's flute outside his window.

God, how vividly he recalled it. And he'd not touched another woman since.

* * *

Quinn insisted they go for a ride, and although Jillian initially resisted, before long she was glad she went. She'd forgotten how charming Quinn was, how easily he could make her laugh. Quinn had come to Caithness the summer after Grimm had arrived. Her father had fostered the two

lads—a chieftain's eldest son and a homeless scavenger—
as equals, although in Jillian's eyes no other boy could ever
have been Grimm's equal.

Quinn had been well mannered and thoughtful, but it
had been Grimm she'd fallen in love with the day she'd met
him—the wild boy living in the woods at the perimeter of
Caithness. It had been Grimm who'd upset her so much
she'd cried hot tears of frustration. It had been Quinn who'd
comforted her when he'd left. Funny, she mused as she
glanced over at the dashing man riding beside her, some
things hadn't changed a bit.

Quinn caught her sidelong glance and grinned easily.
"I've missed you, Jillian. Why is it that we haven't seen one
another in years?"

"Judging from the tales I heard of you, Quinn, you were
too busy conquering the world and the women to spare
time for a simple Lowland lass like me," she teased.

"Conquering the world perhaps. But the women? I think
not. A woman is not to be conquered, but to be wooed and
won. Cherished."

"Tell that to Grimm." She rolled her eyes. "That man
cherishes nothing but his own bad temper. Why does he
hate me so?"

Quinn measured her a moment, as if debating what to
say. Finally he shrugged. "I used to think it was because he
secretly liked you and couldn't let himself show it because
he felt he was a nobody, not good enough for the daughter
of Gibraltar St. Clair. But that doesn't make sense, because
Grimm is now a wealthy man, rich enough for any woman,
and God knows the women desire him. Frankly, Jillian, I
have no idea why he's still cruel to you. I'd thought things
would change, especially now that you're old enough to be
courted. I can't say that I'm sorry, though, because it's less

competition as far as I'm concerned," he finished with a pointed look.

Jillian's eyes widened. "Quinn—" she started, but he waved his hand to silence any protest.

"No, Jillian. Don't answer me now. Don't even make me say the words. Just get to know me again, and then we'll speak of things that may come to be. But come what may, I will always be good to you, Jillian," he added softly.

Jillian tugged her lower lip between her teeth and spurred her mount into a canter, stealing a glance over her shoulder at the handsome Quinn. *Jillian de Moncreiffe*, she thought curiously.

Jillian Alanna Roderick, her heart cried defiantly.

CHAPTER 8

JILLIAN STOOD IN THE LONG, NARROW WINDOW OF THE drum tower a hundred feet above the courtyard and watched Grimm. She'd climbed the winding stairs to the tower, telling herself she was trying to get away from "that man," but she knew she wasn't being entirely honest with herself.

The drum tower held memories, and that's what she'd gone to revisit. Splendid memories of the first summer Grimm had been in residence, that wondrous season she'd taken to sleeping in her princess tower. Her parents had indulged her; they'd had men seal the cracks in the stones and hung tapestries so she'd be warm. Here were all her favorite books, the few remaining dolls that had escaped Grimm's "burials at sea" in the loch, and other love-worn remnants of what had been the best year of her life.

That first summer she'd found the "beast-boy," they'd spent every moment together. He had taken her on hikes and taught her to catch trout and slippery salamanders. He'd sat her on a pony for the first time; he'd built her a snow cave on the lawn their first winter together. He'd been there to raise her up if she wasn't tall enough to see, and he'd been there to pick her up if she fell. Nightly he'd told her outlandish stories until she'd passed into a child's exhausted slumber, dreaming of the next adventure they'd share.

To this day, Jillian could still recall the magic feeling she'd had whenever they'd been together. It had seemed perfectly possible that he might be a rogue angel sent to guard her. After all, she'd been the one who'd discovered him lurking in the thickets of the forest behind Caithness. She'd been the one who'd coaxed him near with a tempting feast, waiting patiently day after day on a rumpled blanket with her beloved puppy, Savanna TeaGarden.

For months he'd resisted her offering, hiding in his bracken and shadows, watching her as intently as she'd watched him. But one rainy day he'd melted out of the mist and come to kneel upon her blanket. He'd gazed at her with an expression that had made her feel beautiful and protected. Sometimes, in the years to follow, despite his cruel indifference, she'd caught that same look in his eyes when he thought she wasn't watching. It had kept her hope alive when it would have been wiser to let it die. She'd grown to young womanhood desperately in love with the fierce boy-turned-man who had a strange way of appearing whenever she needed him, rescuing her repeatedly.

Granted, he hadn't always been gentle while he did it. One time he'd trussed her up, high in an oak's lofty branches, before tearing off through the woods to rescue Savanna from a pack of wild dogs he'd saved Jillian from moments earlier. Lashed to the tree, terrified for her puppy, she'd howled and struggled but had been unable to loosen her bonds. He'd left her there for hours. But sure as the sun always rose and set, he had come back for her—cradling the wounded, but remarkably alive, wolfhound in his arms.

He'd refused to discuss with her how he'd saved her puppy from the rabid pack, but she hadn't worried overmuch. Although Jillian had found it mildly astonishing that he'd been unhurt himself, over the years she'd come to expect that Grimm would suffer no harm. Grimm was her hero. He could do anything.

One year after she'd met Grimm, Quinn de Moncreiffe had arrived to be fostered at Caithness. He and Grimm became close as brothers, sharing a world of adventures from which she was painfully excluded. That had been the beginning of the end of her dreams.

Jillian sighed as Grimm disappeared into the castle. Her back stiffened when he reappeared a few moments later with Zeke. She narrowed her eyes when Zeke slipped his hand trustingly into Grimm's. She could still recall how easy it had been to slide her child's hand into his strong grip. He was the kind of man that children and women wanted to keep around, although for wholly different reasons.

There was certainly a mystery about him. It was as if a swirling black mist had parted the day Grimm Roderick had stepped into existence, and no amount of questioning, no relentless scrutiny could ever illuminate his dark past. He was a deep man, unusually aware of the tiniest nuances in a conversation or interaction. When she'd been a child, he'd always seemed to know exactly how she was feeling, anticipating her feelings before she had understood them herself.

If she was honest with herself, the only truly cruel thing she could accuse him of was years of indifference. He'd never done anything terribly unkind in and of itself. But the

night he'd left, his absolute rejection had caused her to
harden her heart against him.

She watched him swing Zeke up in his arms. What on
earth was he doing? Putting him on a horse? Zeke couldn't
ride, he couldn't see well enough. She opened her mouth to
call down, then paused. Whatever else he might be, Grimm
was not a man who made mistakes. Jillian resigned herself
to watch for a few moments. Zeke was giddy with excitement, and it wasn't often she saw him happy. Several of the
children and their parents had gathered around to watch.
Jillian held her breath. If Grimm's intentions went awry it
would be a painful, public humiliation for Zeke, and one
he'd not live down for a long time.

She watched as Grimm bowed his dark head close to the
horse; it looked as if he was whispering words in the pranc-
ing gray stallion's ear. Jillian suffered a momentary fancy
that the horse had actually nodded his head in response.
When Grimm slipped Zeke on the horse's back, she held
her breath. Zeke sat rigidly at first, then slowly relaxed as
Grimm led the stallion in easy wide circles around the
courtyard. Well, that was all fine and good, Jillian thought,
but now what would Zeke do? He certainly couldn't be led
around all the time. What was the point of putting the child
on a horse when he could never ride on his own?

She quickly decided she'd had enough. Obviously
Grimm didn't understand; he should not be teaching the
boy to want impossible things. He should be encouraging
Zeke to read books, to indulge in safer pursuits, as Jillian
had done. When a child was handicapped, it made no sense
to encourage him to test those limits foolishly in a manner
that might cause him harm. Far better to teach him to appreciate different things and pursue attainable dreams. No
matter that, like any other child, Zeke might wish to run

and play and ride—he had to be taught that he couldn't, that it was dangerous for him to do so with his impaired vision.

She would take Grimm to task over his lapse in judgment immediately, before any more damage was done. Quite a crowd had gathered in the courtyard, and she could already see the parents shaking their heads and whispering among themselves. She promised herself she would handle this problem coolly and rationally, giving the onlookers no cause for gossip. She would explain to Grimm the proper way to treat young Zeke and demonstrate that she wasn't always a witless idiot.

She exited the drum tower quickly and made her way to the courtyard.

* * *

Grimm led the horse in one last slow circle, certain that at any moment Jillian would burst from the castle. He knew he shouldn't spend time with her, yet he found himself deliberately arranging to give Zeke his first riding lesson where she'd be certain to see. Only moments before he had glimpsed a flutter of motion and a fall of golden hair in the tower window. His gut tightened with anticipation as he lifted Zeke down from the stallion. "I suspect you feel comfortable with his gait now, Zeke. We've made a good start."

"He's very easy to ride. But I won't be able to guide him myself, so what's the point? I could never ride by myself."

"Never say never, Zeke," Grimm chided gently. "The moment you say 'never' you've chosen not to try. Rather than worrying about what you can't do, set your mind to thinking of ways that you could do it. You might surprise yourself."

Zeke blinked up at him. "But everybody tells me I canna ride."

"Why do *you* think you can't ride?" Grimm asked, lowering the boy to the ground.

" 'Cause I canna see clearly. I may run your horse smack into a rock!" Zeke exclaimed.

"My horse has eyes, lad. Do you think he'd allow you to run him into a rock? Occam wouldn't let you run him into anything. Trust me, and I'll show you that a horse can be trained to compensate for your vision."

"You really think one day I might be able to ride without your help?" Zeke asked in a low voice, so the onlookers gathered around wouldn't hear the hope in his voice and mock him for it.

"Yes, I do. And I'll prove it to you, in time."

"What madness are you telling Zeke?" Jillian demanded, joining them.

Grimm turned to face her, savoring her flushed cheeks and brilliant eyes. "Go on, Zeke." He gave the lad a gentle nudge toward the castle. "We'll work on this again tomorrow."

Zeke grinned at Grimm, stole a quick look at Jillian's face, and left hurriedly.

"I'm teaching Zeke to ride."

"Why? He can't see well, Grimm. He will never be able to ride by himself. He'll only end up getting hurt."

"That's not true. The lad's been told he can't do a lot of things that he can do. There are different methods for training a horse. Although Zeke may have poor eyesight, Occam here"—Grimm gestured to his snorting stallion—"has keen enough senses for them both."

"What did you just say?" Jillian's brow furrowed.

"I said my horse can see well enough—"

"I heard that part. What did you call your horse?" she demanded, unaware her voice had risen sharply, and the dispersing crowd had halted collectively, hanging on her every word.

Grimm swallowed. He hadn't thought she'd remember! "Occam," he said tightly.

"Occam? You named your horse *Occam*?" Every man, woman, and child in the lower bailey gaped at the uneven timbre of their lady's voice.

Jillian stalked forward and poked an accusing finger at his chest. "Occam?" she repeated, waiting.

She was waiting for him to say something intelligent, Grimm realized. Damn the woman, but she should know better than that. Intelligent just didn't happen when he was around Jillian. Then again, demure and temperate didn't seem to happen when Jillian was around him. Give them a few minutes and they'd be brawling in the courtyard of Caithness while the whole blasted castle watched in abject fascination.

Grimm searched her face intently, seeking some flaw of form that betrayed a weakness of character, anything he could seize upon and stoke into a defense against her charms, but he may as well have searched the seas for a legendary selkie. She was simply perfect. Her strong jaw reflected her proud spirit. Her clear golden eyes shone with truth. She pursed her lips, waiting. Overly full lips, the lower one plump and rosy. Lips that would part sweetly when he took her, lips between which he would slide his tongue, lips that might curve around his . . .

And those lips were moving, but he didn't have the damndest idea what she was saying because he'd taken a dangerous segue into a sensual fantasy involving heated, flushed flesh, Jillian's lips, and a man's need. The roar of blood pounding in his ears must have deafened him. He struggled to focus on her words, which faded back in just in time for him to hear her say

"You lied! You said you never thought about me at all."

He gathered his scattered wits defensively. She was looking much too pleased with herself for his peace of mind. "What are you pecking away at now, little peahen?" he said in his most bored voice.

"Occam," she repeated triumphantly.

"That's my horse," he drawled, "and just what *is* your point?"

Jillian hesitated. Only an instant, but he saw the flicker of embarrassment in her eyes as she must have wondered if he really didn't remember the day she'd discovered the principle of "Occam's Razor," then proceeded to enlighten everyone at Caithness. How could he not recall the child's delight? How could he forget the discomfiture of visiting lords well versed in politics and hunting, yet utterly put off by a woman with a mind, even a lass at the tender age of eleven? Oh, he remembered; he'd been so bloody proud of her it had hurt. He'd wanted to smack the smirks off the prissy lords' faces for telling Jillian's parents to burn her books, lest they ruin a perfectly good female and make her unmarriageable. He remembered. And had named his horse in tribute.

Occam's Razor: The simplest theory that fits the facts corresponds most closely to reality. *Fit this, Jillian—why do I treat you so horribly?* He grimaced. The simplest theory that encompassed the full range of asinine behavior he exhibited around Jillian was that he was hopelessly in love with her, and if he wasn't careful she would figure it out. He had to be cold, perhaps cruel, for Jillian was an intelligent woman and unless he maintained a convincing façade she would see right through him. He drew a deep breath and steeled his will.

"You were saying?" He arched a sardonic brow. Powerful men had withered into babbling idiots beneath the sarcasm and mockery of that deadly gaze.

But not his Jillian, and it delighted him as much as it worried him. She held her ground, even leaned closer, ignoring the curious stares and perked ears of the onlookers. Close enough that her breath fanned his neck and made him want to seal his lips over hers and draw her breath into his lungs so deeply that she'd need him to breathe it back into her. She looked deep into his eyes, then a smile of delight curved her mouth. "You *do* remember," she whispered fiercely. "I wonder what else you lie to me about," she murmured, and he had the dreadful suspicion she was about to start applying a scientific analysis to his idiotic behavior. Then she'd know, and he'd be exposed for the lovestruck dolt he was.

He wrapped his hand around her wrist and clamped his fingers tight, until he knew she understood he could snap it with a flick of his hand. He deliberately let his eyes flash the blazing, unholy look people loathed. Even Jillian backstepped slightly, and he knew that somehow she'd caught the tiniest glimpse of the Berserker in his eyes. It would serve her well to fear him. She *must* be afraid of him— Christ knew, he was afraid of himself. Although Jillian had changed and matured, he still had nothing to offer her. No clan, no family, and no home. "When I left Caithness I swore never to return. *That's* what I remember, Jillian." He dropped her wrist. "And I did not come back willingly, but for a vow made long ago. If I named my horse a word you happen to be familiar with, how arrogant you are to think it had anything to do with you."

"Oh! I am not arrogant—"

"Do you know why your da really brought us here, lass?" Grimm interrupted coldly.

Jillian's mouth snapped shut. It figured that he would be the only one who might tell her the truth.

"Do you? I know you used to have a bad habit of spying, and I doubt much about you has changed."

Her jaw jutted, her spine stiffened, and she threw her shoulders back, presenting him with a clear view of her lush figure—one of the things that had definitely changed about her. She bit her lip to prevent a smug smile when his gaze dropped sharply, then jerked back up.

Grimm regarded her stonily. "Your da summoned the three of us here to secure you a husband, brat. Apparently you're so impossible to persuade that he had to gather Scotia's mightiest warriors to topple your defenses." He studied her stalwart stance and aloof expression a moment and snorted. "I was right—you do still eavesdrop. You aren't at all surprised by my revelation. Seeing as how you know the plan, why doona you just be a good lass for a change; go find Quinn and persuade him to marry you so I can leave and get on with my life?" His gut clenched as he forced himself to say the words.

"That's what you wish me to do?" she asked in a small voice.

He studied her a long moment. "Aye," he said finally. "That's what I wish you to do." He pushed his hands through his hair before grabbing Occam by the reins and leading him away.

Jillian watched him retreat, her throat working painfully. She would not cry. She would never again waste her tears on him. With a sigh, she turned for the castle, only to come smack up against Quinn's broad chest. He was regarding her with such compassion that it unraveled her composure. Tears filled her eyes as he put his arms around her. "How long have you been standing here?" she asked shakily.

"Long enough," he replied softly. "It wouldn't take any persuading, Jillian," Quinn assured her. "I cared deeply for you as a lass—you were as a cherished younger sister to me. I could love you as much more than a sister now."

"What is there to love about me? I'm a blithering idiot!"

Quinn smiled bitterly. "Only for Grimm. But then, you always were a fool for him. As to what one might love about you: your irrepressible spirit, your wit, your curiosity about everything, the music you play, your love for the children. You have a pure heart, Jillian, and that's rare."

"Oh, Quinn, why are you always so good to me?" She affectionately brushed his cheek with her knuckles before she slipped past him and dashed, alone, for the castle.

CHAPTER 9

"WHAT THE HELL IS YOUR PROBLEM?" QUINN DE-manded, bursting into the stables.

Grimm glanced over his shoulder as he slid the halter from Occam. "What are you talking about? I doona have a problem," he replied, waving an eager-to-assist stable boy away. "I'll take care of my own horse, lad. And doona be penning him up in here. I just brought him in to rub him down. *Never* pen him."

Nodding, the stable boy backed away and left quickly.

"Look, McIllioch, I don't care what motivates you to be such a bastard to her," Quinn said, dropping all pretense by using Grimm's real name. "I don't even wish to know. Just stop. I won't have you making her cry. You did it enough when we were young. I didn't interfere then, telling myself that Gavrael McIllioch had had a tough life and maybe he needed some slack, but you don't have a tough life anymore."

"How would you know?"

Quinn glared. "Because I know what you've become. You're one of the most respected men in Scotland. You're no longer Gavrael McIllioch—you're the renowned Grimm Roderick, a legend of discipline and control. You saved the King's life on a dozen different occasions. You've been rewarded so richly that you're worth more than old St. Clair and myself put together. Women fling themselves at your feet. What more could you want?"

Only one thing—the thing I can never have, he brooded. *Jillian*. "You're right, Quinn. As usual. I'm an ass and you're right. So marry her." Grimm turned his back and fiddled with Occam's saddle. He shrugged Quinn's hand off his shoulder a moment later. "Leave me alone, Quinn. You'd make a perfect husband for Jillian, and since I saw Ramsay kissing her the other day, you'd better move fast."

"Ramsay kissed her?" Quinn exclaimed. "Did she kiss him back?"

"Aye," Grimm said bitterly. "And that man has spoiled more than his share of innocent lasses, so do us both a favor and save Jillian from him by offering for her yourself."

"I already have," Quinn said quietly.

Grimm spun sharply. "You did? When? What did she say?"

Quinn shifted from foot to foot. "Well, I didn't exactly out-and-out ask her, but I made my intentions clear."

Grimm waited, one dark brow arched inquiringly.

Quinn tossed himself down on a pile of hay and leaned back, resting his weight on his elbows. He blew a strand of blond hair out of his face irritably. "She thinks she's in love with you, Grimm. She has always thought she was in love with you, ever since she was a child. Why don't you finally come clean with the truth? Tell her who you really are. Let her decide if you're good enough for her. You're heir to a chieftain—if you'd ever go home and claim it. Gibraltar knows exactly who you are, and he summoned you to be one of the contenders for her hand. Obviously he thinks you're good enough for his daughter. Maybe you're the only one who doesn't."

"Maybe he brought me just to make you look good by comparison. You know, invite the beast-boy. Isn't that what Jillian used to call me?" He rolled his eyes. "Then the handsome laird looks even more appealing. She can't be interested in me. As far as Jillian knows, I'm not even titled. I'm a nobody. And I thought you wanted her, Quinn." Grimm turned back to his horse and swept Occam's side with long, even strokes of the brush.

"I do. I'd be proud to make Jillian my wife. Any man would—"

"Do you love her?"

Quinn cocked a brow and eyed him curiously. "Of course I love her."

"No, do you *really* love her? Does she make you crazy inside?" Grimm watched him carefully.

Quinn blinked. "I don't know what you mean, Grimm."

Grimm snorted. "I didn't expect you would," he muttered.

"Oh, hell, this is a snarl of a mess." Quinn exhaled impatiently and dropped onto his back in the fragrant hay. He plucked a stem of clover from the pile and chewed on it thoughtfully. "I want her. She wants you. And you're my closest friend. The only unknown factor in this equation is what you want."

"First of all, I sincerely doubt she wants me, Quinn. If anything, it's the remains of a childish infatuation that, I assure you, I will relieve her of. Secondly, it doesn't matter what I want." Grimm produced an apple from his sporran and offered it to Occam.

"What do you mean, it doesn't matter? Of course it matters." Quinn frowned.

"What *I* want is the most irrelevant part of this affair, Quinn. I'm a Berserker," Grimm said flatly.

"So? Look what it has brought you. Most men would trade their souls to be a Berserker."

"That would be a damned foolish bargain. And there's a lot you doona know that is part and parcel of the curse."

"It's proved quite a boon for you. You're virtually invincible. Why, I remember down at Killarnie—"

"I doona wish to talk about Killarnie—"

"You killed half the damned—"

"Haud yer wheesht!" Grimm's head whipped around. "I doona wish to talk about killing. It seems that's the only thing I'm good for. For all that I'm this ridiculous legend of control, there's still a part of me I can't control, de Moncreiffe. I have no control over the rage. I never have," he admitted roughly. "When it happens, I lose memory. I lose time. I have no idea what I'm doing when I'm doing it, and when it's over, I have to be told what I've done. You know that. You've had to tell me a time or two."

"What are you saying, Grimm?"

"That you must wed her, no matter what I might feel, because I can never be anything to Jillian St. Clair. I knew it then, and I know it now. I will never marry. Nothing has changed. *I* haven't been able to change."

"You *do* feel for her." Quinn sat up on the hay mound, searching Grimm's face intently. "Deeply. And that's why you try to make her hate you."

Grimm turned back to his horse. "I never told you how my mother died, did I, de Moncreiffe?"

Quinn rose and dusted hay from his kilt. "I thought she was killed in the massacre at Tuluth."

Grimm leaned his head against Occam's velvety cheek and breathed deeply of the soothing scent of horse and leather. "No. Jolyn McIllioch died much earlier that morning, before the McKane even arrived." He delivered the words in a cool monotone. "My da murdered her in a fit of rage. Not only did I sink to such foolishness as summoning a Berserker that day, I suffer an inherited madness."

"I don't I believe that, Grimm," Quinn said flatly. "You're one of the most logical, rational men I know."

Grimm made a gesture of impatience. "Da told me so himself the night I left Tuluth. Even if I gave myself latitude, even if I managed to convince myself I didn't suffer an inherited weakness of mind, I'm still a Berserker. Doona you realize, Quinn, that according to ancient law we 'pagan worshipers of Odin' are to be banished? Ostracized, outcast, and murdered, if at all possible. Half the country knows Berserkers exist and seek to employ us; the other half refuses to admit we do while they attempt to destroy us. Gibraltar must have been out of his mind when he summoned me—he couldn't possibly seriously consider me for his daughter's hand! Even if I wanted with all my heart to take Jillian to wife, what could I offer her? A life such as this? That's assuming I'm not addled by birthright, to boot."

"You're not addled. I don't know how you got the ridiculous idea that because your da killed your mother there's something wrong with *you*. And no one knows who you really are except for me, Gibraltar, and Elizabeth," Quinn protested.

"And Hatchard," Grimm reminded. And Hawk and Adrienne, he recalled.

"So four of us know. None of us would ever betray you. As far as the world is concerned you're Grimm Roderick, the King's legendary bodyguard. All that aside, I don't see how it would be a problem for you to admit who you really are. A lot of things have changed since the massacre at Tuluth. And although some people do still fear Berserkers, the majority revere them. You're some of the mightiest warriors Alba has ever produced, and you know how we Scots worship our legends. The Circle Elders say only the purest, most honorable blood in Scotland can actually call the Berserker."

"The McKane still hunt us," Grimm said through his teeth.

"The McKane have always hunted any man they suspected was Berserk. They're jealous. They spend every waking moment training to be warriors and can never match up to a Berserker. So defeat them, and lay it to rest. You're not fourteen anymore. I've seen you in action. Rouse up an army. Hell, I'd fight for you! I know scores of men who would. Go home and claim your birthright—"

"My gift of inherited madness?"

"The chieftainship, you idiot!"

"There might be a small problem with that," Grimm said bitterly. "My crazy, murdering da has the dreadful manners to still be lingering on this earth."

"What?" Quinn was speechless. He shook his head several times and grimaced. "Christ! How can I walk around all these years thinking I know you, only to find out I don't know a blethering thing about you? You told me your da was dead."

It seemed all his close friends were saying the same thing lately, and he wasn't a man given to lying. "I thought he was, for a long time." Grimm ran an impatient hand through his hair. "I will never go home, Quinn, and there are some things about being Berserk that you doona understand. I can't have any degree of intimacy with a woman without her realizing that I'm not normal. So what am I supposed to do? Tell the lucky woman I am one of those savage killing beasts that have gotten such a bad reputation over the centuries? Tell her I can't see blood without losing control of myself? Tell her that if my eyes ever start to seem like they're getting incandescent, to run as far away from me as she can get because Berserkers have been known to turn on friend and foe indiscriminately?"

"You've never once turned on me!" Quinn snapped. "And I've been beside you when it happened many times!"

Grimm shook his head. "Marry her, Quinn. For Christ's sake! Marry her and free me!" He cursed harshly, dropping his head against his stallion.

"Do you really think it will?" Quinn asked angrily. "Will it free any of us, Grimm?"

* * *

Jillian strolled the wall-walk, the dim passage behind the parapet, breathing deeply of the twilight. Gloaming was her favorite hour, the time when dusk blurred into absolute darkness broken only by a silvery moon and cool white stars above Caithness. She paused, resting her arms against the parapet. The scent of roses and honeysuckle carried on the breeze. She inhaled deeply. Another scent teased her senses, and she cocked her head. Dark and spicy; leather and soap and man.

Grimm.

She turned slowly and he was there, standing behind her on the roof, deep in the shadows of the abutting walls watching her, his gaze unfathomable. She hadn't heard a sound as he'd approached, not a whisper of cloth, not one scuffle of his boots on the stones. It was as if he were fashioned of night air and had sailed the wind to her solitary perch.

"Will you marry?" he asked without preface.

Jillian sucked in a breath. Shadows couched his features but for a bar of moonlight illuminating his intense eyes. How long had he been there? Was there a "me," unspoken, at the end of his sentence? "What are you asking?" she said breathlessly.

His smooth voice was bland. "Quinn would make a fine husband for you."

"Quinn?" she echoed.

"Aye. He's golden as you, lass. He's kind, gentle, and wealthy. His family would cherish you."

"And what about yours?" She couldn't believe she dared ask.

"What about mine, what?"

Would your family cherish me? "What is your family like?"

His gaze was icy. "I have no family."

"None?" Jillian frowned. Surely he had some relatives, somewhere.

"You know nothing about me, lass," he reminded her in a low voice.

"Well, since you keep butting your nose into my life, I think I have the right to ask a few questions." Jillian peered intently at him, but it was too dark to see him clearly. How could he seem such a part of the night?

"I'll quit butting my nose. And the only time I butt my nose in is when it looks like you're about to get in trouble."

"I do *not* get into trouble all the time, Grimm."

"So"—he gestured impatiently—"when will you marry him?"

"Who?" She seethed, plucking at the folds of her gown. Clouds passed over the moon, momentarily obscuring him from her view.

His eerily disembodied voice was mildly reproaching. "Try to follow the conversation, lass. Quinn."

"By Odin's shaft—"

"Spear," he corrected with a hint of amusement in his voice.

"I am not marrying Quinn!" she informed the dark corner furiously.

"Certainly not Ramsey?" His voice deepened dangerously. "Or was he such a good kisser that he's already persuaded you?"

Jillian drew a deep breath. She released it and closed her eyes, praying for temperance.

"Lass, you have to wed one of them. Your da demands it," he said quietly.

She opened her eyes. Praise the saints, the clouds had blown by and she could once again discern the outline of his form. There was a flesh-and-blood man in those shadows, not some mythical beast. "You're one of the men my da brought here for me, so I guess that means I could choose you, doesn't it?"

He shook his head, a blur of movement in the gloom. "Never do that, Jillian. I have nothing to offer you but a lifetime of hell."

"Maybe you think that, but maybe you're wrong. Maybe, if you quit feeling sorry for yourself, you'd see things differently."

"I doona feel sorry for myself—"

"Ha! You're drowning in it, Roderick. Only occasionally does a smile manage to steal over your handsome face, and as soon as you catch it you swallow it. You know what your problem is?"

"No. But I have the feeling you're going to tell me, peahen."

"Clever, Roderick. That's supposed to make me feel stupid enough to shut up. Well, it won't work, because I feel stupid around you all the time anyway, so I may as well act stupid too. I suspect your problem is that you're afraid."

Grimm leaned indolently back against the stones of the wall, looking every inch a man who'd never contemplated the word *fear* long enough for it to gain entrance into his vocabulary.

"Do you know what you're afraid of?" she pushed bravely on.

"Considering that I didn't know I was afraid, I'm afraid you've got me at a bit of a disadvantage," he mocked.

"You're afraid you might have a feeling," she announced triumphantly.

"Oh, I'm not afraid of feelings, lass," he said, dark, sensual knowledge dripping from his voice. "It just depends on the kind of feeling—"

Jillian shivered. "Don't try to change the subject—"

"And if the feeling's below my waist—"

"By segueing into a discussion about your debauched—"

"Then I'm perfectly comfortable with it."

"And perverse male needs—"

"Perverse male needs?" he echoed, suppressed laughter lacing his words.

Jillian bit her lip. She always ended up saying too much around him, because he had the bad habit of talking over her, and she lost her head time and again.

"The issue at hand is feelings—as in emotions," she reminded stiffly.

"And you think they're mutually exclusive?" Grimm prodded.

Had she said that? she wondered. By the saints, the man turned her brain into mush. *"What* are you talking about?"

"Feelings and *feelings*, Jillian. Do you think they're mutually exclusive?"

Jillian pondered his question a few moments. "I haven't had a lot of experience in that area, but I would guess they are more often for a man than a woman," she replied at length.

"Not all men, Jillian." He paused, then added smoothly, "Exactly how much experience have you had?"

"What was my point?" she asked irritably, refusing to acknowledge his question.

He laughed. By the saints, he laughed! It was a genuine uninhibited laugh—deeply resonant, rich, and warm. She shuddered, because the flash of white teeth in his shadowed face made him so handsome she wanted to cry at the unfairness of his miserly dispensation of such beauty.

"I was hoping you'd tell me that anytime now, Jillian."

"Roderick, conversations with you never go where I think they're going."

"At least you're never bored. That must count for something."

Jillian blew out a frustrated breath. That was true. She was elated, exhilarated, sensually awakened—but never, never bored.

"So are they mutually exclusive for you?" she dared.

"What?" he asked blandly.

"Feelings and *feelings*."

Grimm tugged restlessly at his dark hair. "I suppose I

haven't met the woman who could make me feel while I was feeling her."

I could, I know I could! she almost shouted. "But you have those other kind of feelings quite frequently, don't you?" she snipped.

"As often as I can."

"There you go with your hair, again. What is it with you and your hair?" When he didn't reply she said childishly, "I hate you, Roderick." She could have kicked herself the moment she said it. She prided herself on being an intelligent woman, yet around Grimm she regressed into a petty child. She was going to have to dredge up something more effective than the same puerile response if she intended to spar with him.

"No you doona, lass." He uttered a harsh curse and stepped forward, doffing the shadows impatiently. "That's the third time you've said that to me, and I'm getting bloody sick of hearing it."

Jillian held her breath as he moved closer, staring down at her with a strained expression. "You wish you could hate me, Jillian St. Clair, and Christ knows you *should* hate me, but you just can't quite bring yourself to hate me all that much, can you? I know, because I've looked in your eyes, Jillian, and where a great big nothing should be if you hated me, there's a fiery thing with curious eyes."

He turned in a swirl of shadows and descended from the roof, moving with lupine grace. At the bottom of the steps, he paused in a puddle of moonlight and tilted his head back. The pale moon cast his bitter expression into stark relief. "Doona ever say those words to me again, Jillian. I mean it—fair warning. Not ever."

Cobblestones crunched beneath his boots as he disappeared into the gardens, comforting her that he was, indeed, of this world.

She pondered his words for a long time after he'd gone, and she was left alone with the bruised sky on the parapet. Three times he'd called her by name—not brat or lass, but Jillian. And although his final words had been delivered in a cool monotone, she had seen—unless the moon was playing tricks with her vision—a hint of anguish in his eyes.

The longer she considered it, the more convinced she became. Logic insisted that love and hate could masquerade behind the same façade. It became an issue of simply peeling back that mask to peer beneath it and determine which emotion truly drove the man in the shadow. A glimmer of understanding pierced the gloom that surrounded her.

Go with your heart, her mother had counseled her hundreds of times. *The heart speaks clearly even when the mind insists otherwise.*

"Mama, I miss you," Jillian whispered as the last stain of purple twilight melted into a raven horizon. But despite the distance, Elizabeth St. Clair's strength was inside her, in her blood. She was a Sacheron *and* a St. Clair—a formidable combination.

Indifferent to her, was he? It was time to see about that.

CHAPTER 10

"WELL, THAT'S IT, THEN—THEY'RE OFF," HATCHARD MUT-
tered, watching the men depart. He finger-combed his
short red beard thoughtfully. He stood with Kaley on the
front steps of Caithness, watching three horses fade into
swirls of dust down the winding road.

"Why did they have to choose Durrkesh?" Kaley asked
irritably. "If they wanted to go catting about, they could
very well have gone to the village right here." She waved at
the small town clustered protectively near the walls of
Caithness that spilled into the valley beyond.

Hatchard shot her a caustic glance. "Although this may
come as a grave shock to your . . . shall we say . . . accommodating nature, not everyone thinks about catting all the
time, Missus Twillow."

"Don't be 'Missus Twillowing' me, Remmy," she snapped.
"I'll not be believing you've lived nearly forty years without doing a bit of catting yourself. But I must say, I find it

appalling that they're off catting when they were brought here for Jillian."

"If you'd listen for a change, Kaley, you might hear what I've been telling you. They went to Durrkesh because Ramsay suggested they go—not for catting, but to acquire wares that can only be purchased in the city. You told me we've run short of peppercorns and cinnamon, and you won't be finding those wares here." He gestured to the village and allowed a significant pause to pass before adding, "I also heard one might find saffron at the city fair this year."

"*Saffron!* Bless the saints, we haven't had saffron since last spring."

"You've kept me perennially aware of the fact," Hatchard said wryly.

"One does what one can to aid an old man's memory." Kaley sniffed. "And correct me if I'm wrong, but don't you usually send your men for the wares?"

"Seeing how Quinn was so avid to buy an elegant gift for Jillian, I certainly wasn't about to stop him. Grimm, I believe, went with them simply to avoid getting stuck alone with the lass," Hatchard added dryly.

Kaley's eyes sparkled, and she clapped her hands together. "A gift for Jillian. So it's to be Jillian de Moncreiffe, is it? A fine name for a fine lass, I must say. And that would keep her nearby in the Lowlands."

Hatchard returned his pensive gaze to the ribbon of road wending through the valley. He watched the last rider disappear around a bend and clucked his tongue. "I wouldn't be so certain, Kaley," he murmured.

"Whatever is that cryptic remark supposed to mean?" Kaley frowned.

"Just that in my estimation the lass has never had eyes for anyone but Grimm."

"Grimm Roderick is the worst possible man for her!" Kaley exclaimed.

Hatchard turned a curious gaze on the voluptuous maid. "Now, why would you say that?"

Kaley's hand flew to her throat, and she fanned herself. "There are men women desire and there are men women marry. Roderick is *not* the kind of man a woman marries."

"Why not?" Hatchard asked, bewildered.

"He's dangerous," Kaley breathed. "Positively dangerous to the lass."

"You think he might harm her in some way?" Hatchard tensed, prepared to do battle if such was the case.

"Without even meaning to, Remmy." Kaley sighed.

* * *

"They've gone where? And for how long did you say?" Jillian's brow puckered with indignation.

"To the city of Durrkesh, milady," Hatchard replied. "I should suppose they'll be gone just shy of a sennight."

Jillian smoothed the folds of her gown irritably. "I wore a dress this morning, Kaley—a pretty one," she complained. "I was even going to ride to the village wearing it instead of Da's plaid, and you know how I hate riding in a dress."

"You look lovely, indeed," Kaley assured her.

"I look lovely for whom? All my suitors have abandoned me."

Hatchard cleared his throat gruffly. "There wouldn't have been one in particular you were hoping to impress, would there?"

Jillian turned on him accusingly. "Did my da put you up to spying on me, Hatchard? You're probably sending him weekly reports! Well, boodle, I'll tell you nothing."

Hatchard had the grace to look abashed. "I'm not sending him reports. I was merely concerned for your welfare."

"You can concern yourself with someone else's. I'm old enough and I worry enough for both of us."

"Jillian," Kaley chided, "crabby does not become you. Hatchard is merely expressing his concern."

"I feel like being crabby. Can't I just do that for a change?" Jillian's brow furrowed as she reflected a moment. "Wait a minute," she said pensively. "Durrkesh, is it? They hold a splendid fair this time of year . . . the last time I went with Mama and Da, we stayed at a perfectly lovely little inn—the Black Boot, wasn't it, Kaley?"

Kaley nodded. "When your brother Edmund was alive the two of you went to the city often."

A shadow flitted across Jillian's face.

Kaley winced. "I'm sorry, Jillian. I didn't mean to bring that up."

"I know." Jillian drew a deep breath. "Kaley, start packing. I've a sudden urge to go a'fairing, and what better time than now? Hatchard, have the horses readied. I'm tired of sitting around letting life happen to me. It's time I make my life happen."

"This doesn't bode well, Missus Twillow," Hatchard told Kaley as Jillian strolled briskly off.

"A woman has as much right to cat about as a man. At least she's catting after a husband. Now we just have to put our heads together and make certain she chooses the right one," Kaley informed him loftily before sauntering after Jillian, twitching her plump hips in a manner that put

Hatchard in mind of a long-forgotten, exceedingly bawdy ditty.

He blew out a gusty breath and headed off to the stables.

* * *

The Black Boot sagged alarmingly at the eaves, but fortunately the rooms Grimm had procured were on the third floor, not the top, which meant they should be reasonably safe from the deluge that had begun halfway through their trip.

Pausing outside the open door to the inn, Grimm fisted double handfuls of his shirt and squeezed it. Water gushed from between his hands and splattered loudly on the great stone slab outside the door.

A thick, swirling mist was settling over the town. Within a quarter hour the dense fog would be impossible to navigate through; they'd arrived just in time to avoid the worst of it. Grimm had settled his horse in the small U-shaped courtyard behind the inn, where a ratty lean-to swayed precariously from the drooping roof. Occam would find sufficient shelter, provided the flood didn't carry him off.

Grimm whisked the beaded water droplets off his plaid before entering the inn. Any weaver worth her salt wove the fabric so tightly it was virtually water-repellant, and the weavers at Dalkeith were some of the finest. He unfastened a length of the woolen fabric and draped it across his shoulder. Quinn and Ramsay were already at the fire, toasting their hands and drying their boots.

"Bloody nasty weather out there, ain't it, lads?" The barkeep beckoned cheerfully through the doorway to the adjoining tavern. "Me, I've got a fire in here s'warm as tha' one, and a fine brew to chase yer chill, so dinna tarry. Me name's Mac," he added with a friendly nod. "Come bide a wee."

Grimm glanced at Quinn, who shrugged. His expression plainly said there wasn't much else to do on such a miserably wet evening than pass it drinking. The three men ducked through the low doorway that partitioned the eatery from the tavern proper and claimed several battered wooden stools at a table by the hearth.

"Seein' as 'tis nearly deserted in here, I may as well pull up a seat once I've seen t' yer drinks. No' many venture out in a downpour such as this." The barkeep ambled unevenly to the bar, then lumbered back to their table, producing a bottle of whisky and four mugs with a flourish.

" 'Tis a fardlin' mess out there, ain't it? An' where be ye travelin'?" he asked, sitting heavily. "Dinna mind me leg, I think the wood's goin' soft," he added as he grabbed a second stool, lifted his wooden leg by the ankle, and dropped it on the slats. "Sometimes it pains me when the weather goes damp. An' in this damn country, tha's all the time, ain't it? Gloomy place, she is, but I love 'er. Y'ever been outside of Alba, lads?"

Grimm glanced at Quinn, who was gazing raptly at the barkeep, his expression a mixture of amusement and irritation. Grimm knew they were both wondering if the lonely little barkeep would ever shut up.

It was going to be a long night.

* * *

A few hours later the rain hadn't abated, and Grimm used the excuse of checking on Occam to escape the smoky tavern and Mac's incessant prattle. Besieged by the same restlessness that had ridden him at Dalkeith, he could scarcely sit still for longer than a few hours. He slipped into the back courtyard of the inn, wondering what Jillian was doing at the moment. A slight smile curved his lips as he

pictured her stomping about, tossing her glorious mane of
hair, outraged that she'd been left behind. Jillian despised
being excluded from anything "the lads" did. But this was
for the best, and she would realize it when Quinn returned
with his gift and made his formal pledge. Grimm could
scarcely look at Quinn without being struck by what a perfect couple they would make, giving birth to perfect,
golden children with aristocratic features and not a touch
of inherited madness. Perhaps by getting the two of them
together he could redeem himself in some small measure,
he mused, although the thought of Jillian with Quinn
caused his stomach to tighten painfully.

"Get out o' me kitchen and dinna be returnin', ye ratty-
ass whelp." A door on the far side of the courtyard suddenly burst open. A child tumbled head over heels into the
night and landed prone in the mud.

Grimm studied the man whose wide frame nearly filled
the doorway. He was a big, beefy man, well over six feet
tall, with a frizzled crown of short-cropped brown curls.
His face was mottled red in patches, either due to rage or
exertion, or more likely both, Grimm decided. He clutched
a wide butcher's knife that gleamed dully in the light.

The lad clambered to his knees, slipping on the sodden
ground. He scrubbed at a spattering of mud on his cheek
with thin, dirty fingers. "But Bannion always gives us the
scraps. Please, sir, we need to eat!"

"I'm no' Bannion, ye insolent whelp! Bannion doesna
work here anymore, and no wonder, if he be giving away to
such as ye. I'm the meat butcher now." The man cuffed the
child with such vigor that the boy collapsed onto his back-
side in the mud, shaking his head dazedly. "Ye think we
spare any cuts fer the likes o' ye? Ye can rot in a gutter,
Robbie MacAuley says. I dinna expect anyone to feed me.

It's the likes o' ye rats that grow up to be thieves and murderers of honest, hardworkin' men." The meat butcher stepped out into the rain, dragged the child from the mud by his scruffy collar, and shook him. When the lad began howling, thè butcher cracked a meaty hand across his face.

"Release him," Grimm said quietly.

"Eh?" The man glanced around, startled. A sneer crossed his red face as his gaze lit on Grimm, who was partially concealed by the shadows. The meat butcher straightened menacingly, suspending the boy by one hand. "What's yer concern wi' me business? Stay out o' it. I dinna ask yer opinion and I dinna want it. I found the l'il whelp stealing me vittles—"

"Nay! I dinna steal! Bannion *gives* us the scraps."

The meat butcher backhanded the lad across the face, and blood sprayed from the child's nose.

In the shadow of the lean-to Grimm stared transfixed at the bleeding child. Memories began to crowd him—the flash of a silver blade, a tumble of blond curls and a blood-stained smock, pillars of smoke—an unnatural wind began to rise, and he felt his body twisting inside, reshaping itself until he was hopelessly lost to the rage within. Far beyond conscious thought, Grimm lunged for the meat butcher, crushing him against the stone wall.

"You son of a bitch." Grimm closed his hands around the man's windpipe. "The child needs food. When I release you, you're going to go in the kitchen and pack him a basket of the finest meat you've got, and then you're going to—"

"Like 'ell I am!" the butcher managed to wheeze. He twisted in Grimm's grip and plunged blindly forward with the knife. As the blade slid home, Grimm's hand relaxed infinitesimally, and the butcher sucked in a whistling breath of air. "There, ye bastard," he cried hoarsely. "Nobody messes wi' Robbie MacAuley. 'At'll be teachin' ye." He shoved Grimm with both hands, twisting the knife as he pushed.

As Grimm swayed back, the butcher started forward, only to fall instinctively backward again, his eyes widening incredulously, for the madman he'd stabbed with a brutality and efficiency that should have caused a mortal wound was smiling.

"Smile. That's it—go on, smile as ye be dyin'," he cried. " 'Cause dyin' ye are, and that's fer sure."

Grimm's smile contained such sinister promise that the meat butcher flattened himself up against the wall of the inn like lichen seeking a deep, shady crevice between the stones. "There's a knife in yer belly, man," the meat butcher hissed, eyeing the protruding hilt of the knife to reassure himself it was, indeed, lodged in his assailant's gut.

Breathing evenly, Grimm grasped the hilt with one hand and removed the blade, calmly placing it beneath the butcher's quivering jowls.

"You're going to get the lad the food he came for. Then you will apologize," Grimm said mildly, his eyes glittering.

"To 'ell with ye," the butcher sputtered. "Any minute now ye'll be falling on yer face."

Grimm leveled the blade below the butcher's ear, flush across his jugular. "Doona count on it."

"Ye should be dead, man. There's a hole in yer belly!"

"Grimm." Quinn's voice cut through the night air.

Pressing gently, with the care of a lover, Grimm pierced the skin on the butcher's neck.

"Grimm," Quinn repeated softly.

"Gawd, man! Get him offa me!" the butcher cried frantically. "He's deranged! His bleedin' eyes are like—"

"Shut up, you imbecile," Quinn said in a modulated, conciliatory tone. He knew from experience that harshly uttered words could escalate the state of Berserkergang. Quinn circled the pair cautiously. Grimm had frozen with the blade locked to the man's throat. The ragged lad huddled at their feet, gazing up with wide eyes.

"He be Berserk," the lad whispered reverently. "By Odin, look at his eyes."

"He be crazed," the butcher whimpered, looking at Quinn. "Do something!"

"I *am* doing something," Quinn said quietly. "Make no loud noises, and for Christ's sake, don't move." Quinn stepped closer to Grimm, making certain his friend could see him.

"The whelp's just a homeless ne'er-do-well. 'Tis not the thing to be killing an honest man for," the butcher whined. "How was I supposed to know he was a fardlin' Berserker?"

"It shouldn't have made any difference whether he was or not. A man shouldn't behave honorably only when there's someone bigger and tougher around to force him," Quinn said, disgusted. "Grimm, do you want to kill this man or feed the boy?" Quinn spoke gently, close to his friend's ear. Grimm's eyes were incandescent in the dim light, and Quinn knew he was deep into the bloodlust that accompanied Berserkergang. "You only want to feed the boy, don't you? All you want to do is to feed the boy and keep him from harm, remember? Grimm—*Gavrael*—listen to me. Look at me!"

* * *

"I hate this, Quinn," Grimm said later as he unbuttoned his shirt with stiff fingers.

Quinn gave him a curious look. "Do you really? What is there to hate about it? The only difference between what you did and what I would have done is that you don't know what you're doing when you're doing it. You're honorable even when you're not fully conscious. You're so damned honorable, you *can't* behave any other way."

"I would have killed him."

"I'm not convinced of that. I've seen you do this before and I've seen you pull out of it. The older you get, the more control you seem to gain. And I don't know if you've realized this, but you weren't completely unaware this time. You heard me when I spoke to you. It used to take a lot longer to reach you."

Grimm's brow furrowed. "That's true," he admitted. "It seems I manage to retain a sliver of awareness. Not much— but it's more than I used to have."

"Let me see that wound." Quinn drew a candle near. "And bear in mind, the meat butcher would have given no thought to beating the lad senseless and leaving him to die in the mud. The homeless children in this city are considered no better than street rats, and the general consensus is the faster they die, the better."

"It's not right, Quinn," Grimm said. "Children are innocent. They haven't had a chance to be corrupted. We'd do better to take the children off somewhere else to raise them properly. With someone like Jillian to teach them fables," he added.

Quinn smiled faintly as he bent over the puckered wound. "She will be a wonderful mother, won't she? Like Elizabeth." Bemused, he drew his fingers over the already-closing cut in Grimm's side. "By Odin's spear, man, how quickly do you heal?"

Grimm grimaced slightly. "Very. It seems to be getting even quicker, the older I get."

Quinn dropped to the bed, shaking his head. "What a blessing it must be. You never have to worry about infection, do you? How *does* one kill a Berserker, anyway?"

"With great difficulty," Grimm replied dryly. "I've tried to drink myself to death, and that didn't work. Then I tried to labor myself to death. Failing that, I just plunged into every battle I could find, and that didn't work either. The only thing left was to try was to fu—" He broke off, embarrassed. "Well, as you can see, that didn't work either."

Quinn grinned. "No harm in trying, though, was there?"

Grimm begrudged a faint curve of his lip.

"Get some sleep, man." Quinn lightly punched him on the shoulder. "Everything looks better in the morning. Well, almost everything," he added with a sheepish grin, "so long as I wasn't too drunk the night before. Then sometimes the wench looks worse. And so do I, for that matter."

Grimm just shook his head and flopped back on the bed. After folding his arms behind his head, he was asleep in seconds.

CHAPTER 11

EVERYTHING LOOKS BETTER IN THE MORNING. WATCHING Jillian from his window, Grimm recalled Quinn's words and agreed wholeheartedly. What lapse of judgment had persuaded him that she wouldn't follow them?

She was breathtaking, he acknowledged as he watched her hungrily, safe in the privacy of his room. Clad in a velvet cloak of amber, she was a vision of flushed cheeks and sparkling eyes. Her blond hair tumbled over her shoulders, casting the sun back at the sky. The rain had stopped— probably just for her, he brooded—and she stood in a puddle of sunshine that shafted over the roof from the east, proclaiming the hour to be shortly before noon. He'd slept like the dead, but he always did after succumbing to the Berserker rage, no matter how brief its duration.

Peering out the narrow casement window, he rubbed the glass until it permitted him an unmarred view. While Hatchard gathered her bags, Jillian linked her arm through

Kaley's and chatted animatedly. When Quinn appeared in
the street below a few moments later, gallantly offered his
arms to both ladies, and escorted them into the inn, Grimm
exhaled dismally.

Ever-gallant, ever-golden Quinn.

Grimm muttered a soft curse and went to feed Occam
before worrying about his own breakfast.

* * *

Jillian mounted the main staircase to her room, glanced
about to ascertain she was alone, then detoured stealthily
down the rear steps, smoothing the folds of her cloak. Biting her lip, she exited into the small courtyard behind the
inn. He was there, just as she'd suspected, feeding Occam a
handful of grain and murmuring quietly. Jillian paused, enjoying the sight of him. He was tall and magnificent, and
his dark hair rippled in the breeze. His plaid was slung too
low for propriety, riding his lean hips with sensual insolence. She could see a peek of his back where his shirt had
obviously been hastily tucked. Her fingers itched to stroke
the smooth olive-tinted skin. When he bent to pick up a
brush, the muscles in his legs rippled, and despite her vow
to make no sound, she exhaled a breath of unadulterated
longing.

Of course, he heard her. She instantly assumed a mask
of indifference and volleyed into questions to head off a
potential verbal sully. "Why don't you ever pen Occam?"
she asked brightly.

Grimm allowed a brief glance over his shoulder, then
started brushing the horse's sleek flank. "He was caught in
a stable fire once."

"He doesn't appear to have suffered for it." Jillian

traversed the courtyard, eyeing the stallion. "Was he injured?" The horse was magnificent, hands taller than most and a glossy, unmarked slate gray.

Grimm stopped brushing. "You never stop with your questions, do you? And what are you doing here, anyway? Couldn't you just be a good lass and wait at Caithness? No, I forgot, Jillian hates being left behind," he said mockingly.

"So who rescued him?" Jillian was determined not to rise to the bait.

Grimm returned his attention to the horse. "I did." There was a pause, filled only with the rasp of bristles against horseflesh. When he spoke again, he released a low rush of words: "Have you ever heard a horse scream, Jillian? It's one of the most bloodcurdling sounds I've ever heard. It cuts through you as cruelly as the sound of an innocent child's cry of pain. I think it has always been the innocence that bothers me most."

Jillian wondered when he'd heard those screams and wanted desperately to ask, but was hesitant to pry at his wounds. She held her tongue, hoping he might continue if she stayed silent.

He didn't. Silently stepping back from the stallion, he made a sharp gesture, accompanied by a clicking noise with his tongue against his teeth. Jillian watched in amazement as the stallion sank to its knees, then dropped heavily to its side with a soft nicker. Grimm knelt by the horse and motioned her closer.

She slipped to her knees beside Grimm. "Oh, poor, sweet Occam," she whispered. The entire underside of the horse was badly scarred. Lightly she ran her fingers over the thick skin, and her brows puckered sympathetically.

"He was burned so badly, they said he wouldn't live," Grimm told her. "They planned to put him down, so I bought him. Not only was he wounded, he was crazed for months afterward. Can you imagine the terror of being trapped in a burning barn, penned in? Occam could run faster than the fleetest horse, could have left the blaze miles behind, but he was imprisoned in a man-made hell. I've never penned him since."

Jillian swallowed and glanced at Grimm. His expression was bitter. "You sound as if you've been trapped in a few man-made hells yourself, Grimm Roderick," she observed softly.

His gaze mocked her. "What would you know about man-made hells?"

"A woman lives most of her life in a man-made world," Jillian replied. "First her father's world, then her husband's, finally her son's, by whose grace she continues on in one of their households should her husband die before her. And in Scotland, the husbands always seem to die before the women in one war or another. Sometimes merely watching the hells men design for each other—that's horror enough for any woman. We feel things differently than you men do." She impulsively laid her hand against his lips to silence him when he started to speak. "No. Don't say anything. I know you think I know little of sorrow or pain, but I've had my share. There are things you don't know about me, Grimm Roderick. And don't forget the battle I watched when I was young." Her eyes widened with disbelief when Grimm lightly kissed the tips of her fingers where they lay across his lips.

"Touché, Jillian," he whispered. He caught her hand in his and placed it gently in her lap. Jillian sat motionless when he curled his own about it protectively.

"If I were a man who believed in wishes on stars, I would wish on all of them that Jillian St. Clair might never suffer the smallest glimpse of any hell. There should only be heaven for Jillian's eyes."

Jillian remained perfectly still, masking her astonishment, exulting in the sensation of his strong, warm hand cupping hers. By the saints, she would have ridden all the way to England through the savagery of a border battle if she'd known *this* was waiting for her at the end of her journey. She fancied her body had taken root where she knelt; to continue being touched by him she would willingly grow old in the small courtyard, suffering wind and rain, hail and snow without the slightest care. Mesmerized by the glimpse of hesitation in his gaze, her head tilted up; his seemed to move forward and down as if nudged by a serendipitous breeze.

His lips were a breath from hers, and she waited, her heart thundering.

"Jillian! Jillian, are you out there?"

Jillian closed her eyes, willing the owner of the intruding voice to hell and farther. She felt the soft brush of Grimm's lips across hers as he quickly, lightly delivered a kiss that was nothing like the one she'd been anticipating. She wanted his lips to bruise hers, she wanted his tongue in her mouth and his breath in her lungs, she wanted everything he had to give.

"It's Ramsay," Grimm said through his teeth. "He's coming out. Get up off your knees, lass. *Now.*"

Jillian stumbled hastily to her feet and stepped back, trying desperately to see Grimm's face, but his dark head had fallen forward to the spot hers had occupied a moment before. "Grimm," she whispered urgently. She wanted him to raise his head; she needed to see his eyes. She had to confirm that she'd truly seen desire in his eyes as he'd gazed at her.

"Lass." He groaned the word, his head still bowed.

"Yes?" she whispered breathlessly.

His hands fisted in the folds of his kilt, and she waited, trembling.

The door clattered open and shut behind them. "Jillian," Ramsay called as he entered the courtyard. "There you are. I'm so pleased you joined us. I thought you might like to accompany me to the fair. What's your horse doing on the ground, Roderick?"

Jillian released her breath in a hiss of frustration and kept her back to Ramsay. "What, Grimm? What?" she entreated in an urgent whisper.

He raised his head. There was a defiant glint in his blue eyes. "Quinn is in love with you, lass. I think you should know that," he said softly.

CHAPTER 12

JILLIAN DEFTLY ELUDED RAMSAY BY TELLING HIM SHE needed to buy "woman things"—a statement that appeared to set his imagination to flight. Thus she was able to spend the afternoon shopping with Kaley and Hatchard. At the silversmith she bought a new buckle for her da. From the tanner she purchased three snowy lambskin rugs—thick as sin and soft as rabbit fur. At the goldsmith's she bartered shrewdly for tiny, hammered-gold stars to adorn a new gown.

But all the while her mind was back in the courtyard, lingering on the dark, sensual man who'd betrayed the first glimpse of a crack in the massive walls around his heart. It had stunned her, bewildered her, and fortified her resolve. Jillian didn't doubt for a moment what she'd seen. Grimm Roderick cared. Buried beneath a mound of rubble—the debris from a past she was beginning to suspect had been more brutal than she could comprehend—there was a very real, vulnerable man.

She'd seen in his stark gaze that he desired her, but more significantly, that he had feelings so deep he couldn't express them, and subsequently did everything in his power to deny them. That was sufficient hope for her to work with. It didn't occur to Jillian, even for a moment, to wonder if he was worth the effort—she knew he was. He had everything to offer that she'd ever wanted in a man. Jillian understood that people didn't come perfect; sometimes they'd been so badly scarred that it took love to heal them and allow them to realize their potential. Sometimes the badly scarred ones had the greatest depth and the most to offer because they understood the infinite value of tenderness. She would be the sun beating down upon the cloak of indifference he'd donned so many years ago, inviting him to walk without defenses.

Her anticipation was so strong, it made her feel shaky and weak. Desire had shimmered in Grimm's gaze when he looked at her, and whether he realized it or not, she'd seen an intense, sensual promise on his face.

Now all she had to do was figure out how to release it. She shivered, rattled by the intuitive knowledge that when Grimm Roderick unleashed his passion, it would definitely be worth waiting for.

"Are you chilled, lass?" Hatchard asked worriedly.

"Chilled?" Jillian echoed blankly.

"You shivered."

"Oh please, Hatchard!" Kaley snorted. "That was a daydreaming shiver. Can't you tell the difference?"

Jillian glanced at Kaley, startled. Kaley merely smiled smugly. "Well, it was, wasn't it, Jillian?"

"How did *you* know?"

"Quinn looked very handsome this morning," Kaley said pointedly.

"So did Grimm," Hatchard snapped immediately. "Didn't you think so, lass? I know you saw him by the stables."

Jillian gaped at Hatchard with a horrified expression. "Were you spying on me?"

"Of course not," Hatchard said defensively. "I just happened to glance out my window."

"Oh," Jillian said in a small voice, her glance darting between her maid and man-at-arms. "Why are you two looking at me like that?" she demanded.

"Like what?" Kaley fluttered her lashes innocently.

Jillian rolled her eyes, disgusted by their obvious matchmaking efforts. "Shall we return to the inn? I promised I'd return in time to have dinner."

"With Quinn?" Kaley said hopefully.

Hatchard nudged the maid. "With Grimm."

"With Occam," Jillian flung over her shoulder dryly.

Hatchard and Kaley exchanged amused glances as Jillian dashed down the street, her arms overflowing with packages.

"I thought she brought *us* to carry," Hatchard observed with a lift of one fox-red eyebrow and a gesture of his empty hands.

Kaley smiled. "Remmy, I suspect she could cart the world off on her shoulders and not feel an ounce. The lass is in love, for certain. My only question is—with which man?"

* * *

"Which one, Jillian?" Kaley asked without preface as she fastened the tiny buttons at the back of Jillian's gown, a creation of lime silk that tumbled in a sensuous ripple from clever ribbons placed at the bodice.

"Which one, what?" Jillian asked nonchalantly. She ran

her fingers through her hair, pulling a sleek fall of gold over her shoulder. She perched on the tiny settle before a blurry mirror in her room at the inn, itching with impatience to join the men in the dining room.

Kaley's reflection met Jillian's with a wordless rebuke. She tugged Jillian's hair back and swept it up into a knot with more enthusiasm than was necessary.

"Ouch." Jillian scowled. "All right, I know what you meant. I just don't wish to answer it yet. Let me see how things go this evening."

Kaley relaxed her grip and smiled. "So you admit to this much—you do intend to select a husband from one of them? You'll heed your father's wishes?"

"Yes, Kaley, oh absolutely yes!" Jillian's eyes sparkled as she leapt to her feet.

"I suppose you could wear your hair down this evening," Kaley begrudged. "Although you should at least allow me to dress and curl it."

"I like it straight," Jillian replied. "It's wavy enough of its own accord, and I don't have time to fuss."

"Oh, now the lass who took over an hour to choose a dress doesn't have time to fuss?" Kaley teased.

"I'm already late, Kaley," Jillian said with a blush as she swept from the room.

* * *

"She's late," Grimm said, pacing irritably. They'd been waiting for some time in the small anteroom that lay between the section of the inn that held private rooms and the public eatery. "By Odin's spear, why doona we just send a tray up to her room?"

"And forgo the pleasure of her company? Not a chance," Ramsay said.

"Stop pacing, Grimm," Quinn said with a grin. "You really need to relax a bit."

"I am perfectly relaxed," Grimm said, stalking back and forth.

"No, you're not," Quinn argued. "You look almost brittle. If I tapped you with my sword, you'd shatter."

"If you tapped me with your sword, I'd bloody well tap you back with mine, and not with the hilt."

"There's no need to get defensive—"

"I am not being defensive!"

Quinn and Ramsay both leveled patronizing gazes at him.

"That's not fair." Grimm scowled. "That's a trap. If someone says 'doona get defensive,' what possible response can a person make except a defensive one? You're stuck with two choices: Say nothing, or sound defensive."

"Grimm, sometimes you think too much," Ramsay observed.

"I'm going to have a drink." Grimm seethed. "Come get me when she's ready, *if* that remarkable event manages to occur before the sun rises."

Ramsay shot Quinn an inquiring look. "He wasn't quite so foul-tempered at court, de Moncreiffe. What's his problem? It's not me, is it? I know we had a few misunderstandings in the past, but I thought they were over and forgotten."

"If memory serves me, the scar on your face is a memento from one of those 'misunderstandings,' isn't it?" When Ramsay grimaced, Quinn continued. "It's not you, Logan. It's how he's always acted around Jillian. But it seems to have gotten worse since she's grown up."

"If he thinks he's going to win her, he's wrong," Ramsay said quietly.

"He's not trying to win her, Logan. He's trying to hate her. And if you think you're going to win her, *you're* wrong."

Ramsay Logan made no reply, but his challenging gaze spoke volumes as he turned away and entered the crowded dining room.

Quinn cast a quick look at the empty stairs, shrugged, and followed on his heels.

* * *

When Jillian arrived downstairs, there was no one waiting for her.

Fine bunch of suitors, she thought. *First they leave me, then they leave me again.*

She glanced back up the stairs, plucking nervously at the neckline of her gown. Should she return for Kaley? The Black Boot was the finest inn in Durrkesh, boasting the best food to be had in the village, yet the thought of walking into the crowded eating establishment by herself was a bit daunting. She'd never gone into a tavern eatery alone before.

She moved to the door and peeked through the opening.

The room was packed with boisterous clusters of patrons. Laughter swelled and broke in waves, despite the fact that half the patrons were forced to stand while eating. Suddenly, as if ordained by the gods, the people faded back to reveal a dark, sinfully handsome man standing by himself near the carved oak counter that served as a bar. Only Grimm Roderick stood with such insolent grace.

As she watched, Quinn walked up to him, handed him a drink, and said something that nearly made Grimm smile. She smiled herself as he caught the expression midway through and quickly terminated any trace of amusement. When Quinn melted back into the crowd, Jillian slipped into the main room and hastened to Grimm's side. He glanced at her and his eyes flared strangely; he nodded but said nothing. Jillian stood in silence, searching for something to say, something witty and intriguing; she was finally alone with him in an adult setting, able to engage in intimate conversation as she'd fantasized so many times.

But before she could think of anything to say, he seemed to lose interest and turned away.

Jillian kicked herself mentally. *Hell's bells, Jillian,* she chided herself, *can't you dredge up a few words around this man?* Her eyes started an adoring journey at the nape of his neck, caressed his thick black hair, wandered over the muscled back straining against the fabric of his shirt as he raised an arm for another draught of ale. She reveled in the mere sight of him, the way the muscles in his shoulders bunched as he gripped an acquaintance by the hand. Her eyes traveled lower, taking in the way his waist narrowed to tight, muscular hips and powerful legs.

His legs were dusted with hair, she noted, drawing a shaky breath, studying the backs of his legs below his kilt, but where did that silky black hair begin and end?

Jillian released a breath she hadn't even known she was holding. Every ounce of her body responded to his with delicious anticipation. Merely standing next to this darkly seductive man, her legs felt weak and her tummy was filled with a shivery sensation.

When Grimm leaned back, momentarily brushing against her in the crowded room, she briefly laid her cheek against his shoulder so softly that he didn't know she'd thieved the touch. She inhaled the scent of him and reached brazenly forward. Her hands found the blades of his shoulders and she scratched gently with her nails, lightly scoring his skin through his shirt.

A soft groan escaped his lips, and Jillian's eyes widened. She scratched gently, stunned that he said nothing. He didn't pull away from her. He didn't spin on his heel and lash out at her.

Jillian held her breath, then inhaled greedily, reveling in the crisp aroma of spicy soap and man. He began to move slightly beneath her nails, like a cat having its chin scratched. Could it be he was actually enjoying her touch?

Oh, can the gods just grant me one wish tonight—to feel the kiss of this man!

She slid her palms lovingly over his back and pressed closer to his body. Her fingers traced the individual muscles in his broad shoulders, slid down his tapered waist, then swept back up again. His body relaxed beneath her hands.

Heaven, this is heaven, she thought dreamily.

"You're looking mighty contented, Grimm." Quinn's voice interrupted her fantasy. "Amazing what a drink can do for your disposition. Where's Jillian gotten off to? Wasn't she just here with you a moment ago?"

Jillian's hands stilled on Grimm's back, which was so broad that it completely shielded her from Quinn's view. She ducked her head, feeling suddenly guilty. The muscles in Grimm's back went rigid beneath her motionless fingers. "Didn't she step outside for a breath of fresh air?" she was stunned to hear Grimm ask.

"By herself? Hell's bells, man—you shouldn't let her go wandering outside by herself!" Quinn's boots clipped smartly on the stone floor as she strode off in search of her.

Grimm whipped around furiously. "What do you think you're doing, peahen?" He snarled.

"I was touching you," she said simply.

Grimm grabbed both her hands in his, nearly crushing the delicate bones in her fingers. "Well, doona be, lass. There is nothing between you and me—"

"You leaned back," she protested. "You didn't seem to be so unhappy—"

"I thought you were a tavern wench!" Grimm said, running a furious hand through his hair.

"Oh!" Jillian was crestfallen.

Grimm lowered his head till his lips brushed her ear, taking pains to make his next words audible over the din in the noisy eatery. "In case you doona recall, it is Quinn who wants you and Quinn who is clearly the best choice. Go find him and touch him, lass. Leave me to the tavern wenches who understand a man like me."

Jillian's eyes sparkled dangerously as she turned away and pushed through the crowded room.

* * *

He would survive the night. It couldn't be too bad; after all, he'd lived through worse. Grimm had been aware of Jillian since the moment she'd entered the room. He had, in fact, deliberately turned away from her when it appeared she'd been about to speak. Little good that had done—as soon as she'd touched him he'd been unable to force himself to step away from the sensual feel of her hands on his back. He'd let it go too far, but it wasn't too late to salvage the situation.

Now he studiously kept his back to Jillian, methodically pouring whisky into a mug. He drank with a vengeance, wiping his lips with the back of his hand, longing for the ability to dull his perfect Berserker senses. Periodically he heard the breathless lilt of her laughter. Occasionally, as the proprietor moved bottles upon shelves, he caught a glimpse of her golden hair in a polished flagon.

But he didn't give a damn, any fool could see that much. He'd pushed her to do what she was currently doing, so how could he care? He didn't, he assured himself, because he was one sane man among a race seemingly condemned to be dragged about by violent, unpredictable emotions that were nothing more than unrelieved lust. Lust, not love, and neither one had a damned thing to do with Jillian.

Christ! Who did he think he was kidding? Grimm closed his eyes and shook his head at his own lies.

Life was hell and he was Sisyphus, eternally condemned to push a boulder of relentless desire up a hill, only to have it flatten him before he reached the crest. Grimm had never been able to tolerate futility. He was a man who resolved things, and tonight he would see to it that Jillian solidified her betrothal to Quinn and that would be the end of his involvement.

He couldn't covet his best friend's wife, could he? So all he had to do was get her wed to Quinn, and that would be the end of his agony. He simply couldn't live with this battle waging within him much longer. If she was free and unwed, he could still dream. If she were safely married, he would be forced to put his fool dreams to rest. So resolved, Grimm stole a covert glance over his shoulder to see how things were progressing. Only peglegged Mac behind the counter heard the hollow whistle of his indrawn breath and noticed the rigid set of his jaw.

Jillian was standing halfway across the room, her golden head tilted back, doing that bedazzling woman-thing to his best friend, which essentially involved nothing more than being what she was: irresistible. A teasing glance, vivacious eyes flashing; a delectable lower lip caught between her teeth. The two were obviously in their own little world, oblivious to him. The very situation he'd encouraged her to seek. It infuriated him.

As he watched, the world that wasn't Jillian—for what was the world without Jillian?—receded. He could hear the rustle of her hair across the crowded tavern, the sigh of air as her hand rose to Quinn's face. Then suddenly the only sound he could hear was the blood thundering in his ears as he watched her slender fingers trace the curve of Quinn's cheek, lingering upon his jaw. His gut tightened and his heart beat a rough staccato of anger.

Mesmerized, Grimm's hand crept to his own face. Jillian's palm feathered Quinn's skin; her fingers traced the shadow beard on Quinn's jaw. Grimm fervently wished he'd broken that perfect jaw a time or two when they'd played as lads.

Deeply oblivious to Mac's fascinated gaze, Grimm's hand traced the same pattern on his own face; he mimicked her touch, his eyes devouring her with such intensity that she might have fled, had she turned to look at him. But she didn't turn. She was too busy gazing adoringly at his best friend.

Behind him a soft snort and a whistle pierced the smoky air. "Man, ye've got it bloody bad, and that's more truth than ye'll find in another bottle o' rotgut mash." Mac's voice shattered the fantasy that Grimm was certainly *not* having. "It's a spot of 'ell wanting yer best friend's wife, now, isn't it?" Mac nodded enthusiastically, warming to the subject. "Me, meself, I had a bit o' thing for one o' me own friend's girl, oh let's see, musta been ten years—"

"She's *not* his wife." The eyes Grimm turned on Mac were not the eyes of a sane man. They were the eyes his villagers had seen before judiciously turning their backs on him so many years ago—the ice-blue eyes of a Viking Berserker who would stop at nothing to get what he wanted.

"Well, she sure as 'ell is his *something*." Mac shrugged off the unmistakable warning in Grimm's eyes with the aplomb of a man who'd survived too many tavern brawls to get overly concerned about one irritable patron. "And yer wishing she wasn't, that's fer sure." Mac removed the empty bottle and picked up a full one that was on the counter. He looked at it curiously. "Now where did this come from?" he asked with a frown. "Och, me mind's getting addled, I dinna even recall openin' this one, though fer sure ye'll be drinking it," Mac said, pouring him a fresh mug. The loquacious barkeep ambled into the room behind the bar and returned a moment later with a heaped basket of brandy-basted chicken. "The way yer drinkin', ye need to be eatin', man," he advised.

Grimm rolled his eyes. Unfortunately, all the whisky in Scotland couldn't dull a Berserker's senses. While Mac tended to a new arrival, Grimm dumped the fresh mug of whisky over the chicken in frustration. He had just decided to go for a long walk when Ramsay sat down next to him.

"Looks like Quinn's making some headway," Ramsay muttered darkly as he eyed the chicken. "Mmm, that looks juicy. Mind if I help myself?"

"Have at it," Grimm said stiffly. "Here—have a drink too." Grimm slid the bottle down the bar.

"No thanks, man. Got my own." Ramsay raised his mug.

Husky, melodic laughter broke over them as Jillian and Quinn joined them at the bar. Despite his best efforts, Grimm's eyes were dark and furious when he glanced at Quinn.

"What do we have here?" Quinn asked, helping himself to the basket of chicken.

"Excuse me," Grimm muttered, pushing past them, ignoring Jillian completely.

Without a backward glance, he left the tavern and melted into the Durrkesh night.

* * *

It was nearly dawn when Grimm returned to the Black Boot. Climbing the stairs wearily, he topped the last step and froze as an unexpected sound reached his ears. He peered down the hallway, eyeing the doors one by one.

He heard the sound again—a whimper, followed by a deeper, husky groan.

Jillian? With Quinn?

He moved swiftly and silently down the corridor, pausing outside Quinn's room. He listened intently and heard it a third time—a husky sigh and a gasp of indrawn air—and each sound ripped through his gut like a double-edged blade. Rage washed over him and everything black he'd ever tried to suppress quickened within. He felt himself slipping over treacherous terrain into the fury he'd first felt fifteen years ago, standing above Tuluth. Something more powerful than any single man could be had taken shape within his veins, endowing him with unspeakable strength and unthinkable capacity for bloodshed—an ancient Viking monster with cold eyes.

Grimm laid his forehead against the cool wood of Quinn's door and breathed in carefully measured gasps as he struggled to subdue his violent reaction. His breathing regulated slowly—sounding nothing like the uncontrolled noises coming from the other side of the door. Christ—he'd encouraged her to marry Quinn, not to go to bed with him!

A feral growl escaped his lips.

Despite his best intentions, his hand found the knob and he turned it, only to meet the defiance of a lock. For a moment he was immobilized, stunned by the barrier. A barrier between him and Jillian—a lock that told him she had chosen. Maybe he had pushed her, but she might have taken a bit more time choosing! A year or two—perhaps the rest of her life.

Aye, she had clearly made her choice—so what right did he have to even consider shattering the door into tiny slivers of wood and selecting the deadliest shard to drive through his best friend's heart? What right had he to do anything but turn away and make his path back down the dark corridor to his own personal hell where the devil surely awaited him with an entirely new boulder to wrestle to the top of the hill: the obdurate stone of regret.

The internal debate raged a tense moment, ending only when the beast within him reared its head, extended its claws, and shattered Quinn's door.

* * *

Grimm's breath rasped in labored pants. He crouched in the doorway and peered into the dimly lit room, wondering why no one had leapt, startled, from the bed.

"Grimm . . ." The word pierced the gloom weakly.

Bewildered, Grimm slipped into the room and moved quickly to the low bed. Quinn was tangled in sodden sheets, curled into a ball—alone. Vomit stained the scuffed planks of the floor. A water tin had been crushed and abandoned, a ceramic pitcher was broken beside it, and the window stood open to the chill night air.

Suddenly Quinn thrashed violently and heaved up from the bed, doubling over. Grimm rushed to catch him before he plunged to the floor. Holding his friend in his arms, he gaped uncomprehendingly until he saw a thin foam of spittle on Quinn's lips.

"P-p-poi-son." Quinn gasped. "H-help . . . me."

"No!" Grimm breathed. "Son of a bitch!" he cursed, cradling Quinn's head as he bellowed for help.

CHAPTER 13

"WHO WOULD POISON QUINN?" HATCHARD PUZZLED. "No one dislikes Quinn. Quinn is the quintessential laird and gentleman."

Grimm grimaced.

"Will he be all right?" Kaley asked, wringing her hands.

"What's going on?" A sleepy-eyed Jillian stood in the doorway. "Goodness," she exclaimed, eyeing the jagged splinters of the door. "What happened in here?"

"How do you feel, lass? Are you well? Does your stomach hurt? Do you have a fever?" Kaley's hands were suddenly everywhere, poking at her brow, prodding her belly, smoothing her hair.

Jillian blinked. "Kaley, I'm fine. Would you stop poking at me? I heard the commotion and it frightened me, that's all." When Quinn moaned, Jillian gasped. "What's wrong with Quinn?" Belatedly she noted the disarray of the room and the stench of illness that clung to the linens and drapes.

"Fetch a physician, Hatchard," Grimm said.

"The barber is closer," Hatchard suggested.

"No barber," Grimm snapped. He turned to Jillian. "Are you all right, lass?" When she nodded, he expelled a relieved breath. "Find Ramsay," he instructed Kaley ominously.

Kaley's eyes widened in comprehension, and she flew from the room.

"What happened?" Jillian asked blankly.

Grimm laid a damp cloth on Quinn's head. "I suspect it's poison." He didn't tell her he was certain; the recent contents of Quinn's stomach pervaded the air, and to a Berserker the stench of poison was obvious. "I think he'll be all right. If it's what I think it is, he would be dead by now had the dose been strong enough. It must have been diluted somehow."

"Who would poison Quinn? Everybody likes Quinn." She unwittingly echoed Hatchard's words.

"I know, lass. Everyone keeps telling me that," Grimm said drolly.

"Ramsay is ill!" Kaley's words echoed down the corridor. "Someone come help me! I can't hold him down!"

Grimm looked toward the hall, then back at Quinn, clearly torn. "Go to Kaley, lass. I can't leave him," he said through his teeth. Some might consider him paranoid, but if his suspicions were correct, it was supposed to have been him lying in a pile of his own vomit, dead.

An ashen-faced Jillian complied quickly.

Biting back a curse, Grimm daubed at Quinn's forehead and sat back to wait for the physician.

* * *

The physician arrived, carrying two large satchels and dashing rain from the thinning web of hair that crowned his pate. After questioning nearly everyone in the inn, he conceded to inspect the patients. Moving with surprising grace for such a rotund man, he paced to and fro, scribbling notes in a tiny book. After peering into their eyes, inspecting their tongues, and prodding their distended abdomens, he retreated to the pages of his tiny booklet.

"Give them barley water stewed with figs, honey, and licorice," he instructed after several moments of flipping pages in thoughtful silence. "Nothing else, you understand, for it won't be digested. The stomach is a cauldron in which food is simmered. While their humors are out of balance, nothing can be cooked, and anything with substance will come back up," the physician informed them. "Liquids only."

"Will they be all right?" Jillian asked worriedly. They'd moved the two men into a clean room adjoining Kaley's for easier tending.

The physician frowned, causing lines to fold his double chin as lugubriously as they creased his forehead. "I think they're out of danger. Neither of them appears to have consumed enough to kill him, but I suspect they'll be weak for some time. Lest they try to rise, you'll want to dilute this with water—it's mandrake." He proffered a small pouch. "Soak cloths in it and place them over their faces." The physician struck a lecturing pose, tapping his quill against his booklet. "You must be certain to cover both their nostrils and mouths completely for several minutes. As they inhale, the vapors will penetrate the body and keep them asleep. The spirits recover faster if the humors rest undisturbed. You see, there are four humors and three spirits . . . ah, but forgive me, I'm quite certain you don't wish to hear all of that. Only one who studies with the zeal of a physician might find such facts fascinating." He snapped his booklet closed. "Do as I have instructed and they shall make a full recovery."

"No bleeding?" Hatchard blinked.

The physician snorted. "Fetch a barber if you have an enemy you wish to murder. Fetch a physician if you have an ill patient you wish to revive."

Grimm nodded vehement agreement and rose to escort the physician out.

"Oh, Quinn," Jillian said, and sighed, placing a hand on his clammy forehead. She fussed at his woolens, tucking them snugly around his fevered body.

Standing behind Jillian on one side of Quinn's bed, Kaley beamed at Hatchard, who was perched across the room, applying cool cloths to Ramsay's brow. *She will choose Quinn, didn't I tell you?* she mouthed silently.

Hatchard merely lifted a brow and rolled his eyes.

* * *

When Grimm checked on the men the following morning, their condition had improved; however, they were still sedated, and not in any condition to travel.

Kaley insisted on acquiring the wares the men had originally come for, so Grimm reluctantly agreed to escort Jillian to the fair. Once there, he rushed her through the stalls at a breakneck pace, despite her protests. When a blanket of fog rolled down from the mountains and sheathed Durrkesh in the afternoon, a relieved Grimm informed Jillian it was time to return to the inn.

Fog always made Grimm uneasy, which proved inconvenient, as Scotland was such foggy terrain. This wasn't a normal fog, however; it was a thick, wet cape of dense white clouds that lingered on the ground and swirled around their feet as they walked. By the time they left the market, he could scarcely see Jillian's face a few feet from him.

"I love this!" Jillian exclaimed, slicing her arms through the tendrils of mist, scattering them with her movement. "Fog has always seemed so romantic to me."

"Life has always seemed romantic to you, lass. You used to think Bertie down at the stables spelling your name in horse manure was romantic," he reminded dryly.

"I still do," she said indignantly. "He learned his letters for the express purpose of writing my name. I think that's very romantic." Her brow furrowed as she peered through the soupy mist.

"Obviously you've never had to fight a battle in this crap," he said irritably. Fog reminded him of Tuluth and irrevocable choices. "It's damned hard to kill a man when you can't see where you're slicing with your sword."

Jillian stopped abruptly. "Our lives are vastly different, aren't they?" she asked, suddenly sober. "You've killed many men, haven't you, Grimm Roderick?"

"You should know," he replied tersely. "You watched me do it."

Jillian nibbled her lip and studied him. "The McKane would have killed my family that day, Grimm. You protected us. If a man must kill to protect his clan, there is no sin in that."

Would that he could absolve himself with such generosity, he thought. She still had no idea that the McKane's attack had not been directed at her family. They'd come to Caithness that foggy day long ago only because they'd heard a Berserker might be in residence. She hadn't known that then, and apparently Gibraltar St. Clair had never revealed his secret.

"Why did you leave that night, Grimm?" Jillian asked carefully.

"I left because it was time," he said roughly, shoving a hand through his hair. "I'd learned all your father could teach me, and it was time to move on. There was nothing to hold me at Caithness any longer."

Jillian sighed. "Well, you should know that none of us ever blamed you, despite the fact that we knew you blamed yourself. Even dear Edmund vowed until his last that you were the most noble warrior he'd ever met." Jillian's eyes misted. "We buried him under the apple tree, just as he'd asked," she added, mostly to herself. "I go there when the heather is blooming. He loved white heather."

Grimm stopped, startled. "Buried? Edmund? What?"

"Edmund. He wished to be buried under the apple tree. We used to play there, remember?"

His fingers closed around her wrist. "When did Edmund die? I thought he was with your brother Hugh in the Highlands."

"No. Edmund died shortly after you left. Nearly seven years ago."

"He was scarcely wounded when the McKane attacked," Grimm insisted. "Even your father said he'd easily recover!"

"He took an infection, then caught a lung complication on top of it," she replied, perplexed by his reaction. "The fever never abated. He wasn't in pain long, Grimm. And some of his last words were of you. He swore you defeated the McKane single-handedly and mumbled some nonsense about you being . . . what was it? A warrior of Odin's who could change shapes, or something like that. But then, Edmund was ever fanciful," she added with a faint smile.

Grimm stared at her through the fog.

"Wh-what?" Jillian stammered, confused by the intensity with which he studied her. When he stepped toward her, she backed up slightly, drawing nearer the stone wall that encircled the church behind her.

"What if creatures like that really existed, Jillian?" he asked, his blue eyes glittering. He knew he shouldn't tread on such dangerous territory, but here was a chance to discover her feelings without revealing himself.

"What do you mean?"

"What if it wasn't fantasy?" he pushed. "What if there really were men who could do the things Edmund spoke of? Men who were part mythical beast—endowed with special abilities, skilled in the art of war, almost invincible. What would you think of such a man?"

Jillian studied him intently. "What an odd question. Do *you* believe such warriors exist, Grimm Roderick?"

"Hardly," he said tightly. "I believe in what I can see and touch and hold in my hand. The legend of the Berserkers is nothing more than a foolish tale told to frighten mischievous children into good behavior."

"Then why did you ask me what I would think if they did?" she persisted.

"It was just a hypothetical question. I was merely making conversation, and it was a stupid conversation. By Odin's spear, lass—*nobody* believes in Berserkers!" He resumed walking, gesturing with an impatient scowl for her to follow.

They walked a few yards in silence. Then, without preamble, Grimm said, "Is Ramsay a fine kisser?"

"What?" Jillian nearly fell over her own feet.

"Ramsay, peahen. Does he kiss well?" Grimm repeated irritably.

Jillian battled the urge to beam with delight. "Well," she drawled thoughtfully, "I haven't had much experience, but in all fairness I'd have to say his kiss was the best I've ever had."

Grimm instantly held her trapped her against him, between his hard body and the stone wall. He tilted her head back with a relentless hand beneath her chin. *By the saints, how could the man move so quickly? And how delicious that he did.*

"Let me help you put it in perspective, lass. But doona think for a minute this means anything. I'm just trying to help you understand there are better men out there. Think of this as a lesson, nothing more. I'd hate to see you wed to Logan simply because you thought he was the best kisser, when such a mistaken perception can be so easily remedied."

Jillian raised her hand to his lips, barring him the kiss he threatened. "I don't need a lesson, Grimm. I can make up my own mind. I loathe the thought of you putting yourself out, suffering on my behalf—"

"I'm willing to suffer a bit. Consider it a favor, since we were once childhood friends." He clasped her hand in his and tugged it away from his lips.

"You were never my friend," she reminded him sweetly. "You chased me away constantly—"

"Not the first year—"

"I thought you didn't remember anything about me or your time at Caithness. Isn't that what you told me? And I don't need any favors from you, Grimm Roderick. Besides, what makes you so certain your kiss will be better? Ramsay's positively took my breath away. I could scarcely stand when he was done," she lied shamelessly. "What if you kiss me and it's not as good as Ramsay's kiss? Then what reason would I have for not marrying him?" Having thrown the gauntlet, Jillian felt as smug as a cat as she waited for the breathtaking kiss she knew would follow.

His expression furious, he claimed her mouth with his.

And the earthquake began beneath his toes. Grimm groaned against her lips as the sensation stripped his waning control.

Jillian sighed and parted her lips.

She was being kissed by Grimm Roderick, and it was everything she'd remembered. The kiss they'd shared so long ago in the stables had seemed a mystical experience, and over the years she'd wondered if she glorified it in her mind, only imagining that it had rocked her entire world. But her memory had been accurate. Her body came alive, her lips tingled, her nipples hardened. She wanted every inch of his body, in every way possible. On top of her, beneath her, beside her, behind her. Hard, muscled, demanding—she knew he was man enough to sate the endless hunger she felt for him.

She twined her fingers in his hair and kissed him back, then lost her breath entirely when he deepened the kiss. One hand cupped her jaw; the other slid down the bow of her spine, cupping her hips, molding her body tightly against his. All thought ceased as Jillian gave herself over to what had long been her greatest fantasy: to touch Grimm Roderick as a woman, as his woman. His hands were at her hips, pushing at her gown—and suddenly her hands were at his kilt, tearing at his sporran to get beneath it. She found his thick manhood and brazenly grasped its hardness through the fabric of his plaid. She felt his body stiffen against hers, and the groan of desire that escaped him was the sweetest sound Jillian had ever heard.

Something exploded between them, and there in the

mist and fog of Durrkesh she was so consumed by the need
to mate her man that she no longer cared that they stood on
a public street. Grimm wanted her, wanted to make love to
her—his body told her that clearly. She arched against him,
encouraging, entreating. The kiss hadn't merely rendered
her breathless, it had depleted the last of her meager supply
of sense.

He caught her questing hand and pinned it against the
wall above her head. Only when he had secured both her
hands did he change the tempo of the kiss, turning it into a
teasing, playful flicker of his tongue, probing, then with-
drawing, until she was gasping for more. He brushed the
length of his body against hers with the same slow, teasing
rhythm.

He tore his lips away from hers with excruciating slow-
ness, catching her lower lip between his teeth and tugging
gently. Then, with a last luscious lick of his tongue, he
drew back.

"So what do you think? Could Ramsay compare to
that?" he asked hoarsely, eyeing her breasts intently. Only
when he ascertained that they didn't rise and fall for a long
moment, that he had indeed managed to "kiss her breathless," did he raise his eyes to hers.

Jillian swayed as she struggled to keep her knees from
simply buckling beneath her. She stared at him blankly.
Words? He thought she could form words after that? He
thought she could *think*?

Grimm's gaze searched her face intently, and Jillian saw
a look of smug satisfaction banked in his glittering eyes.
The faintest hint of a smile curved his lip when she didn't
reply but stood gazing, lips swollen, eyes round. "Breathe,
peahen. You can breathe now."

Still, she stared at him blankly. Valiantly she sucked in a great, whistling breath of air.

"Hmmph" was all he said as he took her hand and tugged her along. She trotted beside him on rubbery legs, occasionally stealing a peek at the supremely masculine expression of satisfaction on his face.

Grimm didn't speak another word for the duration of their walk back to the inn. That was fine with Jillian; she wasn't certain she could have formed a complete sentence if her life had depended on it. She briefly wondered who, if either of them, had won that skirmish. She concluded weakly that she had. He hadn't been unaffected by their encounter, and she'd gotten the kiss she craved.

When they arrived at the Black Boot, Hatchard informed the strangely taciturn couple that the men, although still quite weak, were impatient to be moved out of the inn. Analyzing all the risks, Hatchard had concurred that it was the wisest course. He had procured a wagon for the purpose, and they would return to Caithness at first light.

CHAPTER 14

"TELL ME A STORY, JILLIAN," ZEKE DEMANDED, AMBLING into the solar. "I sore missed you and Mama while you were away." The little boy clambered up onto the settle be-side her and nestled in her arms.

Jillian brushed his hair back from his forehead and dropped a kiss on it. "What shall it be, my sweet Zeke? Dragons? Fairies? The selkie?"

"Tell me about the Berserkers," he said decidedly.

"The what?"

"The Berserkers," Zeke said patiently. "You know, the mighty warriors of Odin."

Jillian snorted delicately. "What is it with boys and their battles? My brothers adored that fairy tale."

" 'Tis not a fae-tale, 'tis true," Zeke informed her. "Mama told me they still prowl the Highlands."

"Nonsense," Jillian said. "I shall tell you a fitting tale for a young boy."

"I don't want a fitting tale. I want a story with knights and heroes and quests. And Berserkers."

"Oh my, you are growing up, aren't you?" Jillian said wryly, tousling his hair.

"Course I am," Zeke said indignantly.

"No Berserkers. I shall tell you, instead, of the boy and the nettles."

"Is this another one of your stories with a *point*?" Zeke complained.

Jillian sniffed. "There's nothing wrong with stories that have a point."

"Fine. Tell me about the stupid nettles." He plunked his chin on his fist and glowered.

Jillian laughed at his sullen expression. "I'll tell you what, Zeke. I shall tell you a story with a point, and then you may go find Grimm and ask him to tell you the story of your fearless warriors. I'm certain he knows it. He's the most fearless man I've ever met," Jillian added with a sigh. "Here we go. Pay attention:

"Once upon time there was a wee lad who was walking through the forest and came upon a patch of nettles. Fascinated by the unusual cluster, he tried to pluck it so he might take it home and show his mama. The plant stung him painfully, and he raced home, his fingers stinging. 'I scarcely touched it, Mama!' the lad cried.

" 'That is exactly why it stung you,' his mama replied. 'The next time you touch a nettle, grab it boldly, and it will be soft as silk in your hand and not hurt you in the least.' " Jillian paused meaningfully.

"That's *it*?" Zeke demanded, outraged. "That wasn't a *story*! You *cheated* me!"

Jillian bit her lip to prevent laughter; he looked like an

offended little bear cub. She was tired from the journey and her storytelling abilities were a bit weak at the moment, but there was a useful lesson in it. Besides, the largest part of her mind was preoccupied with thoughts of the incredible kiss she'd received yesterday. It required every shred of her waning self-control to keep from trundling off to find Grimm herself, nestling on his lap and sweetly begging for a bedtime story. Or, more accurately, just a bedtime. "Tell me what it means, Zeke," Jillian coaxed.

Zeke was quiet a moment as he pondered the fable. His forehead was furrowed in concentration, and Jillian waited patiently. Of all the children, Zeke was the cleverest at isolating the moral. "I have it!" he exclaimed. "I shouldna hesitate. I should grab things boldly. If you're undecided, things may sting you."

"Whatever you do, Zeke," Jillian counseled, "do it with all your might."

"Like learning to ride," he concluded.

"Yes. And loving your mama and working with the horses and studying lessons I give you. If you don't do things with all your might, you may end up being harmed by those things you try halfway."

Zeke gave a disgruntled snort. "Well, it's not the Berserker, but I guess it's all right, from a girl."

Jillian made an exasperated sound and hugged Zeke close, heedless of his impatient squirm. "I'm losing you already, aren't I, Zeke?" she asked when the boy raced from the solar in search of Grimm. "How many lads will grow up on me?" she murmured sadly.

* * *

Jillian checked on Quinn and Ramsay before dinner. The two men were sleeping soundly, exhausted by the return trip to Caithness. She hadn't seen Grimm since their return; he'd settled the patients and stalked off. He'd been silent the entire journey and, stung by his withdrawal, she had retreated to the wagon and ridden with the sick men.

Both Quinn and Ramsay still had an unhealthy pallor, and their clammy skin was evidence of the fever's tenacious grip. She pressed a gentle kiss to Quinn's brow and tucked the woolens beneath his chin.

As she left their chambers, her mind slipped back in time to the summer when she'd been nearly sixteen—the summer Grimm left Caithness.

Nothing in her life had prepared Jillian for such a gruesome battle. Neither death nor brutality had visited her sheltered life before, but on that day both came stampeding in on great black chargers wearing the colors of the McKane.

The moment the guards had sounded the alarm her father had barricaded her in her bedroom. Jillian watched the bloody massacre unfolding in the ward below her window with disbelieving eyes. She was besieged by helplessness, frustrated by her inability to fight beside her brothers. But she knew, even had she been free to run the estate, she wasn't strong enough to wield a sword. What harm could she, a mere lass, hope to wreak upon hardened warriors like the McKane?

The sight of so much blood terrified her. When a crafty McKane crept up behind Edmund, taking him unawares, she screamed and pounded her fists against the window, but what meager noise she managed to make could not compete with the raucous din of battle. The burly McKane crushed her brother to the ground with the flat of his battle-ax.

Jillian flattened herself against the glass, clawing

hysterically at the pane with her nails as if she might break through and snatch him from danger. A deep shuddering breath of relief burst from her lungs when Grimm burst into the fray, dispatching the snarling McKane before Edmund suffered another brutal blow. As she watched her wounded brother struggle to crawl to his knees, something deep within her altered so swiftly that she scarce was aware of it: the blood no longer horrified Jillian—nay, she longed to see every last drop of McKane blood spilled upon Caithness's soil. When a raging Grimm proceeded to slay every McKane within fifty yards, it seemed to her a thing of terrible beauty. She'd never seen a man move with such incredible speed and lethal grace—warring to protect all that was nearest to her heart.

After the battle Jillian was lost in the shuffle as her family fretted over Edmund, tended the wounded, and buried the dead. Feeling dreadfully young and vulnerable, she waited on the rooftop for Grimm to respond to her note, only to glimpse him toting his packs toward the stable.

She was stunned. He couldn't leave. Not now! Not when she was so confused and frightened by all that had transpired. She needed him now more than ever.

Jillian raced to the stables as swiftly as her feet could carry her. But Grimm was obdurate; he bid her an icy farewell and turned to leave. His failure to comfort her was the final slight she could endure—she flung herself into his arms, demanding with her body that he shelter her and keep her safe.

The kiss that began as an innocent press of lips swiftly became the confirmation of her most secret dreams: Grimm Roderick was the man she would marry.

As her heart filled with elation, he pulled away from her

and turned abruptly to his horse, as if their kiss had meant nothing to him. Jillian was shamed and bewildered by his rejection, and the frightening intensity of so many new emotions filled her with desperation.

"You can't leave! Not after *that*!" she cried.

"I must leave," he growled. "And *that*"—he wiped his mouth furiously—"should never have happened!"

"But it did! And what if you don't come back, Grimm? What if I never see you again?"

"That's precisely what I mean to do," he said fiercely. "You're not even sixteen. You'll find a husband. You'll have a bright future."

"I've already found my husband!" Jillian wailed. "You *kissed* me!"

"A kiss is not a pledge of marriage!" he snarled. "And it was a mistake. I never should have done it, but you threw yourself at me. What else did you expect me to do?"

"Y-you didn't want to k-kiss me?" Her eyes darkened with pain.

"I'm a man, Jillian. When a woman throws herself at me, I'm as human as the next!"

"You mean you didn't feel it too?" she gasped.

"Feel what?" he snorted. "Lust? Of course. You're a bonny lass."

Jillian shook her head, mortified. Could she have been so mistaken? Could it truly have been only in her mind? "No, I mean—didn't you feel like the world was a perfect place and . . . and we were meant to be . . ." She trailed off, feeling like the grandest fool.

"Forget about me, Jillian St. Clair. Grow up, marry a handsome laird, and forget about me," Grimm said stonily. With one swift move he tossed himself on the horse's back and sped from the stables.

"Don't leave me, Grimm Roderick! Don't leave me like this! I love you!"

But he rode off as if she hadn't spoken. Jillian knew that he'd heard her every word, though she wished he hadn't. She'd not only flung her body at a man who didn't want her, she'd flung her heart after him as he left.

Jillian sighed heavily and closed her eyes. It was a bitter memory, but the sting had eased somewhat since Durrkesh. She no longer believed she had been mistaken about how the kiss had affected them, for in Durrkesh the same thing had happened and she'd seen in his eyes with a woman's sure knowledge that he'd felt it too.

Now all she had to do was get him to admit it.

CHAPTER 15

AFTER SEARCHING FOR OVER AN HOUR, JILLIAN TRACKED Grimm down in the armory. He was standing near a low wooden table, examining several blades, but she could tell he sensed her presence by the stiffening of his back.

"When I was seventeen, I was near Edinburgh," Jillian informed his rigid back. "I thought I glimpsed you while I was visiting the Hammonds."

"Yes," Grimm replied, intently inspecting a hammered shield.

"It *was* you! I knew it!" Jillian exclaimed. "You were standing near the gatehouse. You were watching me and you looked . . . unhappy."

"Yes," he admitted tightly.

Jillian gazed at Grimm's broad back a moment, uncertain how to vocalize her feelings. It might have helped immensely if she'd understood herself what she wanted to say, but she didn't. It wouldn't have mattered anyway, because he turned and brushed past her with a cool expression that dared her to humble herself by following him.

She didn't.

* * *

She found him later, in the kitchen, scooping a handful of sugar into his pocket.

"For Occam," he said defensively.

"The night I went to the Glannises' ball near Edinburgh," Jillian continued the conversation where, in her mind, it had recently ended, "it was you in the shadows, wasn't it? The fall I turned eighteen."

Grimm sighed heavily. She'd found him yet again. The lass seemed to have a way of knowing where he was, when, and if he was alone. He eyed her with resignation. "Yes," he replied evenly. *That's the fall you became a woman, Jillian. You were wearing ruby velvet. Your hair was uncurled and cascading over your shoulders. Your brothers were so proud of you. I was stunned.*

"When that rogue Alastair—and do you know, I came to find out later he was *married*—took me outside and kissed me, I heard a dreadful racket in the bushes. He said it was likely a ferocious animal."

"And then he told how grateful you should be that you had him to protect you, right?" Grimm mocked. *I almost killed the bastard for touching you.*

"That's not funny. I was truly frightened."

"Were you really, Jillian?" Grimm regarded her levelly. "By which? The man holding you, or the beast in the bush?"

Jillian met his gaze and licked her lips, which were suddenly dry. "Not the beast. Alastair was a blackguard, and had he not been discomfited by the noise, the saints only know what he might have done to me. I was young and, God, I was so innocent!"

"Yes."

"Quinn asked me to marry him today," she announced, watching him carefully.

Grimm was silent.

"I haven't kissed him yet, so I don't know if he's a better kisser. Do you suppose he will be? Better than you, I mean?"

Grimm did not reply.

"Grimm? Will he be a better kisser than you?"

A low rumble filled the air. "Yes, Jillian." Grimm sighed, and went off to find his horse.

* * *

Grimm managed to elude her for almost an entire day. It was late at night before she finally managed to intercept him as he was leaving the ill men's chambers.

"You know, even when I wasn't sure you were really there, I still felt . . . safe. Because you *might* be there."

The hint of an approving smile curved his lips. "*Yes, Jillian.*"

Jillian turned away.

"Jillian?"

She froze.

"Have you kissed Quinn yet?"

"No, Grimm."

"Oh. Well, you'd better get on it, lass."

Jillian scowled.

* * *

"I saw you at the Royal Bazaar."

Finally Jillian had succeeded in getting him all to herself

for more than a few forced moments. With Quinn and
Ramsay confined to bed, she'd asked Grimm to join her for
dinner in the Greathall and had been astonished when he'd
readily consented. She sat on one side of the long table,
peering at his darkly handsome face through the vines of a
candelabrum that held dozens of flickering tapers. They'd
been dining in silence, broken only by the clatter of plates
and goblets. The maids had retreated to deliver broth to the
men upstairs. Three days had passed since they'd returned,
during which she'd tried desperately to recapture the tenderness she'd glimpsed in Durrkesh, to no avail. She hadn't
been able to get him to stand still long enough to try for another kiss.

Nothing in his face moved. Not a lash flickered. "Yes."

If he answered her with one more annoyingly evasive
"yes," she might fly into a rage. She wanted answers. She
wanted to know what really went on inside Grimm's head,
inside his heart. She wanted to know if the single kiss they'd
shared had tilted his world with the same catastrophic force
that had leveled hers. "You were spying on me," Jillian accused, peeping through the candles with a scowl. "I wasn't
being truthful when I said it made me feel safe. It made me
angry," she lied.

Grimm picked up a pewter goblet of wine, drained it,
and carefully rolled the cold metal between his palms. Jillian watched his precise, controlled motion and was overwhelmed with hatred for all deliberate actions. Her life had
been lived that way, one cautious, precise choice after another, with the exception of when she was around Grimm.
She wanted to see him act like she felt: out of control, emotional. Let *him* have an outburst or two. She didn't want
kisses offered on the weak excuse of saving her from bad
choices. She needed to know she could get beneath his skin

the way he penetrated hers. Her hands fisted in her lap, scrunching the fabric of her gown between her fingers.

What would he do if she quit trying to be civil and collected?

She drew a deep breath. "Why did you keep watching me? Why did you leave Caithness, only to follow me all those times?" she demanded with more vehemence than she'd intended, and her words echoed off the stone walls.

Grimm didn't take his eyes from the polished pewter between his palms. "I had to see that all was well with you, Jillian," he said quietly. "Have you kissed Quinn yet?"

"You never breathed a word to me! You'd just come and look at me, and then I'd turn around and you'd be gone."

"I took a vow to keep you from harm, Jillian. It was only natural that I should check on you when you were nearby. Have you kissed Quinn yet?" he demanded.

"Keep me from harm?" Her voice soared with disbelief. "You failed! *You* hurt me worse than anything else ever has in my entire life!"

"Have you kissed Quinn yet?" he roared.

"No! I haven't kissed Quinn yet!" she shouted back. "Is that all you care about? You don't give a damn that *you* hurt *me*."

The goblet clattered to the floor as Grimm lunged to his feet. His hands came down with unbridled fury. Trenchers flew from the table, untouched pottage stew showered the room, chunks of flatbread bounced off the hearth. The candelabrum exploded into the wall and stuck like a cleft foot between the stones. Soapy white candles rained down upon the floor. His rampage didn't stop until the table between them had been swept clean. He paused, panting, his hands splayed wide on the edge of the table, his eyes feverishly bright. Jillian stared at him, stunned.

With a howl of rage, he crashed his hands into the center of six inches of solid oak, and Jillian's hand flew to her throat to smother a cry when the long table split down the middle. His blue eyes blazed incandescently, and she could have sworn he seemed to be growing larger, broader, and more dangerous. She'd certainly gotten the reaction she'd been seeking, and more.

"I know I failed!" he roared. "I know I hurt you! Do you think I haven't had to live with that knowledge?"

Between them, the table creaked and shuddered in an effort to remain whole. The wounded slab tilted precariously. Then, with a groan of defeat, the ends slumped toward the center and it crashed to the floor.

Jillian blinked as she surveyed the wreckage of their meal. No longer seeking to provoke him, she stood dumbfounded by the intensity of his reaction. He knew he'd hurt her? And he cared enough to get this angry at the memory?

"Then why did you come back now?" she whispered. "You could have disobeyed my da."

"I had to see that all is well with you, Jillian," he whispered back across the sea of destruction that separated them.

"I'm well, Grimm," she said carefully. "That means you can go away now," she said, not meaning a breath of it.

Her words evoked no response.

How could a man stand so still that she might think he had been cursed to stone? She couldn't even see his chest rise and fall as she watched him. The breeze blowing in the tall window didn't ruffle him. Nothing touched the man.

God knows she'd never been able to. Hadn't she learned that by now? She'd never been able to reach the real Grimm, the one she'd known that first summer. Why had she believed anything might have changed? Because she was a woman grown? Because she had full breasts and shiny hair and she thought she could entice him near with a man's weakness for a woman? And since he was so damned indifferent to her, why did she even want him?

But Jillian knew the answer to that, even if she didn't understand the how of it. When she'd been a wee lass and tipped her head back to see the wild boy towering above her, her heart had cried welcome. There had been an ancient knowing in her child's breast that had clearly told her no matter what heinous things Grimm stood accused of, she could trust him with her life. She knew he was supposed to belong to her.

"Why don't you just cooperate?" Frustration peeled the words from her lips; she couldn't believe she'd spoken them aloud, but once they were out, she was committed.

"What?"

"Cooperate," she encouraged. "It means to go along. To be obliging."

Grimm stared. "I canna oblige you by leaving. Your da—"

"I am not asking you to leave," she said gently.

Jillian had no idea where she drew her courage from at that moment; she knew only that she was tired of wanting, and tired of being denied. So she stood proudly, moving her body exactly the way it felt whenever Grimm was in the same room: seductive, intense, more alive than at any other time in her life. Her body language must have signified her intent, for he went rigid.

"How would you have me cooperate, Jillian?" he asked in a flat, dead voice.

She approached him, carefully picking her way over broken platters and food. Slowly, as if he were a wild animal, she reached her hand, palm out, toward his chest. He stared at it with a mixture of fascination and mistrust as she placed it upon his chest, over his heart. She felt the heat of him through his linen shirt, felt his body shudder, felt the powerful beating of his heart beneath her palm.

She tilted her head back and gazed up at him. "If you'd truly like to cooperate"—she wet her lips—"kiss me."

It was with a furious gaze that he watched her, but in his eyes Jillian glimpsed the heat he struggled to hide.

"Kiss me," she whispered, never taking her eyes from his. "Kiss me and *then* try to tell me that you don't feel it too."

"Stop it," he ordered hoarsely, backing away.

"Kiss me, Grimm! And not because you think you're doing me a 'favor'! Kiss me because you want to! Once you told me you wouldn't because I was a child. Well, I'm no longer a child, but a woman grown. Other men wish to kiss me. Why not *you*?"

"It isn't like that, Jillian." Both hands moved in frustration to his hair. He buried his fingers deep, then yanked the leather thong off and cast it to the stones.

"Then what is it? Why do Quinn and Ramsay and every other man I've ever known want me, but not you? *Must* I choose one of them? Is it Quinn I should be asking to kiss me? To bed me? To make me a woman?"

He growled, a low warning rumble in his throat. "Stop it, Jillian!"

Jillian tossed her head in a timeless gesture of temptation and defiance. "Kiss me, Grimm, *please*. Just *once*, as if you mean it."

He sprang with such grace and speed that she had no warning. His hands sunk into her hair, pinning her head between his palms and arching her neck back. His lips covered hers and he took the breath from her lungs.

His lips moved over hers with unrestrained hunger, but in the bruising crush of his mouth she sensed a touch of anger—an element she didn't understand. How could he be angry with her when it was so apparent that he'd wanted desperately to kiss her? Of that she was certain. The instant his lips had claimed hers, any doubts she'd previously suffered were permanently laid to rest. She could feel his desire struggling just beneath his skin, waging a mighty battle against his will. *And losing*, she thought smugly as his grip on her hair gentled enough for him to tilt her head, allowing his tongue deeper access to her mouth.

Jillian softened against him, clung to his shoulders, and gave herself over to dizzying waves of sensation. How could a simple kiss resonate in every inch of her body and make it seem the floor was tilting wildly beneath her feet? She kissed him back eagerly and fiercely. After so many years of wanting him, she finally had her answer. Grimm Roderick needed to touch her with the same undeniable need she felt for him.

And she knew that with Grimm Roderick—just once would *never* be enough.

CHAPTER 16

THE KISS SPUN OUT AND DEEPENED. IT WAS FUELED BY years of denied emotion, years of disavowed passion that swiftly clawed to the surface of Grimm's resolve. Standing in the Greathall amidst the wreckage of a feast, kissing Jillian, he realized he hadn't just been denying himself peace, he'd been denying himself life. For this was life, this exquisite moment of blending. His Berserker senses were overwhelmed, stupefied by the taste and touch of Jillian. He exulted in the kiss, becoming a bacchanalian worshiper of her lips as he slipped his hands through her hair, following the silken skein down her back.

He kissed Jillian as he'd never kissed any other woman, driven by hunger sprung from the most profane and the most sacred depths of his soul. He wanted her instinctively and would worship her with the primitiveness of his need. The press of her lips thawed the man, the questing probe of her tongue tamed and humbled the icy Viking warrior who had known no warmth until this moment. Desire flattened all his objections and he crushed her body against his, taking her tongue into his mouth as deeply as he knew she would welcome his body into hers.

They slipped and slid on the bits of food scattered across the stones, stopping only at the stability of the wall. Without lifting his mouth from hers, Grimm slid a hand beneath her hips, braced her shoulders against the wall, and drew her legs around his waist. Years of watching her, forbidding himself to touch her, culminated in a display of frenzied passion. Urgency dictated his movements, not patience or skill. His hands slipped from her ankles as her arms entwined his neck and he pushed her gown up and over her calves, revealing her long, lovely legs. He caressed her skin, groaning against her lips when his thumbs found the soft skin of her inner thighs.

The kiss deepened as he took her mouth the same way he'd laid siege to castles: persistently, ruthlessly, and with single-minded focus. There was only Jillian, warm woman in his hands, warm tongue in his mouth, and she matched him, each wordless demand of his body met by hers. She buried her hands in his hair and kissed him back until he was almost breathless himself. Years of need crashed over him as his hands found her breasts and palmed their curves. Her nipples were hard and peaked; he needed more than her lips—he needed to taste every crevice and hollow of her body.

Cradling his face in her hands with a surprisingly strong grip, Jillian forced him to break the kiss. Grimm stared into her eyes, as if to scry the hidden meaning of her gesture. When she tugged his head down to the curve of her breast, he went willingly. He traced a reverent path with his tongue from peak to peak, tugging gently with his teeth before closing his lips on her nipple.

Jillian cried out in abandon and submission, a breathless sound of capitulation to her own desire. She thrust herself so firmly against his hips that the warm hollow between her thighs snugly fitted him with the sensuous finesse of a velvet glove. The barriers between them incensed him, and ripping his kilt from his waist, he eased her gown aside.

Stop! His mind screamed. *She's virgin! Not like this!*

Jillian moaned and rubbed against him.

"Stop," he whispered hoarsely.

Jillian's eyes slitted open. "Not a chance in hell," she said smugly, a smile curving her lower lip.

Her words ripped through him like a heated iron, raising his blood from molten to boiling. He could feel the beast inside him move, yawning with wicked wakefulness.

The Berserker? Now? There was no blood anywhere . . . yet. What would happen when there was?

"Touch me, Grimm. Here." Jillian placed his hand on her breast and drew his head to hers. He groaned and shifted, rubbing in slow, erotic circles against her open thighs. Dimly he realized that the Berserker was rousing into full awareness, but it was somehow different—not violent, but aroused, violently hard, and violently hungry for every taste of Jillian it could have.

He would have laid her back upon the table, but there was no longer a table, so instead he lowered them both into a chair. He shifted so her legs dangled over its arms, and she sat facing him, her hands on his shoulders, her womanhood bared above him. She needed no encouragement to press herself against him, teasing him with the brush of her peaked nipples across his chest. Jillian dropped her head back, baring the slender arch of her neck, and Grimm froze a long moment, drinking in the vision of his lovely Jillian straddling his lap, her narrow waist curving into those lush hips. Although he'd managed to slide her gown from her shoulders, the fabric pooled at her waist, and she was a goddess rising from a sea of silk.

"Christ, you are the most beautiful woman I've ever seen!"

Jillian's head whipped back, and she stared at him. Her look of disbelief quickly became a look of simple pleasure, then an expression of mischievous sensuality. "When I was thirteen," she said, running her fingers down the arrogant curve of his jaw, "I watched you with a maid and I vowed to myself that one day I would do everything to you that she did. Every kiss." She dropped her mouth to his nipple. Her tongue flicked out as she tasted his skin. "Every touch"—she slipped her hand down his abdomen to his hard shaft—"and every taste."

Grimm groaned and grabbed her hand, preventing her fingers from curling around him. If her lovely hand so much as locked around him one time, he would lose control and be inside her in a heartbeat. Calling upon every ounce of his legendary discipline, he held his body away. He refused to hurt her like that. A confession of his own spilled from his lips. "From the day you began to mature, you drove me crazy. I couldn't close my eyes at night without wanting you beneath me. Without wanting to be beside you, *inside* you. Jillian St. Clair, I hope you're as tough as you like to believe you are, because you're going to need every ounce of strength you possess for me tonight." He kissed her, silencing any reply she might have made.

She melted into his kiss until he pulled back. He regarded her tenderly. "And Jillian," he said softly, "I feel it too. I always did."

His words flung open her heart, and the smile she gave him was dazzling. "I *knew* it!" she breathed.

As his hands slid over her heated skin, Jillian abandoned herself to the sensation. When he palmed her between her thighs, she cried out softly and her body bucked against his hand. "More, Grimm. Give me more," she whispered.

His eyes narrowed as he watched her. Pleasure mingled with amazement and desire on her expressive features. He knew he was large, both in width and length, and she needed to be prepared. When she began to move wildly against his hand, he could deny himself no longer. He positioned her above him. "You're in control this way, Jillian. It will hurt you, but you're in control. If it hurts too much, tell me," he said fiercely.

"It's all right, Grimm. I know it will hurt at first, but Kaley told me that if the man is a skilled lover, he will make me feel something more incredible than I've ever felt."

"*Kaley* told you that?"

Jillian nodded. "Please," she breathed. "Show me what she meant."

Grimm expelled a fascinated breath. His Jillian had no fear. He gently slipped the head of his shaft inside her and eased her down, gauging her every flicker of emotion.

Her eyes flared. Her hand flew down to curl around his shaft. "Big," she said worriedly. "Really big. Are you certain this works?"

A grin of pure delight curved his lip. "Very big," he agreed. "But just right to pleasure a woman." He slipped into her carefully. When he met the resistance of the barrier, he paused. Jillian panted softly. "Now, Grimm. Do it."

He closed his eyes briefly and cupped his hands on her bottom, positioning her above him. When he opened his eyes, resolve glimmered in their depths. With one firm thrust he pierced the barrier.

Jillian gasped. "That wasn't so bad," she breathed after a moment. "I thought it would really hurt." When he began to move slowly, her eyes flared. "Oh!"

She cried out, and he silenced her with a kiss. Moving slowly, he rocked her against him until any trace of pain in her wide eyes disappeared and her face was illuminated by the anticipation of what she sensed was dancing just out of her reach. She initiated an erotic, circular movement with her hips, nipping her lower lip between her teeth.

He watched her, entranced by her innate sensuality. She was abandoned, uninhibited, plunging wholly into their intimate play without reservation. Her lips curved deliciously as a long slow thrust of his hips hinted at the passion to come, and he smiled with wicked delight.

He raised her up and switched places with her, placing her on the chair. Kneeling, he pulled her forward, wrapped her legs around his waist, and slid deep within her, pressing with exquisite friction against the mysterious place deep inside her that would cast her over the edge. He teased the nub between her legs until she squirmed against him, begging with her body for what only he could give her.

The Berserker exulted within him, frolicking in a way he had never thought possible.

When she cried out and shuddered against him, Grimm Roderick made a husky, rich sound that was more than laughter; it was the resonant knell of liberation. His triumph quickly became a groan of release. The sensation of her body shuddering around him so tightly was more than he could resist, and he exploded inside her.

Jillian clung to him, gasping as an unfamiliar sound penetrated her reeling mind. Her muscles fused to molten uselessness, her head fell forward, and she peered through her hair at the nude warrior-man kneeling before her.

"Y-you can laugh! Really, truly laugh!" she exclaimed breathlessly.

He traced his thumbs up the inside of her thighs, over the light skein of blood. Blood of her virginity marked her pale thighs. "Jillian, I . . . I . . . oh . . ."

"Don't freeze up on me, Grimm Roderick," Jillian said instantly.

He began shaking violently. "I can't help it," he said tightly, knowing they weren't talking about the same thing at all. "The Greathall," he muttered. "I am such an ass. I am so damned—"

"Stop it!" Jillian grabbed his head with both hands, leveling him with a furious look. "I wanted this," she said intensely. "I waited for this, I needed this. Don't you dare regret it! I don't, and I never will."

Grimm froze, transfixed by the blood that marked her thighs, waiting for the sensation of lost time to begin. It wouldn't be long before the darkness claimed him and the violence ensued.

But moments ticked by, and it didn't happen. Despite the raging energy that flooded his body, the madness never came.

He gazed at her, dumbfounded. The beast within him was fully awakened, yet tame. How could that be? No bloodlust, no need for violence, all the good things the Berserker brought—and none of the danger.

"Jillian," he breathed reverently.

CHAPTER 17

"How are you feeling?" Grimm asked quietly. Punching the pillows, he maneuvered Quinn to a sitting position. The window fittings were tied loosely back, swags framed the casements, and the crescent moon cast enough light that his heightened vision allowed him to function as if it were broad daylight.

Quinn blinked groggily at Grimm and peered through the gloom. "Please don't." He groaned when Grimm reached for a cloth.

Grimm stopped in mid-reach. "Doona what? I was merely going to wipe your brow."

"Don't smother me with any more of that blasted mandrake," Quinn muttered. "Half the reason I feel so lousy is because Kaley keeps knocking me out."

One bed over, Ramsay rumbled assent. "Don't let her make us sleep anymore, man. My head is splitting from that crap and my tongue feels as if some wee furry beastie crawled in, kicked over on its back, and died there. Three days ago. And now it's rotting—"

"Enough! Do you have to be so descriptive?" Quinn made a face of disgust as his empty stomach heaved.

Grimm raised his hands in a gesture of assent. "No more mandrake. I promise. So how are you two feeling?"

"Like bloody hell," Ramsay groaned. "Light a candle, would you? I can't see a thing. What happened? Who poisoned us?"

A dark expression flitted across Grimm's face. He stepped into the hallway to light a taper, then lit several candles by the bedside and returned to his seat. "I suspect it was meant for me, and my guess is the poison was in the chicken."

"The chicken?" Quinn exclaimed, wincing as he sat up straight. "Didn't the barkeep bring it? Why would the barkeep try to poison you?"

"I doona think it was the barkeep. I think it was the butcher's attempt at revenge. My theory is that if either of you had consumed the entire basket, you would have died. It was intended for me. But the two of you split it."

"That doesn't make any sense if the butcher meant it for you, Grimm," Quinn protested. "He'd seen you in action. Any man knows you can't poison a Ber—"

"Bastard as ornery as myself," Grimm roared, drowning out Quinn's last word before Ramsay heard it.

Ramsay clutched his head. "Och, man, quit bellowing! You're killing me."

Quinn mouthed a silent "sorry" at Grimm, followed by an apologetic whisper: "It's the lingering effects of the mandrake. I'm stupid right now."

"Eh? What?" Ramsay said. "What are you two whispering about?"

"Even between the two of us we didn't even eat all the chicken," Quinn continued, evading Ramsay's query. "And I thought the innkeeper dismissed the butcher after that incident. I asked him to do it myself."

"What incident?" Ramsay asked.

"Apparently not." Grimm ran a hand through his hair and sighed.

"Did you get his name?" Ramsay asked.

"Who? The innkeeper?" Quinn gave him a puzzled look.

"No, the butcher." Ramsay rolled his eyes.

"Why?" Quinn asked blankly.

"Because the bastard poisoned a Logan, you fool. That doesn't happen without recompense."

"No vengeance," Grimm warned. "Just forget it, Logan. I've seen what you do when you focus on vengeance. The two of you came out of this bungled attempt unharmed. That does not justify murdering a man, no matter how much he might deserve it for other things."

"Where's Jillian?" Quinn changed the subject quickly. "I have these foggy memories of a goddess hovering over my bed."

Ramsay snorted. "Just because you think you were making some progress before we were both poisoned doesn't mean you've won her, de Moncreiffe.

Grimm winced inwardly and sat in pensive silence while Quinn and Ramsay argued back and forth about Jillian. The men were still at it some time later and didn't even notice when Grimm left the room.

* * *

Having spent the early hours of dawn with Quinn and Ramsay, Grimm checked in on Jillian, who was still sleeping soundly as he'd left her, curled on her side beneath a mound of blankets. He longed to ease himself into bed beside her, to experience the pleasure of waking up to the sensation of holding her in his arms, but he couldn't risk being seen leaving Jillian's chambers once the castle roused.

So, as morning broke over Caithness, he nodded to Ramsay, who'd managed to stumble down the stairs in search of solid food, whistled to Occam, and swung himself onto the stallion's bare back. He headed for the loch, intending to immerse his overheated body in icy water. The completion he'd experienced with Jillian had only whetted his appetite for her, and he was afraid if she so much as smiled at him today he would fall on her with all the slathering grace of a starved wolf. Years of denied passion were free, and he realized he possessed a hunger for Jillian that could never be sated.

He nudged Occam around a copse of trees and paused, savoring the quiet beauty of the morning. The loch rippled, a vast silvery mirror beneath rosy clouds. Lofty oaks waved black branches against the red sky.

Strains of a painfully off-key song carried faintly on the breeze, and Grimm circumvented the loch carefully, guiding his horse past sinkholes and rocky terrain, following the sound until, rounding a thick cluster of growth, he saw Zeke hunched near the water. The lad's legs were tucked up, his forearms resting on his knees, and he was rubbing his eyes.

Grimm drew Occam to a halt. Zeke was half crying the broken words of an old lullaby. Grimm wondered who had managed to hurt his feelings this early in the morning. He watched the lad, trying to decide what was the best way to approach him without offending the child's dignity. As he hesitated in the shadows, any decision on his part was rendered obsolete as the crackling of brush and bracken alerted him to an intruder. He scanned the surrounding forest, but before he had detected the source, a snarling animal sprang from the woods a few feet behind Zeke. A great, mangy mountain cat burst onto the bank of the loch, thick white spittle foaming on its snout. It snarled, baring lethal white fangs. Zeke turned, and his song warbled to a stop. His eyes widened in horror.

Grimm instantly flung himself from Occam's back, yanked his *sgain dubh* from his thigh, and drew it across his hand, causing blood to well in his palm. In less than a heartbeat, the sight of the crimson beads roused the Viking warrior and set the Berserker free.

Moving with inhuman speed, he snatched Zeke up and tossed him on his stallion and smacked Occam on the rump. Then he did what he so despised . . . he lost time.

✴ ✴ ✴

"Somebody help!" Zeke shrieked as he rode into the bailey on Occam's back. "You must help Grimm!"

Hatchard burst from the castle to find Zeke perched on Occam's back, hanging on to his mane with whitened knuckles. "Where?" he shouted.

"The loch! There's a crazed mountain cat and it almost ate me and he threw me on the horse and I rode by myself but it attacked Grimm and he's going to be hurt!"

Hatchard sped off for the loch, unaware of two other people who'd been alerted by the shouting and were hot on his heels.

✴ ✴ ✴

Hatchard found Grimm standing motionless, a black shadow against the misty red sky. He was facing the water,

standing amidst the scraps of what had once been an animal. His arms and face were covered with blood.

"Gavrael," Hatchard said quietly, using his real name in
hopes of reaching the man within the beast.

Grimm did not reply. His chest rose and fell rapidly. His
body was pumped up with the massive quantities of oxy-
gen a Berserker inhaled to compensate for the preternatural rage. The veins in his corded forearms pulsed dark
blue against his skin, and, Hatchard marveled, he seemed
twice as large as he normally was. Hatchard had seen
Grimm in the thick of Berserker rage several times when
he'd trained the fosterling, but the mature Grimm wore it
far more dangerously than the stripling lad had.

"Gavrael Roderick Icarus McIllioch," Hatchard said.
He approached him from the side, trying to enter Grimm's
line of vision in as innocuous a manner as possible. Behind
him, two figures stopped in the shadows of the forest. One
of them gasped softly and echoed the name.

"Gavrael, it's me, Hatchard," Hatchard repeated gently.

Grimm turned and looked directly at the chief man-
at-arms. The warrior's blue eyes were incandescent,
glowing like banked coals, and Hatchard received a dis-
concerting lesson in what it felt like to have someone look
straight through him.

A strangled noise behind him compelled Hatchard's attention. Turning, he realized Zeke had trailed him.

"Ohmigod," Zeke breathed. He trundled closer, peering
intently at the ground, then paused mere inches from
Grimm. His eyes widened enormously as he scanned the
small bits of what had once been a rabid mountain cat, savage enough to shred a grown man and, driven by the blood
sickness, mad enough to attempt it. His astonished gaze
drifted upward to Grimm's brilliant blue eyes, and he

nearly rose on his tiptoes, staring. "He's a Berserker!" Zeke breathed reverently. "Look, his eyes are glowing! They *do* exist!"

"Fetch Quinn, Zeke. Now," Hatchard commanded. "Bring *no one else but Quinn*, no matter what. Do you understand? And not a word of this to anyone!"

Zeke stole one last worshiping look. "Aye," he said, then fled to get Quinn.

CHAPTER 18

"I TRULY DOUBT HE RIPPED THE ANIMAL TO PIECES, Zeke. It isn't healthy to exaggerate," Jillian reprimanded, masking her amusement to protect the boy's sensitive feelings.

"I didn't exaggerate," Zeke said passionately, "I told the truth! I was down by the loch and a rabid mountain cat attacked me and Grimm threw me on his horse and caught the beastie in mid-leap and killed it with one flick o' his wrist! He's a Berserker, he is! I *knew* he was special! Hmmph!" The little boy snorted. "He doesn't need to be a puny laird—he's king o' the warriors! He's a legend!"

Hatchard took Zeke firmly by the arm and tugged him away from Jillian. "Go find your mother, lad, and do it *now*." He fixed Zeke with a glower that dared him to disobey, then snorted as the boy fled the room. He met Jillian's gaze and shrugged. "You know how wee lads are. They must have their fairy tales."

"Is Grimm all right?" Jillian asked breathlessly. Her entire body ached in a most pleasurable way. Every move was a subtle reminder of the things he'd done to her, the things she'd begged him to do before the night had ended.

"Right as rain," Hatchard replied dryly. "The animal was indeed rabid, but don't worry, it didn't manage to bite him."

"Did Grimm kill it?" A rabid mountain cat could decimate an entire herd of sheep in less than a fortnight. They wouldn't usually attack a man, but apparently Zeke had been small enough and the beast had been sick enough to try it.

"Yes," Hatchard replied tersely. "He and Quinn are burying it now," he lied with cool aplomb. There hadn't been enough left to bury, but neither love nor gold could have persuaded Hatchard to tell Jillian that. He winced inwardly. Had the infected mountain cat bitten Zeke even once, the boy would have been contaminated by the ferocious animal's blood sickness and died within days, foaming at the mouth in excruciating agony. Praise the saints Grimm had been there, and praise Odin for his special talents, or Caithness would have been singing funeral dirges and weeping.

"Zeke rode Occam all by himself," Jillian marveled aloud.

Hatchard glanced up and smiled faintly. "That he did, and it saved his life, milady."

Jillian's expression was thoughtful as she headed for the door. "If Grimm hadn't believed in the lad enough to try to teach him, Zeke might never have been able to escape."

"Where are you going?" Hatchard said quickly.

Jillian paused at the entrance. "Why, to find Grimm, of course." To tell him she was wrong to have doubted him. To see his face, to glimpse the newfound intimacy in his eyes.

"Milady, leave him be for a time. He and Quinn are talking and he needs to be alone."

In a flash Jillian felt thirteen again, excluded from the company of the man she loved. "Did he say that? That he needed to be alone?"

"He's washing up in the loch," Hatchard said. "Just give him time, all right?"

Jillian sighed. She would wait for him to come to her.

* * *

"Grimm, I didn't want to say anything before, but I paid that innkeeper a small fortune to get rid of the butcher," Quinn said as he paced the edge of the loch. Grimm rose from the icy water, finally clean again, and scowled at the remains of the animal.

Quinn caught his look and said, "Don't even start. You saved his life, Grimm. I won't hear one word of your self-loathing for being a Berserker. It's a gift, do you hear me? A gift!"

Grimm exhaled dismally and made no response.

Quinn continued where he'd left off. "As I was saying, I paid the man. If he didn't get rid of the butcher, then I'm going to be heading back to Durrkesh to get some answers."

Grimm waved his hand, dismissing Quinn's concern. "Doona bother, Quinn. It wasn't the butcher."

"What? What do you mean, it wasn't the butcher?"

"It wasn't even the chicken. It was the whisky."

Quinn blinked rapidly several times. "Then why did you say it was the chicken?"

"I trust *you*, Quinn. I doona know Ramsay. The poison was root of thmsynne. The root loses its poisonous properties if simmered, broiled, or roasted. It must be crushed and diluted, and its effect is enhanced by alcohol. Besides, I found the remainder of the bottle downstairs the next morning. Whoever it was wasn't very thorough."

"But I didn't drink any whisky with you," Quinn protested.

"You didn't know you drank whisky." Grimm gave him a wry, apologetic twist of his lips. "I dumped my final mug of whisky, poured from the drugged bottle, over the chicken to get rid of it because I was sick of drinking and getting ready to leave. The poison is odorless until digested, and even my senses couldn't pick it up. Once it mixes with the body's fluids, however, it takes on a noxious odor."

"Christ, man!" Quinn gave him a dark look. "Of all the luck. So who do you think did it?"

Grimm studied him intently. "I've given that a lot of thought over the past few days. The only thing I can conclude is that the McKane have ferreted me out again somehow."

"Don't they know poison doesn't work on a Berserker?"

"They've never succeeded in taking one alive to question."

"So they may not know what feats one of you is capable of? Even they don't know how to kill you?"

"Correct."

Quinn mulled this new information over a moment. Then his eyes clouded. "If that's the case, if the McKane have indeed found you again, Grimm, what's to stop them from following you to Caithness?" Quinn asked carefully. "Again."

Grimm raised his head with a stricken look.

* * *

Jillian didn't see Grimm the rest of the day. Quinn informed her that he'd gone riding and would likely not return until nightfall. Night came and the castle retired. Peering out the casement window, she spied Occam wandering the bailey. Grimm had returned.

Draping a plush woolen over her chemise, Jillian slipped from her chambers. The castle was quiet, its occupants sleeping.

"Jillian."

Jillian stopped in mid-step. She turned, suppressing her impatience. She needed to see Grimm, to touch him again, to investigate their newfound intimacy and to revel in her womanhood.

Kaley Twillow was hurrying down the corridor toward her, tugging a wrapper around her shoulders in the chilly air. The older woman's chestnut curls were unpinned and rumpled, and her face was flushed with sleep.

"I heard your door open," Kaley said. "Did you want something from the kitchen? You should have called for me. I'll be happy to get it for you. What did you want? Shall I prepare you a mug of warm milk? Some bread and honey?"

Jillian demurred and patted Kaley's shoulder reassuringly. "Don't worry, Kaley. You go back to bed. I'll get it."

"It's no problem. I was considering a snack myself." Worried eyes flickered over Jillian's impromptu robe of soft woolen.

"Kaley," Jillian tried again, "you needn't worry about me. I'll be fine. Really, I'm just a bit restless and—"

"You're going to see Grimm."

Jillian flushed. "I must. I need to speak with him. I can't sleep. There are things I must say—"

"That can't wait until the morning light?" Kaley eyed

the sheer chemise peeking from beneath the woolen. "You're not even properly dressed," she said reprovingly. "If you find him clad in that, you'll get more than you bargained for."

"You don't understand," Jillian said, sighing.

"Oh, but my dear lass, I do. I saw the remains of the Greathall this morning."

Jillian swallowed and said nothing.

"Shall we cut to the quick of it?" Kaley said tersely. "I'm not so old that I can't recall what it's like. I loved a man like him once. I understand what you're feeling, perhaps even more so than you do, so let me put it into plain words. Quinn is sexual. Ramsay Logan is sexual, and the power they exude promises a rollicking good time." Kaley took Jillian's hands in hers and regarded her soberly. "But Grimm Roderick, ah, he's an entirely different animal, he's not merely sexual. He drips sensual power, and Jillian, sensual power can reshape a woman."

"You *do* know what I mean!"

"I'm flesh and blood too, lass." Kaley laid a gentle hand against her cheek. "Jillian, I've watched you mature with pride, love, and lately a touch of fear. I'm proud because you have a good, fearless heart and a strong will. I'm fearful because your will can make you headstrong beyond compare. Heed my words before you commit yourself to a course that is irrevocable: Sexual men can be forgotten, but a sensual man lingers in a woman's heart forever."

"Oh, Kaley, it's too late," Jillian confessed. "He's in there already."

Kaley drew her into her arms. "I was afraid of that. Jillian, what if he leaves you? How will you handle that? How will you go on? A man like Quinn would never leave. A man like Grimm, well, the men who are larger than life are also the most dangerous to a woman. Grimm is unpredictable."

"Do you regret yours?"

"My what?"

"Your man like Grimm."

Kaley's features softened rapturously, and her expression was answer enough.

"And there you have it," Jillian pointed out gently. "Kaley, if I knew that I could only have a few nights in that man's arms or nothing, I would take those magic nights and use them to keep me warm for the rest of my life."

Kaley swallowed audibly, her eyes filled with empathy. She smiled faintly. "I understand, lass," she said finally.

"Good night, my dear Kaley. Go back to bed, and permit me the same sweet dreams you once dreamt yourself."

"I love you, lass," Kaley said gruffly.

"I love you too, Kaley," Jillian replied with a smile as she slipped down the corridor to find Grimm.

* * *

Jillian entered his chambers quietly. He wasn't there. She sighed, frustrated, and moved restlessly about his room. His chambers were spartan, as clean and disciplined as the man. Nothing was out of order except for a mussed pillow. Smiling, she stepped to the bed and picked it up to plump it. She pressed it to her face for a moment and inhaled his crisp masculine scent. Her smile faltered and became quiet wonder when she spied the tattered book the pillow had been concealing. *Aesop's Fables*. It was the illustrated manuscript she'd given him nearly a dozen years before, that first snowy Christmas they'd spent together. She dropped the pillow and gathered the manuscript, stroking it tenderly with her fingertips. The pages were frayed, the illustrations faded, and little notes and oddities peeked out from the binding. He'd been carrying it all these years, tucking in his mementos, much as she had done with her volume. She cradled it wonderingly. This book told her everything she needed to know. Grimm Roderick was a warrior, a hunter, a guard, an often hard man who carried a tattered copy of *Aesop's Fables* wherever he went, occasionally secreting dried flowers and verses between the pages. She flipped through, stopping at a note that had been crumpled and resmoothed dozens of times. *I will be on the roof at gloaming. I must speak to you tonight, Grimm!*

He'd never forgotten her.

Sensitive yet strong, capable yet vulnerable, earthy and sensual. She was hopelessly in love with him.

"I kept it."

Jillian spun around. Once again she hadn't heard a sound when he'd entered the room. He was framed in the doorway, his eyes dark and unreadable.

"I see that," she replied in a hushed voice.

He crossed the room and dropped himself into a chair before the fire, his back to her. Jillian stood, hugging the precious book to her chest in silence. They were so close to the intimacy she'd always wanted from him that she was afraid to break the spell with words.

"I can't believe you're not bombarding me with questions," he said carefully. "Like why did I keep it?"

"Why did you keep it, Grimm?" she asked, but it really didn't matter why. He had carried it with him to this day, and that was enough.

"Come here, lass."

Jillian gently placed the book on a table and approached him slowly. She hesitated a few paces from his side.

Grimm's hand shot out and fastened on her wrist. "Jillian, please." His voice was so low, it was almost inaudible.

"Please what?" she whispered.

Swiftly he flicked his wrist and she was standing before him, captured between his thighs. His eyes were fixed in the vicinity of her navel, as if he couldn't summon the strength to raise them. "Kiss me, Jillian. Touch me. Show me I'm alive," he whispered back.

Jillian bit her lip as his words slammed into her heart. The most valiant, intense man she'd ever known was afraid he wasn't fully alive. He raised his head and she cried out softly at his expression. It was dark, his eyes swirling with shadows, memories of times she couldn't even begin to comprehend. She cradled his face between her hands and kissed him, lingering on his lower lip, savoring the sensual curve.

"You're the most incredibly alive man I've ever known."

"Am I, Jillian? Am I?" he asked desperately.

How could he wonder about such a thing? His lips were warm and vital, his hands moved across her skin, awakening nerve endings she'd never suspected existed. "Why did you keep the book, Grimm?"

His hands fastened possessively on her waist. "I kept it to remind me that although there is evil, there is sometimes beauty and light. You, Jillian. You were always my light."

Jillian's heart soared. She'd come seeking confirmation of their fragile intimacy, to prove to herself that the tenderness and physical affection Grimm had offered her the night before had not been an isolated instance. She'd never dreamed that he might offer her words of . . . love? For what else were words like that if not words of love?

Her dreams were finally being realized. She'd always known there was a bond between herself and her wild-eyed beast-boy, but coming together as man and woman exceeded all her childhood fantasies.

Rising to his feet, Grimm pulled her against the muscled length of his body, unselfconsciously offering her the powerful evidence of his desire. The mere brush of him between her thighs made her shiver breathlessly.

"I can't get enough of you, Jillian," he breathed, fascinated by the sensual widening of her eyes, by the instinctive way her tongue wet the fullness of her lower lip. He captured it and kissed her slowly with scorching, lingering, mind-stealing kisses as he backed her toward the bed. Halfway there, he seemed to change his mind. He cupped her shoulders in his strong hands and turned her in his arms. Jillian had thought the sensation of him pressed against her thighs was too exciting to bear, but now the hard length of him rose hot against her, and she pushed back into him in a wordless plea. His hands began a languid journey over her body. He caressed the soft curve of her hips, slid his palms up the bow of her back, then slipped his arms around her to catch her breasts, finding the sensitive nipples and tugging them gently through the thin fabric of her chemise.

Gathering her hair in his hand, he tenderly tugged it to the side and kissed the exposed nape of her neck. The brief nip of his teeth caused her to arch her back and surge against him.

He edged her forward, guiding her past the bed and toward the wall. Pressing her close to the smooth stones, he twined his fingers between hers with his palms flush to the backs of her hands. He placed her palms against the wall above her head.

"Doona remove your hands from the wall, Jillian. No matter what I do, hold on to the wall and simply feel . . ."

Jillian held on to the wall as if it were her last hold on sanity. When he slipped her chemise from her body, she shivered as the cool air met her heated skin. His hands brushed the firm underside of her breasts, trailed over her waist, and hesitated on her hips. Then his fingers tightened on her skin and his tongue traced a lingering path down the hollow of her spine. She leaned against the wall, her palms flat, swaying with pleasure. By the time he was done, there was not one inch of her skin he hadn't kissed or caressed with the velvety stroke of his tongue.

Now she understood why he'd told her to hold on to the wall. It had nothing to do with the wall itself and everything to do with preventing her from touching him. Being touched by Grimm Roderick, yet being unable to touch back, overwhelmed her senses and forced her to accept pure pleasure with no distractions.

He dropped to his knees behind her, and he told her—both with his hands and with a low rush of words—how beautiful she was, what she did to him, and how very much he wanted her, *needed* her.

He slid his hands up the insides of her thighs, trailing slow, heated kisses across the round curves of her bottom. A sudden gasp of pleasure escaped her when his hand found the sensitive center between her legs. As his fingers stroked her with an irresistible friction that coaxed a whimper from her throat, he nipped her buttock.

"Grimm!" she gasped.

Laughter laced with something dangerously erotic heightened her arousal even further. "Hands on the wall," he reminded when she started to turn. He eased her thighs apart and maneuvered himself so that he was on the floor, gazing up at her, his face only inches from the part of her that was aching for his touch. She opened her mouth to protest his being so intimately positioned, when the heat of his tongue silenced any admonishment she may have made. Her neck arched and it took every ounce of her will not to scream from the stunning pleasure he ignited within her.

Then her gaze was drawn down to the magnificent warrior kneeling between her thighs. The vision of his face, intense with passion, coupled with the incredible feelings he was coaxing forth, shortened her breath to tiny, helpless pants. She rocked softly against him, making small, breathless cries unlike any sound she'd ever thought to make before.

"I'm going to fall," she gasped.

"I'll catch you, Jillian."

"But I don't think we should—oh!"

"Don't think," he agreed.

"But my legs . . . won't . . . hold!"

He laughed, and with a swift tug yanked her down on top of him. They tumbled onto a woven rug in a press of heated skin and tangled limbs. "And to think you were afraid to fall," he teased.

She savored the incredible closeness of their bodies, and at that moment she fully let go. As she fell against him, she fell even more completely in love with him, into a mindless passion. He *would* always catch her—that she knew without a doubt. They rolled across the rug in a playful skirmish for the superior position, then he flipped her so suddenly that she landed on her hands and knees. In an instant he was behind her, nudging into the cleft between the soft curves of her bottom, and she gasped aloud.

"Now," she cried.

"Now," he agreed, and drove into her.

She felt him deep inside her, filling her, joining them together. Cupping her breasts, he thrust inside her, and she felt so connected to him that it took her breath away. She made a sound of supreme dismay when he slipped out, leaving an ache deep inside her, and she purred with pleasure when he filled her again so deeply that she arched her back and rose up against him, her shoulders pressing against his hard chest

He must have awakened something inside her, Jillian decided, because it took only a few more thrusts for her body to break free and shatter into a thousand quivering pieces. She would *never* get enough of him.

* * *

Hours later, a sated Jillian was lying in a puddle of contentment on his bed. When his hands began their sensual dance upon her body, she sighed. "I couldn't possibly feel that again, Grimm," she protested weakly. "I haven't a muscle left in my body, and I simply couldn't . . ."

Grimm smiled wickedly. "When I was younger I stayed with Gypsies for a time."

Jillian lay back against the pillow, wondering what this had to do with the earth-shattering explosions he'd been lavishing upon her.

"They had a strange ceremony they practiced to induce 'Vision.' It didn't rely upon a mixture of herbs and spices or the smoking of a pipe. It relied upon sexual excess to achieve a state that transcended the everyday frame of mind. They would place one of their seers in a tent with a dozen women, who repeatedly brought him to climax until he was begging for no more pleasure. The Rom claim climax releases something in the body that causes the spirit to soar, ripping it free from its earthly mooring, opening it to the extraordinary."

"I believe that." Jillian was fascinated. "It makes me feel as if I've drunk too much sweet wine—my head gets swimmy and my body feels weak and strong at the same time." When his fingers found the juncture of her thighs, she shivered. With a few deft movements, he had her tingling, hungering all over again, and when he brought her to a swift release with his hands, it was even more exquisite than the last. "Grimm!" Heat erupted inside her, and she shuddered. He didn't remove his hand, but cupped her gently until she calmed. Then he began again, moving his fingers in a light teasing motion over the sensitive nub.

"And again, my sweet Jillian, until you can no longer look at me without knowing what I can do to you, where I can take you, how many times I can take you there."

* * *

For Grimm there was no rest that night. He paced the stone floor, kicking at the lambskin rugs, wondering how he was going to bring himself to do the right thing this time. Never in his life had he allowed himself to get too attached to anything or anyone, because he'd always known that at any moment he might have to leave, fleeing the hunt the McKane perpetuated against any man suspected of being Berserk.

They'd found him in Durrkesh. Quinn was right. What was to prevent them from coming to Caithness? They could have easily followed the lumbering cart upon which they'd transported the sick men. And if they descended upon Caithness again, what harm would this blessed place suffer? What harm might they do to Jillian's home and Jillian herself? Edmund had died as a result of the last McKane attack. Maybe he'd caught a lung fever, but if he hadn't been wounded to begin with, he would never have caught the disease that had claimed his young life.

Grimm couldn't live with the thought of bringing harm—again—to Caithness and Jillian.

He stopped by the bed, gazed down at her, and watched her with his heart in his eyes. *I love you, Jillian,* he willed to her sleeping form. *Always have, and always will. But I'm Berserk, and you—you're the best of life. I have an insane old da and a crumbling pile of rocks to call home. It's no life for a lady.*

He forced his dark thoughts away, scattering them with his formidable will. Sinking into her body was all he wanted to contemplate. These past two days with Jillian had been the best two days of his life. He should be content with that, he told himself.

She rolled over in her sleep, her hand falling palm open, fingers slightly curled. Her golden hair fanned out across the white pillows, her full breasts spilled above the downy linen. Just one more day, he promised himself, and one more blissful, magical, incredible night. Then he'd leave, before it was too late.

CHAPTER 19

QUINN AND RAMSAY SACKED THE KITCHENS OF CAITH-
ness at dawn. Not one piece of fruit, not one slab of meat,
not a single savory morsel was spared.

"Christ, I feel like I haven't eaten solid food in weeks!"

"We damn near haven't. Broth and bread don't count as
real food." Ramsay tore off a chunk of smoked ham with
his teeth. "I haven't had an appetite until now. That damn
poison made me so sick, I thought I might never want to
eat again!"

Quinn palmed an apple and bit into it with relish. Platters were piled haphazardly atop every available surface.
The maids would faint when they discovered the men had
wiped out all the food that had been prepared for the coming weekend.

"We'll hunt and replenish." Quinn felt mildly guilty as
his gaze swept the decimated larder. "You up to a bit of
hunting, Ram, my man?"

"So long as it's wearing a skirt," Ramsay said with a gusty sigh, "and answers to the name of Jillian."

"I don't think so," Quinn replied acerbically. "Perhaps you didn't notice, but Jillian obviously has a bit of a *tendre* for me. If I hadn't gotten sick at Durrkesh, I would have proposed marriage and we would be betrothed by now."

Ramsay took a deep slug of whisky and placed the bottle on the counter with a thump. "You really are dense, aren't you, de Moncreiffe?"

"Don't tell me you think it's you." Quinn rolled his eyes.

"Of course not. It's that bastard Roderick. It always has been, ever since we got here." Ramsay's dark expression was murderous. "And after what happened two nights ago . . ."

Quinn stiffened. "What happened two nights ago?"

Ramsay took another swallow, swished it over his tongue, and brooded a silent moment. "Did you notice the long table in the hall is gone, Quinn?"

"Now that you mention it, yes, it is. What happened to it?"

"I saw pieces of it out back behind the bothy. It was shattered down the center."

Quinn said nothing. He knew of only one man who could shatter a table of such massive proportions with his bare hands.

"I came down yesterday to find the maids sweeping food off the floor. One of the candelabra was wedged into the wall. Someone had a helluva fight in there two nights ago. But nobody has breathed a word about it, have they?"

"What are you saying, Logan?" Quinn asked grimly.

"Just that the only two people who were well enough to dine in the hall two nights ago were Grimm and Jillian. They obviously fought, but today Grimm didn't seem bitter. And Jillian, why, the woman has been wreathed in smiles and good humor. Matter of fact, just as a little test, what say we go wake Grimm right now and talk to him about it? That is, if he's not otherwise occupied."

"If you're insinuating that Jillian might be in his chambers, you're a stupid bastard and I'll call you out for it," Quinn snapped. "And maybe there was a fight in the hall between them, but I guarantee you that Grimm is far too honorable to seduce Jillian. Besides, he can't even bring himself to say a civil word to her. He certainly couldn't be nice to her long enough to seduce her."

"You don't find it curious that just when it seemed like you were making progress with her, you and I get poisoned and put out of the running, but he doesn't?" Ramsay asked. "I'd say it was suspiciously convenient. I think it's damned odd that he didn't get sick too."

"He didn't consume any of the poison," Quinn defended.

"Maybe that's because he knew what was poisoned in advance," Ramsay argued.

"That's enough, Logan!" Quinn snapped. "It's one thing to accuse him of wanting Jillian. Hell, we all want her. But it's entirely another to accuse him of trying to kill us. You don't know a damn thing about Grimm Roderick."

"Maybe you're the one who doesn't know him," Ramsay countered. "Maybe Grimm Roderick pretends to be something he's not. I, for one, plan to wake him right now and find out." Ramsay stalked from the room, muttering under his breath.

Quinn shook his head and vaulted after him. "Logan, would you cool your heels—"

"No! You're so convinced of his innocence, I say let's make him prove it!" Ramsay took the stairs to the west wing three at a time, and Quinn had to lope to keep up. As

Logan sped down the long corridor, Quinn overtook him and placed a restraining hand on his shoulder, but Ramsay shook it off.

"If you're so convinced he wouldn't do it, what are you afraid of, de Moncreiffe? Let's just go rouse him."

"You're not thinking clearly about this, Ram—" Quinn broke off abruptly as the door to Grimm's chambers eased opened.

When Jillian slipped out into the hallway, his eyes widened incredulously. There was unequivocally no reason for Jillian to be leaving Grimm's chambers in the wee hours of the morning but for the reason Ramsay had suggested. She was his lover.

Quinn instantly ducked back, pulling Ramsay with him into the shadowed alcove of a doorway.

Her hair was disheveled, and she wore only a woolen draped about her shoulders. Although it trailed nearly to the floor, it left little doubt that there was nothing beneath it.

"Odin's balls," he whispered.

Ramsay favored him with a mocking smile as they lurked in the dark alcove. "Not the honorable Grimm Roderick, right, Quinn?" he whispered.

"That son of a bitch." Quinn's gaze lingered on Jillian's sweet curves as she disappeared down the hallway. The early rays of dawn coming in the tall windows colored his eyes with a strangely crimson glint as he stared at Ramsay.

"Some best friend, eh, de Moncreiffe? He knew you wanted her. He doesn't even offer her marriage. He just takes it for free."

"Over my dead body he will," Quinn vowed.

"Her da brought three men here so she could choose a husband. And what does he do? Both you and I would do the honorable thing, marry her and give her a name, babes, and a life. Roderick tups her and will likely saunter off into the sunset, and you know it. That man has no intention of wedding her. If he possessed one honorable intention, he would have left her to you or me, men who would do right by her. I'm telling you, you don't know him as well as you think."

Quinn scowled, and the minute Jillian disappeared from view, he stalked off muttering beneath his breath.

* * *

The day passed in a haze of happiness for Jillian. The only moment it was marred was when she encountered Quinn at breakfast. He was distant and aloof, not his normal self at all. He eyed her strangely, fidgeted over his breakfast, and finally stalked off in silence.

Once or twice she brushed past Ramsay, who was also behaving oddly. Jillian didn't spare much thought for it; they were probably still suffering the aftereffects of the poison and would be fine in time.

The world was a magnificent place, in her opinion. She was even feeling magnanimous toward her da for having brought her true love back to her. In a burst of generosity she decided he was as wise as she'd once thought. She would wed Grimm Roderick and her life would be perfect.

CHAPTER 20

"WELL?" RONIN MCILLIOCH DEMANDED.

Elliott shuffled forward, clutching a sheaf of crisp parchments in his hand. "Tobie did well, milord, although we couldn't risk moving in too close to Caithness. Your son possesses the same remarkable senses you have. Still, Tobie managed to capture his likeness on several occasions: riding, saving a small boy, and twice with the woman."

"Let me see." Ronin thrust an impatient hand at Elliott. He rifled through the pages one by one, absorbing every detail. "He's a bonny lad, isn't he, Elliott? Look at those shoulders! Tobie dinna exaggerate, did he?" When Elliott shook his head, Ronin smiled. "Look at that power. My son's every inch a legendary warrior. The lasses must swoon over him."

"Aye, he's a legend, your son is. You should have seen him kill the mountain cat. He cut his own hand to bring on the Berserker rage, to save the child."

Ronin passed the sketches to the man at his side. Two pairs of ice-blue eyes studied every line.

"By Odin's spear!" Ronin exhaled slowly as he reached the last two drawings. "She's the loveliest thing I've ever seen."

"Your son thinks so," Elliott said smugly. "He's every bit as besotted as you were with Jolyn. She's 'the one,' milord, no doubt about it."

"Have they . . . ?" Ronin trailed off meaningfully.

"Judging by the wreck Gavrael made of the Greathall, I'd say yes." Elliott grinned.

Ronin and the man at his side exchanged pleased glances. "The time is at hand. Get with Gilles and start the preparations for him to be comin' home."

"Yes, milord!"

The man sitting next to Ronin raised ice-blue eyes to the McIllioch's. "Do you really think it's goin' to happen as the old woman foretold?" Ronin's brother, Balder, asked softly.

"Cataclysmic changes," Ronin murmured. "She said this generation would suffer more greatly than any McIllioch, but promised that so, too, would this generation advance, and know greater happiness. The old seer swore that my son would see sons of his own, and I believe that. She vowed that when he chose his mate, his mate would be bringin' him home to Maldebann."

"And how will you transcend his hatred for you, Ronin?" his brother asked.

"I doona know." Ronin sighed heavily. "Maybe I'm hoping for a miracle, that he'll listen and forgive me. Now that he's found his mate he may be sympathetic to my plight. He may be capable of understandin' why I did what I did. And why I let him go."

"Doona be so hard on yourself, Ronin. The McKane would have followed you to him if you'd gone after him. They were waiting for you to betray his hidin' place. They know you won't breed more sons. They doona know I even exist. It's Gavrael they're determined to destroy, and the time is quickenin'. If they discover he's found his mate, they'll stop at nothin'."

"I know. He was well hidden at Caithness for years, so I thought it best to leave well enough alone. Gibraltar trained him better than I could have at the time." Ronin met Balder's gaze. "But I always thought that at some point he would come home of his own volition; out of curiosity or confusion about what he was if nothing else, and long before now. When he didn't, when he never once looked west to Maldebann . . . ah, Balder, I fear I grew bitter. I couldna believe he hated me so completely."

"What makes you think he'll be forgivin' you now?"

Ronin raised his hands in a gesture of helplessness. "A fool's fancy? I must believe. Or else I'd have no reason to go on."

Balder clasped his shoulder affectionately. "You have a reason to go on. The McKane must be defeated once and for all and you must ensure the safety of your son's sons. That in itself is reason enough."

"And it will be done," Ronin vowed.

*   *   *

Grimm spent the day riding, scouring every inch of Caithness for some sign that the McKane had found him. He knew how they operated: They would set up camp on the perimeter of the estate and wait for the right moment, any moment of vulnerability. Grimm rode the entire circumference, searching for anything: the remains of a recent fire, missing livestock commandeered and slaughtered, word of strangers among the crofters.

He found nothing. Not one shred of evidence to support his suspicion that he was being watched.

Still, a prickling of unease lurked at the base of his neck where he always felt it when something was wrong. There was a threat, unidentified and unseen, somewhere at Caithness.

He rode into the bailey at dusk, battling an overwhelming desire to slip from his horse, race into the castle, and rush to Jillian. To sweep her into his embrace, carry her to his chambers, and make love to her until neither of them could move, which for a Berserker was a very long time.

Leave, his conscience pricked. *Leave this moment. Doona even pack a satchel, doona even say goodbye, just get out now.*

He felt like he was being torn in half. In all the years he'd dreamed of Jillian, he'd never imagined he could feel this way; she completed him. The Berserker had risen in him and been humbled by her presence. She could make him clean again. Merely being with her soothed the beast he'd learned to hate, the beast she didn't even know existed.

He grimaced inwardly as hope, the treacherous emotion he'd never permitted himself to feel, jockeyed for position with his premonition of danger. Hope was a luxury he could ill afford. Hope made men do foolish things, such as staying at Caithness when all his heightened senses were clamoring that despite finding no sign of McKane, he was being watched and a confrontation was imminent. He knew how to handle danger. He didn't know how to handle hope.

Sighing, he entered the Greathall and picked at a platter of fruit near the hearth. Selecting a ripe pear, he dropped into a chair before the fire and brooded into the flames, battling his urge to seek her out. He had to make some decisions. He had to find a way to behave honorably, to do the right thing, but he no longer knew what the right thing was. Nothing was black and white anymore; there were no easy answers. He knew it was dangerous to remain at Caithness, but he wanted to remain more than anything he'd ever desired in his life.

He was so lost in thought, he didn't hear Ramsay approach until the Highlander's deep, rumbling voice jarred him. That alone should have warned him that he'd allowed his guard to slip dangerously.

"Where've you been, Roderick?"

"Riding."

"All day? Damn it, man, there's a beautiful woman in the castle and you go out riding all day?"

"I had some thinking to do. Riding clears my head."

"I'd say you have some thinking to do," Ramsay muttered beneath his breath.

With his heightened hearing, Grimm heard each syllable. He turned and faced Ramsay levelly. "Just what is it you think I should be thinking about?"

Ramsay looked startled. "I'm standing a dozen paces from you! There's no way you could have heard that. It was scarcely audible."

"Obviously I did," Grimm said coolly. "So what is it you presume to tell me I should be thinking about?"

Ramsay's dark eyes flickered, and Grimm could see he was trying to suppress his volatile temper. "Let's try honor, Roderick," Ramsay said stiffly. "Honoring our host. And his daughter."

Grimm's smile was dangerous. "I'll make you a deal, Logan. If you doona bring up my honor, I won't drag yours out of the pigsty where it's been bedding down for years."

"My honor—" Ramsay began hotly, but Grimm cut him off impatiently. He had more important things to occupy his mind than arguing with Ramsay.

"Let's just get to the point, Logan. How much gold do you owe the Campbell? Half of what Jillian's worth? Or is it more? From what I hear, you're into him so deeply you may as well have put yourself six feet under. If you bag the St. Clair heiress, you'll be able to clear your debts and live in extravagance for a few years. Isn't that right?"

"Not all men are as wealthy as you, Roderick. For some of us, whose people are vast in number, it's a struggle to take care of our clan. And I care for Jillian," Ramsay growled.

"I'm sure you do. The same way you care for seeing your belly filled with the finest food and the best whisky. The same way you care for riding a pure-blooded stallion, the same way you like to show off your wolfhounds. Maybe all those expenses are why you've been having a hard time maintaining your people. How many years did you fritter away at court, spending gold as liberally as your clan procreates?"

Ramsay turned stiffly and was silent a long moment. Grimm watched him, every muscle in his body tensed to spring. Logan had a violent temper—Grimm had experienced it before. He berated himself for antagonizing the man, but Ramsay Logan's tendency to put his own needs above those of his starving clan infuriated him.

Ramsay drew a deep breath and turned around, astonishing Grimm with a pleasant smile. "You're wrong about me, Roderick. I confess, my past isn't so exemplary, but I'm not the same man I used to be."

Grimm watched him, skepticism evident in every line on his face.

"See? I'm not losing my temper." Ramsay raised his hands in a conciliatory gesture. "I can see how you might believe such things of me. I was a wild, self-centered reprobate once. But I'm not any longer. I can't prove it to you. Only time will prove my sincerity. Grant me that much, will you?"

Grimm snorted. "Sure, Logan. I'll grant you that much. You may be different." *Worse*, Grimm added in the privacy of his thoughts. He turned his gaze back to the flames.

As Grimm heard Ramsay turn to leave the room, he was unable to prevent himself from asking, "Where's Jillian?"

Logan stopped in mid-step and shot a cool glance over his shoulder. "Playing chess with Quinn in the study. He intends to propose marriage to her tonight, so I suggest you give them privacy. Jillian deserves a proper husband, and if she won't have him, I intend to offer in his stead."

Grimm nodded stiffly. After a few moments of attempting to block all thoughts of Jillian from his mind—Jillian ensconced in the cozy study with Quinn, who was proposing marriage—and failing, he stalked back out into the night, more disturbed by Ramsay's words than he wished to admit.

* * *

Grimm wandered the gardens for nearly half an hour before he was struck by the realization that he'd seen no sign of his stallion. He'd left him in the inner ward less than an hour ago. Occam rarely wandered far from the castle.

Puzzled, Grimm searched the inner and outer wards, whistling repeatedly, but he heard nary a nicker, no thunder of hooves. He turned his thoughtful gaze to the stables that graced the edge of the outer bailey. Instinct quickened inside him, warning him, and he set off at a run for the outbuilding.

He burst into the stables and drew to an abrupt halt. It was abnormally silent, and an odd odor pervaded the air. Sharp, acrid, like the stench of rotten eggs. Peering into the gloom, he catalogued every detail of the room before stepping in. Hay tumbled in piles across the floor—normal. Oil lamps suspended from the rafters—also normal. All the gates shut—still normal.

Scent of a thing sulfuric—definitely not normal. But not much to go on either.

He stepped gingerly into the stables, whistled, and was rewarded with a muffled neigh from the stall at the farthest end of the stables. Grimm forced himself not to lurch forward.

It was a trap.

While he couldn't fathom the exact nature of the threat, danger fairly dripped from the rafters of the low outbuilding. His senses bristled. What was amiss? Sulfur?

He narrowed his eyes thoughtfully, paced forward and gently scuffed at the hay beneath his boot, then stooped to push aside a thick sheaf of clover.

He expelled a low whistle of amazement.

He pushed at more hay, moved forward five paces, did the same, moved left five paces, and repeated the motion. Sweeping his hand across the dusty stone floor beneath the hay, he came up with a fistful of finely corned black powder.

Christ! The entire floor of the stable had been evenly sprinkled with a layer of black powder. Someone had liberally doused the stones, then spread loose hay atop it. Black powder was made from a combination of saltpeter, charcoal, and sulfur. Many clans cultivated their own saltpeter in or near the stables to fashion the weapon, but the stuff spread on the floor was fully processed black powder, painstakingly corned to uniform granules, possessing lethal explosive properties, and planted deliberately. It was a far cry from the raw version of fermenting manure from which saltpeter was derived. Coupled with the flammability of the hay and the natural abundance of fresh manure, the stables were an inferno waiting to blow. One spark would send the entire stable up with the force of a massive bomb. If one of the oil lanterns fell or so much as coughed up an oily spark, the building—and half the outer ward—would be rocked by the explosion.

Occam nickered, a sound of frustrated fear. He was muzzled, Grimm realized. Someone had muzzled his horse and penned him in a deadly trap.

He would never permit his horse to be burned again, and whoever had designed this trap knew him well enough to know his weakness for the stallion. Grimm stood, absolutely motionless, ten paces inside the door—not too far to flee for safety if the hay started to smolder. But Occam was in a locked stall, fifty yards from safety, and therein lay the problem.

A coldhearted man would turn his back and leave. What was a horse, after all? A beast, used for man's purposes. Grimm snorted. Occam was a regal, beautiful creature, possessing intelligence and the same capacity to suffer pain and fear as any human being.

No, he could never leave his horse behind.

He had barely completed that thought when something hurtled through the window to his left and the straw caught fire in an instant.

Grimm lunged into the flames.

* * *

In the coziness of the study, Jillian laughed as she moved her bishop into a position of checkmate. She stole a surreptitious peek toward the window, as she had a dozen times in the past hour, seeking some sign that Grimm had returned. Ever since she'd glimpsed him riding out this morning, she'd been watching for him. The moment Occam's great gray shape lumbered past the study, Jillian feared she would surge to her feet, giddy as a lass, and be off at a run. Memories of the night she'd spent entangled with Grimm's hard, inexhaustible body brought a flush to her skin, heating her in a way a fire never could.

"Not fair! How can I concentrate? Playing you when you were a wee lass was far easier," Quinn complained. "I can't think when I play you now."

"Ah, the advantages of being a woman," Jillian drawled mischievously. She was certain she must be radiating her newfound sensual knowledge. "Is it my fault your attention wanders?"

Quinn's gaze lingered on her shoulders, bared by the gown she wore. "Absolutely," he assured her. "Look at you, Jillian. You're beautiful!" His voice dropped to a confidential tone. "Jillian, lass, there's something I wish to discuss with you—"

"Quinn, hush." She placed a finger against his lips and shook her head.

Quinn brushed her hand away. "No, Jillian, I've kept my silence long enough. I know what you feel, Jillian." He paused deliberately to lend emphasis to his next words. "And I know what's going on with Grimm." He held her gaze levelly.

Jillian was immediately wary. "What do you mean?" she evaded.

Quinn smiled in an effort to soften his words. "Jillian, he's not the marrying kind."

Jillian bit her lip and averted her gaze. "You don't know that for certain. That's like saying Ramsay's not the marrying kind because, from the tales I've heard, he's been a consummate womanizer. But only this morning he convinced me of his troth. Merely because a man has shown no past inclination to wed doesn't mean he won't. People change." Grimm had certainly changed, revealing the tender, loving man she'd always believed he really was.

"Logan asked you to marry him?" Quinn scowled.

Jillian nodded. "This morning. After breakfast he approached me while I was walking in the gardens."

"He offered for you? He knew I planned to do so myself!" Quinn cursed, then mumbled a hasty apology. "Forgive me, Jillian, but it makes me angry that he'd go behind my back like that."

"I didn't accept, Quinn, so it hardly matters."

"How did he take it?"

Jillian sighed. The Highlander hadn't taken it well at all; she had the feeling she'd barely escaped a dangerous display of temper. "I don't think Ramsay Logan is accustomed to being rebuffed. He seemed furious."

Quinn studied her a moment, then said, "Jillian, lass, I wasn't going to tell you this, but I think you should be informed so you can make a wise decision. The Logan are land rich but gold poor. Ramsay Logan needs to marry, and marry well. You would be a godsend to his impoverished clan."

Jillian gave him an astonished look. "Quinn! I can't believe that you would try to discredit my suitors. Heavens! Ramsay spent a quarter hour this morning trying to discredit you and Grimm. What's with you men?"

Quinn stiffened. "I am not trying to discredit your suitors. I'm telling you the truth. Logan needs gold. His clan is starving, and has been for many years. They've scarcely managed to hold on to their own lands lately. In the past, the Logan hired out as mercenaries to get coin, but there've been so few wars in recent years that there is no mercenary work to be found. Land takes coin, and coin is something the Logan have never had. You are the answer to their every prayer. Excuse my crass way of wording it, but if Logan could bag the rich St. Clair bride, his clan would herald him as their savior."

Jillian nibbled her lip thoughtfully. "And you, Quinn de Moncreiffe, why do you wish to wed me?"

"Because I care deeply for you, lass," Quinn said simply.

"Perhaps I should ask Grimm about *you*."

Quinn closed his eyes and sighed.

"Just what's wrong with Grimm as a candidate?" she pressed, determined to have it all out.

Quinn's gaze was compassionate. "I don't mean to be cruel, but he will never marry you, Jillian. Everyone knows that Grimm Roderick has vowed never to wed."

Jillian refused to let Quinn see how his words affected her. She bit her lip to prevent any rash words from escaping. She had nearly worked up the courage to ask him why, and if Grimm had actually said such a thing recently, when a tremendous explosion rocked the castle.

The windows rattled in their frames, the very castle shuddered, and both Jillian and Quinn leapt to their feet.

"What was that?" she gasped.

Quinn flew to the window and peered out. "Christ!" he shouted. "The stables are on fire!"

CHAPTER 21

JILLIAN RACED INTO THE COURTYARD AFTER QUINN, crying Grimm's name over and over, heedless of the curious eyes of the staff and the shocked gazes of Kaley and Hatchard. The explosion had roused the castle. Hatchard was standing in the courtyard shouting orders, organizing an attack against the hostile flames that were devouring the stables and moving east to ravage the castle.

The autumn weather had been dry enough that the fire would quickly rage out of control, gobbling buildings and crops. The teeming village of daub-and-wattle huts would ignite like dry grass if the flames encroached that far. A few stray sparks carried on the breeze could destroy the whole valley. Jillian frantically pushed that concern to the perimeter of her thoughts; she had to find Grimm.

"Where's Grimm? Has anyone seen Grimm?" Jillian pushed through the throng of people, peering into faces, desperate to catch a glimpse of his proud stance, his intense blue eyes. Her eyes were peeled for the shape of a great, gray stallion. "Don't be a hero, don't be a hero," she muttered under her breath. "For once, just be a man, Grimm Roderick. Be *safe*."

She didn't realize she'd said the words aloud until Quinn, who'd surfaced in the throng beside her, looked at her sharply and shook his head. "Och, lass, you love him, don't you?"

Jillian nodded as tears filled her eyes. "Find him, Quinn! Make him be safe!"

Quinn sighed and nodded. "Stay here, lass. I'll find him for you. I promise."

The eerie scream of a trapped horse split the air, and Jillian pivoted toward the stables, chilled by a sudden, terrible knowledge. "He couldn't be in there, could he, Quinn?"

Quinn's expression plainly echoed her fear. But of course he could, and would. Grimm could not stand by and watch a horse be burned. She knew that; he'd said as much that day at Durrkesh. In his mind, the innocent cry of an animal was as intolerable as the cry of wounded child or a frightened woman.

"No man could survive that." Jillian eyed the inferno. Flames shot up, tall as the castle, brilliant orange against the black sky. The wall of fire was so intense that it was nearly impossible to look at. Jillian narrowed her eyes in a desperate bid to make out the low rectangular shape of the stable, to no avail. She could see nothing but fire.

"You're right, Jillian," Quinn said slowly. "No *man* could."

As if in a dream, she saw a shape coalesce within the flames. Like some nightmare vision the white-orange flames shimmered, a blurred form of darkness rippled behind them, and a rider burst forth, wreathed in flames, streaking straight for the loch, where both horse and rider plunged into the cool waters, hissing as they submerged. She held her breath until horse and rider surfaced.

Quinn spared her a quick nod of reassurance before racing off to join the fight against the inferno that threatened Caithness.

Jillian darted for the loch, tripping over her feet in her haste to reach his side. As Grimm rose from the water and led Occam up the rocky bank, she flung herself at him, burrowed into his arms, and buried her face against his sodden chest. He held her for a long moment until she stopped shuddering, then drew back, wiping gently at her tears.

"Jillian," he said sadly.

"Grimm, I thought I'd lost you!" She pressed frantic kisses to his face while she searched his body with her hands to assure herself he was unharmed. "Why, you're not even burned," she said, puzzled. Although his clothing hung in charred tatters and his skin was a bit pinkened, there wasn't so much as a blister marring his smooth skin. She peered past him at Occam, who also seemed to have been spared. "How can this be?" she wondered.

"His coat has been singed, but overall he's fine. We rode fast," Grimm said quickly.

"I thought I'd lost you," Jillian repeated. Gazing into his eyes, she was struck by the sudden and terrible understanding that although he'd burst from the flames, miraculously whole, her words had never been truer. She *had* lost him. She had no idea how or why, but his glittering gaze was teeming with distance and sorrow. With goodbye.

"No," she shouted. "No. I won't let you go. You are *not* leaving me!"

Grimm dropped his gaze to the ground.

"No," she insisted. "Look at me."

His gaze was dark. "I have to go, lass. I will not bring destruction to this place again."

"What makes you think this fire is about you?" she demanded, battling her every instinct that told her the fire had indeed been about him. She didn't know why, but she knew it was true. "Oh! You are so arrogant," she pressed on bravely, determined to convince him that the truth was not the truth. She would use every weapon, fair or unfair, to keep him.

"Jillian." He blew out a breath of frustration and reached for her.

She beat at him with her fists. "No! Don't touch me, don't hold me, not if it means you're going to say goodbye!"

"I must, lass. I've tried to tell you—Christ, I tried to tell myself! I have nothing to offer you. You doona understand; it can never be. No matter how much I might wish to, I can't offer you the kind of life you deserve. Things like this fire happen to me all the time, Jillian. It's not safe for anyone to be around me. They hunt me!"

"Who hunts you?" she wailed as her world crumbled around her.

He made an angry gesture. "I can't explain, lass. You'll simply have to take my word on this. I'm not a normal man. Could a normal man have survived that?" He flung his arm toward the blaze.

"Then what are you?" she shouted. "Why don't you just tell me?"

He shook his head and closed his eyes. After a long pause, he opened them. His eyes were burning, incandescent, and Jillian gasped as a fleeting memory surfaced. It was the memory of a fifteen-year-old who'd watched this man battle the McKane. Watching as he'd seemed to grow larger, broader, stronger with every drop of blood that was shed. Watching his eyes burn like banked coals, listening to his chilling laughter, wondering how any man could slay so many yet remain unharmed.

"What *are* you?" she repeated in a whisper, begging him for comfort. Begging him to be nothing more than a man.

"The warrior who has always—" He closed his eyes. *Loved you.* But he couldn't offer her those words, because he couldn't follow up on what they promised. "Adored you, Jillian St. Clair. A man who isn't quite a man, who knows he can never have you." He drew a shuddering breath. "You must marry Quinn. Marry him and free me. Doona marry Ramsay—he's not good enough for you. But you must let me go, because I cannot suffer your death on my hands, and that's all that could ever come of you and me being together." He met her gaze, wordlessly beseeching her not to make his leaving any harder than it already was.

Jillian stiffened. If the man was going to leave her, she was going to make certain it hurt like hell. She narrowed her eyes, shooting him a wordless challenge to be brave, to fight for their love. He averted his face.

"Thank you for these days and nights, lass. Thank you for giving me the best memories of my life. But say good-bye, Jillian. Let me go. Take the splendor and wonder that we've shared and let me go."

Her tears started then. He had already made up his mind, had already begun putting distance between them. "Just tell me, Grimm," she begged. "It can't be so bad. Whatever it is, we can deal with it together."

"I'm an animal, Jillian. You doona know me!"

"I know you're the most honorable man I've ever met! I

don't care what our life would be like. I would live *any* kind of life, so long as I lived it with you," she hissed.

As Grimm backed away slowly, she watched the life disappear from his eyes, leaving his gaze wintry and hollow. She felt the moment she lost him; something inside her emptied completely, leaving a void she suspected she might die from. "No!"

He backed away. Occam followed, nickering gently.

"You said you adored me! If you truly cared for me, you would fight to stay by my side!"

He winced. "I care about you too much to hurt you."

"That's weak! You don't know what caring is," she shouted furiously. "Caring is love. And love fights! Love doesn't look for the path of least resistance. Hell's bells, Roderick, if love was that easy everyone would have it. You're a coward!"

He flinched, and a muscle jumped furiously in his jaw. "I am doing the honorable thing."

"To *hell* with the honorable thing," she shouted. "Love has no pride. Love looks for ways to endure."

"Jillian, stop. You want more from me than I'm capable of."

Her gaze turned icy. "Obviously. I thought you were heroic in every way. But you're not. You're just a man after all." She cast her gaze away and held her breath, wondering if she'd goaded him far enough.

"Goodbye, Jillian."

He leapt on his horse, and they seemed to melt into one beast—a creature of shadows disappearing into the night.

She gaped in disbelief at the hole he'd left in her world. He'd left her. He'd really left her. A sob welled up within her, so painful that she doubled over. "You coward," she whispered.

CHAPTER 22

RONIN INSERTED THE KEY INTO THE LOCK, HESITATED, then squared his shoulders firmly. He eyed the towering oak door that was banded with steel. It soared over his head, set in a lofty arch of stone. *Deo non fortuna* was chiseled in flowing script above the arch—"By God, not by chance." For years Ronin had denied those words, refused to come to this place, believing God had forsaken him. *Deo non fortuna* was the motto his clan had lived by, believing their special gifts were God-given and had purpose. Then his "gift" had resulted in Jolyn's death.

Ronin expelled an anxious breath, forcing himself to turn the key and push open the door. Rusty hinges shrieked the protest of long disuse. Cobwebs danced in the doorway and the musty scent of forgotten legends greeted him. *Welcome to the Hall of Lords,* the legends clamored. *Did you really think you could forget us?*

One thousand years of McIllioch graced the hall. Carved deep into the belly of the mountain, the chamber

soared to a towering fifty feet. The curved walls met in a
royal arch and the ceilings were painted with graphic de-
pictions of the epic heroes of their clan.

His own da had brought him here when he'd turned sixteen. He'd explained their noble history and guided Ronin
through the change—guidance Ronin had been unable to
provide his own son.

But who would have thought Gavrael would change so
much sooner than any of them had? It had been totally unexpected. The battle with the McKane following so quickly
on the heels of Jolyn's savage murder had left Ronin too
exhausted, too numbed by grief to reach out to his son.
Although Berserkers were difficult to kill, if one was
wounded badly enough it took time to heal. It had taken
Ronin months to recover. The day the McKane had murdered Jolyn they'd left a shell of a man who hadn't wanted
to heal.

Immersed in his grief, he'd failed his son. He'd been
unable to introduce Gavrael to the life of a Berserker, to
train him in the secret ways of controlling the bloodlust. He
hadn't been there to explain. He'd failed, and his son had
run off to find a new family and a new life.

As the passing years had weathered Ronin's body he'd
greeted each weary bone, each aching joint, and each
newly discovered silver hair with gratitude, because it carried him one day closer to his beloved Jolyn.

But he couldn't go to Jolyn yet. There were things yet
undone. His son was coming home, and he would not fail
him this time.

With effort, Ronin forced his attention away from his
deep guilt and back to the Hall of Lords. He hadn't even
managed to cross the threshold. He squared his shoulders.

Clutching a brightly burning torch, Ronin pushed his way through the cobwebs and into the hall. His footsteps echoed like small explosions in the vast stone chamber. He skirted a few pieces of moldy, forgotten furniture and followed the wall to the first portrait that had been etched in stone over one thousand years ago. The oldest likenesses were stone, painted with faded mixtures of herbs and clays. The more recent portraits were charcoal sketches and paintings.

The women in the portraits shared one striking characteristic. They were all breathtakingly radiant, positively brimming with happiness. The men shared a single distinction as well. All nine hundred and fifty-eight males in this hall had eyes of blue ice.

Ronin moved to the portrait of his wife and raised the torch. He smiled. Had some pagan deity offered him a bargain and said, "I will take away all the tragedy you have suffered in your life, I will take you back in time and give you dozens of sons and perfect peace, but you can never have Jolyn," Ronin McIllioch would have scoffed. He would willingly embrace every bit of tragedy he'd endured to have loved Jolyn, even for the painfully brief time they'd been allotted.

"I won't fail him this time, Jolyn. I swear to you, I will see Castle Maldebann secured and filled with promise again. Then we'll be together to smile down upon this place." After a long pause, he whispered fiercely, "I miss you, woman."

Outside the Hall of Lords, an astonished Gilles entered the connecting hallway and paused, eyeing the open door in disbelief. Rushing down the corridor, he burst into the long-sealed hall, barely suppressing a whoop of delight at the sight of Ronin, no longer stooped but standing proudly erect beneath a portrait of his wife and son. Ronin didn't turn, but Gilles hadn't expected him to; Ronin always knew who was in his immediate circumference.

"Have the maids set to cleaning, Gilles," Ronin commanded without taking his eyes off the portrait of his smiling wife. "Open this place up and air it out. I want the entire castle scrubbed as it hasna been since my Jolyn was alive. I want this place sparklin'." Ronin opened his arms expansively. "Light the torchères and henceforth keep them burnin' in here as they did years ago, day and night. My son is coming home," he finished proudly.

"*Yes*, milord!" Gilles exclaimed as he hastened off to obey a command he'd been waiting a lifetime to hear.

* * *

Where to now, Grimm Roderick? he wondered wearily. Back to Dalkeith to see if he might lure destruction to those blessed shores?

His hands fisted and he longed for a bottomless bottle of whisky, although he knew it wouldn't grant him the oblivion he sought. If a Berserker drank quickly enough, he might feel drunk for the sum total of about three seconds. That wouldn't work at all.

The McKane always found him eventually. He knew now that they must have had a spy in Durrkesh. Likely someone had seen the rage come over him in the courtyard of the tavern, then tried to poison him. The McKane had learned over the years to attack stealthily. Cunning traps or sheer numbers were the only possible ways to take a Berserker, and neither of them was foolproof. Now that he had escaped the McKane twice, he knew the next time they struck they would descend in force.

First they'd tried poison, then the fire at the stables.

Grimm knew if he had remained at Caithness they might have destroyed the entire castle, taking out all the St. Clair in their blind quest to kill him. He'd become acquainted with their unique fanaticism at an early age, and it was a lesson he'd never forgotten.

They'd blessedly lost track of him during the years he'd been in Edinburgh. The McKane were fighters, not royal arse-kissers, and they devoted little attention to the events at court. He'd hidden in plain sight. Then, when he'd moved from court to Dalkeith, he'd encountered few new people, and those he had met were abjectly loyal to Hawk. He'd started to relax his guard and begun to feel almost . . . normal.

What an intriguing, tantalizing word: normal. "Take it away, Odin. I was wrong," Grimm whispered. "I doona wish to be Berserk any longer."

But Odin didn't seem to care.

Grimm had to face the facts. Now that the McKane had found him again, they would tear the country apart looking for him. It wasn't safe for him to be near other people. It was time for a new name, perhaps a new country. His thoughts turned to England, but every ounce of Scot in him rebelled.

How could he live without ever touching Jillian again? Having experienced such joy, how could he resume his barren existence? Christ, it would have been better if he'd never known what his life might have been like! On that fateful night above Tuluth, at the foolish age of fourteen, he'd called a Berserker, begging for the gift of vengeance, never realizing how complete that vengeance would be. Vengeance didn't bring back the dead, it deadened the avenger.

But there was really little point in regret, he mocked

himself, for he owned the beast and the beast owned him, and it was that simple. Resignation blanketed him, and only one issue remained. *Where to now, Grimm Roderick?*

He nudged Occam to the only place left to go: in the forbidding Highlands he could disappear into the wilderness. He knew every empty hut and cave, every source of shelter from the bitter winter that would soon ice white caps around the mountains.

He would be so cold again.

Guiding Occam with his knees, he plaited war braids into his hair and wondered if an invincible Berserker could die from something so innocuous as a broken heart.

* * *

Jillian gazed sadly at the blackened lawn of Caithness. Everything was a reminder. It was November, and the hated lawn would be black until the first snowfall came to smother it. She couldn't step outside the castle without being forced to remember that night, the fire, Grimm leaving. The lawn sloped and rolled in a vast, never-ending carpet of black ash. All her flowers were gone. Grimm was gone.

He'd abandoned her because he was a coward.

She'd tried to make excuses for him, but there were none to be made. The most courageous man she'd ever known was afraid to love. *Well, to hell with him!* she thought defiantly.

She felt pain; she wouldn't deny it. The mere thought of living without him for the rest of her life was unbearable, but she refused to dwell on it. That would be the sure path to emotional collapse. So she stoked her anger against him, clutching it like a shield to her wounded heart.

"He's not coming back, lass," Ramsay said gently.

Jillian clenched her jaw and spun to face him. "I think I've figured that out, Ramsay," she said evenly.

Ramsay studied her in stalwart stance. When she moved to leave, his hand shot out and wrapped around her wrist. She tried to snatch it away, but he was too strong. "Marry me, Jillian. I swear to you, I'll treat you like a queen. I will never abandon you."

Not so long as there's coin in keeping me, she thought. "Let go of me," she hissed.

He didn't budge. "Jillian, consider your situation. Your parents will be back any day now and expect you to wed. They'll likely force you to choose when they return. I would be good to you," he promised.

"I will never wed," she said with absolute conviction.

His demeanor altered instantly. When his sneering gaze slid over her abdomen, she was shocked; when he spoke, she was rendered momentarily speechless.

"If a bastard quickens in your belly you may think differently, lass," he said with a smirk. "Then your parents will force you to wed, and you'll be counting your blessings if any decent man will have you. There's a name for women like you. You're not so pure," he spat.

"How dare you!" she cried. The instinct to slap the smirk from his face was overwhelming, and she acted upon it reflexively.

Ramsay's face whitened with rage, and the red welt from her blow stood out in stark relief. He caught her other wrist and pulled her close, bristling with anger. "You'll regret that one day, lass." He shoved her away so savagely, she stumbled. For an instant she saw something so brutal in his eyes that she feared he might force her to the ground and beat her, or worse. She scrambled to her feet and dashed for the castle on trembling legs.

* * *

"He's not coming back, Jillian," Kaley said gently.

"I know that! For God's sake, could everyone please just quit saying that to me? Do I look dense? Is that it?"

Kaley eyes filled with tears, and Jillian was instantly remorseful. "Oh, Kaley, I didn't mean to yell at you. I haven't been myself lately. It's just that I'm worried about . . . things . . ."

"Things like babies?" Kaley said carefully.

Jillian stiffened.

"Is it possible . . ." Kaley trailed off.

Jillian averted her gaze guiltily.

"Oh, lass." Kaley wrapped her in her ample embrace. "Oh, lass," she echoed helplessly.

* * *

Two weeks later, Gibraltar and Elizabeth St. Clair returned.

Jillian was torn by mixed emotions. She was elated to have them home, yet she dreaded seeing them, so she hid in her chambers and waited for them to come to her. And they did, but not until the next morning. In retrospect, she realized she'd been a fool to give her clever da any time to ferret out information before confronting her.

When the summons finally came, she shivered, and the last vestige of excitement at seeing her parents turned to pure dread. She dragged her feet all the way to the study.

* * *

"Mama! Da!" Jillian exclaimed. She vaulted into their arms, greedily snatching hugs before they could launch the interrogation she knew was coming.

"Jillian." Gibraltar terminated the hug so quickly, Jillian knew she was in dire straits indeed.

"How's Hugh? And my new nephew?" she asked brightly.

Gibraltar and Elizabeth exchanged glances, then Elizabeth sank into a chair near the fire, abandoning Jillian to deal with Gibraltar by herself.

"Have you chosen a husband yet, Jillian?" Gibraltar skirted all niceties.

Jillian drew a deep breath. "That's what I wished to speak with you about, Da. I've had a lot of time to think." She swallowed nervously as Gibraltar eyed her dispassionately. Dispassionate never boded well for her—it meant her da was furious. She cleared her throat anxiously. "I have decided, after much consideration, I mean, I've really thought this through . . . that I . . . um—" Jillian broke off. She had to stop warbling like an idiot—her da would never be swayed by tepid protests. "Da . . . I really don't plan to wed. *Ever.*" There, it was out. "I mean, I appreciate everything you and Mama have done for me, never think I don't, but marriage is just not for me." She punctuated her words with a confident nod.

Gibraltar regarded her with an unnerving mixture of amusement and condescension. "Nice try, Jillian. But I'm not playing games anymore. I brought three men here for you. Only two are left, and you will marry one of them. I've had it with your shenanigans. You're going to be twenty-two in a month, and either de Moncreiffe or Logan will make a perfectly good husband. There will be no more moping about and no crafty little ploys. *Which one will you wed?*" he demanded, a bit more forcefully than he'd intended.

"Gibraltar!" Elizabeth protested. She rose from her chair, ruffled by his high-handed tone.

"Stay out of this, Elizabeth. She's played me for a fool for the last time. Jillian will summon up one reason after another why she can't wed until we're both too old to do anything about it."

"Gibraltar, we will *not* force her to wed someone she doesn't want." Elizabeth stamped a dainty foot to punctuate her decree.

"She's going to have to accept the fact that she can't have the man she wants, Elizabeth. He was here and he left. And that's the end of the matter." Gibraltar sighed, eyeing his daughter's rigid back as she stood plucking at the folds of her gown. "Elizabeth, I tried. Don't you think I tried? I knew how Jillian felt about Grimm. But I won't force the man to wed her, and even if I did, what good would that do? Jillian doesn't want a forced husband."

"You knew I loved him?" Jillian exclaimed. She almost ran to him, but caught herself and stiffened further.

Gibraltar almost laughed; a broom handle couldn't have been more rigid than his daughter's spine. Stubborn just like her mother. "Of course, lass. I've seen it in your eyes for years. So I brought him here for you. And now Kaley tells me that he left a sennight ago and told you to marry Quinn. Jillian, he's gone. He's made his feelings clear." Gibraltar drew himself up. "I am not going to fling my daughter at some inconsiderate bastard who's too much a fool to see what kind of treasure he'd be getting. I will not gift my Jillian to a man who can't appreciate how rare a woman she is. What kind of father would I be to chase a man down and throw my daughter after him?"

Elizabeth sniffed, blinking back a tear. "You brought him because you knew she loved him," she cooed. "Oh,

Gibraltar! Even though I didn't think he was right for her, you saw through it all. You knew what Jillian wanted."

Gibraltar's pleasure at his wife's adoration quickly evaporated when Jillian's shoulders slumped in defeat.

"I never knew you knew how I felt, Da," Jillian said in a small voice.

"Of course I did. Just as I know how you feel now. But you have to face the facts. He left, Jillian—"

"I know he left! *Must* you all keep reminding me?"

"Yes, if you persist in trying to fritter your life away. I gave him the chance, and he was too much a fool to take it. You must move on with your life, lass."

"He didn't think he was good enough for me," Jillian murmured.

"Is that what he said?" Elizabeth asked quickly.

Jillian blew a tendril of hair from her face. "Sort of. He said that I couldn't possibly understand what would happen if he married me. And he's right. Whatever terrible thing he thinks it is, I can't even begin to guess. He acts like there's some dreadful secret about him, and Mama, I can't convince him otherwise. I can't even begin to imagine what horrible thing he thinks is wrong with him. Grimm Roderick is the best man I've ever known, except for you, Da." Jillian smiled weakly at her father before crossing to the window to stare out at the blackened lawn.

Gibraltar's eyes narrowed and he gazed thoughtfully at Elizabeth, who had raised her eyebrows in surprise.

She still doesn't know. Tell her, Elizabeth mouthed, shooting a glance at her daughter's stiff back.

That he's a Berserker? Gibraltar mouthed back, disbelieving. *He must tell her himself.*

He can't. He's not here!

He refuses. And I won't fix it for him. If he can't bring

himself to trust her, she shouldn't marry him. He's obviously not man enough for my Jillian.

Our *Jillian*.

He shrugged. Crossing the study, he cupped Jillian's shoulders with comforting hands. "I'm sorry, Jillian. I truly am. I thought maybe he'd changed over the years. But he hasn't. Still, it doesn't alter that fact that you must wed. I'd like it to be Quinn."

She stiffened and hissed softly. "I am not marrying anyone."

"Yes, you are," Gibraltar enunciated sternly. "I am posting the banns tomorrow, and in three weeks' time you are going to marry *someone*."

Jillian whirled around to face him, her eyes flashing. "You should know I became his lover."

Elizabeth fanned herself furiously.

Gibraltar shrugged.

Elizabeth gaped, first at Jillian, then at her unresponsive husband.

"That's all? A shrug?" Jillian blinked at her father disbelievingly. "Well, while you may not care, I hardly think my husband-to-be would cheerily accept it, do you, Da?"

"I wouldn't mind," Quinn said quietly, startling them all with his unannounced presence. "I'd marry you on any terms, Jillian."

All eyes flew to Quinn de Moncreiffe, whose broad golden frame filled the doorway.

"Good man," Gibraltar said firmly.

"Oh, Quinn!" Jillian said sadly. "You deserve better . . ."

"I've told you as much before, lass. I'll take you on any terms. Grimm's a fool, but I'm not. I'll marry you happily. No regrets. I've never understood why a woman's supposed to be untouched when a man's expected to be as touched as possible."

"Then it's settled," Gibraltar concluded quickly.

"No, it's not!"

"Yes, it is, Jillian," Gibraltar said sternly. "You will marry in three weeks. Period. End of conversation." He turned away.

"You can't do this to me!"

"Wait." Ramsay Logan stepped into the doorway behind Quinn. "I'd like to offer for her too."

Gibraltar assessed the two men in the doorway and slowly turned his regard to his daughter, who stood, mouth ajar.

"You have twelve hours to choose, Jillian. I post the banns at dawn."

"Mama, you can't let him do this!" Jillian wailed.

Elizabeth St. Clair drew herself erect and sniffed before following Gibraltar from the study.

* * *

"What on earth do you think you're doing now, Gibraltar?" Elizabeth demanded.

Gibraltar leaned back, resting on the sill of the window in their bedroom, the hair on his chest glinting gold between the folds of his silk robe in the soft glow of the firelight.

Elizabeth reclined on the bed nude and, Gibraltar marveled, breathtaking. "By Odin's spear, woman, you know I can refuse you nothing when I see you like that."

"Then don't make Jillian wed, love," Elizabeth said simply. There were no games between her and her husband, and there never had been. Elizabeth firmly believed most problems in a relationship could be cleared up or avoided entirely by clear, concise communication. Games invited unnecessary discord.

"I don't plan to," Gibraltar replied with a faint smile. "It will never go that far."

"Whatever do you mean?" Elizabeth removed the pins from her hair, allowing it to cascade in golden waves over her bare breasts. "Is this another one of your infamous plans, Gibraltar?" she asked with lazy amusement.

"Yes." He sank to the edge of the bed beside her. He ran his hand down the smooth shape of her side, contouring the lovely indentation of her waist, soaring over the lush curve of her hip. "If she hadn't admitted that she'd become his lover, I might not have felt so confident. But he's a Berserker, Elizabeth. There is only one true mate for each Berserker, and they know it. He cannot allow the wedding to take place. A Berserker would die first."

Elizabeth's eyes brightened, and understanding penetrated her sensual languor. "You're posting the banns to antagonize him. Because it's the most effective way to force him to declare himself."

"As always, we understand each other perfectly, don't we, my dear? What better way to bring him back at a run?"

"How clever. I hadn't thought of that. There's no way a Berserker would allow his mate to wed another."

"Let's just hope all the legends about those warriors are true, Elizabeth. Gavrael's da told me years ago that once a Berserker makes love with his own true mate, he can no longer mate another woman. Gavrael is even more Berserk than his da. He'll come for her, and when he does, he'll have no choice but to tell her the truth. We'll get our wedding in three weeks, no doubt about it, and it will be to the man she wants—Grimm."

"What about Quinn's feelings?"

"Quinn doesn't really believe she'll marry him. He is also of the opinion that Grimm will come. I spoke with Quinn before I made Jillian choose, and he agreed to do this. Although I must admit, Ramsay certainly surprised me with his offer."

"You mean you had this all planned out before you confronted her?" Elizabeth was amazed once again by the twists and turns of her husband's brilliant scheming mind.

"It was one of several possible plans," Gibraltar corrected. "A man must anticipate every possibility when the women he loves are concerned."

"My hero." Elizabeth fluttered her eyelashes.

Gibraltar covered her body with his. "I'll show you a hero," he growled.

* * *

Gibraltar hadn't thought that even his cosseted Jillian could pout, sulk, and be nasty for three solid weeks.

She could.

Ever since the morning she'd slipped a note bearing one word, "Quinn," under her parents' bedroom door, she'd refused to speak to him in anything but single-word replies. Everyone else in the castle she harangued with the same questions: how many banns had been posted, when, and where.

"Were they posted in Durrkesh, Kaley?" Jillian fretted.

"Yes, Jillian."

"What about Scurrington and Edinburgh?"

"Yes, Jillian." Hatchard sighed, knowing it was futile to remind her he'd answered the same question the day before.

"And the smaller villages in the Highlands? When were they posted there?"

"Days ago, Jillian." Gibraltar interrupted her interrogation. Jillian sniffed and turned her back on her da.

"Why do you care where the banns have been posted?" Gibraltar provoked.

"Just curious," Jillian said lightly as she strode regally from the room.

* * *

"He'll come, Mama. I know he will."

Elizabeth smiled and smoothed Jillian's hair, but weeks passed and Grimm didn't come.

Even Quinn started to get a little nervous.

* * *

"What will we do if he doesn't show?" Quinn asked. He paced the study, moving his long legs silently. The wedding was tomorrow and no one had heard a word from Grimm Roderick.

Gibraltar poured them both a drink. "He has to come."

Quinn picked up the goblet and sipped thoughtfully. "He must know the wedding is tomorrow. The only way he could possibly not know is if he is no longer in Scotland. We posted those blasted banns in every village of over fivescore inhabitants."

Gibraltar and Quinn stared at the fire and drank for a time in silence.

"If he doesn't come, I'll go through with it."

"Now, why would you be doing that, lad?" Gibraltar asked gently.

Quinn shrugged. "I love her. I always have."

Gibraltar shook his head. "There's love and then there's

love, Quinn. And if you're not ready to kill Grimm simply for touching Jillian, then it's not the marrying kind of love you're feeling. She's not for you."

When Quinn made no reply, Gibraltar laughed aloud and slapped him on the thigh. "Oh, she's *definitely* not for you. You didn't even argue with me."

"Grimm said something very similar. He asked me if I *really* loved her—if she made me crazy inside."

Gibraltar smiled knowingly. "That's because she *does* make him crazy inside."

"I want her to be happy, Gibraltar," Quinn said fervently. "Jillian is special. She's generous and beautiful and so . . . och, so damned in love with *Grimm*!"

Gibraltar raised his goblet to Quinn's and smiled. "That she is. If push comes to shove, I'll stop the ceremony and give her a choice. But I won't let her marry you without giving her that choice." As he drank, he regarded Quinn thoughtfully. "Actually, I'm not sure I'd let her marry you even then."

"You wound me," Quinn protested.

"She's my baby girl, Quinn. I want love for her. Real love. The kind that makes a man crazy inside."

* * *

Jillian curled into a ball on the window ledge of the drum tower and stared, unseeing, into the night. Thousands of stars dimpled the sky, but she saw none of them. Staring into the night was like staring into a great vacuum—her future without Grimm.

How could she wed Quinn?

How could she refuse? Grimm obviously wasn't coming.

The banns had been posted throughout the country. There was absolutely no way he could *not* know that tomorrow Jillian St. Clair was going to wed Quinn de Moncreiffe. The whole blasted country knew it.

Three weeks ago she might have run away.

But not tonight, not three weeks late for her monthly flow, not with no word from Grimm. Not after believing in him and being proven a lovesick fool.

Jillian rested her palm on her stomach. It was possible she was pregnant, but she wasn't absolutely certain. Her monthly flow had often been irregular and she had been later than this in the past. Mama had told her that many things besides pregnancy could affect a woman's courses: emotional turmoil . . . or a woman's own devout wish that she was pregnant.

Was that it? Did she so long to be pregnant with Grimm Roderick's child that she'd fooled herself? Or was there truly a baby growing inside her? How she wished she knew for certain. She drew a deep breath and expelled it slowly. Only time would tell.

She'd considered striking out on her own, tracking him down, and fighting for their love, but a defiant shred of pride coupled with good common sense made her refuse. Grimm was in the thick of a battle with himself, and it was a battle *he* had to win or lose. She'd offered her love, told him she would accept any kind of life as long as they lived it together. A woman shouldn't have to fight the man she loved for his love. He had to choose to give it freely, to learn that love was the one thing in this world that *wasn't* frightening.

He was an intelligent man and a brave one. He would come.

Jillian sighed. God forgive her, but she still believed.

He *would* come.

CHAPTER 23

HE DIDN'T COME.

The day of her wedding dawned cloudy and cold. Sleet started falling at dawn, coating the charred lawn with a layer of crunchy black ice.

Jillian stayed in bed, listening to the sounds of the castle preparing for the wedding feast. Her stomach rumbled a welcome to the scents of roasting ham and pheasant. It was a feast to wake the dead, and it worked; she stumbled from the bed and groped her way through the dimly lit room to the mirror. She stared at her reflection. Dark shadows marred the delicate skin where her cheekbones met her tilted amber eyes.

She would marry Quinn de Moncreiffe in less than six hours.

The rumble of voices carried clearly into her chambers; half the county was in residence, and had been since yesterday. Four hundred guests had been invited and five hundred had arrived, crowding the massive castle and spilling over into less accommodating lodgings in the nearby village.

Five hundred people, more than she would ever have at her funeral, tramping around the frozen black lawn.

Jillian squeezed her eyes tightly shut and refused to cry, certain she'd weep blood if she allowed even one more tear to fall.

* * *

At eleven o'clock Elizabeth St. Clair dabbed prettily at her tears with a dainty hanky. "You look lovely, Jillian," she said with a heartfelt sigh. "Even more so than I did."

"You don't think the bags under my eyes detract, Mama?" Jillian asked acerbically. "How about the grim set of my mouth? My shoulders droop and my nose is beet red from crying. You don't think anyone will find my appearance a bit suspect?"

Elizabeth sniffed, plunked a headpiece on Jillian's hair, and tugged a thin fall of sheer blue gossamer over her daughter's face. "Your da thinks of everything," she said with a shrug.

"A veil? Really, Mama. No one wears a veil in these modern times."

"Just think of it, you'll start a new fashion. By the end of the year, everyone will be wearing them again," Elizabeth chirped.

"How can he do this to me, Mama? Knowing the kind of love you and he share, how can he justify condemning me to a loveless marriage?"

"Quinn does love you, so it won't be loveless."

"It will be on my part."

Elizabeth perched on the edge of the bed. She studied the floor a moment, then raised her eyes to Jillian's.

"You do care," Jillian said, somewhat mollified by the sympathy in Elizabeth's gaze.

"Of course I care, Jillian. I'm your mother." Elizabeth regarded her a pensive moment. "Darling, don't fret, your da has a plan. I hadn't intended to tell you this, but he doesn't plan to make you go through with it. He thinks Grimm will come."

Jillian snorted. "So did I, Mama. But it's ten minutes to the hour and there's no sign of the man. What's Da going to do? Halt the wedding in the middle if he doesn't show up? In front of five hundred guests?"

"You know your da has never been afraid of making a spectacle of himself—or of anyone else, for that matter. The man abducted me from my wedding. I do believe he's hoping the same will happen to you."

Jillian smiled faintly. The story of her mama's "courtship" by her da had enthralled her since she'd been a child. Her da was a man who could give Grimm lessons. Grimm Roderick shouldn't be battling himself about her, he should be battling the world *for* her. Jillian drew a deep breath, hoping against hope, imagining such a scene for herself.

* * *

"We are gathered here today in the company of family, friends, and well-wishers to unite this man and woman in the holy, unbreakable bonds. . . ."

Jillian blew furiously at her veil. Although it puffed a bit, it didn't clear her view. The preacher was slightly blue, Quinn was slightly blue. Irritably she plucked at the veil. No rose-colored hues for her on her wedding day, and why should there be? Outside the tall windows, sleet fell in vaguely blue sheets.

She stole a glance at Quinn, who stood at her side. She
was eye level with his chest. Despite her despair, she conceded he was a magnificent man. Regally clad in ceremonial tartan, he'd pulled his long hair back from his chiseled
face. Most women would be thrilled to be standing beside
him, saying the vows of a lifetime, accompanying him to
be mistress of his estate, to give him bonny blond bairns
and live in splendor for the rest of their days.

But he was the wrong man. *He'll come for me, he'll
come for me, I know he will,* Jillian repeated silently as if it
were a magic spell she could weave from the fibers of sheer
redundancy.

* * *

Grimm plucked another bann from the wall of a church as
he sped by. He crumpled it and crammed it in a satchel that
was overflowing with balled-up parchment. He'd been in
the tiny highland village of Tummas when he'd seen the
first bann, nailed to the side of a ramshackle bothy. Twenty
paces beyond it he'd found the second, then the third and
the fourth.

Jillian St. Clair was marrying Quinn de Moncreiffe.
He'd cursed furiously. How long had she waited? Two days?
He hadn't slept that night, consumed by a rage so violent
that it had threatened to release the Berserker without any
bloodshed to bring it on.

The rage had only intensified, goading him to Occam's
back, sending him in circles around the Highlands. He'd
ridden to the edge of Caithness, turned around, and come
back, ripping down banns all the way, ranging like a mad-
dened beast from Lowland to Highland. Then he turned
around again, compelled to Caithness by a force beyond
his understanding, a force that reached into the very mar-

row of his bones. Grimm tossed his braids out of his face and growled. In the forest nearby, a wolf responded with a mournful howl.

He'd had the dream again last night. The one in which Jillian watched him turn Berserk. The one in which she laid her palm against his chest and looked into his eyes and they connected—Jillian and the beast. In his dream, Grimm had realized the beast loved Jillian as deeply as the man, and was just as incapable of ever harming her. In the light of day, he no longer feared that he might hurt Jillian, not even with the threat of his da's madness. He knew himself well enough to know that not even in the wildest throes of Berserkergang could he harm her.

But in his dream, as Jillian had searched his blazing, unholy eyes, fear and revulsion had marked her lovely features. She'd extended a hand palm out to stay him, begging him to go far away as quickly as Occam could carry him.

The Berserker had made a pathetic sound while the man's heart slowly iced over, cooler than the ice-blue eyes that had witnessed so much loss. In his dream, he'd fled for the cover of darkness to hide from her horrified gaze.

Once Quinn had asked him what could kill a Berserker, and now he knew.

A thing so slight as the look on Jillian's face.

He'd woken from the dream filled with despair. Today was Jillian's wedding, and if dreams were portents, she would never forgive him for what he was about to do should she ever uncover his true nature.

But need she ever know?

He would hide the Berserker inside him forever if necessary. He would never again save anyone, never fight, never view blood; he would never reveal himself. He would live as a mere man. They would stop at Dalkeith, where the

Hawk stored a considerable fortune for Grimm, and, with enough gold to buy her a castle in any country, they would flee far from the treacherous McKane and those who knew his secret.

If she would still have him.

He knew what he was about to do was not the honorable thing, but truth be told, he no longer cared. God forgive him—he was a Berserker who likely suffered his da's madness somewhere in his veins, but he could not stand by and permit Jillian St. Clair to wed another man while he still lived and breathed.

Now he understood what she'd known instinctively, years ago, the day he'd stepped out of the woods and stood looking down at her.

Jillian St. Clair was his.

* * *

The hour was approaching noon and he was no more than three miles from Caithness when he was ambushed.

CHAPTER 24

YE GODS! JILLIAN DRIFTED BACK FROM HER WANDERING thoughts, alarmed. The pudgy priest was almost to the "I do" part. Jillian craned her neck, searching frantically for her father, with no success. The Greathall was crammed to overflowing; guests angled up the staircase, hung over the balustrade, and were stuffed into every nook and cranny.

Fear gripped her. What if her mother had made up the story of her father's plan merely as a ruse to get her to stand up in front of the crowd? What if her mama had deliberately lied, wagering that once they got to the vows, Jillian wouldn't have the nerve to dishonor her parents and Quinn, not to mention herself, by refusing to wed him?

"If there are any here today who know some reason why these two should remain separate, speak now or forever haud yer wheesht."

The hall was silent.

The pause stretched over the length of several heartbeats.

As it lengthened intolerably into minutes, people began to yawn, shuffle their feet, and stretch impatiently.

Silence.

Jillian puffed at her veil and peeked at Quinn. He stood ramrod straight beside her, his hands clasped. She whispered his name, but either he didn't hear or he refused to acknowledge it. She peered at the priest, who seemed to have fallen into a trance, gazing at the bound volume in his hands.

What on earth was going on? She tapped her foot and waited for her da to say something to bring this debacle to a screeching halt.

"I said, if there are any here who see some reason . . ." the priest intoned dramatically.

More silence.

Jillian's nerves stretched to breaking. What was she doing? If her da wouldn't rescue her, to hell with him. She refused to be cowed by fear of scandal. She was her father's daughter, by God, and he'd never genuflected to the false idol of propriety. She puffed at her veil, flipped it back impatiently, and scowled at the priest. "Oh, for goodness' sake—"

"Don't get snippy with me, missy," the priest snapped. "I'm just doing my job."

Jillian's courage was momentarily quaffed by his unexpected rebuke.

Quinn caught her hand in his. "Is something wrong, Jillian? Are you feeling unwell? Your face is flushed." His gaze was full of concern and . . . sympathy?

"I—*can't marry you*" is what she started to say when the doors to the Greathall burst open, crushing several unsuspecting people against the wall. Her words were swallowed in the din of indignant squeals and yelps.

All eyes flew to the entrance.

A great gray stallion reared up in the doorway, its breath frosting the air with puffs of steam. It was a scene from every fairy-tale romance she'd ever read: the handsome prince bursting into the castle astride a magnificent stallion, ablaze with desire and honor as he'd declared his undying love before all and sundry. Her heart swelled with joy.

Then her brow puckered as she scrutinized her "prince." Well, it was almost like a fairy tale. Except this prince was dressed in nothing but a drenched and muddy tartan with blood on his face and hands and war braids plaited at his temples. Although determination glittered in his gaze, a declaration of undying love didn't appear to be his first priority.

"Jillian!" he roared.

Her knees buckled. His voice brought her violently to life. Everything in the room receded and there was only Grimm, blue eyes blazing, his massive frame filling the doorway. He was majestic, towering, and ruthless. *Here* was her fierce warrior ready to battle the world to gain her love.

He urged Occam into the crowd, making his way toward the altar.

"Grimm," she whispered.

He drew up beside her. Sliding from Occam's back, he dropped to the floor next to the bride and groom. He looked at Quinn. The two men gazed at each other a tense moment, then Quinn inclined his head the merest fraction and stepped back a pace. The Greathall hushed as five hundred guests stood riveted by the unfolding spectacle.

Grimm was at a sudden loss for words. Jillian was so beautiful, a goddess clad in shimmering satin. He was covered with blood, mud-stained and filthy, while behind them stood the incomparable Quinn, impeccably attired, titled and noble—Quinn, who had all he lacked.

The blood on his hands was a relentless reminder that despite his fervent vows to conceal the Berserker, the McKane would always be there. They'd been lying in wait for him today. What if they attacked when he was traveling with Jillian? Four had escaped him. The others were dead. But those four were trouble enough—they would round up more men and continue hunting Grimm until either the last McKane was dead, or he was. Along with anyone traveling with him.

What could he hope to accomplish by taking her now? What fool's dream had possessed him to come here today? What desperate hope had convinced him he might be able to hide his true nature from her? And how would he survive the look on her face when she saw him for what he really was? "I'm a bloody fool," he muttered.

A smile curved Jillian's lip. "Yes, that you've been on more than one occasion, Grimm Roderick. You were most foolish when you left me, but I do believe I might forgive you now that you've come back."

Grimm sucked in a harsh breath. Berserker be damned, he had to have her.

"Will you come with me, Jillian?" *Say yes, woman,* he prayed.

A simple nod was her immediate response.

His chest swelled with unexpected emotion. "I'm sorry, Quinn," Grimm said. He wanted to say more, but Quinn shook his head, leaned close, and whispered something in Grimm's ear. Grimm's jaw tensed, and they stared at each other in silence. Finally Grimm nodded.

"Then you go with my blessing," Quinn said clearly.

Grimm extended his arms to Jillian, who slipped into his embrace. Before he could succumb to the urge to kiss her senseless, he tossed her on Occam's back and mounted behind her.

Jillian scanned the worried faces around her. Ramsay was gazing at Grimm with a shocking amount of hatred in his eyes, and she was momentarily flustered by the intensity of it. Quinn's expression was a blend of concern and reluctant understanding. She finally spotted her da where he stood with her mother a dozen feet away. Elizabeth's face was grim. Gibraltar held her gaze a moment, then nodded encouragingly.

Jillian leaned back into Grimm's broad chest and gave a small sigh of pleasure. "I would live any kind of life I had to live, so long as I lived it with you, Grimm Roderick."

It was all he needed to hear. His arms tightened around her waist, he kneed Occam forward and together they fled Caithness.

✳ ✳ ✳

"Now that's my idea of how a man takes a woman to wife," Gibraltar observed with satisfaction.

AN ILLYOCH PROPHECY

*L*egend tells that the Clan Illyoch will prosper for one thousand years, birthing warriors who will accomplish great good for Alba.

In the fertile vale of Tuluth a castle shall rise around the Hall of Gods and many shall covet what belongs to Scotia's blessed race.

The seers warn that an envious clan shall pursue the Illyoch until they are but three. The three will be scattered like seeds uprooted by the wind of betrayal, cast far and wide, and all will appear to be lost. Much grief and despair will descend upon the holy vale.

But harken to hope, sons of Odin, for the three shall be gathered by his far-reaching grasp. When the young Illyoch finds his true mate, she shall bring him home, the enemy shall be vanquished, and the Illyoch shall thrive for a thousand years more.

CHAPTER 25

THEY RODE HARD UNTIL EARLY EVENING, WHEN GRIMM drew Occam to a stop in a copse of trees. Upon leaving Caithness, he'd tugged a plaid from his pack and secured it tightly around Jillian's body, forming a nearly waterproof barrier between her and the elements.

He hadn't uttered a word since then. His face had been so grim that she'd kept her silence, allowing him time and privacy to muddle through his thoughts. She'd nestled back against him, contentedly savoring the press of his hard body against hers. Grimm Roderick had come for her. While such an inauspicious beginning might not be the perfect way to start a life together, it would do. For Grimm Roderick to steal a woman from her wedding, he must intend to care for her the rest of her life, and that's all she'd ever desired—a life with him.

By the time he drew Occam to a halt, the freezing rain had abated but the temperature had plummeted. Winter was encroaching, and she suspected they were headed directly for the Highlands, where the chill winds gusted with twice the vigor as in the Lowlands. She clutched the plaid snugly around her, sealing out the cold air.

Grimm dismounted, lowered her from the saddle, and held her for a moment. "God, I missed you, Jillian." The words exploded from him.

She tossed her head, delighted. "What took you so long, Grimm?"

His expression was impossible to interpret. He glanced self-consciously at his hands, which were badly in need of a washing. He busied himself with a flagon of water and a scrap of clean plaid for a moment, removing the worst of the stains. "I had a wee bit of a skirmish on the way and . . ." he mumbled inaudibly.

She studied his disheveled clothing but decided not to ask him about it then. The mud and blood appeared to be from a recent fight, but what had happened in the last few days wasn't her first concern. "That's not what I meant. It took you over a month. Was it so difficult for you to decide if you wanted me?" She forced a teasing smile to camouflage the wounded part of her that was utterly serious.

"Never think that, Jillian. I wake up wanting you. I fall asleep wanting you. I watch a magnificent sunrise and can think only of sharing it with you. I glimpse a piece of amber and see your eyes. Jillian, I've caught a disease, and the fever abates only when I'm near you."

She flashed him a radiant smile. "You're nearly forgiven. So tell me—what took you so long? Is it that you think you're not good enough for me, Grimm Roderick? Because you're not titled, I mean." When he didn't respond, she hastened to reassure him. "I don't care, you know. A title doesn't make the man, and you're certainly the finest man that I've ever known. What on earth do you think is wrong with you?"

His stubborn silence didn't serve as the deterrent he intended; she scurried down an alternate route of inquiry. "Quinn told me that you think your father is mad and you're afraid you've inherited the madness. He said it was nonsense and I must tell you I agree, because you're the most intelligent man I've ever met—except for the times when you don't trust me, which evidences a glaring lapse in your customary good judgment."

Grimm stared at her, disconcerted. "What else did Quinn tell you?"

"That you love me," she said simply.

He swept her into his embrace in one swift move. He buried his hands in her hair and kissed her urgently. She savored the rock-hard press of his body against hers, his teasing tongue, his strong hands cupping her face. Jillian melted against him, wordlessly demanding more. The past month without him, followed by hours pressed against his muscled body as they'd ridden, had begun a slow burn of desire within her. For the past hour, her skin had tingled at every point of contact with his body, and a trembling heat had gathered in her midsection, seeping lower, awakening shockingly intense feelings of desire. She'd been oblivious to the terrain, her mind fully occupied with imagining, in blush-inducing detail, the many different ways she wanted to make love with him.

Now she practically vibrated with need, and she responded wildly to his kiss. Her body was already prepared for him, and she pressed encouragingly against his hips.

He stopped kissing her as suddenly as he'd begun. "We must continue riding," he said tightly. "We have a long way to go, lass. I doona wish to keep you out here in the cold any longer than I must."

He pulled away so abruptly that Jillian gaped at him and nearly screamed with frustration. She was so heated from his kiss that the chill air was inconsequential, and she certainly had no intention of waiting even a moment longer to make love with him again.

She let her eyes flutter slowly closed and swayed a bit. Grimm eyed her intently. "Are you feeling all right, lass?"

"No," Jillian replied, casting him a sidelong glance beneath her lowered lashes. "Frankly, I feel decidedly odd, Grimm, and I don't know what to make of it."

He moved back to her side instantly, and she prepared to spring her trap.

"Where do you feel odd, Jillian? Have I—"

"Here." She swiftly took his hand and placed it on her breast. "And here." She guided his other hand to her hips.

Grimm took several deep breaths and blew them out, willing his thundering heart to slow, to quit pumping so much blood to his loins and perhaps let his brain in on the bargain so he might entertain a coherent thought. "Jillian," he said, exhaling a frustrated breath.

"Well, my," she said mischievously, moving her hands over his body. "You seem to be suffering the same ailment." Her hand closed over him through his plaid, and he made a low, growling sound deep in his throat.

They both spoke at once.

"It's freezing out here, lass. I won't subject you—"

"I'm not—"

"—to the cold for my own selfish needs—"

"—fragile, Grimm. And what about *my* selfish needs?"

"—and I can't make love to you properly outside!"

"Oh, and is *properly* the only way you've ever wanted me?" she mocked.

His gaze locked with hers, and his eyes darkened with desire. He seemed immobilized, obtusely assessing the cold, considering all of her needs—except for the one that really mattered.

In a low voice she said, "Do it. Take me. *Now.*"

His eyes narrowed and he sucked in a harsh breath. *"Jillian."* A storm gathered in his ice-blue eyes, and she wondered for a moment what she'd called forth. A beast—*her* beast. And she wanted him exactly the way he was.

The force of his passion hit her like a sea gale, hot and salty and primitive in its power, holding nothing back. They exploded against each other, driving their bodies as close together as they could. He backed her against a tree, thrust her gown up, and pushed his plaid aside, all the while kissing her eyelids, her nose, her lips, plunging his tongue so deeply into her mouth that she felt herself drowning in the man's sensuality.

"I need you, Jillian St. Clair. Ever since I tossed you up on my horse I've been wanting nothing more than to drag you back off it and bury myself in you, without a word of explanation or apology—because I need you."

"Yes," she whispered fervently. *"That's* what I want!"

With a swift stroke he plunged deeply into her, but the storm was in her body and it raged with the devastating fury of a hurricane.

She tossed her head back and freed her voice, crying out to him, only the creatures of the wilderness to hear. She moved against him urgently, her hips rising to meet every thrust. Her hands clawed at his shoulders and she raised her legs, wrapping them tightly around his waist, locking her ankles over his muscled hips. With each thrust he pressed her back against the tree trunk and she used it to rock herself back into him, taking him as deeply into her body as she could. Only the sounds of passion escaped their lips; words simply weren't needed. Bonding and pledging through contact, their bodies spoke in a tongue ancient and unmistakable.

"Jillian!" he roared as he exploded inside her. An unfettered laugh of delight escaped her as the rush of his liquid warmth inside her pushed her over the edge of pleasure, and she bucked against him.

They held on to each other for a reverent moment. Leaning against her in a soft crush, he seemed reluctant to move, as if he wanted to stay joined to her forever. And when he began to stiffen inside her, she knew she'd convinced him that a little cold air was good for the soul.

* * *

Grimm whistled for Occam. Summoning his horse from the woods, he tightened the tethers on the packs. It was full dark, and they needed to be on their way. There was no shelter to be secured tonight, but by the following day they would be far enough into the Highlands that he could provide shelter for them each night to come. He glanced over his shoulder at Jillian. It was imperative to him that he keep her happy, warm, and safe. "Are you hungry, Jillian? Are you dry enough? Warm enough?"

"No, yes, and yes. Where are we going, Grimm?" she asked, still feeling dreamy from their intense lovemaking.

"There's an abandoned cottage a day's ride from here."

"I didn't mean now, I meant where are you taking me after that?"

Grimm pondered his answer. He'd originally planned to ride directly to Dalkeith, then leave as soon as they'd gathered his fortune and loaded the horses. But he'd begun to think running might not be necessary. He'd spent much of their time on the ride from Caithness mulling over something Quinn had said. *Hell, man, rouse an army and fight the McKane once and for all. I know scores of men who would fight for you. I would.* As would the Hawk's army, as well as many of the men he'd known at court, men who fought for hire.

Grimm loathed the idea of taking Jillian away from Scotland, from her family. He knew what it was like to be without a clan. If he triumphed over the McKane, he could purchase an estate near her family and have only one demon to battle. He could devote his energy to concealing his nature and making Jillian a fine husband.

Promise me you'll tell her the truth, Quinn had demanded in a low, urgent whisper against his ear.

Grimm had nodded.

But he hadn't said when, he prevaricated lamely as he studied her innocent features. Maybe next year, or a lifetime from now. In the meantime, he had other battles to wage.

"Dalkeith. My good friend and his wife are laird and lady there. You'll be safe with them."

Jillian snapped to attention, dreamy reverie squashed by the thought of an impending separation. "What do you mean, I will be safe there? Don't you mean *we* will be safe there?"

Grimm fidgeted with Occam's saddle.

"Grimm—*we,* right?"

He muttered, deliberately incoherent.

Jillian eyed him a moment and snorted delicately.

"Grimm, you don't plan to take me to Dalkeith and leave me there by myself, do you?" Her eyes narrowed, forecasting a tempest if such was his intention.

Without raising his head from an intent inspection of Occam's tethers, he replied, "Only for a time, Jillian. There's something I must do, and I need to know you'll be safe while I'm doing it."

Jillian watched him fidget and considered her options. "His good friend and his wife," he'd said, people who would know something about her man of mystery. That was promising, if not her preference. She wished he would confide in her, tell her what kept him solitary, but she would work with what she could get. Maybe what had happened in his past was too painful for him to discuss. "Where is Dalkeith?"

"In the Highlands."

"Near where you were born?"

"Past there. We have to circle around Tuluth to get to Dalkeith."

"Why circle around it? Why not ride through it?" Jillian fished.

"Because I've never gone back to Tuluth and I doona plan to now. Besides, the village was destroyed."

"Well, if it was destroyed, that makes it even odder to ride around it. Why avoid nothing?"

Grimm raised a brow. "Must you always be so logical?"

"Must you always be so evasive?" she countered, arching a brow of her own.

"I just doona wish to ride through it, all right?"

"Are you certain it's in ruins?"

When Grimm buried a hand in his hair, Jillian finally understood. The only time Grimm Roderick started messing with his hair was when she asked him a question he didn't want to answer. She almost laughed; if she continued questioning him he might rip it out by the handfuls. But she needed answers, and occasionally her digging resulted in a few treasures. What could possibly make him avoid Tuluth like the darkest plague? "Oh, my goodness," she breathed as intuition pointed an unerring finger toward the truth. "Your family is still alive, aren't they, Grimm?"

Ice-blue eyes flew to hers, and she watched him struggle to avoid her question. He toyed with his war braids and she bit her lip, waiting.

"My da is still alive," he conceded.

Although she'd already arrived at such a conclusion herself, his admission threw her off balance. "What else didn't you tell me, Grimm?"

"That Quinn told you the truth. He's an insane old man," Grimm said bitterly.

"Truly insane, or do you mean you just disagree about things, like most people do with their parents?"

"I doona wish to talk about it."

"How old is your da? Have you other family I don't know about?"

Grimm walked away and started pacing. "No."

"Well, what is your home like? In Tuluth."

"It's not in Tuluth," he said through set teeth. "My home was in a bleak, dreary castle carved into the mountain above Tuluth."

Jillian wondered what other astonishing things might be revealed if he kept answering her questions. "If your home was in the castle, then you must be either a servant—" She eyed him from head to toe and shook her head as comprehension crashed over her. "Oh! Here I am prattling on about titles and you don't even say anything! You're a chieftain's son, aren't you? You wouldn't, by chance, be his oldest son, would you?" she asked, mostly in jest. When he quickly averted his gaze, she exclaimed, "You mean you'll be the laird one day? There's a clan awaiting your return?"

"Never. I will never return to Tuluth, and that's the end of this discussion. My da is a batty old bastard and the castle is in ruins. Along with the village, half my clan was destroyed years ago, and I'm certain the remaining half scattered to escape the old man and rebuild elsewhere. I doubt there's anyone left in Tuluth at all—it's likely nothing but ruins." He stole a surreptitious glance at Jillian to see how she was taking his confession.

Jillian's mind was whirling. Something didn't make sense, and she knew she was lacking vital information. Grimm's childhood home lay between here and their destination, and answers lay in the moldering old ruin. A "batty old da" and insight that would show her the way to Grimm's deepest heart.

"Why did you leave?" she asked gently.

He faced her, his blue eyes glittering in the fading light. "Jillian, please. Not so many questions at once. Give me time. These things . . . I haven't spoken of them since they happened." His eyes wordlessly pleaded with her for patience and understanding.

"Time, I can give. I'll be patient, but I won't give up."

"Promise me that." He was suddenly grave. "Promise me you'll never give up, no matter what."

"On you? I wouldn't. Goodness, as mean as you were to me when I was a wee lass, I still didn't give up on you," she said lightly, hoping to brighten his somber expression.

"On *us*, Jillian. Promise me you'll never give up on us." He tugged her back into his arms and gazed down at her so intensely, it nearly took her breath away.

"I promise," she breathed. "And I take my honor as seriously as any warrior."

He relaxed infinitesimally, hoping he'd never need to remind her of her words.

"Are you certain you're not hungry yet?" He changed the subject swiftly.

"I can wait until we stop for the night," she assured him absently, too occupied with her thoughts to consider physical demands. She no longer wondered why he had appeared so late, bloody and mud-stained. He had come, and that was enough for now.

There were other, bigger questions she needed answered.

As they remounted, he drew her against him and she relaxed, relishing the feel of his hard body.

A few hours later, she reached a decision. *A lass has to do what a lass has to do*, she told herself firmly. By morning she planned to acquire a sudden case of inexplicable illness that would demand they secure permanent shelter long before they reached Dalkeith. She had no idea that, by morning, serendipity would take charge of events for her with a twisted sense of humor.

CHAPTER 26

JILLIAN ROLLED OVER, STRETCHED, AND PEERED
through the dim light at Grimm. Furs hung over the windows of the cottage. They barred entrance to the bitter
wind, but also permitted little light. The fire had burned
down to embers hours ago, and in the amber glow that
remained he looked like a bronzed warrior, a heroic,
mighty Viking stretched out on the pallet of furs with
one arm bent behind his head, the other curled about her
waist.

By the saints, but the man was beautiful! In repose, his
face had the kind of perfection that made one think of an
archangel, created by a joyous God. His brows winged in
black arches above eyes that were fringed with thick
lashes. Although tiny lines splayed out from the corners of
his eyes, he had few laugh lines around his mouth, a lack
she intended to remedy. His nose was straight and proud,
his lips . . . she could spend a day just gazing at those firm
pink lips that curved sensually even in his sleep. She

dropped a whisper-light kiss upon the stubborn cleft in his chin.

When they'd arrived the night before, Grimm had built a roaring fire and melted buckets of snow for a bath. They'd shared a tub, shivering in the frigid air until the heat of passion had warmed them to the bone. On a lush pile of furs, they'd wordlessly renewed their pledge to each other. The man was patently inexhaustible, she thought contentedly. Her body ached pleasantly from the marathon lovemaking. He'd shown her things that made her cheeks flame and her heart race in anticipation of more.

Steamy thoughts decamped abruptly when her stomach chose that moment to lurch alarmingly. Rendered momentarily breathless from the sudden nausea, she curled on her side and waited for the feeling to recede. As they'd had little to eat last night and been very active, she concluded she was probably hungry. An aching tummy would certainly make her plan to convince Grimm she was too sick to ride to Dalkeith easier to enact. What illness could she claim? An upset stomach might not be convincing enough to make him consider stopping in a village he'd sworn never to see again.

Conveniently, another wave of nausea gripped her. She scowled as the possibility occurred to her that she'd actually made herself ill merely by planning to pretend she was. She lay motionless, waiting for the discomfort to subside, and conjured visions of her favorite food, hoping that imagination would quaff the hunger pains.

Thoughts of Kaley's pork roast nearly doubled her over. Baked fish in wine sauce had her gagging in an instant. Bread? That didn't sound so bad. The crustier the better. She tried to inch away from Grimm to snatch the satchel where she'd seen a loaf of brown bread the night before, but in his sleep he tightened his arm around her waist. Stealthily she worked at his fingers, but they were like iron vises. As a fresh wave of nausea assaulted her, she moaned and curled into a ball, clutching her stomach. The sound woke Grimm instantly.

"Are you all right, lass? Did I hurt you?"

Afraid he was referring to their excessive lovemaking, she hastened to reassure him. She didn't wish to give him any reason to think twice before bestowing such pleasure on her again. "I'm only a bit sore," she said, then groaned as her stomach heaved again.

"What is it?" Grimm shot up in bed, and despite her misery she marveled at his beauty. His black hair fell about his face, and although the thought of food made her feel impossibly queasy, his lips still looked inviting.

"Did I harm you in my sleep?" he asked hoarsely. "What is it? Talk to me, lass!"

"I just don't feel well. I don't know what's wrong. My stomach hurts."

"Would food help?" He scuffled through the packs rapidly. Uncovering a large piece of greasy, salted beef, he thrust it beneath her nose.

"Oh, *no*!" she wailed, lunging to her knees. She scuttled away from him as quickly as possible, but made it only a few feet before retching. He was at her side in a heartbeat, smoothing the hair back from her face. "Don't," she cried. "Don't even look at me." Jillian hadn't been sick much in her life, but when she had she loathed anyone seeing her weakened by forces beyond her control. It made her feel helpless.

She was probably being punished for planning to be deceitful. That was hardly fair, she thought crossly. She'd never been deceitful in her life—surely she was entitled to one time, especially since it was for a such good cause. They had to stop at Tuluth. She needed answers that she suspected could be found only by returning to Grimm's roots.

"Hush, lass, it's all right. What can I do? What do you need?" It couldn't be poison, Grimm thought frantically. He'd prepared the food they'd eaten last night himself, of venison he'd tracked and cured while up in the Highlands. Then what was it? he wondered, deluged by a flood of emotions: helplessness, fear, realization that this woman in his arms meant everything to him and that he would take whatever sickness she had and bear it himself, if he could.

She convulsed again in his arms, and he held her trembling body.

It was some time before she stopped heaving. When she finally calmed, he wrapped her in a warm blanket and heated some water over the fire. She lay absolutely still while he washed her face. He was transfixed by her beauty; despite her illness Jillian certainly did seem radiant, her skin a translucent ivory, her lips deep pink, her cheeks flushed with rose.

"Are you feeling better, lass?"

She took a deep breath and nodded. "I think so. But I'm not certain I can ride very far today. Is there a place we might stop between here and Dalkeith?" she asked plaintively.

"Perhaps we shouldn't go at all," he hedged, but they had to move on, and he knew it. Lingering here another day was the most dangerous thing he could do. If the McKane were following, one more day might well cost them their lives. He closed his eyes and pondered the dilemma. What

if they started off again and she became sicker? Where
could he take her? Where they could they hide away until
she was well enough to travel?

Of course, he thought sardonically.

Tuluth.

CHAPTER 27

AS THEY NEARED THE VILLAGE OF HIS BIRTH, GRIMM lapsed into a protracted silence.

They'd ridden at an easy gait through the day, and Jillian had rapidly recovered her customary vigor. Despite her improved health, she forced herself to continue the charade. They were too close to Tuluth for her to waffle in indecision.

They had to go to Tuluth. It was necessary, whether she condoned her methods or not. She suffered no delusions that Grimm would return voluntarily. If he had his way he'd forget the village ever existed. While she accepted the fact that Grimm couldn't bring himself to talk about his past, she had a suspicion that returning to Tuluth might be more necessary for him than it was for her. It was possible he needed to confront his memories in order to lay them to rest.

For her part, she needed to examine the evidence with her own eyes and hands, speak with his "batty" da, and fish for information. In the rubble and debris of the destroyed castle she might find clues to help her understand the man she loved.

Jillian glanced down at his hand, so big it nearly cupped both of hers, while he guided Occam with the other one. What could he possibly think was wrong with him? He was noble and honest, with the exception of speaking about his past. He was strong, fearless, and one of the best warriors she'd ever seen. The man was virtually invincible. Why, he put the legends of those mythical beasts, the Berserkers, to shame.

Jillian smiled, thinking men like Grimm were where such legends were born. Why, he even had the legendary fierce blue eyes. If such beings truly existed, he might have been one of those mighty warriors, she thought dreamily. She hadn't been surprised to learn he was the son of a chieftain; nobility was evident in every line of his magnificent face. She released a sigh of pleasure and leaned back into his chest.

"We're nearly there, lass," he said comfortingly, misinterpreting the sigh.

"Will we be going to the castle?" she asked weakly.

"No. There are some caves where we can take shelter on a cliff called Wotan's Cleft. I played there when I was a boy. I know them well."

"Wouldn't the castle be warmer? I'm so cold, Grimm." She shivered in what she hoped was a convincing manner.

"If my memory serves me, Maldebann is a shambles." He tucked the plaid more securely about her shoulders and cradled her in the heat from his body. "I'm not certain any of the walls are standing. Besides, if my da is still around anywhere he probably haunts those crumbling halls."

"Well, how about the village? Surely some of your people remained?" She refused to succeed in her bid to reach Tuluth but be denied contact with people who might know something about her Highland warrior.

"Jillian, the entire valley was wiped out. I suspect it will be completely deserted. We'll be lucky if the caves are still passable. A lot of the passageways shifted, even collapsed into rubble during the years I played there."

"More reason to go to the castle," she said quickly. "It sounds as if the caves are dangerous."

Grimm expelled a breath. "You're persistent, aren't you, lass?"

"I'm just so cold," she whimpered, pushing away the guilt she felt about being deceitful. It was for a good cause.

His arms tightened around her. "I'll take care of you, Jillian, I promise."

* * *

"Where are they, Gilles?" Ronin asked.

"Nearly three miles east, milord."

Ronin plucked nervously at his tartan and turned to his brother. "Do I look all right?"

Balder grinned. " 'Do I look all right?' " he mocked in falsetto, preening for an imaginary audience.

Ronin punched him in the arm. "Stop it, Balder. This is important. I'm meetin' my son's wife today."

"You're seein' your *son* today," Balder corrected.

Ronin cast his gaze to the stones. "Aye, that I am," he said finally. His head whipped back and he glanced at Balder anxiously. "What if he still hates me, Balder? What if he rides up, spits in my face, and leaves?"

The grin faded from Balder's lips. "Then I'll beat the lad senseless, tie him up, and we'll both be talkin' to him. Persuasively and at our leisure."

Ronin's face brightened considerably. "Now, there's a plan," he said optimistically. "Maybe we could do that straightaway, what say you?"

"*Ronin.*"

Ronin shrugged. "It just seems the most direct course," he said defensively.

Balder assessed his brother, his nervous, callused fingers smoothing the ceremonial tartan. His sleekly combed black hair, liberally sprinkled with silver. His jeweled *sgain dubh* and velvet sporran. His wide shoulders and not-so-trim waist. He stood taller and with more pride than Balder had seen him stand in years. His blue eyes reflected joy, hope, and . . . fear. "You look like every inch a fine laird, brother," Balder said gently. "Any son would be proud to call you da."

Ronin took a deep breath and nodded tightly. "Let's hope you're right. Are the banners hung, Gilles?"

Gilles grinned and nodded. "You do look regal, milord," he added proudly. "And I must say Tuluth has made a fine showing for us. The valley fairly sparkles. Any lad would be pleased to see this as his future demesne."

"And the Hall of Lords, has it been cleaned and opened? Are the torches lit?"

"Yes, milord, and I've hung the portrait in the dining hall."

Ronin gulped a breath of air and began pacing. "The villagers have been informed? All of them?"

"They're waitin' in the streets, Ronin, and the banners have been hung throughout Tuluth as well. It's a fine homecoming you've planned," Balder said.

"Let's just hope he thinks so," Ronin muttered, pacing.

* * *

Grimm's fingers tightened on Jillian's waist as Occam carefully picked his way up the back pass to Wotan's Cleft.

He had no intention of taking Jillian to the cold damp caves where a fire could smoke them out if the wind suddenly changed course down one of the tunnels, but from the Cleft he could assess the village and the castle. If any part of it was still standing, he could scan for smoke from a hearth if anyone inhabited the ghost village. Besides, he preferred Jillian to see immediately what a desolate place it was so she might wish to hurry on to Dalkeith as soon as she was able. She seemed to be making a rapid recovery, although she was still weak and complained of intermittent queasiness.

The sun topped the peak of the Cleft. It wouldn't set for several more hours, allowing him ample time to assess the potential dangers and secure shelter somewhere in the ruined village. If Jillian was well tomorrow morning they could race for the shores of Dalkeith. To avoid leading the McKane to the Douglas estate, he planned to stop in a nearby village and send a messenger for Hawk. They would meet discreetly to discuss the possibility of raising an army and plan Jillian's and his future.

As the tall standing stones of Wotan's Cleft came into view, Grimm's chest tightened painfully. He forced himself to take deep, even breaths as they navigated the rocky path. He hadn't anticipated the force with which his bitter memories would resurface. He'd last climbed this path fifteen years ago and it had forever changed his life. *Hear me, Odin! I summon the Berserker* . . . He'd ascended a boy and descended a monster.

His hands fisted. How could he have considered coming back here? But Jillian snuggled against him, seeking warmth, and he knew he would enter Tuluth willingly even if it were occupied by hordes of demons, to keep her safe and warm.

"Are you all right, Grimm?"

How typically Jillian, he marveled. Despite her own sickness, her concern was for him. "I'm fine. We'll be warm soon, lass. Just rest."

He sounded so worried that Jillian had to bite her tongue to prevent an instant confession from escaping.

"In just a moment you'll be able to see where the village used to be," he said, sorrow roughening his voice.

"I can't imagine what it would be like to see Caithness destroyed. I didn't mean to bring you back to a place that is so painful . . ."

"It happened many years ago. It's almost as if it happened in another lifetime."

Jillian sat up straight as they topped the crest and searched the landscape with curious eyes.

"There." Grimm directed her attention to the cliff. "From the promontory the whole valley comes into view." He smiled faintly. "I used to come up here and look out over the land, thinking that a lad had never been born luckier than I."

Jillian winced. Occam moved forward, his gait steady. Jillian held her breath as they approached the edge.

"The caves lie behind us, beyond that tumble of stones where the slope of the mountain is steepest. My best friend Arron and I once vowed we would map out every tunnel, every chamber in that mountain, but the passages seemed to go on forever. We'd nearly mapped out a quarter of it before . . . before . . ."

Remorse for dragging him back to face his demons flooded her. "Was your friend killed in the battle?"

"Aye."

"Was your da hurt in the battle?" she asked gently.

"He should have died," Grimm said tightly. "The McKane buried a battle-ax in his chest clear to the hilt. It's amazing he survived. For several years after, I assumed he had died."

"And your mother?" she said in a whisper.

There was a silence, broken only by the sound of shale crushing beneath Occam's hooves. "We'll be able to see it any moment, lass."

Jillian's gaze fixed on the cliff's edge where the rock terminated abruptly and became the horizon. Hundreds of feet down she would find the ashes of Tuluth. She drew herself up straighter, nearly tumbling from the horse in her anxiety, and braced herself for the grim scene.

"Hold, lass," Grimm soothed as they took the last few steps to the cliff and gazed out over the lifeless valley.

For nearly five minutes he didn't speak. Jillian wasn't certain he breathed. On the other hand, she wasn't certain she did either.

Below them, nestled around a crystalline river and several sparkling lochs, a vibrant city teemed with life, white huts washed to soft amber by the afternoon sun. Hundreds of homes dotted the valley in even rows along meticulously maintained roads. Smoke from cozy fires spiraled lazily from flues, and although she couldn't hear the voices, she could see children running and playing. People walked up and down the roads where an occasional lamb or cow wandered. Two wolfhounds played in a small garden. Along the main roadway that ran down the center of the city, brilliantly colored banners waved and flapped in the breeze.

Astonished, she scanned the valley, following the river to the face of the mountain. It bubbled from an underground source at the mountain's base, the castle towering in stone above it. Her hand flew to her lips to smother a cry of shock. This was not what she'd expected to see.

A bleak and dreary castle, he'd called it.

Nothing could have been further from the truth. Castle Maldebann was the most beautiful castle she'd ever laid eyes on. With its exquisitely carved towers and regal face, it looked as if it had been liberated from the mountain by the hammer and chisel of a visionary sculptor. Constructed of pale gray stone, it rose in mighty arches to a breathtaking height. The mountain effectively sealed the valley at that end and the castle sprawled along the entire width of the closure, wings stretching east and west from the castle proper.

Its mighty towers made Caithness look like a summer cottage—nay, like a child's tree loft. No wonder Castle Maldebann had been the focus of an attack; it was an incredible, enviable stronghold. The guard walk at the top was dotted with dozens of uniformed figures. The entrance was visible beyond the portcullis and postern and soared nearly fifty feet. Brightly clad women dotted the lower walkways, scurrying to and fro with baskets and children.

"Grimm?" Jillian croaked his name. Ruins? Her brow furrowed in consternation as she wondered how this could possibly be. Was it possible Grimm had misunderstood who lost that fateful battle years ago?

A huge banner with bold lettering rippled above the entrance to the castle. Jillian narrowed her eyes and squinted, much as she chided Zeke for doing, but she couldn't make out the words. "What does it say, Grimm?" she managed in a hushed whisper, awed by the unexpected vista of peace and prosperity stretching before her eyes.

For a long moment he didn't answer. She heard him

swallow convulsively behind her, his body as rigid as the rocks Occam shifted his hooves upon.

"Do you think maybe some other clan took over this valley and rebuilt?" she offered faintly, latching on to any reason she could find to make sense of things.

He released a whistling breath, then punctuated it with a groan. "I doubt it, Jillian."

"It's possible, isn't it?" she insisted. If not, Grimm might genuinely suffer his da's madness, for only a madman could call this magnificent city a ruin.

"No."

"Why? I mean, how can you be certain from here? I can't even make out their plaids."

"Because that banner says 'Welcome home, son,' " he whispered with horror.

CHAPTER 28

"HOW AM I SUPPOSED TO MAKE SENSE OF THIS, GRIMM?"
Jillian asked as the tense silence between them grew. He
was staring blankly down at the valley. She felt suddenly
and overwhelmingly confused.

"How are *you* supposed to make sense of it?" He slid
from Occam's back and lowered her to the ground beside
him. "You?" he echoed incredulously. He couldn't find one
bit of sense in it either. Not only wasn't his home a ruin of
ashes scattered across the valley floor as it was supposed to
be, there were bloody welcome banners flapping from the
turrets.

"Yes," she encouraged. "Me. You told me this place had
been destroyed."

Grimm couldn't tear his eyes away from the vision in
the valley. He was stupefied, any hope of logic derailed by
shock. Tuluth was five times the size it had once been, the
land tilled in neatly patterned sections, the homes twice as

large. Weren't things supposed to seem smaller when one got bigger? His mind objected, with a growing sense of disorientation. He scanned the rocks behind him, seeking the hidden mouth of the cave to reassure himself that he was standing upon Wotan's Cleft and that it was indeed Tuluth below him. The river flowing through the valley was twice as wide, bluer than lapis—hell, even the mountain seemed to have grown.

Castle Maldebann was another matter. Had it changed colors? He recalled it as a towering monolith carved from blackest obsidian, all wicked forbidding angles, dripping moss and gargoyles. His gaze roved disbelievingly over the flowing lines of the pale gray, inviting structure. Fully occupied, cheerily functional, decorated—by God—with banners.

Banners that read "Welcome home."

Grimm sank to his knees, opened his eyes as wide as he could, closed and rubbed them, then opened them again. Jillian watched him curiously.

"It's still there, isn't it?" she said matter-of-factly. "I tried it too," she sympathized.

Grimm snatched a quick glance at her and was stunned to see a half-smile curving her lip. "Is there something amusing about this, lass?" he asked, unaccountably offended.

Instant compassion flooded her features. She laid a gentle hand on his arm. "Oh, no, Grimm. Don't think I'm laughing at you. I'm laughing at how stunned we both are, and partly with relief. I was expecting a dreadful scene. This is the last thing we expected to see. I know the shock must be doubly hard for you to absorb, but I was thinking it's funny because you look like I felt when you first came back to Caithness."

"How is that, lass?"

"Well, when I was little you seemed so big. I mean huge, monstrous, the biggest man in the world. And when you came back, since I was bigger, I expected you to finally look smaller. Not smaller than me, but at least smaller than you did the last time I'd seen you up close."

"And?" he encouraged.

She shook her head, bewildered. "You didn't. You looked bigger."

"And your point is?" He tore his gaze from the valley and peered at her.

"Well, you were expecting smaller, weren't you? I suspect it's probably much bigger. Shocking, isn't it?"

"I'm still waiting for your point, lass," he said dryly.

"I can see someone should have told you more fables when you were young," she teased. "My point is, memory can be a deceptive thing," she clarified. "Perhaps the village never was completely destroyed. Perhaps it just seemed that way when you left. Did you leave at night? Was it too dark to see clearly?"

Grimm took her hands in his as they knelt together on the cliff's edge. It *had* been night when he'd left Tuluth, and the air had been thick with smoke. It had been a horrifying scene to the fourteen-year-old lad. He'd left believing his village and home destroyed and himself a dangerous beast. He'd left filled with hatred and despair, expecting little of life.

Now, fifteen years later, he crouched upon the same ridge, holding the hands of the woman he loved beyond life itself, gazing upon impossible sights. If Jillian hadn't been with him he might have tucked tail and run, never permitting himself to wonder what strange magic had been worked in this vale. He raised her hand to his lips and kissed it. "My memory of you was never deceptive. I always remembered you as the best that life had to offer."

Jillian's eyes widened. She tried to speak but ended up making a small choked sound instead. Grimm stiffened, interpreting her sound for a cry of discomfort. "Here I am, keeping you out in the cold when you're ill."

"That's not what . . . no," she stammered. "Truly, I feel much better now." When he eyed her suspiciously, she added, "Oooh, but I do need to get somewhere warm soon, Grimm. And that castle certainly looks warm." She eyed it hopefully.

Grimm's gaze darted back to the valley. The castle did look warm. And well fortified. Damn near the safest place he could take her, and why not? There were "welcome home" banners draped in dozens of locations. If the McKane were following him, what better place to stand and fight? How strange it was to return to Tuluth after all these years, with the McKane on his heels once again. Would the pattern finally come full circle and end? Perhaps they wouldn't need to go to Dalkeith to raise an army to fight the McKane after all.

But he'd have to face his da. He blew out a frustrated breath and weighed their options. How could he descend into this valley that cradled all his deepest fears? But how could he explain to Jillian if he turned and rode away? What if her illness returned? What if the McKane caught them? He was confounded by the onslaught of questions with no clear answers. Discovering Tuluth was this . . . this glorious place . . . it was too shocking for his mind to absorb.

Jillian winced and rubbed her stomach. His hands

tightened on hers and he invoked his legendary willpower, aware that before this day was through he would need every ounce of it.

He had no choice. They swiftly remounted and began the descent.

* * *

"They're comin'!"

Ronin looked ready to bolt.

"Relax, man," Balder chided. "It's goin' to be fine, you'll see."

The McIllioch grimaced. "Easy for you to say. He's not your son. I tell you, he's goin' to spit in my face."

Balder shook his head and tried not to laugh. "If that's your worst concern, old man, you have nothin' to worry about."

* * *

Grimm and Jillian descended the back of Wotan's Cleft, circled around the base of it, and picked up the wending road into the mouth of the valley. Five huge mountains formed a natural fortress around the valley, rising like the gentle fingers of an unfurled hand. The city filled its protected palm, verdant, teeming with life. Jillian quickly concluded that when the McKane had attacked Tuluth years ago, they must have been either thoroughly arrogant or impossibly vast in numbers.

As if he'd read her mind, Grimm said, "We weren't always this great in numbers, Jillian. In the past fifteen years, Tuluth seems to have not only regained the men lost in the battle with the McKane, but increased by"—his dumbfounded gaze swept the valley—"nearly five times." He whistled, and shook his head. "Someone has been rebuilding."

"Are you certain your da is insane?"

Grimm grimaced. "Yes." *As certain as I am of anything at the moment,* he appended silently.

"Well, for an insane man, he certainly seems to have done wonders here."

"I doona believe he has. Something else must be going on."

"And the 'Welcome back, son' banner? I thought you said you have no brothers."

"I doona," he replied stiffly. He realized they would soon be in clear sight of the first of those banners and he hadn't told Jillian the truth: that there was absolutely no mistaking who was expected because he hadn't been entirely truthful before—the dozens of banners hung throughout the city really read "Welcome back, Gavrael."

Jillian squirmed, trying to get a better view. Despite his concerns, her lush hips wriggling against his loins sent a bolt of lust through his veins. Memories of last night teased the periphery of his mind, but he could afford no distractions. "Be still," he growled.

"I just want to see."

"You're going to be seeing the sky from your back if you keep wiggling like that, lass." He tugged her against him so she could feel what her squirming had accomplished. He'd love nothing more than to lose himself in the passion of Jillian and, when she was sleepily sated, spirit her miles in the other direction.

They had come within reading distance of the banners when Jillian leaned forward again. Grimm swallowed and braced himself for the questions he knew would follow.

"Why, it's not about you at all, Grimm," she said wonderingly. "This banner doesn't say 'Welcome home, son.' It says 'Welcome home, Gavrael.' " She paused, nibbling her lip. "Who's Gavrael? And how could you manage to read it from so far away yet mistake the word 'son' for 'Gavrael'? The words don't look anything alike."

"Must you be so logical?" he said with a sigh. He reconsidered turning Occam about and tearing off in the other direction without offering an explanation, but he knew it would be only a temporary reprieve. Ultimately, Jillian would bring him back, one way or another.

It was time to face his demons—apparently, all of them at the same time. For winding down the road toward him was a parade of people, replete with a band of pipes and drums, and—if his memory could be trusted on anything at all—the one in front bore a marked resemblance to his da. And so did the man who rode beside him. Grimm's gaze darted back and forth between them, searching for some clue that might tell him which one was his father.

Suddenly a worse realization struck him, one which, stunned to temporary senselessness by the condition of his home, he'd managed to overlook entirely. The moment he'd glimpsed the thriving Tuluth, the shock of it all had caused his deepest fear to recede deceptively to the back of his mind. Now it returned with the force of a tidal wave, flooding him with quiet desperation.

If his memory could be trusted—and that did seem to be the question of the day—familiar faces were approaching, which meant some of the people riding toward them knew he was a Berserker.

In an instant, they could betray his terrible secret to Jillian, and he would lose her forever.

CHAPTER 29

GRIMM DREW OCCAM TO SUCH AN ABRUPT HALT THAT the stallion spooked and reared. Mustering the most soothing sounds he could manage in his agitated condition, Grimm calmed the startled gray and slipped from its back.

"What are you doing?" Jillian was bewildered by his rapid dismount.

Grimm studied the ground intently. "I need you to remain here, lass. Come forward when I beckon, but no sooner. Promise me you'll wait until I summon you."

Jillian studied his bent head. After a brief internal debate, she reached out and caressed his dark hair. He turned his face into her hand and kissed her palm.

"I haven't seen these people in fifteen years, Jillian."

"I'll stay, I promise."

He gave her a wordless thank-you with his eyes. He was torn by conflicting emotions, yet he knew he had to approach alone. Only when he had wrung an oath from the villagers to protect his secret would he lead Jillian into the

city and address her comfort. Had she been dangerously ill,
he would have risked losing her love to save her life, but
she was hardly incapacitated, and although he regretted
any discomfort she might suffer he was not willing to face
the fear and revulsion he'd glimpsed in his dreams. He
couldn't afford to take any chances.

Satisfied that she would wait at this distance until he
summoned her, Grimm turned and sprinted down the dirt
road toward the approaching melee. His heart seemed to
have lodged in the vicinity of his throat, and he felt as if he
were being wrenched in two. Behind him was the woman
he loved; in front of him was the past he'd vowed never to
confront by light of day.

At the forefront of the cluster rode two men of equal
height and girth, both with thick shocks of black hair, liberally threaded with silver. Both had strong, craggy faces and
clefts in their proud chins, both had a similar expression
of joy on their features. What was going on here? Grimm
wondered.

It was as if everything he'd ever believed had been a lie.
Tuluth had been destroyed, but Tuluth was a thriving city.
His da had been insane, but someone with a stable mind
and a strong back had rebuilt this land. His da seemed ex-
traordinarily happy to see him, and though Grimm had not
intended to return, his father apparently had been expecting him. How? Why? Thousands of questions flashed
through his mind in the short time it took him to span the
distance between them.

The parade of people began roaring as he drew near,
their faces wreathed in smiles. How was a man expected to
walk into such an exuberant crowd with hatred in his
heart?

And why were they so damned happy to see him?

He stopped his sprint a dozen feet from the front line. Unable to hold still, he resorted to jogging in place, breathing harshly, not from the run but from the dreaded encounter to come.

The two men who looked so similar broke away from the crowd. One of them raised a hand to the entourage and the crowd fell silent, maintaining a respectful distance as they rode forward. Grimm sneaked a glance over his shoulder to make certain Jillian hadn't followed him. With relief he saw she had obeyed his command, although if she leaned any farther over Occam's head toward the crowd he'd have to peel her from the road.

"Gavrael."

The deep voice so like his own whipped his head around. He stared up at the two men, uncertain which one had spoken.

"Grimm," he corrected instantly.

The man on the right erupted into an immediate bluster. "What the bletherin' hell kind of name is Grim? Why not be namin' yourself Depressed, or Melancholy? Nay, I have it—Woebegone." He cast a disgusted glance at Grimm and snorted.

"It's better than McIllioch," Grimm said stiffly. "And it's not Grim with one *m*. It's Grimm with two."

"Well, why would you be changin' your name at all, lad?" The man on the left did little to disguise his wounded expression.

Grimm searched their faces, trying desperately to decide which one was his father. He didn't have the faintest clue what he might do when he figured it out, but he'd really like to know which one to treat to the venom he'd been storing for years uncounted. No, not uncounted, he corrected himself—fifteen years of angry words he wanted to fling at the man, words that had festered for half his lifetime.

"Who are you?" he demanded of the man who'd most recently spoken.

The man turned to his companion with a mournful look. "Who am I, he's asking me, Balder. Can you be believin' that? Who am I?"

"At least he dinna spit," Balder said mildly.

"You're Ronin," Grimm accused. If the one was named Balder, the other had to be his da, Ronin McIllioch.

"I'm not Ronin to you," the man exclaimed indignantly. "I'm your da."

"You're no father to me," Grimm remarked in a voice so chill it vied with the bitterest Highland wind.

Ronin gazed accusingly at Balder. "I told you so."

Balder shook his head, arching a bushy brow. "He still dinna spit."

"What the hell does spitting have to do with anything?"

"Well, lad," Balder drawled, "that's the excuse I'm lookin' for to tie your spiteful arse up and drag you back to the castle, where I can be poundin' some good common sense and respect for your elders into you."

"You think you could?" Grimm challenged coolly. His dangerous mix of emotions clamored lustily for a fight.

Balder laughed, the sound a joyous shout rumbling from his thick chest. "I love a good fight, lad, but a man like me could eat a pup like you in one snap of his jaws."

Grimm leveled a dark look at Ronin. "Does he know what I am?" Arrogance underscored the question.

"Do you know what *I* am?" Balder countered softly.

Grimm's eyes swept back to his face. "What do you mean?" he asked so quickly it came out sounding like one word. He studied Balder intently. Mocking ice-blue eyes met his levelly. *Impossible!* In all his years, he'd never encountered another Berserker!

Balder shook his head and sighed. He exchanged glances with Ronin. "The lad is dense, Ronin. I'm tellin' you, he's thick through and through."

Ronin puffed himself up indignantly. "He is not. He's my son."

"The lad doesn't know the first thing about himself, even after all these—"

"Well, how could he, bein' that—"

"And any dolt should have figured—"

"That doesn't mean he's dense—"

"Haud yer wheesht!" Grimm roared.

"There's no need to be roarin' my head off, boy," Balder rebuked. "It's not as if you're the only one with a Berserker's temper here."

"I am not a boy. I am not a lad. I am not a dolt," Grimm said evenly, determined to take control of the erratic conversation. There would be time later to discover how Balder had become a Berserker. "And when the woman who is behind me approaches, you will kindly make it clear to the servants, the villagers, and the entire clan that I am *not* a Berserker, do you understand me?"

"Not a Berserker?" Balder's eyebrows rose.

"Not a Berserker?" Ronin's brow furrowed.

"Not a Berserker."

"But you *are*," Ronin argued obtusely.

Grimm glared at Ronin. "But she doesn't know that. And if she discovers it, she'll leave me. And if she leaves me, I'll have no choice but to kill you both," Grimm said matter-of-factly.

"Well," Balder huffed, deeply offended. "There's no need to be gettin' nasty about things, lad. I'm sure we'll find a way to sort things out."

"I doubt it, Balder. And if you call me lad one more time, you're going to have a problem. I'll spit, and give you the reason you've been looking for, and we'll just see if an aging Berserker can take one in his prime."

"Two agin' Berserkers," Ronin corrected proudly.

Grimm's head snapped around, and he stared at Ronin. Identical ice-blue eyes. The day kept dishing out one bewildering revelation after another. He found sanctuary in sarcasm: "What the hell is this, the valley of the Berserkers?"

"Somethin' like that, Gavrael," Balder muttered, dodging a nudge from Ronin.

"My name is *Grimm*."

"How do you plan to be explainin' the name on the banners to your wife?" Ronin asked.

"She's not my wife," Grimm evaded. He hadn't figured that out yet.

"What?" Outraged, Ronin nearly rose to his feet in the stirrups. "You've brought a woman here in dishonor? No son of mine cavorts with his mate without offerin' her the proper union."

Grimm buried his hands in his hair. His world had gone mad. This was the most absurd conversation he could recall holding. "I haven't had the *time* to marry her yet! I only recently abducted her—"

"Abducted her?" Ronin's nostrils flared.

"With her consent!" Grimm said defensively.

"I thought there was a wedding at Caithness," Ronin argued.

"There nearly was, but not to me. And there will be one

as soon as I can. Lack of time is the only reason she's not my wife. And you"—he pointed furiously at Ronin—"you haven't been a father to me for fifteen years, so doona think you can start acting like one now."

"I haven't been a father to you because you wouldn't come home!"

"You know why I wouldn't come home." Grimm spoke furiously, his eyes blazing.

Ronin flinched. He drew a deep breath, and when he spoke again he seemed deflated by Grimm's anger. "I know I failed you," he said, his eyes brimful of regret.

"Failed me is putting it lightly," Grimm muttered. He was badly thrown off balance by his da's response. He'd expected the old man to rage right back, maybe attack him like the batty bastard he was. But there was genuine regret in his gaze. How was he supposed to deal with that? If Ronin had raged back, he could have released his pent-up anger by fighting with him. But Ronin didn't. He simply sat his horse and gazed sadly down at him, and it made Grimm feel even worse.

"Jillian is ill," Grimm said gruffly. "She needs a warm place to stay."

"She's ill?" Balder trumpeted. "By Odin's spear, lad, did you have to wait until now to say the most important thing?"

"Lad?" The way Grimm uttered the single word made his threat clear.

But Balder was unruffled. His mouth twisted with a sneer. "Listen up, son of the McIllioch, you doona frighten me. I'm far too old to be put off by a young pup's growl. You won't let me call you by your God-given name, and I refuse to call you that ridiculous appellation you've chosen, so it's either goin' to be 'lad' or it's goin' to be 'arsehole.' Which do you prefer?" The older man's grin was menacing.

Grimm caught himself on the verge of a faint smile. If he hadn't been so hell-bent on hating this place, he would have liked blustering old Balder. The man commanded respect and clearly took guff from no one.

"You can call me lad on one condition," he relented. "Take care of my woman and keep my secret. And make sure the villagers do the same."

Ronin and Balder exchanged glances and sighed. "Done."

"Welcome home, lad," Balder added.

Grimm rolled his eyes.

"Aye, welcome—" Ronin began, but Grimm raised a warning finger.

"And you, old man," he said to Ronin. "If I were you, I'd be giving me a lot of breathing room," he warned.

Ronin opened his mouth, then closed it, his blue eyes dark with pain.

CHAPTER 30

JILLIAN COULDN'T STOP SMILING. IT WAS NEARLY IMPOS-
sible not to in the midst of such excitement. How Grimm
managed to continue looking so somber was beyond her
comprehension.

She spared a glance at him, which she nearly begrudged
because everywhere else she looked she found something
enchanting and Grimm looked so miserable it depressed
her. She knew she should feel more compassion for his
plight, but it was difficult to feel empathy when his family
was so overjoyed to welcome him back into the fold. And
what a magnificent fold it was.

Gavrael, she corrected herself silently. Rather than motioning her to join them after he'd greeted his da, he'd
sprinted back to get her so they could ride in together. Surrounded by the cheering crowd, he'd explained to her that
when he'd left Tuluth years ago he'd assumed a new name.
His real name, although he insisted she continue calling
him Grimm, was Gavrael Roderick Icarus McIllioch.

She sighed dreamily. Jillian Alanna McIllioch; said aloud it was a tumble of *l*'s that rolled euphonically. She had no doubt that Grimm would marry her once they'd settled in.

Grimm tightened his grip on her hand and whispered her name to get her attention. "Jillian, come back from wherever you are. Balder's going to show us to our chambers, and we'll get you warm and fed."

"Oh, I feel much better, Grimm," she said absently, marveling over a beautiful sculpture that adorned the hall. She trundled after Balder and an assortment of maids happily holding Grimm's hand. "This castle is enormous, breathtaking. How could you have ever thought it was dark and dreary?"

He gave her a glum look. "I haven't a blethering clue," he muttered.

"Here's your room, Gavrael—" Balder began.

"Grimm."

"Lad." Balder stared him down levelly. "And Merry here will see Jillian to hers," he said pointedly.

"What?" Grimm was momentarily dumbfounded. Now that she was his, how could he sleep without Jillian in his arms?

"Room." Balder gestured impatiently. "Yours." He turned abruptly to a dainty maid. "And Merry here will show Jillian to *hers*." His blue eyes reflected a cool challenge.

"I will see Jillian to hers myself," Grimm begrudged after a tense pause.

"As long as you see yourself right back out of it, lad, go on ahead. But you're not married, so doona be thinkin' you can act like you are."

Jillian flushed.

"No reflection on you, lass," Balder hastened to assure

her. "I can see you're a fine lady, but this boy is randy as a goat around you and it's plain to see. If he seeks the joys of wedded bliss, he can wed you. Without a weddin' he'll be havin' no bliss."

Grimm flushed. "Enough, Balder."

Balder arched a brow and frowned. "And try to be a bit nicer to your da, lad. The man did give you life, after all." With that he turned and blustered down the hall, his proud chin jutting like the prow of a ship breaking waves.

Grimm waited until he had disappeared from sight, then sought directions from the maid. "I'll escort Jillian to her chambers," he informed the elfin-looking Merry. To the cluster of maids he said, "See to it that we have a steaming tub and"—he glanced at Jillian worriedly—"what kind of food might your stomach tolerate, lass?"

Anything and everything, Jillian thought. She was famished. "Lots," she said succinctly.

Grimm smiled faintly, finished giving the maids instructions, and escorted Jillian to her rooms.

As they entered the rooms, Jillian exhaled a sigh of pleasure. Her chambers were every bit as luxuriously appointed as the rest of Maldebann. Four tall windows graced the west wall of the bedroom, and from there she could watch the sun set over the mountains. Snowy lambskin rugs covered the floors. The bed was carved of burnished cherry that had been polished to a vibrant luster and canopied with sheer white linen. A cheery fire burned in an enormous fireplace.

"How are you feeling, Jillian?" Grimm shut the door and drew her into his arms.

"I'm much better now," she assured him.

"I know this must all be quite shocking—"

Jillian kissed him, silencing further words. He seemed

startled by the gesture, then kissed her back so urgently it caused her toes to curl with anticipation. She clung to the kiss, spinning it out as long as she could, trying to imbue him with courage and love, for she suspected he'd be needing it. Then she forgot her noble intentions as desire sizzled between them.

A sharp rap on the door dampened it quickly.

Grimm pulled back and stalked to the door, unsurprised to find Balder standing there. "I forgot to tell you, lad, we have supper at eight," Balder said, peering beyond him at Jillian. "Has he been kissin' you, lass? You just tell me and I'll take care of it."

Grimm closed the door without replying, and locked it. Balder sighed so loudly outside the door that Jillian nearly laughed.

As Grimm walked back to her side, she studied him. The strain of the day was evident; even his usual proud posture seemed bowed. When she considered all the man had been through in the past few hours, she felt terrible. He was busy tending to her when he could probably use nothing more greatly than some time alone to sort through all the shocks the day had delivered. She brushed his cheek with her hand. "Grimm, if you don't mind, do you think I could rest a bit before I meet any more people? Perhaps I could take dinner in my room tonight and face the castle tomorrow?"

She hadn't been wrong. His expression was a mixture of concern and relief.

"Are you certain you doona mind being on your own? Are you certain you're well enough?"

"Grimm, I feel wonderful. Whatever was wrong with me this morning has passed. Now I'd just like to relax, soak in a long bath, and sleep. I suspect you probably have people and places you'd like to reacquaint yourself with."

"You're remarkable, do you know that, lass?" He smoothed her hair and tucked a stray tendril behind her ear.

"I love you, Grimm Roderick," she said intensely. "Go meet your people and see your home. Take your time. I will always be here for you."

"What did I do to deserve you?" The words exploded from him.

She brushed her lips against his lightly. "I ask myself the same question all the time."

"I want to see you tonight, Jillian. I need to see you."

"I'll leave my door unlocked." She flashed him a dazzling smile that promised the moon and the stars when he came.

He gave her one last tender look and left.

* * *

"Go to him. I can't," Ronin said urgently.

The two men peered out the window at Grimm, sprawled on the wall in front of the castle, gazing out over the village. Night had fallen, and tiny lights in the village twinkled like a reflection of the stars that dotted the sky. The castle had been constructed to provide an unimpeded view of the village. A wide stone terrace lined the perimeter, east and west. It sloped in tiers down to the fortifying walls, the terrace itself surrounded by a low wall at such a height that from atop it one could look straight out over the valley. Grimm had been sitting alone on the wall for hours, alternating his gaze between the castle behind him and the valley before him.

"What would you like me to be sayin'?" Balder grunted.

"He's your son, Ronin. You're goin' to have to speak with him at some point."

"He hates me."

"So speak with him and try to help him get past it."

"It's not that easy!" Ronin snapped, but in his blue eyes Balder saw fear. Fear that if Ronin spoke with his son, he might lose him all over again.

Balder eyed his brother for a moment and then sighed. "I'll try, Ronin."

* * *

Grimm watched the valley batten down for the night. The villagers had begun to light candles and pull shutters, and from his perch on the low wall he could hear the faint strains of parents calling their children into cozy cottages and farmers rounding up animals before venturing to bed themselves. It was a scene of peace and harmony. He stole an occasional glance over his shoulder at the castle, but not one gargoyle lurked. It was possible, he conceded, that at fourteen he'd been fanciful. It was possible that years of running and hiding had colored his perceptions until all seemed desolate and barren, even a past that had once been bright. His life had changed so abruptly on that fateful day, it might well have skewed his memories.

He could accept that he'd forgotten what Tuluth was really like. He could accept that the castle had never been truly menacing. But what was he to make of his da? He'd seen him with his own eyes, crouched over his mother's body. Had he, in his shock and grief, misconstrued that event too? Once the possibility presented itself, he studied it from every angle, his confusion deepening.

He'd found his da in the south gardens in the early

morning, the time Jolyn strolled the grounds and greeted the day. He'd been on his way to meet Arron to go fishing. The scene was painstakingly etched on his mind: Jolyn beaten and battered, her face a mass of bruises, Ronin crouched above her, snarling, blood everywhere, and that damned incriminating knife in his hand.

"Beautiful, isn't it?" Balder interrupted his internal debate.

"Aye," Grimm replied, mildly surprised Balder had joined him. "I doona remember it like this, Balder."

Balder placed a comforting hand on his shoulder. "That's because it wasn't always like this. Tuluth has grown tremendously over the years, thanks to your da's efforts."

"Come to think of it, I doona remember you either," Grimm said thoughtfully. "Did I know you when I was a lad?"

"No. I've spent most of my life wanderin'. I visited Maldebann twice when you were young, but only briefly. Six months ago the ship I was sailin' broke up in a storm, washin' me ashore old Alba. I figured that meant it was time to check on what remained of my clan. I'm your da's older brother, but I had a fancy to see the world, so I bullied Ronin into bein' laird, and a fine one he's made."

Grimm scowled. "That's debatable."

"Doona be so hard on Ronin, lad. He's wanted nothin' more than for you to come home. Maybe your memories of him are as discolored as your memories of Tuluth."

"Maybe," Grimm allowed tightly. "But maybe not."

"Give him a chance, that's all I'm askin'. Get to know him again and make a fresh judgment. There were things he dinna have time to explain to you before. Let him tell you now."

Grimm shrugged his hand off his shoulder. "Enough, Balder. Leave me alone."

"Promise me you'll give him a chance to talk to you, lad," Balder persisted, undaunted by Grimm's dismissal.

"I haven't left yet, have I?"

Balder inclined his head and retreated.

* * *

"Well, that dinna last long," Ronin complained.

"I said my piece. Now do your part," Balder grumbled.

"Tomorrow." Ronin procrastinated.

Balder glared.

"You know it's foolish to try talkin' about things when people are tired, and the lad must be exhausted, Balder."

"Berserkers only get tired when they've been in a rage," Balder said dryly.

"Quit actin' like my older brother," Ronin snapped.

"Well, quit actin' like my younger brother." Two pairs of ice-blue eyes battled, and Balder finally shrugged. "If you won't face that problem, then turn your mind to this one. Merry overheard Jillian tellin' the lad she'd leave her door unlocked. If we doona come up with somethin', that lad o' yours will be samplin' the pleasures without payin' the price."

"But he already has sampled them. We know that."

"That doesn't make it right. And bein' denied may encourage him to wed her all the sooner," Balder pointed out.

"What do you suggest? Lock her in the tower? The boy's a Berserker, he'll get past anythin'."

Balder thought a moment, then grinned. "He won't be gettin' past righteous indignation, will he, now?"

* * *

The hour was past midnight when Grimm hastened down the corridor to Jillian's chambers. Merry had assured him that Jillian passed a restful evening with no further bouts of illness. She'd eaten like a woman famished, the elfin maid had said.

He let his lips curve in the full smile he felt whenever he thought of Jillian. He needed to touch her, to tell her that he wanted to marry her if she would still have him. He longed to confide in her. She had a logical mind; perhaps she could help him see things he couldn't make sense of by dint of being too near the subjects involved. He stood firm on his position that she must never know what he really was, but he could talk with her about much of what had happened— or *seemed* to have happened—fifteen years ago, without betraying his secret. His gait quickened as he turned down the hall leading to her chambers, and he nearly sprinted around the corner.

He halted abruptly when he spotted Balder, energetically plastering a crack in the stone with a mixture of clay and crushed stone.

"What are you doing here?" Grimm scowled indignantly. "It's the middle of the night."

Balder shrugged innocently. "Tendin' this castle is a full-time job. Fortunately, I doona require much sleep anymore. But come to think of it, what are you doin' here? Your rooms are that way"—he leveled a half-full trowel in the other direction—"in case you've forgotten. You wouldn't be lookin' to spoil an innocent young lass, now, would you?"

A muscle twitched in Grimm's jaw. "Right. I must have gotten turned around."

"Well, turn back around, lad. I expect I'll be workin' on this wall all night," Balder said evenly. "The *whole* night."

* * *

Twenty minutes later, Jillian poked her head out the door. "Balder!" She tugged her wrapper about her shoulders, peering at him peevishly.

Balder grinned. She was lovely, flushed with sleep and obviously intent upon sneaking to Grimm's room.

"Do you need somethin', lass?"

"What on earth are you doing?"

He gave her the same lame excuse he'd given Grimm and plastered heartily away.

"Oh," Jillian said in a small voice.

"Do you wish me to escort you to the kitchens, lass? Can I give you a wee tour? I'm usually up all night, and the only thing I plan to do is plaster here. Wee cracks between the stones can become great cracks in the blink of an eye if left untended."

"No, no." Jillian waved him away. "I just heard a noise and wondered what it was." She bid him good night and retreated.

After she'd closed the door, Balder rubbed his eyes. By the saints, it was going to be a bloody long night.

* * *

High above Tuluth, men gathered. Two of them broke away from the main group and moved toward the bluff, talking quietly.

"The ambush didn't work, Connor. Why the hell did you send a mere score of men after a Berserker?"

"Because you said he was probably on his way back to Tuluth," Connor shot back. "We dinna wish to waste too many that we might be needing later. Besides, how many kegs of our black powder did you waste, only to be failing, yourself?"

Ramsay Logan scowled. "I hadn't thought it through as well as I should have. He won't escape the next time."

"Logan, if you kill Gavrael McIllioch there will be gold enough to last you the rest of your days. We've been trying for years. He's the last one left that can breed. That we know of," he added.

"Are all their children born Berserkers?" Ramsay watched the lights flicker and fade in the valley.

Connor's lip curled in disgust. "Only the sons of direct descent from the laird. The curse confines itself to the primary, paternal line. Over the centuries our clan has gathered as much information about the McIllioch as we could. We know they have only one true mate, and once their mate dies they remain celibate for the duration of their years. So the old man is no longer a threat. To the best of our knowledge, Gavrael is his only son. When he dies, that's the end. However, during various times over the centuries they've managed to hide a few from us. That's why it's imperative that you get inside Castle Maldebann. I want the last McIllioch destroyed."

"Do you suspect the castle is crawling with concealed blue-eyed boys? Is it possible Ronin had other sons besides Gavrael?"

"We don't know," Connor admitted. "Over the years we've heard there is a hall, a place of pagan worship to Odin. It's supposed to be right in the heart of the mountain." His face grew taut with fury. "Damned heathens, it's a Christian land now! We've heard they practice pagan ceremonies there. And one of the maids we captured—before she died—said that they record each and every one of their unholy spawn in that hall. You must find it and verify Gavrael is the last."

"You expect me to slip into the lair of such creatures and spy? How much gold did you say was in this for me?" Ramsay bargained shrewdly.

Connor regarded him with the fanaticism of a purist. "If you prove he's the last and succeed in killing him, you can name your price."

"I'll get into the castle and take the last Berserker down," Ramsay said with relish.

"How? You've failed three times now."

"Don't worry. I'll not only get to the hall, I will take his mate, Jillian. It's possible she's pregnant—"

"By Christ's blessed tears!" Connor shuddered with disgust. "After you use her, kill her," he ordered.

Ramsay raised a hand. "No. We will wait to see if she's pregnant."

"But she's been tainted—"

"I want her. She's part of my price," Ramsay insisted. "If she's carrying his child, I'll keep her under close guard until she gives birth."

"If it's a son you kill it, and I'll be there to watch. You say you hate the Berserkers, but if you thought you could breed them into your clan, you might feel differently."

"Gavrael McIllioch killed my brothers," Ramsay said tightly. "Religion or not, I'll suffer no qualms about killing his son. Or daughter."

"Good." Connor McKane looked down into the valley at the sleeping village of Tuluth. "The city is much larger now, Logan. What's your plan?"

"You mentioned there are caves in the mountain. Once I've captured the woman I'll give you a piece of the clothing she's wearing. You'll take it and confront the old man and Gavrael. They won't fight as long as they know I have Jillian. You'll send him to the caves, and I'll take care of it from there."

"How?"

"I said I will take care of it from there," Ramsay growled.

"I want to see his dead body with my own eyes."

"You will." Ramsay joined Connor behind the shelter of a bluff. The two of them stared down at Castle Maldebann.

"Such a waste of beauty and strength on heathens. When they are defeated the McKane will take Maldebann," Connor breathed.

"When I have done as I promised, the *Logan* take Maldebann," Ramsay said with an icy gaze that dared Connor to disagree.

CHAPTER 31

WHEN JILLIAN AWOKE THE NEXT MORNING, SHE IMMEDI-
ately became aware of two things: She missed Grimm
terribly, and she had what women called "breeding woes."
As she curled on her side and cradled her stomach, she
couldn't believe she had failed to recognize her malady the
previous morning. Although she'd suspected she was pregnant, she must have been so distracted by worries of how
she would maneuver Grimm to Maldebann that she hadn't
pieced the facts together and realized she had the morning
nausea the maids at Caithness had often complained of.
The thought of suffering it every morning depressed her,
but the confirmation that she was carrying Grimm's child
replaced her discomfort with elation. She couldn't wait to
share the wonderful news with him.

A sudden alarming ache in her stomach nearly made
her reevaluate her joy. She indulged herself in a loud, self-
pitying groan. Curling into a ball helped, as did the conso-

lation that from what she'd heard, such illness was usually of brief duration.

And it was. After about thirty minutes it passed as suddenly as it had assaulted her. She was surprised to discover she felt hearty and hale, as if she'd not suffered a moment of queasiness. She brushed her long hair, tied it back in a ribbon, then sat gazing sadly at the ruins of her wedding gown. They'd left Caithness with nothing but the dress on her body. The only items of clothing in her chambers were that and the Douglas plaid that Grimm had bundled around her. Well, she wasn't going to be denied breakfast by a lack of clothing, she decided swiftly. Not when her tummy was so temperamental.

A few moments and a few strategic knots later, she was wrapped Scots-style in a plaid and ready to make her way to the Greathall.

* * *

Ronin, Balder, and Grimm were already at breakfast, eating in strained silence. Jillian chirped a cheery good morning; the morose group clearly needed a stiff dose of gaiety.

The three men leapt to their feet, jostling for the honor of seating her. She bestowed it upon Grimm with a bright smile. "Good morning," she purred, her eyes wandering over him hungrily. She wondered if her newfound knowledge of their child growing within her glittered in her eyes. She simply *had* to get him alone soon!

He froze, her chair half pulled out. "Morning," he whispered huskily, stupidly, dazzled by her radiance. "Och, Jillian, you have no other clothes, do you?" He eyed her clad in his plaid and smiled tenderly. "I recall you dressing like this when you were wee. You were determined to be just like your da." He seated her, his hands lingering on her shoulders. "Balder, can you set the maids to finding something Jillian might wear?"

It was Ronin who replied. "I'm certain some of Jolyn's gowns could be altered. I had them sealed away . . ." His eyes clouded with sorrow.

Jillian was astonished when Grimm's jaw tensed. He dropped into his seat and fisted his hand around his mug so tightly, his knuckles whitened. Although Grimm had told her a few things about his family, he'd not told her how Jolyn had died. Nor had he told her what Ronin had done to carve such a chasm between the two of them. From what she'd seen of his da, there was nothing remotely strange or mad about him. He seemed a gentle man, filled with regrets and longing for a better future with his son. She realized Balder was watching Grimm as intently as she was.

"Did you ever hear the fable of the wolf in sheep's clothing, lad?" Balder asked, eyeing Grimm with displeasure.

"Aye," he growled. "I became well acquainted with that moral at an early age." Again he flashed a look of fury at Ronin.

"Then you should be understandin' sometimes it works in reverse—there's such a thing as a sheep in wolf's clothing too. Sometimes appearances can be misleadin'. Sometimes you have to reexamine the facts with mature eyes."

Jillian eyed them curiously. There was a message being conveyed that she didn't understand.

"Jillian loves fables," Grimm muttered, urging the subject in a new direction.

"Well, tell us one, lass," Ronin encouraged.

Jillian blushed. "No, really, I couldn't. It's the children who love fables so much."

"Bah, children, she says, Balder!" Ronin exclaimed. "My Jolyn loved fables and told us them often. Come on, lass, give us a story."

"Well . . ." she demurred.

"Tell us one. Go on," the brothers urged.

Beside her Grimm took a deep swallow from his mug and slammed it down on the table.

Jillian flinched inwardly but refused to react. He'd been stomping and glowering ever since they'd arrived, and she couldn't fathom why. Seeking a way to lessen the palpable tension, she rummaged through her stock of fables and, struck by an impish impulse, selected a tale.

"Once there was a mighty lion, heroic and invincible. He was king of the beasts, and he knew it well. A bit arrogant, one might say, but a good king just the same." She paused to smile warmly at Grimm.

He scowled.

"This mighty lion was walking in the forest of the lowlands one evening when he spied a lovely woman—"

"With waves of golden hair and amber eyes," Balder interjected.

"Why, yes! How did you know? You've heard this one, haven't you, Balder?"

Grimm rolled his eyes.

Jillian stifled an urge to laugh and continued. "The mighty lion was mesmerized by her beauty, by her gentle ways, and by the lovely song she was singing. He padded forward quietly so he wouldn't startle her. But the maiden wasn't frightened—she saw the lion for what he was: a powerful, courageous, and honorable creature with an often-fearsome roar who possessed a pure, fearless heart. His arrogance she could overlook, because she knew from watching her own father that arrogance was often part and parcel of extraordinary strength." Jillian sneaked a quick glance at Ronin; he was grinning broadly.

Drawing succor from Ronin's amusement, she looked directly at Grimm and continued. "The lion was besotted. The next day he sought out the woman's father and pledged his heart, seeking her hand in marriage. The woman's father was concerned about the lion's beastly nature, despite the fact that his daughter was perfectly comfortable with it. Unknown to the daughter, her father agreed to accept the lion's courtship, provided the lion king allowed him to pluck his claws and pull his teeth, rendering him tame and civilized. The lion was hopelessly in love. He agreed, and so it was done."

"Another Samson and Delilah," Grimm muttered.

Jillian ignored him. "When the lion then pressed his case, the father drove him from his home with sticks and stones, because the beast was no longer a threat, no longer a fearsome creature."

Jillian paused significantly, and Balder and Ronin clapped their hands. "Wonderfully told!" Ronin exclaimed. "That was a favorite of my wife's as well."

Grimm scowled. "That's the end? Just what the hell was the point of that story?" he asked, offended. "That loving makes a man weaker? That he loses the woman he loves when she sees him unmanned?"

Ronin gave him a disparaging glance. "No, lad. The point of that fable is that even the mighty can be humbled by love."

"Wait—there's more. The daughter," Jillian said quietly, "moved by his willingness to trust so completely, fled her da's house and wed her lion king." She understood Grimm's fear now. Whatever secret he was hiding, he was afraid that once she discovered it, she would leave him.

"I still think it's a terrible story!" Grimm thundered, waving his hand angrily. It caught his mug and sent it flying across the table, spraying Ronin with cider wine. Grimm stared at the bright red stain spreading on his da's white linen for a long, strained moment. "Excuse me," he said roughly, pushing his chair back and without another glance loping from the room.

"Ah, lass, he can be a handful sometimes, I fear," Ronin said with an apologetic look, mopping at his shirt with a cloth.

Jillian poked at her breakfast. "I wish I understood what was going on." She shot a hopeful glance at the brothers.

"You haven't asked him, have you?" Balder remarked.

"I want to ask him, but . . ."

"But you understand he may not be able to give you answers because he doesn't seem to have them himself, does he?"

"I just wish he'd talk to me about it! If not to me, then at least to *you*," she said to Ronin. "There's so much pent up inside him, and I have no idea what to do but give him time."

"He loves you, lass," Ronin assured her. "It's in his eyes, in the way he touches you, in the way he moves when you're around. You're the center of his heart."

"I know," she said simply. "I don't doubt that he loves me. But trust is part and parcel of love."

Balder turned a piercing gaze on his brother. "Ronin is going to speak with him today, aren't you, brother?" He rose from the table. "I'll get you a fresh shirt," he added, and left the Greathall.

Ronin removed his cider-soaked shirt, draped it over a chair, and mopped his body with a linen cloth. The cider had doused him thoroughly.

Jillian watched him curiously. His torso was well defined and powerful. His chest was broad, darkened by years of Highland sun and dusted with hair like Grimm's. And like Grimm's, it was free of scars or birthmarks, a vast unblemished expanse of olive-tinted skin. She couldn't help herself; she stared, perplexed by the fact that there was not a single scar on the torso of a man who'd allegedly fought dozens of battles while wearing no more protection than his plaid, if he fought in the usual Scots manner. Even her father had a scar or two on his chest. She stared uncomprehendingly until she realized Ronin wasn't moving, but was watching her watch him.

"The last time a pretty lass looked at my chest was over fifteen years ago," he teased.

Jillian's gaze flew to his face. He was regarding her tenderly. "Was that how long ago your wife died?"

Ronin nodded. "Jolyn was the loveliest woman I've ever seen. And a truer heart I've never known."

"How did you lose her?" she asked gently.

Ronin regarded her impassively.

"Was it in the battle?" she persisted.

Ronin studied his shirt. "I fear this shirt's ruined."

She tried another route, one he might be willing to discuss. "But surely in fifteen years you've met other women, haven't you?"

"There's only one for us, lass. And after she's gone there can never be another."

"You mean you've never been with . . . in fifteen years you've—" She broke off, embarrassed by the direction the conversation was taking, but she couldn't suppress her curiosity. She knew men often remarried after their wives died. If they didn't, it was considered natural that they took mistresses. Was this man saying he'd been utterly alone for fifteen years?

"There's only one in here." Ronin thumped a fist against his chest. "We only love once, and we're no good to a woman without love," he said with quiet dignity. "My son knows that, at least."

Jillian's eyes fixed on his chest again, and she remarked upon the cause of her consternation. "Grimm said the McKane split your chest open with a battle-ax."

Ronin's eyes darted away. "I heal well. And it's been fifteen years, lass." He shrugged, as if that should explain all.

Jillian stepped closer and stretched out a wondering hand.

Ronin moved away. "The sun darkenin' my skin covers a lot of scars. And there's the hair as well," he said quickly.

Too quickly, for Jillian's peace of mind. "But I don't even see the *hint* of a scar," she protested. According to Grimm, the ax had been buried to the thick wedge of the hilt. Not only couldn't most men survive that, such an injury would have left a thick ridge of hard white tissue. "Grimm said you'd been in many battles. One would think you'd have at least one or two scars to show. Come to think of it," she wondered aloud, "Grimm doesn't have any scars either. Anywhere. As a matter of fact, I don't think I have ever even seen a small cut on that man. Does he never hurt himself? Slip while shaving that stubborn jaw? Stub his toe? Tear a hangnail?" She knew her voice was rising but couldn't help it.

"We McIllioch enjoy excellent health." Ronin fidgeted with his tartan, unrolled a fold, and draped it across his chest.

"Apparently," Jillian responded, her mind far away. She forced herself back with an effort. "Milord—"

"Ronin."

"Ronin, is there something you'd like to tell me about your son?"

Ronin sighed and regarded her somberly. "Och, and is there," he admitted. "But I canna, lass. He must tell you himself."

"Why doesn't he trust me?"

"It's not you he doesn't trust, lass," Balder said, entering the Greathall with a fresh shirt. Like Grimm, he moved silently. "It's that he doesn't trust himself."

Jillian eyed Grimm's uncle. Her gaze darted between him and Ronin. There was something indefinable nagging at the back of her mind, but she simply couldn't put her finger on it. They were both watching her intently, almost hopefully. But what were they hoping for? Baffled, Jillian finished her cider and placed the goblet on a nearby table. "I suppose I should go find Grimm."

"Just doona go looking down the central hall, Jillian," Balder said quickly, regarding her intently. "He rarely goes there, but if he does, it's because he's wishin' for some privacy."

"The central hall?" Jillian's brow furrowed. "I thought this was the central hall." She waved her arm at the Greathall, where they'd dined.

"No, this is the front hall. I mean the one that runs off the back of the castle. Actually, it tunnels right into the heart of the mountain itself. It's where he used to run to when he was a boy."

"Oh." She inclined her head. "Thank you," she added, but had no idea what she was thanking him for. His cryptic comment seemed to have been issued as a deterrent, but it sounded suspiciously like an invitation to snoop. She shook her head briskly and excused herself, consumed by curiosity.

After she left, Ronin grinned at Balder. "He never went there when he was a boy. He hasn't even seen the Hall of Lords yet! You're a sneaky bastard, you are," he exclaimed admiringly.

"I always told you I got the lion's share o' brains in the family." Balder preened and poured them both another glass of cider. "Are the torches lit, Ronin? You left it unlocked, didn't you?"

" 'Course I did! You dinna get *all* the brains. But Balder, what if she can't figure it out? Or worse, can't accept it?"

"That woman has a head on her shoulders, brother. She's fairly burstin' with questions, but she keeps her tongue. Not because she's meek, but out of love for your boy. She's dyin' to know what happened here fifteen years ago, and she's waitin' patiently for Gavrael to tell her. So we'll be givin' her the answers another way to be certain she's prepared when he finally speaks." Balder paused and regarded his brother sternly. "You dinna used to be such a coward, Ronin. Stop waitin' for him to come to you. Go to him as you wish you had years ago. Do it, Ronin."

* * *

Jillian made a beeline for the central hall, or as much of a beeline as she was capable of given that wandering around inside Castle Maldebann was akin to roaming an uncharted city. She navigated confusing corridors, proceeding in the direction she hoped led back toward the mountain, determined to find the central hall. It was obvious Balder and Ronin wished her to see it. Would it give her answers about Grimm?

After thirty minutes of frustrated searching, she looped through a series of twisting hallways and around a corner that opened into a second Greathall, even larger than the one she'd breakfasted in. She stepped forward hesitantly; the hall was definitely old—perhaps as ancient as the standing stones erected by the mystical Druids.

Someone had conveniently lit torches—the interfering brothers, she concluded gratefully—for there was not one window in this part of the structure, and how could there be? This Greathall was actually inside the belly of the mountain. She shivered, rattled by the idea. She crossed the huge room slowly, drawn by the mysterious double doors set into the wall at the other end. They towered above her, wrapped in bands of steel, and above the arched opening bold letters had been chiseled.

"Deo non fortuna," she whispered, driven by the same impulse to speak in hushed tones that she'd suffered in Caithness's chapel.

She pressed against the massive doors and held her breath as they swung inward, revealing the central hall Balder had spoken of. Wide-eyed, she moved forward with the dreamy gait of a sleepwalker, riveted by what lay before her. The flowing lines of the hall commanded the eyes upward, and she pivoted slowly, arching her head back and marveling at the ceiling. Pictures and murals covered the vast expanse, some of them so vibrant and realistic that her hands begged to touch them. A chill coursed through her as she tried to comprehend what she was seeing. Was she gazing up at centuries of the history of the McIllioch? She dragged her gaze downward, only to discover new wonders. The walls of the hall held portraits. Hundreds of them!

Jillian glided along the wall. It took only a few moments for her to realize she was walking down a historical genealogy, a time line done in portraits. The first pictures were chiseled in stone, some directly into the wall, with names carved beneath them—odd names she couldn't begin to pronounce. As she worked her way down the wall, the methods of depiction became more modern, as did the clothing. It was apparent that much care had been given to repainting and restoring the portraits to maintain their accuracy over the centuries.

As she progressed down the time line toward the present, the portraits became more graphically detailed, which deepened her growing sense of confusion. Colors were brighter, more painstakingly applied. Her eyes darting between portraits, she moved forward and back again, comparing portraits of children to their subsequent adult portraits.

She must be mistaken.

Incredulous, Jillian closed her eyes a minute, then opened them slowly and stepped back a few paces to study an entire section. It couldn't be. Grabbing a torch, she moved nearer, peering intently at a cluster of boys at their mothers' skirts. They were beautiful boys, dark-haired, brown-eyed boys who would certainly grow into dangerously handsome men.

She moved to the next portraits and there they were again: dark-haired, blue-eyed, dangerously handsome men.

Eyes didn't change color.

Jillian retraced her steps and studied the woman in the last portrait. She was a stunning auburn-haired woman with five brown-eyed boys at her skirts. Jillian then moved to her right; it was either the same woman or her identical twin. Five men clustered around her in various poses, all looking directly at the artist, leaving no doubt as to the color of their eyes. Ice blue. The names beneath the portraits were the same. She moved farther down the hall, bewildered.

Until she found the sixteenth century.

Unfortunately, the portraits raised more questions than they answered, and she sank to her knees in the hall for a long time, thinking.

Hours passed before she managed to sort through it all to her satisfaction. When she had, no question remained in her mind—she was an intelligent woman, able to exercise her powers of deductive reasoning with the best of them. And those powers told her that, though it defied her every rational thought, there was simply no other explanation. She was sitting on her knees, clad in a disheveled plaid, clutching a nearly burned-out torch in a hall filled with Berserkers.

CHAPTER 32

GRIMM PACED THE TERRACE, FEELING LIKE A FOOL. HE'D sat across the table and shared food with his da, managing to make civil conversation until Jillian had arrived. Then Ronin had mentioned Jolyn, and he'd felt fury rise up so quickly he'd nearly lunged across the table and grabbed the old man by the throat.

But Grimm was intelligent enough to realize that much of the anger he felt was at himself. He needed information and was afraid to ask. He needed to talk to Jillian, but what could he tell her? He had no answers himself. *Confront your da,* his conscience demanded. *Find out what really happened.*

The idea terrified him. If he discovered he was wrong, his entire world would look radically different.

Besides, he had other things to worry about. He had to make certain Jillian didn't discover what he was, and he needed to warn Balder that the McKane were on his heels. He needed to get Jillian somewhere safe before they attacked, and he needed to figure out why he, his uncle, and his da were all Berserkers. It just seemed too coincidental, and Balder kept alluding to information he didn't possess. Information he couldn't ask for.

"Son."

Grimm spun around. "Doona call me that," he snapped, but the protest didn't carry its usual venom.

Ronin expelled a gust of air. "We need to talk."

"It's too late. You said all you had to say years ago."

Ronin crossed the terrace and joined Grimm at the wall. "Tuluth is beautiful, isn't she?" he asked softly.

Grimm didn't reply.

"Lad, I . . ."

"Ronin, did you . . ."

The two men looked at each other searchingly. Neither noticed as Balder stepped out onto the terrace.

"Why did you leave and never come back?" The words burst from Ronin's lips with the pent-up anguish of fifteen years of waiting to say them.

"Why did I leave?" Grimm echoed incredulously.

"Was it because you were afraid of what you'd become?"

"What *I* became? I never became what you are!"

Ronin gaped at him. "How can you be sayin' that when you have the blue eyes? You have the bloodlust."

"I know I'm a Berserker," Grimm replied evenly. "But I'm *not* insane."

Ronin blinked. "I never said you were."

"You did too. That night at the battle, you told me I was just like you," he reminded bitterly.

"And you are."

"I am not!"

"Yes, you are—"

"You killed my mother!" Grimm roared, with all the anguish built up from fifteen years of waiting.

Balder moved forward instantly, and Grimm found himself the uncomfortable focus of two pairs of intense blue eyes.

Ronin and Balder exchanged a glance of astonishment. "*That's* why you never came home?" Ronin said carefully.

Grimm breathed deeply. Questions exploded from him, and now that he'd begun asking he thought he might never stop. "How did I get brown eyes to begin with? How come you're both Berserkers too?"

"Oh, you really are dense, aren't you?" Balder snorted. "Come on, canna you put two and two together yet, lad?"

Every muscle in Grimm's body spasmed. Thousands of questions collided with hundreds of suspicions and dozens of suppressed memories, and it all coalesced into the unthinkable. "Is someone else my father?" he demanded.

Ronin and Balder watched him, shaking their heads.

"Well, then why did you kill my mother?" he roared. "And doona be telling me we're born this way. You may have been born crazy enough to kill your wife, but I'm not."

Ronin's face stiffened with fury. "I canna believe you think I killed Jolyn."

"I found you over her body," Grimm persisted. *"You were holding the knife."*

"I removed it from her heart." Ronin gritted. "Why would I kill the only woman I ever loved? How could you, of all people, possibly think I could kill my true mate? Could you kill Jillian? Even in the midst of Berserker-gang, could you kill her?"

"Never!" Grimm thundered the word.

"Then you realize you misunderstood."

"You lunged for me. I would have been next!"

"You are my son," Ronin breathed. "I *needed* you. I needed to touch you; to know you were alive; to reassure myself that the McKane hadn't gotten you too."

Grimm stared at him blankly. "The McKane? Are you telling me the McKane killed mother? The McKane didn't even attack until sundown. Mother died in the morning."

Ronin regarded him with a mixture of amazement and anger. "The McKane had been waiting in the hills all day. They had a spy among us and had discovered Jolyn was pregnant again."

A look of horror crossed Grimm's face. "Mother was pregnant?"

Ronin rubbed his eyes. "Aye. We'd thought she wouldn't bear more children—it was unexpected. She hadn't gotten pregnant since you, and that had been nearly fifteen years. It would have been a late child, but we were so lookin' forward to havin' another—" Ronin broke off abruptly. He swallowed several times. "I lost everythin' in one day," he said, his eyes glittering brightly. "And all these years I thought you wouldn't come home because you dinna understand what you were. I despised myself for havin' failed you. I thought you hated me for makin' you what you are and for not bein' there to teach you how to deal with it. I spent years fightin' my urge to come after you and claim you as my son, to prevent the McKane from trackin' you. You'd managed to pretty effectively disappear. And now . . . now I discover that all these years I've been watchin' you, waitin' for you to come home, you were hatin' me. You were out there thinkin' I killed Jolyn!" Ronin turned away bitterly.

"The McKane killed my mother?" Grimm whispered. "Why would they care if she was pregnant?"

Ronin shook his head and looked at Balder. "How did I raise a son who was so thickheaded?"

Balder shrugged and rolled his eyes.

"You still doona get it, do you, Gavrael? What I was tryin' to tell you all those years ago: We—the McIllioch men—we're *born* Berserk. Any son born of the Laird's direct line is a Berserker. The McKane have hunted us for a thousand years. They know our legends nearly as well as we do. The prophecy was that we would be virtually destroyed, whittled down to three." He waved his arms in a gesture that encompassed the three of them. "But one lad would return home, brought by his true mate, and destroy the McKane. The McIllioch would become mightier than ever before. *You* are that lad."

"B-b-born Berserk?" Grimm stuttered.

"Yes," both men responded in a single breath.

"But I turned into one," Grimm floundered. "Up on Wotan's Cleft. I called on Odin."

Ronin shook his head. "It just seemed that way. It was first blood in battle that brought the Berserker out. Normally our sons doona turn until sixteen. First battle accelerated your change."

Grimm sank to a seat on the wall and buried his face in his hands. "Why did you never tell me what I was before I changed?"

"Son, it's not like we hid it from you. We started tellin' you the legends at a young age. You were entranced, remember?" Ronin broke off and laughed. "I recall you runnin' around, tryin' to 'become a Berserker' for years. We were pleased you welcomed your heritage with such open arms. Go, go look in the blasted Hall of Lords, Gavrael—"

"Grimm," Grimm corrected stubbornly, holding on to some part of his identity—any part.

Ronin continued as if he hadn't been interrupted. "There are ceremonies we hold, when we pass on the secrets and teach our sons to deal with the Berserker rage. Your time was approachin', but suddenly the McKane attacked. I lost Jolyn and you left, never once lookin' west to Maldebann, to me. And now I know you were hatin' me, accusin' me of the most vile thing a man could do."

"We train our sons, Gavrael," Balder said. "Intense discipline: mental, emotional, and physical trainin'. We instruct them to command the Berserker, not be commanded by it. You missed that trainin', yet I must say that even on your own you did well. Without any training, without any understandin' of your nature, you remained honorable and have grown into a fine Berserker. Donna be thrashin' yourself for seein' things at fourteen with the half-opened eyes of a fourteen-year-old."

"So I'm supposed to repopulate Maldebann with Berserkers?" Grimm suddenly fixated on Ronin's words about the prophecy.

"It's been foretold in the Hall of Lords."

"But Jillian doesn't know what I am," Grimm said despairingly. "And any son she has will be just like me. We can never—" He was unable to finish the thought aloud.

"She's stronger than you think she is, lad," Ronin replied. "Trust in her. Together you can learn about our heritage. It is an honor to be a Berserker, not a curse. Most of Alba's greatest heroes have been our kind."

Grimm was silent a long time, trying to recolor fifteen years of thinking. "The McKane are coming," he said finally, latching on to one solid fact in an internal landscape deluged by intangibles.

Both men's eyes flew to the surrounding mountains. "Did you see something move on the mountains?"

"No. They've been following me. They've tried three times now to take me. They've been on our heels since we left Caithness."

"Wonderful!" Balder rubbed his hands together in gleeful anticipation.

Ronin looked delighted. "How far behind you were they?"

"I suspect scarcely a day."

"So they'll be here anytime. Lad, you must go find Jillian. Take her to the heart of the castle and explain. Trust her. Give her the chance to work through things. If you had known the truth years ago, would fifteen years have been wasted?"

"She'll hate me when she discovers what I am," Grimm said bitterly.

"Are you as certain of that as you were that I killed Jolyn?" Ronin asked pointedly.

Grimm's eyes flew to his. "I'm no longer certain of anything," he said bleakly.

"You're certain you love her, lad," Ronin said. "And I'm certain she's your mate. Never has one of our true mates rejected our heritage. Never."

Grimm nodded and turned for the castle.

"Be certain she stays in the castle, Gavrael," Ronin called to his back. "We canna risk her in battle."

After Grimm had disappeared into Maldebann, Balder smiled. "He dinna try to correct you when you called him Gavrael."

Ronin's smile was joyous. "I noticed," he said. "Prepare the villagers, Balder, and I'll rouse the guards. We put an end to the feuding today. All of it."

CHAPTER 33

IT WAS EARLY AFTERNOON WHEN JILLIAN FINALLY ROSE to her feet in the Hall of Lords. A sense of peace enveloped her as she laid the last of her questions to rest. Suddenly so many things she'd overheard her brothers and Quinn saying when Grimm had been in residence made sense, and upon reflection she suspected a part of her had always known.

Her love was a legendary warrior who had grown to despise himself, cut off from his roots. But now that he was home and given the time to explore those roots, he might be able to make peace with himself at long last.

She strolled the hall a final time, not missing the radiant expressions of the McIllioch brides. She stood for a long moment beneath the portrait of Grimm and his parents. Jolyn had been a chestnut-haired beauty; love radiated from her patient smile. Ronin was gazing adoringly at her. In the portrait, Grimm was kneeling before his seated parents, looking like the happiest brown-eyed boy in the world.

Her hands moved to her belly in a timeless feminine

celebration as she wondered what it would be like to bring another boy like Grimm into the world. How proud she would be, and together with Grimm, Balder, and Ronin, they would teach him what he could be, and how special he was—one of Alba's own private warriors.

"Och, lass, tell me you're not breeding!" a voice filled with loathing spat.

Jillian's scream ricocheted off the cold stone walls as Ramsay Logan's hand closed on her shoulder in a painful, viselike grip.

* * *

"I can't find her," Grimm said tightly.

Ronin and Balder turned as one when he stormed into the Greathall. The guards were ready, the villagers had been roused, and to the last man Tuluth was prepared to fight the McKane.

"Did you check in the Hall of Lords?"

"Aye, a brief glance, enough to assure myself she wasn't there." If he'd looked longer he might never have dragged himself back out, so fascinated was he by his previously unknown heritage.

"Did you search the whole castle?"

"Aye." He buried his hands in his hair, voicing his worst fear. "Is it possible the McKane got in here and took her somehow?"

Ronin expelled a gust of air. "Anythin's possible, lad. There were deliveries from the village this afternoon. Hell, anyone could have sneaked in with 'em. We've grown a bit lax in fifteen years of peace."

A sudden cry from the guardhouse compelled their instant attention.

"The McKane are comin'!"

* * *

Connor McKane rode into the vale waving a flag of Douglas plaid, which, while it confused most of the McIllioch, filled Grimm with rage and fear. The only piece of Douglas plaid a McKane could have obtained was the one from Jillian's body. She'd worn the blue and gray fabric at breakfast only this morning.

The villagers were bristling to fight, eager to demand satisfaction for the loss of their loved ones fifteen years past. As Ronin prepared to order them forward, Grimm laid a restraining hand on his arm.

"They have Jillian," he said in a voice that sounded like death.

"How can you be sure?" Ronin's gaze flew to his.

"That's my plaid they're waving. Jillian was wearing it at breakfast."

Ronin closed his eyes. "Not again," he whispered. "Not again." When he opened his eyes, they burned with the inner fire of determination. "We won't lose her, lad. Bring the McKane laird forward," he commanded the guard.

The McIllioch troops emanated hostility but drew back to permit his approach. When Connor McKane drew up in front of Ronin he scowled. "I knew you'd heal from the battle-ax, you devil, but I didn't think you'd recover so well from me killing your pretty whore of a wife." Connor bared his teeth in a smile. "*And* your unborn child."

Although Ronin's hand fisted around his claymore, he didn't free the sword. "Let the lass go, McKane. She has nothin' to do with us."

"The lass may be breeding."

Grimm went rigid on Occam's back. "She's not," he countered coolly. *Surely she would have told him!*

Connor McKane searched his face intently. "That's what she says. But I don't trust either of you."

"Where is she?" Grimm demanded.

"Safe."

"Take me, Connor, take me in her stead," Ronin offered, stunning Grimm.

"You, old man?" Connor spat. "You're not a threat anymore—we saw to that years ago. You won't be having any more sons. Now, him"—he pointed to Grimm—"he's a problem. Our spies tell us he is the last living Berserker, and the woman who may or may not be pregnant is his mate."

"What do you want from me?" Grimm said quietly.

"Your life," the McKane said simply. "To see the last of the McIllioch die is all I've ever wanted."

"We're not the monsters you think we are." Ronin glowered at the McKane chieftain.

"You're pagans. Heathens, blasphemers to the one true religion—"

"You're hardly one to judge!" Ronin exclaimed.

"Dinna think to debate the Lord's word with me, McIllioch. The voice of Satan will not tempt me from God's course."

Ronin's lip drew back in a snarl. "When man thinks he knows God's course better than God himself is when hundreds die—"

"Free Jillian and you may have my life," Grimm interrupted. "But she goes free. You will entrust her to"—Grimm glanced at Ronin—"my da." He tried to meet Ronin's gaze when he named him his sire, but couldn't.

"I dinna recover you to lose you again, lad," Ronin muttered harshly.

"What a touching reunion," Connor remarked dryly.

"But lose him you will. And if you want her, Gavrael McIllioch—last of the Berserkers—free her yourself. She's up there." He pointed to Wotan's Cleft. "In the caves."

Horrified, Grimm scanned the jagged face of the cliff. "Where in the caves?" Dread filled him at the thought of Jillian wandering in the darkness, skirting dangers she couldn't even know were there: collapsed tunnels, rock slides, dangerous pits.

"Find her yourself."

"How do I know this isn't a trap?" Grimm's eyes glittered dangerously.

"You don't," the McKane said flatly. "But if she is in there, it's very dark and there are a lot of dangerous chasms. Besides, what would I gain by sending you off into the caves?"

"They could be set to explode," Grimm said tightly.

"Then I guess you better get her out fast, McIllioch," the McKane provoked.

Ronin shook his head. "We need proof that she's in there. And alive."

Connor dispatched a guard with a low rush of words.

Some time later, that proof was offered. Jillian's piercing scream ripped through the tense air of the valley.

* * *

Ronin watched in silence as Grimm climbed the rocky pass to Wotan's Cleft.

Balder was far back in the ranks, his features concealed by a heavy cloak to prevent the McKane from realizing there was yet another unmated Berserker still alive. Ronin had insisted they not reveal his existence unless it was necessary to save lives.

From different vantages, the brothers admired the young

man mounting the cleft. He'd left Occam behind and was scaling the sheer face of the cliff with a skill and ease that revealed the preternatural prowess of the Berserker. After years of hiding what he was, he now flaunted his superiority to the enemy. He was a warrior, at one with the beast, born to survive and endure. When he topped the cliff and disappeared over the edge the two clans sat their horses in battle lines, staring across the space that separated them with hatred so palpable it hung in the air as thick and oppressive as the smoke that had filled the vale fifteen years past.

Until Jillian and Grimm—or, God forbid, a McKane— topped the edge of the cliff, neither side would move. The McKane hadn't come to Tuluth to lose any more of their clan; they'd come to take Gavrael and eliminate the last of the Berserkers.

The McIllioch didn't move out of fear for Jillian.

The time stretched painfully.

* * *

Grimm entered the tunnel silently. His every instinct demanded he bellow for Jillian, but that would only alert whoever was holding her to his presence. The memory of her terrible scream both chilled his blood and made it boil for vengeance.

He eased into the tunnel, gliding with the silent stealth of a mountain cat, sniffing the air like a wolf. All his animal instincts roused with chill, predatory perfection. Somewhere torches were burning; the scent was unmistakable. He followed the odor down twisting corridors, his hands outstretched in the darkness. Although the interior of the tunnels was pitch black, his heightened vision enabled him to discern the slope of the floor. Skirting deep pits and ducking beneath crumbling ceilings, he navigated the musty tunnels, following the scent.

He rounded a bend where the tunnel opened into a long straight corridor, and there she was, her golden hair gleaming in the torchlight.

"Stop right there," Ramsay Logan warned. "Or she dies."

It was a vision from one of his worst nightmares. Ramsay had Jillian at the end of the tunnel. He'd gagged and bound her. She was wearing the McKane tartan, and the sight of it on her body filled him with fury. The question of who had stripped and reclothed her tortured him. He assessed her quickly, assuring himself that whatever had made her scream had not drawn blood or left visible sign of injury. The blade Logan was holding to her throat had not pierced her delicate skin. Yet.

"Ramsay Logan." Grimm gave him a chilling smile.

"Not surprised to see me, eh, Roderick? Or should I say McIllioch?" He spat the name as if he'd found a foul thing lying on his tongue.

"No, I can't say I'm surprised." Grimm moved stealthily nearer. "I always knew what kind of man you are."

"I said stop, you bastard. I won't hesitate to kill her."

"And then what would you do?" Grimm countered, but drew to a halt. "You'll never make it past me, so what would killing Jillian accomplish?"

"I'd get the pleasure of ridding the world of McIllioch monsters yet to be. And if I don't come out, the McKane will destroy you when you do."

"Let her go. Release her and you can have me," Grimm offered. Jillian thrashed in Ramsay's tight grip, making it clear that she wanted no such thing.

"I'm afraid I can't do that, McIllioch."

Grimm said nothing, his eyes murderous. A score of yards lay between them, and Grimm wondered if the Berserker rage could get him across it and free Jillian before Ramsay could slice with the knife.

It was too risky to chance, and Ramsay was counting on that to stay him. But something didn't make sense. What did Logan hope to gain? If he killed Jillian, Ramsay knew Grimm would go Berserk and rip him to shreds. What was Logan's plan? He began to ask questions, trying to buy precious minutes. "Why are you doing this, Logan? I know we've had our disagreements in the past, but they were minor."

"It has nothing to do with our disagreements and everything to do with what you are." Ramsay sneered. "You're not human, McIllioch."

Grimm closed his eyes, unwilling to see the look of horror he was certain would be on Jillian's face. "When did you figure it out?" Keeping Ramsay talking might give him insight into what the bastard wanted. If it was his life and his alone, and he could assure Jillian's safety by giving it, he would gladly die. But if Ramsay planned to kill them both, Grimm would die fighting for her.

"I figured it out the day you killed the mountain cat. I was standing in the trees and saw you after you transformed. Hatchard called you by your real name." Ramsay shook his head in disgust. "All those years at court I never knew. Oh, I knew who Gavrael McIllioch was—hell, I think everyone does but your lovely bitch here." He laughed when Grimm stiffened. "Careful, or I cut."

"So you aren't the one who tried to poison me?" Grimm inched forward so gracefully he didn't appear to be moving.

Ramsay roared with laughter. "That was a fine fix. Hell

yes, I tried to poison you. Even that backfired; you switched it somehow. But I didn't know you were a Berserker then, or I wouldn't have wasted my time."

Grimm winced. It was out. But Jillian's face was turned to the side, away from the knife, and he couldn't make out her expression.

"No," Ramsay continued. "I had no idea. I just wanted you out of the running for Jillian. You see, I need the lass."

"I was right. You need her dowry."

"But you don't know the half of it. I'm in to Campbell so deeply, he's holding the titles to my land. In years past the Logans hired out as mercenaries, but there haven't been any good wars lately. Do you know when we hired out as mercenaries last? Stop moving!" he bellowed.

Grimm stood impassively. "When?"

"Fifteen years ago. To the McKane, you bastard. And fifteen years ago, Gavrael McIllioch killed my da and three of my brothers."

Grimm hadn't known. The battle was a blur in his mind, his first Berserker rage. "In fair battle. And if your clan hired out they weren't even fighting for a cause, but murdering for coin. If they were in Tuluth, they were attacking my home and slaughtering my people—"

"You're not people. You're not *human*."

"Jillian's not part of this. Let her go. It's me you want."

"She's part of it if she's breeding, McIllioch. She swears she's not, but I think I'll keep her just to make sure. The McKane told me a lot about you monsters. I know the boys are born Berserkers but don't change until they get older. A boy slips out of her womb, he's dead. If it's a girl, who knows. I may let it live. She could be a pretty toy."

Grimm finally managed to get a glimpse of Jillian's

face. It was drawn in a mask of horror. So it was out. She knew, and it was over. The fear and revulsion he'd glimpsed in his nightmares had indeed been a portent. The fight nearly fled him when he saw it, and would have had she not been in danger. He could die now. He may as well, because inside he already had. But not Jillian; she must live.

"She's not pregnant, Ramsay."

Wasn't she? Memories of her sudden nausea at the cottage surfaced in his mind. Of course Ramsay couldn't know, but the mere possibility of Jillian carrying his child sent a primitive thrill of exultation through Grimm's body. His need to protect her, already all-consuming, became the singular focus of his mind. Ramsay might have the upper hand, but Grimm refused to let him win.

"As if you would tell me the truth." Logan scoffed. "There's only one way to find out. Besides, whether she is or isn't, she'll still be wedding me. I want the gold she brings as her dowry. Between her and what the McKane pay me, I'll never have to worry about wealth again. Don't worry, I'll keep her alive. So long as she breathes, Gibraltar will do anything to keep her happy, which means an endless supply of coin."

"You son of a bitch. Just let her go!"

"You want her? Come and get her." Ramsay taunted.

Grimm stepped forward, eyeing the distance. In the instant he hesitated, Ramsay moved the blade, pricking Jillian's skin, and drops of crimson blood fell.

The Berserker, simmering with rage, erupted.

Even as he wondered why Ramsay would dare goad the Berserker into appearing, instinct plunged him forward. He had been considering cutting himself to bring on the rage, when Ramsay had done it for him. One leap brought him ten paces forward. He tried to stop, sensing an unknown trap, but the floor of the cave disappeared beneath his feet and he plunged into a chasm that hadn't existed when he'd played these tunnels as a boy. A chasm deep enough to kill even a Berserker.

"Good riddance, you bastard," Ramsay said with a smile. He held the torch above the previously concealed pit and peered as deep as the flames would permit. He waited a full five minutes but heard no sound. When he'd selected his trap, he'd tossed stones into the chasm to test the depth. None of the stones had yielded a sound, so deep was the aperture yawning into the core of the earth. If Grimm hadn't been ripped to shreds on rocky slag, the fall itself would crush every bone in his body. Skirting the pit, he dragged Jillian from the caves.

* * *

"It's done!" Ramsay Logan cried. "The McKane!" he roared. He stood on the edge of Wotan's Cleft, raised his arm, and bellowed a cry of victory that was instantly echoed by all the McKane. The valley resounded with triumphant thunder. Exuberant, Ramsay released Jillian's hands and removed her gag. His took her mouth in a triumphant, brutal kiss. She stiffened, revolted, and struggled against him. Angered by her resistance, he shoved her away, and Jillian crumpled to her knees.

"Get up, you stupid bitch," Ramsay shouted, nudging at her with his foot. "I said get up!" he roared again when she responded to his kick by curling into a ball. "I don't need you right now anyway," he muttered, gazing down at the valley that would be his home. Adulation lay in the valley, a reflection of his mighty conquest. He waved his arm again, elated by the kill.

Ramsay Logan had taken a Berserker single-handed. His name would live in legends. The chasm was so deep that not even one of Odin's monsters could survive the fall. He'd carefully covered it with thin sheaves of wood, then scattered stone dust atop it. It had been brilliant, if he had to say so himself.

"Brilliant," Ramsay informed the night.

Behind Ramsay, Grimm blinked, trying to clear the red haze of bloodlust. A part of his mind that seemed lost down an endless corridor reminded him that he wanted to attack the man standing near the balled-up woman, not the woman herself. The woman was his world. When he sprang he must be careful, very careful, for to even touch her with the strength of Berserkergang could kill her. A slight brush of his hand could shatter her jaw, the merest caress of her breast could crush her ribs.

To those sitting the horses in the valley below, listening to Ramsay Logan's victory cry, the creature seemed to explode out of the night with such speed it was impossible to identify. A blur of motion surged through the air, grabbed Ramsay Logan by the hair, and neatly severed his head before anyone could so much as shout a warning.

Because she was on the ground, the clans gathered below couldn't see Jillian roll over, startled by the slight hissing sound the blade made as it whisked through the air for Ramsay's throat. But the creature on the cliffs saw her move, and he waited for her judgment, resigned to condemnation.

It was the worst Jillian might ever see of him, the beast realized. In the full throes of Berserkergang, he towered over her, his blue eyes blazing incandescently. He was bruised and bloody from a fall that had halted abruptly on a jagged outcropping, and he held Ramsay Logan's severed head in one hand. He stared at her, pumping great gasps of air into his chest, waiting. Would she scream? Spit at him, hiss and renounce him? Jillian St. Clair was all he'd ever wanted in his entire life, and as he waited for her to shriek in horror of him, he felt something inside him trying to die.

But the Berserker wouldn't go down so easily. The wildness in him rose to its full height and stared down at her through vulnerable ice-blue eyes, wordlessly beseeching her love.

Jillian raised her head slowly and gazed at him a long, silent moment. She drew herself upright into a sitting position and tilted her head back, her eyes wide.

Berserker.

The truth he'd struggled so hard to hide hung between them, fully exposed.

Although Jillian had known what Grimm was before that moment, she was briefly immobilized by the sight of him. It was one thing to know that the man she loved was a Berserker—it was another thing entirely to behold it. He regarded her with such an inhuman expression that if she hadn't peered deep into his eyes, she might have seen nothing of Grimm at all. But there, deep in the flickering blue flames, she glimpsed such love that it rocked her soul. She smiled up at him through her tears.

A wounded sound of disbelief escaped him.

Jillian gave him the most dazzling smile she could muster and placed her fist to her heart. "And the daughter wed the lion king," she said clearly.

An expression of incredulity crossed the warrior's face. His blue eyes widened and he stared at her in stunned silence.

"I love you, Gavrael McIllioch."

When he smiled, his face blazed with love. He tossed his head back and shouted his joy to the sky.

* * *

The last of the McKane died in the vale of Tuluth, December 14, 1515.

CHAPTER 34

"THEY'RE COMING, HAWK!" ADRIENNE SPED INTO THE Greathall where Hawk, Lydia, and Tavis were busy decorating for the wedding. As the ceremony was being held on Christmas Day, they'd combined the customary decorations with the gaily colored greens and reds of the season. Exquisite wreaths fashioned of pinecones and dried berries had been decorated with brilliant velvet bows and shimmering ribbons. The finest tapestries adorned the walls, including one Adrienne had helped to weave over the past year that featured a Nativity scene with a radiant Madonna cradling the infant Jesus while proud Joseph and the magi looked on.

Today the hall was clear of rushes, the stones scoured to a spotless gray. Later, only moments before the wedding, they would strew dried rose petals across the stones to release a springy floral aroma into the air. Sprigs of mistletoe dangled from every beam and Adrienne eyed the foliage, peering up at Hawk, who stood on a ladder, fastening a wreath to the wall.

"What are those lovely sprigs you've hung, Hawk?" Adrienne asked, the picture of innocence.

Hawk glanced down at her. "Mistletoe. It's a Christmas tradition."

"How is it associated with Christmas?"

"The legends say the Scandinavian god of peace, Balder, was slain by an arrow fashioned of mistletoe. The other gods and goddesses loved Balder so greatly, they begged his life be restored and mistletoe be endowed with special meaning."

"What kind of special meaning?" Adrienne blinked expectantly up at him.

Hawk slid swiftly down the ladder, happy to demonstrate. He kissed her so passionately that the embers of desire, always at a steady burn around her husband, roared into flame. "One who passes beneath the mistletoe must be kissed thoroughly."

"Mmm. I like this tradition. But what happened to poor Balder?"

Hawk grinned and planted another kiss on her lips. "Balder was returned to life and the care of mistletoe was bequeathed to the goddess of love. Each time a kiss is given beneath mistletoe, love and peace gain a stronger foothold in the world of mortals."

"How lovely," Adrienne exclaimed. Her eyes sparkled mischievously. "So essentially, the more I kiss you under this branch"—she pointed up—"the more good I'm doing the world. One might say I'm helping all of humankind, doing my duty—"

"Your duty?" Hawk arched a brow.

Lydia laughed and tugged Tavis beneath the branch as well. "It sounds like a good idea to me, Adrienne. Maybe if we kiss them enough we'll lay all the silly feuding in this land to rest."

The next few minutes belonged to lovers, until the door burst open and a guard announced the arrival of their guests.

Adrienne's gaze darted about the Greathall as she fretted over anything that might be yet undone. She wanted everything to be perfect for Grimm's bride. "How do I say it again?" she asked Lydia frantically. She'd been trying to perfect her Gaelic so she could greet them with a proper "Merry Christmas."

"*Nollaig Chridheil,*" Lydia repeated slowly.

Adrienne repeated it several times, then linked her arm through Hawk's and smiled beatifically. "My wish came true, Hawk," she said smugly.

"What was that blasted wish, anyway?" Hawk said, disgruntled.

"That Grimm Roderick find the woman who would heal his heart as you healed mine, my love." Adrienne would never call a man "radiant"; it seemed a feminine word. But when her husband gazed down at her with his eyes glowing so lovingly, she whispered a fervent "thank you" in the direction of the Nativity scene. Then she added a silent benediction for any and all other beings responsible for the events that had carried her across five hundred years to find him. Scotland was a magical place, rich in legends, and Adrienne embraced them because the underlying themes were universal: Love endured, and it could heal all.

* * *

It was a traditional wedding, if such could be between a woman and a man of legend—a Berserker no less, with two more of the epic warriors in attendance. The women fussed and the men shared toasts. At the last minute, Gibraltar and Elizabeth St. Clair arrived. They had ridden like the devil the moment they'd received the message that Jillian was to be wed at Dalkeith-Upon-the-Sea.

Jillian was elated to see her parents. Elizabeth and Adrienne helped her dress while they resolved that both "das" should escort the bride to the groom's side. Ronin had already been solicited for the honor, but Elizabeth maintained that Gibraltar would never recover if he wasn't allowed to escort her too. Yes, she knew that Jillian hadn't expected them to be able to make it in time, but they had and that was the end of it.

The bride and groom didn't see one another until the moment Gibraltar and Ronin escorted Jillian down the elaborate staircase into the Greathall, after a long pause at the top that permitted all and sundry to exclaim over the radiant bride.

Jillian's heart was thundering as her two "das" lifted her hands from their forearms and tucked her arm through the elbow of the man who was to be her husband. Grimm looked magnificent, clad in ceremonial tartan, his black hair neatly queued. Jillian didn't miss it when Ronin's gaze flickered over the plaid. He looked momentarily astonished, then elated, for Grimm had donned the full dress of the McIllioch for his wedding day.

She hadn't thought the day could be any more perfect until the priest began the ceremony. After what seemed like years of traditional benedictions and prayers, he moved onto the vows:

"Do you, Grimm Roderick, promise—"

Grimm's deep voice interrupted him. Pride underscored each word. "My name is Gavrael." He took a deep breath, then continued, enunciating his name clearly. "Gavrael Roderick Icarus McIllioch."

Chills swept up her spine. Tears misted Ronin's eyes and the hall fell silent for a moment. Hawk grinned at Adrienne, and far in the back of the hall where few had as yet seen him, Quinn de Moncreiffe nodded, satisfied. At long last, Grimm Roderick was at peace with who and what he was.

"Do you, Gavrael Roderick—"

"I do."

Jillian nudged him.

He arched a brow and frowned. "Well, I *do*. Must we go through all this? I do. I swear a man has never 'I do'd' more fervently than I. I just want to be *married* to you, lass."

Ronin and Balder exchanged amused glances. Keeping them apart had certainly heightened Gavrael's enthusiasm for the matrimonial bonds.

Guests tittered, and Jillian smiled. "Let the priest have his turn, because I would like to hear you say it all. Especially the 'loving and cherishing me' part."

"Oh, I'll love and ravish you, lass," Gavrael said close to her ear.

"Cherish! And behave." She teasingly swatted at him and nodded encouragingly to the priest. "Do continue."

And so they were wed.

* * *

Kaley Twillow jostled for room, rising to her toes and peering over heads anxiously. Her precious Jillian was getting married and she couldn't see a dratted thing. It just wouldn't do.

"Watch where yer pokin'," an irate guest barked as she strategically jabbed her elbow in a few tender spots to squeeze past.

"Wait your turn to greet the bride!" another one complained when she stepped on his toes.

"I practically raised the wee bride, and I'll be damned if I'm sitting in back unable to see, so *move* your arse!" She glowered.

A small path appeared as they reluctantly permitted her passage.

Wedging her ample bosom and hips between a cluster of guards created a small furor as dozens of men eyed the shapely woman with interest. Finally she pushed through, crested the last wave of guests, and surfaced beside a man whose handsome height and girth took her breath away. His thick black hair was streaked with silver, revealing his mature years, which, in her experience, meant mature passion.

She peered coquettishly at the black-haired man from the corner of her eye, then turned her head to savor him fully. "My, my, and just who might you be?" She fluttered her long lashes admiringly.

Balder's ice-blue eyes crinkled with pleasure as he beheld the voluptuous woman who was obviously delighted to see him. "The man who's been waiting for you all his life, lass," he said huskily.

* * *

The wedding celebration began the moment the vows had been exchanged. Jillian longed to slip off with her husband the instant the ceremony ended. With Balder and

Ronin strictly monitoring her time with Gavrael for the past two weeks, they'd been able to spend no time alone at all. But she didn't wish to hurt Adrienne's feelings when she had obviously taken great care to ensure Jillian's wedding day was the stuff of dreams, so she dutifully lingered and greeted and smiled. The moment she and Gavrael had sealed their union with a kiss, she'd been snatched from his lips, tugged in one direction by the joyous crowd and able to do nothing but watch helplessly as her husband was dragged in the other.

They were married, the older and wiser had counseled, and they would have plenty of time to spend with each other. Jillian had rolled her eyes and pasted a smile on her face, accepting congratulations.

Finally, the flatbread was broken and the feasting commenced, drawing attention away from the newlyweds. Adrienne helped Jillian slip out of the hall, but instead of showing her to their chambers as she'd expected, the stunning, unusual woman had led her to Dalkeith's study. The light from oil globes and dozens of candles coupled with a cheery fire made the room a welcoming and warm haven despite the banks of fluffy white snow drifting outside the windows.

"It looks like we may get a real doozy." Adrienne eyed the drifts as she bustled about, poking up the fire.

Jillian blinked. "A what?"

"Doozy. Oh . . ." Adrienne paused, then laughed. "A big storm. You know, we might get snowed in for a time."

"You're not from this part of the country, are you?" Jillian frowned, trying to place her strange accent.

Again her hostess laughed. "Not quite." She beckoned Jillian to join her before the fire. "Just tell me, are those two of the hunkiest men you've ever laid eyes on?" Adrienne eyed a picture above the hewn-oak mantel and sighed dreamily.

Jillian followed her hostess's gaze upward to a beautifully rendered portrait of Gavrael and the Hawk. "Oh my. I don't know what 'hunkiest' means, but they certainly are the most handsome men I've ever seen."

"That's it," Adrienne agreed. "Do you know they complained the entire time this was being painted? Men." She rolled her eyes and gestured at the painting. "How could they blame a woman for wanting to immortalize such raw masculine splendor?"

The women spoke quietly for a time, unaware Hawk and Gavrael had entered the study behind them. Gavrael's eyes lingered on his wife and he started to move forward, determined to claim her before someone else dragged him off.

"Relax." Hawk placed a restraining hand on his sleeve. Enough distance separated the men from their wives that the women hadn't heard them yet, but Adrienne's voice carried clearly:

"It was all that fairy's fault. He dragged me back through time—not that I'm complaining a bit, mind you. I love it here and I adore my husband, but I'm originally from the twentieth century."

Both men grinned when Jillian did a double take. "Five hundred years from now?" she exclaimed.

Adrienne nodded, her eyes dancing. Jillian studied her intently, then leaned closer. "My husband's a Berserker," she confided.

"I know. He told us right before he left for Caithness, but I didn't get a chance to ask him any questions. Can he change shapes?" Adrienne looked as if she were about to reach for paper and ink and start scribbling notes. "In the twentieth century there's a great deal of dispute over just what they were and what they were capable of." Adrienne paused as she became aware of the two men standing in the doorway. Her eyes twinkled mischievously, and she winked at her husband. "However, there *was* a general consensus on one thing, Jillian." She smiled impishly. "It was commonly held that Berserkers were known for their legendary stamina—both in battle and in the b—"

"We get the point, Adrienne." Hawk cut her off, his black eyes sparkling with amusement. "Now, perhaps we should let Gavrael show her the rest himself."

* * *

Gavrael and Jillian's chambers were on the third floor of Dalkeith. Adrienne and Hawk escorted them, dropping not-so-subtle hints that the newlyweds could make as much noise as they wished; with the intervening floors, the revelers below would be none the wiser.

When the door closed behind them and they were finally alone, Gavrael and Jillian gazed at each other across the downy expanse of a wide mahogany bed. A fire leapt and crackled in the hearth while fluffy snowflakes fell beyond the window.

Grimm regarded her tenderly and his eyes slipped down, as they'd frequently done lately, to the scarcely noticeable swell of her abdomen. Jillian caught the possessive glance and gave him a dazzling smile. Ever since the night of the attack, when she'd told him they were going to have a baby, she'd caught him smiling at odd times with little or no provocation. It delighted her, his intense delight about the baby growing inside her. When she'd told him, after they'd returned from the caves to Maldebann, he'd sat blinking and shaking his head, as if he couldn't believe it was true. When she'd cradled his face in her hands and drawn his head close to kiss him, she'd been stunned by the glimpse of moisture in his eyes. Her husband was the best of men: strong yet sensitive, capable yet vulnerable—and how she loved him!

As she watched him now, his eyes darkened with desire, and anticipation shivered through her.

"Adrienne said we might get snowed in for a while," Jillian said breathlessly, feeling suddenly awkward. Being chaperoned these past weeks had nearly driven her crazy; to compensate, she'd tried to push her unruly steamy thoughts into a secluded corner of her mind. Now they resisted their confines, broke free, and demanded attention. She wanted her husband *now*.

"Good. I hope it snows a dozen feet." Gavrael moved around the bed. All he wanted to do was bury himself inside her, reassure himself that she was indeed his. This day had been the culmination of all his dreams—he was married to Jillian St. Clair. Gazing down at her, he marveled at how much she had changed his life: He had a home, a clan, and a father, the wife he'd always dreamed of, a precious child on the way, and a bright future. He, who had always felt like an outcast, now belonged. And he owed it all to Jillian. He came to a stop inches from her and flashed her a lazy, sensual smile. "I doona suppose you have any noises you'd like to be making while we're snowbound? I'd hate to disappoint our hosts."

Jillian's awkwardness melted away in a flash. Skirting all niceties, she slipped her hand up his muscular thigh and tugged his plaid away from his body. Her fingers flew over the buttons of his shirt, and within moments he stood before her as nature had fashioned him—a mighty warrior with hard angles and muscled planes.

Her gaze dropped lower and fixed upon what must have

surely been nature's most generous boon. She wet her lip, a wordless gesture of desire, unaware of the effect it had on him.

Gavrael groaned and reached for her. Jillian slipped into his arms, wrapped her hand around his thick shaft, and nearly purred with delight.

His eyes flared, then narrowed as he moved with the grace and power of a mountain cat, dragging her down onto the bed. A rough sigh escaped him. "Ah, I missed you, lass. I thought I was going to go crazy from wanting you. Balder wouldn't even let me kiss you!" Gavrael worked swiftly at the tiny buttons on her wedding gown. When she tightened her fingers around him, he quickly secured her hands, trapping them with one of his. "I can't think when you do that, lass."

"I didn't ask you to think, my big brawny warrior," she teased. "I have other uses for you."

He tossed her an arrogant look that clearly warned her he was in charge for the moment. With her distracting hands temporarily restrained, he lingered over her buttons, tracing kisses over each inch of skin as it was revealed. When his lips returned to hers, he kissed her with a savage intensity. Their tongues met, retreated, then met again. He tasted of brandy and cinnamon; Jillian followed his tongue, caught it with her own, and drew it into her mouth. When he stretched full length on top of her, muscled body to silken skin, her softness accommodating his hardness in perfect symmetry, she sighed her pleasure.

"Please," she begged, shifting her body enticingly beneath him.

"Please what, Jillian? What would you like me to do? Tell me exactly, lass." His heavy-lidded eyes glittered with interest.

"I want you to . . ." She gestured.

He nibbled her lower lip, drew back, and blinked innocently. "I'm afraid I doona understand. What was that?"

"Here." She gestured again.

"Say it, Jillian," he whispered huskily. "Tell me. I am yours to command, but I follow only very explicit instructions." The wicked grin he flashed loosened the last of her restraints, leaving her free to indulge in a bit of wickedness of her own.

So she told him, the man who was her own private legend, and he fulfilled her every secret desire, tasting and touching and pleasing her. He worshipped her body with his passion, celebrated their child in her womb with gentle kisses, kisses that lost their gentleness and became hot and hungry against her hips and blazed into flowing heat between her thighs.

Plunging her hands into his thick dark hair, she rose up against him, crying his name over and over.

Gavrael.

And after she'd run out of demands—or simply had been sated beyond coherent thought—he knelt on the bed, pulled her astride him, and wrapped her long legs around his waist. Her nails scored his back as he lowered her onto his hard shaft one exquisite inch at a time.

"You can't harm the baby, Gavrael," she assured him, panting softly as he held her away, giving her but a tiny taste of what she so desperately wanted.

"I'm not worried about that," he assured her.

"Then why . . . are . . . you . . . going so *slow*?"

"To watch your face," he said with a lazy smile. "I love to watch your eyes when we make love. I see every bit of pleasure, every ounce of desire reflected in them."

"They'll look even better if you'll just—" She pushed

against him with her hips and, laughing, he held her away with his strong hands on her waist.

Jillian nearly wailed. "Please!"

But he took his sweet time—and how sweet it was—until she thought she could no longer bear it. Then, abruptly, he buried himself deep within her. "I love you, Jillian McIllioch." His accompanying smile was uninhibited, his white teeth flashing against his dark face.

She laid a finger to his lips. "I know," she assured him.

"But I wanted to say the words." He caught her finger between his lips and kissed it.

"I see," she teased. "You get to say all the love words while I have to say all the bawdy ones."

He made a rumble low in his throat. "I *love* it when you tell me what you want me to do to you."

"Then do this . . ." Her low rush of words dissolved into a satisfied cry as he fulfilled her demand.

Hours later, her last conscious thought was that she should not forget to mention to Adrienne that the "general consensus" about Berserkers could not even begin to touch the reality.

EPILOGUE

"I DOONA UNDERSTAND IT," RONIN SAID, WATCHING THE lads. He shook his head. "It's never happened before."

"I doona either, Da. But something is different about me from any of the McIllioch males before. Either that, or there's something different about Jillian. Perhaps it's both of us."

"How do you keep up with them?"

Gavrael laughed, a rich sound. "Between Jillian and me, we manage."

"But with them being, you know, the way they are so young, aren't they constantly getting into mischief?"

"Not to mention impossibly high places. They're forever pulling off incredible feats, and if you ask me, they're just a little too damned smart for anyone's good. It's almost more than any one Berserker could be expected to keep up with. That's why I think it would be useful to have their grandda around too," Gavrael said pointedly.

The flush of pleasure on Ronin's cheeks was unmistakable. "You mean you want me to stay here with you and Jillian?"

"Maldebann is home, Da. I know you felt Jillian and I needed the privacy of newlyweds, but we wish you would come home for good. Both you and Balder; the lads need their great-uncle too. Remember, we McIllioch are the stuff of legends, and how will they come to understand the legends without the finest of our Berserkers to teach them? Quit visiting all those people you've been dropping in on and *come home*." Gavrael studied him out of the corner of his eyes and knew Ronin would not leave Maldebann again. The thought gave him great satisfaction. His sons should know their grandda. Not merely as an intermittent visitor, but as a steady influence.

In a contented silence that bordered on awe, Gavrael and Ronin watched the three young boys playing on the lawn. When Jillian stepped out into the sunshine, her sons looked up as one, as if they could sense her presence. They stopped playing and ranged in around their mother, vying for attention.

"Now, there's a beautiful sight," Ronin said reverently.

"Aye," Gavrael agreed.

Jillian laughed as she tousled the heads of her three young sons and smiled into three pairs of ice-blue eyes.

A NORSE LEGEND
(THE TWILIGHT OF THE GODS)

Legend tells that *Ragnarok*—the final battle of the gods—will herald the end of the world.

Destruction will rage in the kingdom of the gods. In the last battle, Odin will be devoured by a wolf. The earth will be destroyed by fire, and the universe will sink into the sea.

Legend holds that this final destruction will be followed by rebirth. The earth will reemerge from the water, lush and teeming with new life. It is prophesied the sons of the dead Aesir will return to Asgard, the home of the gods, and reign again.

In the mountains of Scotland, the Circle Elders say Odin doesn't believe in taking any chances, that he schemes to defy fate by breeding his warrior race of Berserkers into the Scottish bloodlines, deeply hidden. There they await the twilight of the gods, at which time he will summon them to fight for him once more.

Legend tells that there are Berserkers walking among us, even still. . . .

About the Author

KAREN MARIE MONING graduated from Purdue University with a bachelor's degree in Society & Law. Her novels have been *USA Today* bestsellers and have appeared on the *New York Times* expanded bestseller list. They have won numerous awards, including the prestigious RITA Award. She can be reached at www.karenmoning.com.

Visit our website at www.bantamdell.com.

*Don't miss the greatest
adventure in the
Highlander series*

the immortal
highlander

by

karen marie
moning

A Delacorte hardcover on sale in August

Please read on for a preview....

the immortal highlander

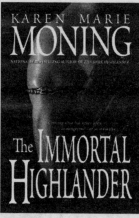

Adam Black raked a hand through his long black hair and scowled as he stalked down the alley.

Three eternal months he'd been human. Ninety-seven horrific days, to be exact. Two thousand three hundred twenty-eight interminable hours. One hundred thirty-nine thousand six hundred eighty thoroughly offensive minutes.

He'd become obsessed with increments of time. It was an embarrassingly mortal affliction. Next thing he knew, he'd be wearing a watch.

Never.

He'd been certain Aoibheal would have come for him by now. Would have staked his very essence on it; not that he had much left to stake.

But she hadn't, and he was sick of waiting. Not only were

humans allotted a ridiculously finite slice of time to exist, their bodies had requirements that consumed a great deal of that time. Sleep alone consumed a full third of it. Although he'd mastered those requirements, over the past few months, he resented being slave to his physical form. Having to eat, wash, dress, sleep, piss, shave, brush his hair and teeth, for Christ's sake! He wanted to be himself again. Not at the queen's bloody convenience, but *now.*

Hence he'd left London and journeyed to Cincinnati (the infernally long way—by plane) looking for the half-Fae son he'd sired over a millennium ago, Circenn Brodie, who'd married a twenty-first-century mortal and usually resided here with her.

Usually.

Upon arriving in Cincinnati, he'd found Circenn's residence vacant, and had no idea where to look for him next. He'd taken up residence there himself, and had been killing time since—endeavoring grimly to ignore that, for the first time in his timeless existence, time was returning the favor—waiting for Circenn to return. A half-blooded Tuatha Dé, Circenn had magic Adam no longer possessed.

Adam's scowl deepened. What paltry power the queen had left him was virtually worthless. He'd quickly discovered that she'd thought through his punishment most thoroughly. The spell of the *féth fiada* was one of the most powerful and perception-altering that the Tuatha Dé possessed, employed to permit a Tuatha Dé full interaction with the human realm, while keeping him or her undetectable by humans. It cloaked its wearer in illusion that affected short-term memory and generated confusion in the minds of those in the immediate vicinity.

If Adam toppled a newsstand, the vendor would blithely blame an unseen wind. If he took food from a diner's plate, the person merely decided he/she must have finished. If he procured new clothing for himself at a shop, the owner would register an inventory error. If he snatched groceries from a passerby and flung the bag to the ground, his hapless victim would turn on the nearest bystander and a bitter fight would ensue (he'd done that a few times for a bit of sport). If he plucked the purse from a woman's arm and dangled it before her face, she would simply walk through both him and it (the moment he touched a thing, it, too, was sucked into the illusion cast by the *féth fiada* until he released it), then head in the opposite direction, muttering about having forgotten her purse at home.

There was nothing he could do to draw attention to himself. And he'd tried everything. To all intents and purposes, Adam Black didn't exist. Didn't even merit his own measly slice of human space.

He knew why she'd chosen this particular punishment: Because he'd sided with humans in their little disagreement, she was forcing him to taste of being human in the worst possible way. Alone and powerless, without a single distraction with which to pass the time and entertain himself.

He'd had enough of a taste to last an eternity.

Once an all-powerful being that could sift time and space, a being that could travel anywhere and anywhen in the blink of an eye, he was now limited to a single useful power: He could sift place over short distances, but no more than a few miles. It'd surprised him the queen had left him even that much power, until the first time he'd almost been run down by a careening bus in the heart of London.

She'd left him just enough magic to stay alive. Which told him two things: one, she planned to forgive him eventually, and two, it was probably going to be a long, long time. Like, probably not until the moment his mortal form was about to expire.

Fifty more years of this would drive him bloody frigging nuts.

Problem was, even when Circenn *did* return, Adam still hadn't figured out a way to communicate with him. Because of his mortal half, Circenn wouldn't be able to see past the *féth fiada* either.

All he needed, Adam brooded for the thousandth time, was one person. Just one person who could see him. A single person who could help him. He wasn't entirely without options, but he couldn't exercise a damned one of them without someone to aid him.

And that sucked too. The almighty Adam Black needed help. He could almost hear silvery laughter tinkling on the night breeze, blowing tauntingly across the realms, all the way from the shimmering silica sands of the Isle of Morar.

With a growl of caged fury, he stalked out of the alley.

$$* \quad * \quad *$$

Gabby indulged herself in a huge self-pitying sigh as she got out of her car. Normally on nights like this, when the sky was black velvet, glittering with stars and a silver-scythe moon, warm and humid and alive with the glorious scents and sounds of summer, nothing could depress her.

But not tonight. Everyone but her was out somewhere having a life, while she was scrambling to clean up after the latest fairy debacle. Again.

It seemed like all she ever did anymore.

She wondered briefly what her ex was doing tonight. Was he out at the bars? Had he already met someone new? Someone who wasn't still a virgin at twenty-four?

And *that* was the Fae's fault too.

She slammed the car door harder than she should have, and a little piece of chrome trim fell off and clattered to the pavement. It was the third bit of itself her aging Corolla had shed that week, though she was pretty sure the antenna had been assisted by bored neighborhood kids. With a snort of exasperation, she locked the car, kicked the little piece of trim beneath the car—she refused to clean up even one more thing—and turned toward the building.

And froze.

A fairy male had just stalked out of the alley and was standing by the bench in the small courtyard oasis near the entrance to her office building. As she watched, it stretched out on the bench on its back, folded its arms behind its head, and stared up at the night sky, looking as if it had no intention of moving for a long, long time.

Damn and double-damn!

She was still in such a stew over the day's events that she wasn't sure she could manage to walk by it without giving in to the overwhelming urge to *kick* it.

It.

Fairies were "its," never "hims" or "hers." Gram had taught her at a young age not to personify them. They weren't human. And it was dangerous to think of them, even in the privacy of her thoughts, as if they were.

But heavens, Gabby thought, staring, he—*it*—was certainly male.

So tall that the bench wasn't long enough for it to fully stretch out on, it had propped one leg on the back of the bench and bent the other at the knee, its legs spread in a basely masculine position. It was clad in snug-fitting, faded jeans, a black T-shirt, and black leather boots. Long, silky black hair spilled over its folded arms, falling to sweep the sidewalk. In contrast to the golden angelic ones she'd seen earlier that day, this one was dark and utterly devilish-looking.

Gold armbands adorned its muscular arms, showcasing

its powerful rock-hard biceps, and a gold torque encircled its neck, gleaming richly in the amber glow of the gaslights illuming the courtyard oasis.

Royalty, she realized with a trace of breathless fascination. Only those of a royal house were entitled to wear torques of gold. She'd never seen a member of one of the Ruling Houses before.

And "royal" was certainly a good word for him, er . . . it. Its profile was sheer majesty. Chiseled features, high cheekbones, strong jaw, aquiline nose, all covered with that luscious gold-velvet fairy skin. She narrowed her eyes, absorbing details. Unshaven jaw sculpted by five-o'clock shadow. Full mouth. Lower lip decadently full. Sinfully so, really. (Gabby, quit *thinking* that!)

She inhaled slowly, exhaled softly, holding utterly still, one hand on the roof of her car, the other clutching her keys.

It exuded immense sexuality: base, raw, scorching. From this distance she should not have been able to feel the heat from its body, but she could. She should not have gotten a bit dizzy from its exotic scent, but she had. As if it were twenty times more potent than any she'd encountered before; a veritable powerhouse of a fairy.

She was never going to be able to walk past it. Just wasn't happening. Not today. There was only so much she was capable of in a given day, and Gabby O'Callaghan had exceeded her limits.

Still . . . it hadn't moved. In fact, it seemed utterly oblivious to its surroundings. It couldn't hurt to look a little longer. . . .

Besides, she reminded herself, she had a duty to surreptitiously observe as much as possible about any unknown fairy specimen. In such fashion did the O'Callaghan women protect themselves and the future of their children—by learning about their enemy. By passing down stories. By adding new information, with sketches when possible, to the multivolume *Books of the Fae,* thereby providing future generations greater odds of escaping detection.

This one didn't have the sleekly muscled body of most fairy males, she noted; this one had the body of a warrior. Shoulders much too wide to squeeze onto the bench. Arms bunched with muscle, thick forearms, strong wrists. Cut abdomen rippling beneath the fabric of its T-shirt each time it shifted position. Powerful thighs caressed by soft faded denim.

No, not a warrior, she mused, that wasn't quite it. A shadowy image was dancing in the dark recesses of her mind and she struggled to bring it into focus.

More like . . . ah, she had it! Like one of those blacksmiths of yore who'd spent their days pounding steel at a scorching forge, metal clanging, sparks flying. Possessing massive brawn, yet also capable of the delicacy necessary to craft intricately embellished blades, combining pure power with exquisite control.

There wasn't a spare ounce of flesh on it, just rock-hard male body. It had a finely honed, brutal strength that, coupled with its height and breadth, could feel overwhelming to a woman. Especially if it were stretching all that rippling muscle on top of—

Stop that, O'Callaghan! Wiping tiny beads of sweat from her forehead with the back of her hand, she drew a shaky breath, struggling desperately for objectivity. She felt as hot as the forge she could imagine him bending over, hard body glistening, pounding . . . pounding . . .

Go, Gabby, a faint inner voice warned. *Go now. Hurry.*

But her inner alarm went off too late. At that precise moment it turned its head and glanced her way.

She should have looked away. She tried to look away. She couldn't.

Its face, full-on, was a work of impossible masculine beauty—exquisite symmetry brushed by a touch of savagery—but it was the eyes that got her all tangled up. They were ancient eyes, immortal eyes, eyes that had seen more than she could ever dream of seeing in a thousand lifetimes. Eyes full of intelligence, mockery, mischief, and—her breath caught in her throat as its gaze dropped down her body, then raked slowly back up—unchained sexuality. Black as midnight beneath slashing brows, its eyes flashed with gold sparks.

Her mouth dropped open and she gasped.

But, but, but, a part of her sputtered in protest, *it doesn't have fairy eyes! It can't be a fairy! They have iridescent eyes. Always. And if it's not a fairy, what* is *it?*

Again its gaze slid down her body, this time much more slowly, lingering on her breasts, fixing unabashedly at the juncture of her thighs. Without a shred of self-consciousness, it shifted its hips to gain play in its jeans, reached down, and blatantly adjusted itself.

Helplessly, as if mesmerized, her gaze followed, snagging on that big dark hand tugging at the faded denim. At the huge swollen bulge cupped by the soft worn fabric. For a moment it closed its hand over itself and rubbed the thick ridge, and she was horrified to feel her own hand clenching. She flushed, mouth dry, cheeks flaming.

Suddenly it went motionless and its preternatural gaze locked with hers, eyes narrowing.

"Christ," it hissed, surging up from the bench in one graceful ripple of animal strength, "you see me. You're *seeing* me!"

"No I'm not," Gabby snapped instantly. Defensively. Stupidly. *Oh, that was good, O'Callaghan, you dolt!*

Snapping her mouth shut so hard her teeth clacked, she unlocked the car door and scrambled in faster than she'd ever thought possible.

Twisting the key in the ignition, she threw the car into reverse.

And then she did another stupid thing: She glanced at it again. She couldn't help it. It simply commanded attention.

It was stalking toward her, its expression one of pure astonishment.

For a brief moment she gaped blankly back. Was a fairy *capable* of being astonished? According to O'Callaghan sources, they experienced no emotion. And how could they? They had no hearts, no souls. Only a fool would think some kind of higher conscience lurked behind those quixotic eyes. Gabby was no fool.

It was almost to the curb. Heading straight for her.

With a startled jerk she came to her senses, slammed the car into drive, and jammed the gas pedal to the floor.

✳   ✳   ✳

Adam was so caught off guard that it didn't occur to him to do a series of short jumps and follow the woman, until it was too late.

By the time he'd tensed to sift, the dilapidated vehicle had sped off, and he had no idea where it had gone. He popped about in various directions for a time but was unable to pick it up again.

Shaking his head, he returned to the bench and sat down, cursing himself in half a dozen languages.

Finally, someone had *seen* him.

And what had he done? Let her get away. Undermined by his disgusting human anatomy.

It had just been made excruciatingly clear to him that the human male brain and the human male cock couldn't both sustain sufficient amounts of blood to function at the same time. It was one or the other, and the human male apparently didn't get to choose which one.

As a Tuatha Dé, he would have been in complete control of his lust. Desirous yet cool-headed, perhaps even a touch bored (it wasn't as if he could do something he hadn't done before; given a few thousand years, a Tuatha Dé got around to trying everything).

But as a human male, lust was far more intense, and his body was apparently slave to it. A simple hard-on could turn him into a bloody Neanderthal.

How *had* mankind survived this long? For that matter, how had they ever managed to crawl out of their primordial swamps to begin with?

Blowing out an exasperated breath, he rose from the bench and began pacing a stunted space of cobbled courtyard.

There he'd been, lying on his back, staring up at the stars, wondering where in the hell Circenn might have hied himself off to for so long, when suddenly he'd suffered a prickly sensation, as if he were the focus of an intense gaze.

He'd glanced over, half-expecting to see a few of his brethren laughing at him. In fact, he'd hoped to see his brethren. Laughing or not. In the past ninety-seven days he'd searched high and low for one of his race, but hadn't caught so much as a glimpse of a Tuatha Dé. He'd finally concluded that the queen must have forbidden them to spy upon him, for he could find no other explanation for their absence. He knew full well there were those of his race that would savor the sight of his suffering.

He'd seen—not his brethren—but a woman. A human woman, illumed by that which his kind didn't possess, lit from within by the soft golden glow of her immortal soul.

A young, lushly sensual woman at that, with the look of the Irish about her. Long silvery-blond hair twisted up in a clip, loose shorter strands spiking about a delicate heart-shaped face. Huge eyes uptilted at the outer corners, a pointed chin, a full lush mouth. A flash of fire in her catlike green-gold gaze, proof of that passionate Gaelic temper that always turned him on. Full round breasts, shapely legs, luscious ass.

He'd gone instantly, painfully, hard as a rock.

And for a few critical moments, his brain hadn't functioned at all. All the rest of him had. Stupendously well, in fact. Just not his brain.

Cursed by the *féth fiada,* he'd been celibate for three long, hellish months now. And his own hand didn't count.

Lying there, imagining all the things he would do to her if only he could, he'd completely failed to process that she was not only standing there looking in his general direction, but his first instinct had been right: He *was* the focus of an intense gaze. She was looking directly at him.

Seeing him.

By the time he'd managed to find his feet, to even remember that he had feet, she'd been in her car.

She'd escaped him.

But not for long, he thought, eyes narrowing. He would find her.

She'd seen him. He had no idea how or why she'd been able to, but frankly he didn't much care. She had, and now she was going to be his ticket back to Paradise.

And, he thought, lips curving in a wicked erotic grin, he was willing to bet she'd be able to *feel* him too. Logic dictated that if she was immune to one aspect of the *féth fiada,* she would be immune to them all.

For the first time since the queen had made him human, he threw back his head and laughed. The rich dark sound rolled—despite the human mouth shaping it—not entirely human, echoing in the empty street.

He turned and eyed the building behind him speculatively. He knew a great deal about humans from having walked among them for so many millennia, and he'd learned even more about them in the past few months. They were creatures of habit; like plodding little Highland sheep, they dutifully trod the same hoof-beaten paths, returning to the same pastures day after day.

Undoubtedly, there was a reason she'd come to this building this evening.

And undoubtedly, there was something in that building that would lead him to her.

The luscious little Irish was going to be his savior.

She would help him find Circenn and communicate his plight. Circenn would sift dimensions and return him to the Fae Isle of Morar, where the queen held her court. And Adam would persuade her that enough was enough already.

He knew Aoibheal wouldn't be able to look him in the eye and deny him. He merely had to get to her, see her, touch her, remind her how much she favored him and why.

Ah, yes, now that he'd found someone who could see him, he'd be his glorious immortal self again in no time at all.

In the meantime, pending Circenn's return, he now had much with which to entertain himself. He was no longer in quite the same rush to be made immortal again. Not just yet. Not now that he suddenly had the opportunity to experience sex in human form. Fae glamour wasn't nearly as sensitive as the body he currently inhabited, and—sensual to the core— he'd been doubly pissed off at Aoibheal for making him unable to explore its erotic capabilities. She could be such a bitch sometimes.

If a simple hard-on in human form could reduce him to a primitive state, what would burying himself inside a woman do? What would it feel like to come inside her?

There was no doubt in his mind that he would soon find out.

Never had the mortal woman lived and breathed who could say no to a bit of fairy tail.

beyond the
highland mist

Adrienne sighed, shook her head, and ordered her muscles
to relax. She had nearly succeeded, when overhead a floor-
board creaked. Tension reclaimed her instantly. She dropped
Moonie on a stuffed chair and eyed the ceiling intently as the
creaking sound repeated.

Perhaps it was just the house settling.

She really had to get over this skittishness.

How much time had to pass until she stopped being afraid
that she would turn around and see Eberhard standing there
with his faintly mocking smile and gleaming gun?

Eberhard was dead. She was safe, she knew she was.

So why did she feel so horridly vulnerable? For the past
few days she'd had the suffocating sensation that someone
was spying on her. No matter how hard she tried to reassure

herself that anyone who might wish her harm was either dead—or didn't know she was alive—she was still consumed by a morbid unease. Every instinct she possessed warned her that something was wrong—or about to go terribly wrong. Having grown up in the City of Spooks—the sultry, superstitious, magical New Orleans—Adrienne had learned to listen to her instincts. They were almost always right on target.

Her instincts had even been right about Eberhard. She'd had a bad feeling about him from the beginning, but she'd convinced herself it was her own insecurity. Eberhard was the catch of New Orleans; naturally, a woman might feel a little unsettled by such a man.

Only much later did she understand that she'd been lonely for so long, and had wanted the fairy tale so badly, she'd tried to force reality to reflect her desires, instead of the other way around. She'd told herself so many white lies before finally facing the truth that Eberhard wasn't the man she'd thought he was. She'd been such a fool.

Adrienne breathed deeply of the spring air that breezed gently in the window behind her, then flinched and spun abruptly. She eyed the fluttering drapes warily. Hadn't she closed that window? She was sure of it. She'd closed all of them just before closing the French doors. Adrienne edged cautiously to the window, shut it quickly, and locked it.

It was nerves, nothing more. No face peered in the window at her, no dogs barked, no alarms sounded. What was the use of taking so many precautions if she couldn't relax? There couldn't *possibly* be anyone out there.

She forced herself to turn away from the window. As she padded across the room, her foot encountered a small object and sent it skidding across the faded Oushak rug, where it clunked to a rest against the wall.

Adrienne glanced at it and flinched. It was a piece from

Eberhard's chess set, the one she'd swiped from his house in New Orleans the night she'd fled. She'd forgotten all about it after she'd moved in. She'd tossed it in a box—one of those piled in the corner that she'd never gotten around to unpacking. Perhaps Moonie had dragged the pieces out, she mused; there were several of them scattered across the rug.

She retrieved the piece she'd kicked and rolled it gingerly between her fingers. Waves of emotion flooded her: a sea of shame and anger and humiliation, capped with a relentless fear that she still wasn't safe.

A draft of air kissed the back of her neck and she stiffened, clutching the chess piece so tightly that the crown of the black queen dug cruelly into her palm. Logic insisted that the windows behind her were shut—she *knew* they were—still, instinct told her otherwise.

The rational Adrienne *knew* there was no one in her library but herself and a lightly snoring kitten. The irrational Adrienne teetered on the brink of terror.

Laughing nervously, she berated herself for being so jumpy, then cursed Eberhard for making her this way. She would *not* succumb to paranoia.

Dropping to her knees without sparing a backward glance, she scooped the scattered chess pieces into a pile. She didn't really like to touch them. A woman couldn't spend her childhood in New Orleans—much of it at the feet of a Creole storyteller who'd lived behind the orphanage—without becoming a bit superstitious. The set was ancient, an original Viking set; an old legend claimed it was cursed, and Adrienne's life had been cursed enough. The only reason she'd pilfered the set was in case she needed quick cash. Carved of walrus ivory and ebony, it would command an exorbitant price from a collector. Besides, hadn't she earned it, after all he'd put her through?

Adrienne muttered a colorful invective about beautiful

men. It wasn't morally acceptable that someone as evil as Eberhard had been so nice to look at. Poetic justice demanded otherwise—shouldn't people's faces reflect their hearts? If Eberhard had been as ugly on the outside as she'd belatedly discovered he was on the inside, she never would have ended up at the wrong end of a gun. Of course, Adrienne had learned the hard way that any end of a gun was the wrong end.

Eberhard Darrow Garrett was a beautiful, womanizing, deceitful man—and he'd ruined her life. Clutching the black queen tightly, she made herself a firm promise. "I will never go out with a beautiful man again, so long as I live and breathe. I hate beautiful men. Hate them!"

* * *

Outside the French doors at 93 Coattail Lane, a man who lacked substance, a creature manmade devices could neither detect nor contain, heard her words and smiled. His choice was made with swift certainty—Adrienne de Simone was definitely the woman he'd been searching for.

to tame a
highland warrior

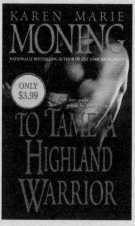

It wasn't easy for Jillian to hide in her chambers all day. She wasn't the cowering sort. Nor, however, was she the foolish sort, and she knew she must have a plan before she subjected herself to the perils of her parents' nefarious scheme. As afternoon faded into evening and she'd yet to be struck by inspiration, she discovered she was feeling quite irritable. She hated being cooped up in her chambers. She wanted to play the virginal, she wanted to kick the first person she saw, she wanted to visit Zeke, she wanted to eat. She'd thought someone would appear by lunchtime, she'd been certain loyal Kaley would come check on her if she didn't arrive at dinner, but the maids didn't even appear to clean her chambers or light the fire. As the solitary hours passed, Jillian's ire increased. The angrier she became, the less objectively she considered her plight, ultimately concluding she would simply ignore the three men and go about her life as if nothing were amiss.

Food was her priority now. Shivering in the chilly evening air, she donned a light but voluminous cloak and pulled the hood snug around her face. Perhaps if she met up with one of the oversized brutes, the combination of darkness and concealing attire would grant her anonymity. It probably wouldn't fool Grimm, but the other two hadn't seen her with clothes *on* yet.

Jillian closed the door quietly and slipped into the hallway. She opted for the servants' staircase and carefully picked her way down the dimly lit, winding steps. Caithness was huge, but Jillian had played in every nook and cranny and knew the castle well; nine doors down and to the left was the kitchen, just past the buttery. She peered down the long corridor. Lit by flickering oil lamps, it was deserted, the castle silent. Where was everyone?

As she moved forward, a voice floated out of the darkness behind her. "Pardon, lass, but could you tell me where I might find the buttery? We've run short of whisky and there's not a maid about."

Jillian froze in mid-step, momentarily robbed of speech. How could all the maids disappear and that man appear the very instant she decided to sneak from her chambers?

"I asked you to leave, Grimm Roderick. What are you still doing here?" she said coolly.

"Is that you, Jillian?" He stepped closer, peering through the shadows.

"Have so many other women at Caithness demanded you depart that you're suffering confusion about my identity?" she asked sweetly, plunging her shaking hands into the folds of her cloak.

"I didn't recognize you beneath your hood until I heard

you speak, and as to the women, you know how the women around here felt about me. I assume nothing has changed."

Jillian almost choked. He was as arrogant as he'd always been. She pushed her hood back irritably. The women had fallen all over him when he'd fostered here, lured by his dark, dangerous looks, muscled body, and absolute indifference. Maids had thrown themselves at his feet, visiting ladies had offered him jewels and lodgings. It had been revolting to watch. "Well, you are older," she parried weakly. "And you know as a man gets older his good looks can suffer."

Grimm's mouth turned faintly upward as he stepped forward into the flickering light thrown off by a wall torch. Tiny lines at the corners of his eyes were whiter than his Highland-tanned face. If anything, it made him more beautiful.

"You are older too." He studied her through narrowed eyes.

"It's not nice to chide a woman about her age. I am *not* an old maid."

"I didn't say you were," he said mildly. "The years have made you a lovely woman."

"And?" Jillian demanded.

"And what?"

"Well, go ahead. Don't leave me hanging, waiting for the nasty thing you're going to say. Just say it and get it over with."

"What nasty thing?"

"Grimm Roderick, you have never said a single nice thing to me in all my life. So don't start faking it now."

Grimm's mouth twisted up at one corner, and Jillian realized that he still hated to smile. He fought it, begrudged it, and rarely did one ever break the confines of his eternal self-control. Such a waste, for he was even more handsome when he smiled, if that was possible.

He moved closer.

"Stop right there!"

Grimm ignored her command, continuing his approach.

"I said *stop*."

"Or you'll do what, Jillian?" His voice was smooth and amused. He cocked his head at a lazy angle and folded his arms across his chest.

"Why, I'll . . ." She belatedly acknowledged there wasn't much of anything she could do to prevent him from going anywhere he wished to go, in any manner he wished to go there. He was twice her size, and she'd never be his physical match. The only weapon she'd ever had against him was her sharp tongue, honed to a razor edge by years of defensive practice on this man.

He shrugged his shoulders impatiently. "Tell me, lass, what will you do?"

the highlander's touch

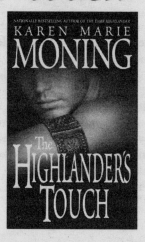

Lisa awoke abruptly, uncertain of where she was or what had awakened her. Then she heard men's voices in the hallway outside the office.

Galvanized into action, Lisa leaped to her feet and shot a panicked glance at her watch. It was 5:20 A.M.—she would lose her job! Instinctively she dropped to the floor and took a nasty blow to her temple on the corner of the desk in the process. Wincing, she crawled under the desk as she heard a key in the lock, followed by Steinmann's voice: "It's impossible to get decent help. Worthless maid didn't even lock up. All she had to do was press the button. Even a child could do it."

Lisa curled into a silent ball as the men entered the office.

"Here it is." Steinmann's spotlessly buffed shoes stopped inches from her knees.

"What amazing detail. It's beautiful." The second voice was hushed.

"Isn't it?" Steinmann agreed.

"Wait a minute, Steinmann. Where did you say this chest was found?"

"Beneath a crush of rock near a riverbank in Scotland."

"That doesn't make any sense. How did it remain untouched by the elements? Ebony is obdurate wood, but it isn't impervious to decay. This chest is in mint condition. Has it been dated yet?"

"No, but my source in Edinburgh swore by it. Can you open it, Taylor?" Steinmann said.

There was a rustle of noise. A softly murmured "Let's see . . . How do you work, you lovely little mystery?"

Lisa battled an urge to pop out from under the desk, curiosity nearly overriding her common sense and instinct for self-preservation.

There was a long pause. "Well? What is it?" Steinmann asked.

"I have no idea," Taylor said slowly. "I've neither translated tales of it nor seen sketches in my research. It doesn't look quite medieval, does it? It almost looks . . . why . . . futuristic," he said uneasily. "Frankly, I'm baffled."

"Perhaps you aren't as much of an expert as you would have me believe, Taylor."

"No one knows more about the Gaels and Picts than I do," he replied stiffly. "But some artifacts simply aren't mentioned in any records. I assure you, I will find the answers."

"And you'll have it examined?" Steinmann said.

"I'll take it with me now—"

"No. I'll call you when we're ready to release it."

There was a pause, then: "You plan to invite someone else to examine it, don't you?" Taylor said. "You question my ability."

"I simply need to get it cataloged, photographed, and logged into our files."

"And logged into someone else's collection?" Taylor said tightly.

"Put it back, Taylor." Steinmann closed his fingers around Taylor's wrist, lowering the flask back to the cloth. He slipped the tongs from Taylor's hand, closed the chest, and placed the tongs beside it.

"Fine," Taylor snapped. "But when you discover no one else knows what it is, you'll be calling me. You can't move an artifact that can't be identified. I'm the only one who can track this thing down, and you know it."

Steinmann laughed. "I'll see you out."

"I can find my own way."

"But I'll rest easier knowing I've escorted you," Steinmann said softly. "It wouldn't do to leave such a passionate antiquity worshiper as yourself wandering the museum on his own."

The shoes retreated with muffled steps across the carpet. The click of a key in the lock jarred Lisa into action. *Damn and double-damn!* Normally when she left, she depressed the button latch on the door—no lowly maid was entrusted with keys. Steinmann had bypassed the button latch and actually used a key to lock the dead bolt. She jerked upright and banged her head against the underside of the desk. "Ow!" she exclaimed softly. As she clutched the edge and drew herself upright, she paused to look at the chest.

Fascinated, she touched the cool wood. Beautifully engraved, the black wood gleamed in the low light. Bold letters were seared into the top in angry, slanted strokes. What did the chest contain that had perplexed two sophisticated purveyors of antiquities? Despite the fact that she was locked in Steinmann's office and had no doubt that he would return in moments, she was consumed by curiosity. *Futuristic?* Gingerly, she ran her fingers over the chest, seeking the square pressure latch they'd mentioned, then paused. The strange letters on the lid seemed almost to . . . pulse. A shiver of foreboding raced up her spine.

Silly goose—open it! It can't hurt you. They *touched it.*

Resolved, she isolated the square and depressed it with her thumb. The lid swung upward with the faint popping sound she'd heard earlier. A flask lay inside, surrounded by dusty tatters of ancient fabric. The flask was fashioned of a silver metal and seemed to shimmer, as if the contents were energized. She cast a nervous glance at the door. She knew she had to get out of the office before Steinmann returned, yet she felt strangely transfixed by the flask. Her eyes drifted from door to flask and back again, but the flask beckoned. It said, *Touch me,* in the same tone all the artifacts in the museum spoke to Lisa. *Touch me while no guards are about, and I will tell you of my history and my legends. I am knowledge. . . .*

Lisa's fingertips curled around the flask.

The world shifted on its axis beneath her feet. She stumbled, and suddenly she . . .

Couldn't . . .

Stop . . .

Falling . . .

kiss of the highlander

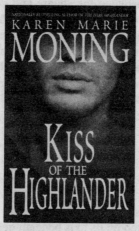

NATIONALLY BESTSELLING AUTHOR OF *THE DARK HIGHLANDER*

KAREN MARIE

MONING

KISS
OF THE
HIGHLANDER

She'd fallen on a body. One that, considering she hadn't disturbed it, must be dead. *Or,* she worried, *perhaps I killed it when I fell.*

When she managed to stop screaming, she found that she'd pushed herself up and was straddling it, her palms braced on its chest. Not its chest, she realized, but *his* chest. The motionless figure beneath her was undeniably male.

Sinfully male.

She snatched her hands away and sucked in a shocked breath.

However he'd managed to get here, if he was dead, his demise had been quite recent. He was in perfect condition and—her hands crept back to his chest—warm. He had the sculpted physique of a professional football player, with wide shoulders, pumped biceps and pecs, and washboard abs. His hips beneath her were lean and powerful. Strange symbols were tattooed across his bare chest.

She took slow, deep breaths to ease the sudden tightness in her chest. Leaning cautiously forward, she peered at a face that was savagely beautiful. His was the type of dominant male virility women dreamed about in dark, erotic fantasies but knew didn't *really* exist. Black lashes swept his golden skin, beneath arched brows and a silky fall of long, black hair. His jaw was dusted with a blue-black shadow beard; his lips were pink and firm and sensually full. She brushed her finger against them, then felt mildly perverse, so she pretended she was just checking to see if he was alive and shook him, but he didn't respond. Cupping his nose with her hand, she was relieved to feel a soft puff of breath. *He isn't dead, thank God.* It made her feel better about finding him so attractive. Palm flush to his chest, she was further reassured by his strong heartbeat. Although it wasn't beating very often, at least it was. He must be deeply unconscious, perhaps in a coma, she decided. Whichever it was, he couldn't help her.

Her gaze darted back up to the hole. Even if she managed to wake him and then stood on his shoulders, she still wouldn't be near the lip of the hole. Sunshine streamed over her face, mocking her with a freedom that was so near, yet so impossibly far, and she shivered again. "Just what am I supposed to do now?" she muttered.

Despite the fact that he was unconscious and of no use, her gaze swept back down. He exuded such vitality that his condition baffled her. She couldn't decide if she was upset that he was unconscious, or relieved. With his looks he was surely a womanizer, just the kind of man she steered away from by instinct. Having grown up surrounded by scientists, she had no experience with men of his ilk. On the rare occasions she'd glimpsed a man like him sauntering out of Gold's Gym, she'd gawked surreptitiously, grateful that she was safely in her car. So much testosterone made her nervous. It couldn't possibly be healthy.

Cherry picker extraordinaire. The thought caught her off guard. Mortified, she berated herself, because he was injured and there she was, sitting on him, thinking lascivious thoughts. She pondered the possibility that she'd developed some kind of hormonal imbalance, perhaps a surfeit of perky little eggs.

She eyed the designs on the man's chest more closely, wondering if one of them concealed a wound. The strange symbols, unlike any tattoos she'd ever seen, were smeared with blood from the abrasions on her palms.

Gwen leaned back a few inches so a ray of sunshine spilled across his chest. As she studied him, a curious thing happened: the brightly colored designs blurred before her eyes, growing indistinct, as if they were fading, leaving only streaks of her blood to mar his muscled chest. But that wasn't possible. . . .

Gwen blinked as, undeniably, several symbols disappeared entirely. In a matter of moments all of them were gone, vanished as if they'd never existed.

Perplexed, she glanced up at his face and sucked in an astonished breath.

His eyes were open and he was watching her. He had remarkable eyes that glittered like shards of silver and ice, sleepy eyes that banked a touch of amusement and unmistakable masculine interest. He stretched his body beneath hers with the self-indulgent grace of a cat prolonging the pleasure of awakening, and she suspected that although he was rousing physically, his mental acuity was not fully engaged. His pupils were large and dark, as if he'd recently had his eyes dilated for an exam or taken some drug.

Oh, God, he's conscious and I'm straddling him! She could imagine what he was thinking and could hardly blame him for it. She was as intimately positioned as a woman astride her lover, knees on either side of his hips, her palms flat against his rock-hard stomach.

She tensed and tried to scramble off him, but his hands clamped around her thighs and pinned her there. He didn't speak, merely secured and regarded her, his eyes dropping to linger appreciatively on her breasts. When he slid his hands up her bare thighs, she seriously regretted having put on her short-shorts this morning. A slip of a lilac thong was all that was beneath them, and his fingers were toying with the hem of her shorts, perilously close to slipping inside. . . .

the dark highlander

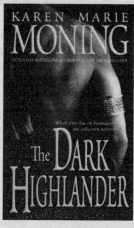

Some days Dageus felt as ancient as the evil within him.

As he hailed a cab to take him to The Cloisters to pick up a
copy of one of the last tomes in New York that he needed to
check, he didn't notice the fascinated glances women walking
down the sidewalk turned his way. Didn't realize that, even in
a metropolis that teemed with diversity, he stood out. It was
nothing he said or did; to all appearances he was but another
wealthy, sinfully gorgeous man. It was simply the essence of
the man. The way he moved. His every gesture exuded power,
something dark and . . . forbidden. He was sexual in a way that
made women think of deeply repressed fantasies therapists
and feminists alike would cringe to hear tell of.

But he realized none of that. His thoughts were far away,
still mulling over the nonsense penned in the Book of Leinster.

It was there in the peaches-and-cream complexion and the huge aquamarine eyes—eyes that still regarded the world with wonder, he noticed with a faintly mocking smile. It was there in a fire that simmered just beneath the surface of her flawless skin. Wee, lusciously plump where it counted, with a trim waist and shapely legs hugged by a snug skirt, the lass was an exiled Highlander's dream.

He wet his lips and stared, making a noise deep in his throat that was more animal than human.

When she leaned back in through the open window of the car to say something to the driver, the back of her skirt rode up a few inches. He inhaled sharply, envisioning himself behind her. His entire body went tight with lust.

Christ, she was lovely. Lush curves that could make a dead man stir.

She leaned forward a smidgen, showing more of that sweet curve of the back of her thigh.

His mouth went ferociously dry.

No' for me, he warned himself, gritting his teeth and shifting to lessen the pressure on his suddenly painfully hard cock. He took only experienced lasses to his bed. Lasses far older in both mind and body. Not reeking, as she did, of innocence. Of bright dreams and a bonny future.

Sleek and worldly, with jaded palates and cynical hearts—they were the ones a man could tumble and leave with a bauble in the morn, no worse for the wear.

She was the kind a man kept.

"Go," he murmured to the driver, forcing his gaze away.

Och, what he wouldn't give for his da's library.

In lieu of it, he'd been systematically obtaining what manuscripts still existed, exhausting his present possibilities before pursuing riskier ones. Risky, like setting foot on the isles of his ancestors again, a thing fast seeming inevitable.

Thinking of risk, he made a mental note to return some of the volumes he'd "borrowed" from private collections when bribes had failed. It wouldn't do to have them lying about too long.

He glanced up at the clock above the bank. Twelve forty-five. The cocurator of The Cloisters had assured him he would have the text delivered first thing that morn, but it hadn't arrived and Dageus was weary of waiting.

He needed information, *accurate* information about the Keltar's ancient benefactors, the Tuatha Dé Danaan, those "gods and not gods," as the Book of the Dun Cow called them. They were the ones who had originally imprisoned the dark Druids in the in-between, hence it followed that there was a way to reimprison them.

It was imperative he find that way.

As he eased into the cab—a torturous fit for a man of his height and breadth—his attention was caught by a lass who was stepping from a car at the curb in front of them.

She was different, and it was that difference that drew his eye. She had none of the city's polish and was all the lovelier for it. Refreshingly tousled, delightfully free of the artifice with which modern women enhanced their faces, she was a vision.

"Wait," he growled at the driver, watching her hungrily.

His every sense heightened painfully. His hands fisted as desire, never sated, flooded him.

Somewhere in her ancestry the lass had Scots blood. It was there in the curly waves of copper-and-blond hair that tumbled about a delicate face with a surprisingly strong jaw.